THE LIE

Other books by Michael Weaver

Deceptions
Impulse

THE LIE

MICHAEL WEAVER

WARNER BOOKS

A Time Warner Company

Copyright © 1997 by Michael Weaver
All rights reserved.

Warner Books, Inc., 1271 Avenue of the Americas,
New York, NY 10020

W A Time Warner Company

First Printing: March 1997
10 9 8 7 6 5 4 3 2 1

Library of Congress Cataloging-in-Publication Data

Weaver, Michael
    The lie / Michael Weaver.
        p.   cm.
    ISBN 0-446-51814-X
    I. Title.
    PS3573.E1788L5   1997
    813'.54—dc20   96-26373
                                                              CIP

For Dorothy Kaiser . . . simply a lovely lady.

A special thanks to my editor, Susan Sandler.
Warm. Gracious. Intelligent.

Chapter 1

IT WAS WELL PAST MIDNIGHT when she saw the light in the upstairs bedroom go out, leaving the house dark.

By that time she had been waiting almost two hours in the deeper part of the surrounding woods, and she would probably wait another hour before going in. Since she had been waiting eighteen years for what lay just ahead, these last few hours only added to the anticipation, to the excitement, and to the fear and trembling.

She sat with her back to a tree, feeling the damp earth beneath her and the roughness of the bark through the fabric of her shirt. The night was warm, with little wind. Patches of mist drifted from the Bay of Salerno off to the west. In the distance, she saw the lights of a late plane starting its final descent toward Naples.

When the lights disappeared, her hand went to the automatic she carried inside the belt of her slacks. She fingered its butt, trigger guard, and safety for perhaps the fifth time in the past half hour. It was the only visible sign of her nervousness.

Then she just sat holding the gun in both hands like a supplicant making an offering to a god she could not see but, she knew with absolute certainty, was out there someplace.

Her name was Kate Dinneson.

Kate made her move at a quarter to two, rising up out of the woods and silently approaching the rear of the house. As she walked, the slender, delicately put together young woman in dark shirt, slacks, and gloves slipped on an equally dark ski mask.

The mask was her tacit admission of uncertainty. It was the only sign she gave, even to herself, that she wasn't totally committed to any single course of action.

She had done a dry run earlier, while it was still light, so she knew exactly where the wires, alarm, and points of entry were. Now, working deftly, she neutralized the system in five minutes. Still, when she had finished her face was damp under the mask and her throat was stiflingly dry.

The few tools she needed were in a small canvas belt bag. She used a glass cutter and rubber suction cup to let herself in through a basement window.

Inside, she used a pinpoint flash to find the smooth stone stairs and reached the first floor without a sound.

Turning off her light, she stood in the translucent dark of the entrance hall, letting her eyes pick out the shape and placement of things. She drew the automatic from her belt, flicked off the safety, and climbed the curving flight of steps to the second-floor landing.

Their bedroom was directly ahead, the door open. They slept curled together in a wash of blue starlight. A nightgown was tossed across a chair. The sheet lay partly on the floor. A pistol lay on the night table near Peter Walters's side of the bed. She knew it would have to be taken care of at once. Walters's first move on waking would be pure reflex, and she didn't want to have to shoot him in response.

Kate reached the gun in two silent steps, slipped it into her belt, and backed off. Then she switched on a small lamp and waited.

Peter Walters's eyelids stirred, fluttered briefly, and opened. They were the only part of him that moved.

He looked at the slender, masked figure pointing an automatic at his head. Shifting his glance, he did not see the gun that he always kept on the table beside him.

Still watching the girl, he reached for and found his wife's hand. He pressed it to wake her as gently as possible.

"Peg?" he said. "We have company."

His voice, too, was gentle. He spoke in unaccented English. Although he and his wife had been living in Positano for twenty-seven years, they were American.

Peggy Walters came awake. Her eyes blinked against the light and she gasped as she saw the masked, dark-clothed figure pointing a gun. Then she just lay there, gripping her husband's hand.

"Who are you?" Walters asked in Italian.

Kate Dinneson swallowed twice. "I'm the daughter of Angelo and Patty Falanga."

Her answer, also in Italian, contained the exact words she had imagined herself saying for as long as she could remember.

Walters stared at the knitted fabric of her mask.

"In case it's slipped your mind," Kate said, "eighteen years ago last month you killed them."

"Who told you I was the one who did it?" Walters asked.

"Someone who obviously knew."

Walters was silent.

"Do you deny it?"

"Would you believe me if I did?"

"No."

He sighed and slowly shook his head. "It took you eighteen years to get here?"

"I found out it was you only ten days ago."

"And now all you want is to kill me?"

"If that was all I wanted, you would be dead right now."

"What else do you want?"

"To hear your side. If you have one."

"You mean and *then* you'll kill me?"

Kate Dinneson said nothing.

Walters glanced at his wife, who lay white-faced yet composed under the sheet beside him. He was still holding her hand. Then he looked once more at Kate's eyes. "May I take my cigarettes and lighter?"

"Very carefully."

He lifted them from the night table and lit up.

Watching, her gun leveled, Kate pulled over a straight-backed chair and eased into it. Despite herself, her legs were trembling. She was working hard to remain calm, cool, controlled, wishing she could be dispassionate and afraid she never would be.

"So what did this person, this someone who supposedly knew, tell you about me?" Peter Walters asked.

He was sitting up in bed now, smoking. The sheet had slipped away from his naked upper body, and Kate saw an incredible number of welted puncture scars scattered across his chest, abdomen, sides, and arms. Some were from bullets and shrapnel. Others were from cutting blades. His life history, she thought.

"He told me you had been a contract killer for the United States Central Intelligence Agency. That you did work for them all over Europe. Do you deny that?"

"No. That's true."

"He told me you shot my mother and father in cold blood. He said you killed them as they were coming out to surrender, unarmed, with their hands over their heads."

Kate Dinneson felt oddly numb. She wondered what had become of all the anger she had been storing up and carrying for so many years. This man had robbed her of a lifetime of love. He had stolen her mother and father. He had murdered them, along with all the good things that were supposed to come to her from them. Yet looking at him now, all she saw was a battered, aging man, the force in him long faded and gone. Beside him, his aging wife, who had yet to say a word, waited in silence for whatever was going to happen next.

Peter Walters slowly shook his head. "That part is a lie. It wasn't like that at all. I'm sure you've been told about your parents," he said. "You must know who and what they were."

"I've been told and I've known all my life. Now I'm waiting to hear what *you* have to tell me about them."

Peggy Walters spoke for the first time. "You said all this was eighteen years ago. I can't see your face but you must have been just a child. Whatever you've heard had to have come from others. Please. This isn't fair."

Kate ignored her. "Go ahead," she told Walters. "Talk to me."

"Your mother and father were the most deadly terrorists of their day," said Walters. "They killed hundreds. Innocents. Is that what you knew about them?"

"They fought for a cause. Sadly, there were sacrifices."

Walters looked at the ceiling and the walls. "I saw some of those sacrifices. Have you ever seen *pieces* of children? And as for my killing your parents in cold blood, that just wasn't so. They came out shooting from behind a white flag after promising to give themselves up. Three of my scars are from their bullets."

This was the version Kate had grown up with, this legend of her mother and father choosing a martyr's death over a prison cell. She had heard the new story from the one man who had finally been able to name Peter Walters as her parents' killer. The romantic in her preferred the original. She preferred it, too, because if she did accept it, she would not feel so compelled to make payment.

"Why should I believe you?" she said. "Staring into the muzzle of a gun, you would say anything."

"I wasn't alone when it happened. I had two men as backup. One of them used a camera to record what was supposed to be a peaceful surrender. They were both killed when your parents came out blazing at us with machine pistols. But I do have a couple of pictures of how it was."

Kate was silent. Peggy Walters stirred in bed, pulling her attention.

"She's not here to look at your pictures," Peggy told her husband. "She's just here to shoot you."

"Where are they?" Kate asked.

"In a wall safe behind that mirror. If you let my wife out of bed she'll open it for you."

Kate saw the mirror hanging over a dresser on Peter Walters's side of the bed. The pictures might or might not be in the safe, but there would certainly be a gun waiting there.

"What's the combination?" she asked.

"Twice around to the right to four . . . left to ten . . . right to six."

"Here's what I want you to do," said Kate. "I want you to

carefully get out of bed, take the mirror off the wall, and open the safe without putting a hand inside. All right?"

"Yes."

"Then I want you back in bed with your hands on your head while I look at the pictures." Kate paused. "If there *are* any pictures."

Peter Walters was silent.

"Are they the only pictures in the safe?" Kate Dinneson asked him.

"Yes."

"Why did you save just them? What made my parents so special?"

"Because they killed two of my men and almost killed me. Because no one else ever made me look that stupid, and I didn't want to forget it."

Kate stared at him. He might be telling the truth. Some of the tightness went out of her chest and her breathing.

"All right. You can get out of bed and open the safe."

"I'm naked."

"I'll try not to get too excited," Kate said.

He did not smile. Moving with care, Walters got out of bed, lifted the mirror off the wall, and worked the exposed safe's dial until Kate heard a click.

"That's it," she said. "I'll take it from here. Now just get back into bed and put your hands on your head."

Kate watched as he followed her instructions.

"You too," she told his wife. "Hands on your head."

"Are you also going to shoot *me?*" asked Peggy Walters. "Or just my husband?"

Kate Dinneson stood up and looked at the woman. "Right now I'm not shooting anyone," she said, and was half turning toward the safe even as she realized that the woman's hands were still not on her head. One hand lay at her side, while the other remained where it had been all along. Somewhere beneath the sheet.

Kate saw the slight narrowing of Peggy Walters's eyes and the sudden look of terror on her face. When Kate saw her expression she was terrified too.

The terror made her move, sent her diving off to the left an instant before a gun exploded under the sheet and its bullet whistled past her ear.

Kate landed on her shoulder and rolled, not holding still for the second shot, which ricocheted off the tile floor. She spun about until she was able to lift her gun and get off a couple of shots of her own, just barely glimpsing the woman's face over the barrel, seeing her eyes widen now as she sat up in bed, holding her suddenly visible pistol with both hands until her face and eyes seemed to dissolve in a red haze.

Then her husband appeared in her place, his naked body riding the air in a flat-out leap, his hands reaching for Kate's automatic. His mouth was wide open, yelling something Kate could not understand.

She squeezed off just one shot, all she had time for, as Peter Walters's full weight took her squarely in the chest. Kate fought for breath and they lay there like exhausted lovers.

Straining, Kate worked herself free. Walters's unseeing eyes were open. Bright arterial blood spurted from a hole in the left side of his chest.

My one shot.

Kate looked across the bed and saw Peggy Walters lying on her back, her face a scarlet mask. Still in one hand was the pistol that had started it all. Kate struggled up from the floor, took the woman's wrist, and felt for a pulse that was no longer there.

I didn't want it this way.

She held her forehead for a moment, trying to calm herself. Then she went to the safe that she had turned toward only moments before and pulled open the steel door.

An automatic lay right in front. The safety was off and it was ready to be fired. At least she had been right about that. As for the alleged photographs, they were probably nothing but a ploy to let Walters or his wife grab the gun, whirl, and blow her away.

Kate Dinneson looked anyway, foraging through half a dozen envelopes until she finally opened one and found herself staring at pictures of her mother and father.

Surprise.

There were, indeed, two pictures. They were both en-largements, taken from good negatives, so that the details were clear and without distortion.

How young they were, Kate thought, and saw them dashing side by side, machine pistols blazing during what would soon turn out to be the final seconds of their lives. She saw their sun-bronzed skin, and their white teeth bared in grins that were not really grins at all, but frightening grimaces in the face of certain death.

Kate wondered what they were thinking during these last seconds before all thinking stopped. Or had they reached the point where they were functioning purely on instinct?

I wish I could talk to you, she told them. *I wish I had been older when you were with me. I wish I had known you better.*

What she knew now was that Peter Walters had been telling the truth. He had not shot her mother and father in cold blood while they were coming out to surrender, un-armed, with their hands over their heads.

Why had Walters's wife made that crazy move with her gun and gotten them both killed?

Had she perhaps not known about the pictures and thought her husband was just bluffing? Or had she expected that she and Walters would be shot anyway, so what was there to lose?

Too bad.

Because this slight, masked young woman knew very well by now that if she had not been driven to it, she would never have shot anyone at all here tonight.

Kate Dinneson lifted the ski mask from her sweated face and took a long, hard look at what she had done.

She felt a chill, and an emptiness, and the total silence of the house. With all her long-held dreams of vengeance, these two were the first human lives she had ever been re-sponsible for taking.

It was very different from fantasy.

Dear God, yes.

Have you ever seen pieces of children? Walters had asked.

Well, no. She hadn't. Nor did she ever want or intend

to. Whatever her parents had believed and done had nothing to do with her. They had lived and died marching to their own particular drummer. She was still straining to hear the first, faint beat of hers.

There was nothing more for her here, but Kate could not bring herself to leave. As though tangled in the shrouds of those she had killed, she seemed to lack the will to tear loose. What else did she want from them? Absolution? If it was a joke, she was not laughing. All she did was replace the pictures, lock the safe, and cover it with the mirror.

In the end, Kate Dinneson turned on her tiny light and began drifting through the house like a restless spirit. She went downstairs and walked the rooms of the newly dead. Chancing on a collection of family photographs, she stopped to punish herself with them. Along with happily smiling pictures of Peggy and Peter Walters were shots of an unsmiling, dark-haired little boy. More pictures followed of the same boy grown older. And older still. Until he evolved into a tall, lean, striking young man with dark, deep-set eyes and a haunting stare. He still had the same determined solemnity, as if not even the camera could coax him into the faintest of smiles.

On a wall beside the photographs hung a strongly brushed oil painting of the same young man. It evidently was a self-portrait since he was shown holding a palette and brushes. Scrawled in English across the bottom of the canvas was an inscription: *For Mom and Dad—with love—Paulie.*

I've orphaned him, Kate realized.

So he was an artist, as his father apparently had been.

A large, skylighted studio offered plenty of evidence. Canvases were scattered everywhere. Inasmuch as it was Peter Walters's studio, almost all the paintings were his. But a few were signed by his son, Paulie. Once Kate noticed the first of these, the others stabbed at her.

How many of this Paulie's paintings were there? Three? Five? Seven? It didn't matter. The message remained the same.

Life was better than death, and peace was better than war.

Yet death watched. So if you had a moment of joy, it was

better to conceal it. When your heart beat loudly with hope, you kept that as quiet as possible also.

Curiously, although they were all war paintings, not a single dead body was visible in any of them. Yet it made a rare kind of sense. War was over for the dead. It existed only in the faces of the living, which was where Paulie Walters had looked for it—in the eyes and mouths of those in trouble, in the way flesh acted in grief and pain and shock. He had looked for it too, in the wounded reaching for each other, or giving comfort with the terrible tenderness people can show in the darkest places. He had found it even in those odd moments of laughter, in the rare joy that is the underside of the deepest anguish.

Kate was stunned.

How had someone so young learned so much?

No wonder he looked so solemn.

Kate Dinneson went back and stood once more in front of Paulie Walters's unsmiling self-portrait. For several long moments she felt herself at the absolute center of his thoughts.

I'm sorry about what I did to you here tonight, Kate told him. *If I could change it, I would.*

She finally left his parents' house shortly before dawn.

Chapter 2

PAULIE WALTERS WAS FOLLOWING a Serbian army staff car through mountains that had once been part of greater Yugoslavia, but whose current ownership was much less certain. He had been tailing the car for almost three hours, ever since it had left the military barracks in Banja Luka at two-thirty that morning. He was waiting for it to make its first rest stop.

Only one road ran through this part of the mountains, which allowed Paulie to maintain a good, safe tailing distance of close to two kilometers. Also, he had the added advantage of knowing exactly where the staff car was going. This in itself let him feel relaxed enough to watch the sky beginning to lighten in the east.

It was beautiful country even in the dark, with a deep blue haze over the summits, and the shadows falling to purple between some of the lower pine-covered slopes. Normally, Paulie Walters would have been enjoying the purity of the air while imagining how he would paint what he saw. He called it mind-painting, something his father had taught him when he was five years old. But right now his thoughts were on more pressing things.

At best, the operation was risky, delicately balanced. Orders had come straight from the top out of Langley, Virginia, and once Tommy Cortlandt himself was involved, Paulie never argued or tried to second-guess him. In a line of work where trust and honesty were in depressingly short supply, he had never known the director to disappoint. Still, given a choice, this was one job Paulie would have been just as happy to pass on.

His orders were to either set a man free of those holding him or, failing that, to kill him. Perhaps worst of all, the man in question, Stefan Tutsikov, was one of the few out here in this Balkan charnel house who was on the side of the angels.

Even Cortlandt had been sympathetic. "I don't like having to stick you with this one," the director had told him. "But I know of no one else I'd trust it to, or who could do it as well."

Unabashed flattery. Yet Paulie had felt himself respond like Pavlov's dog. Tommy Cortlandt's face had offered more than his words. It always did. That marvelous face, with its ice-blue eyes and the look of a born conspirator.

Paulie Walters had never met Stefan Tutsikov, and he had seen him only a few times from a distance. He thought of him now sitting in that Serbian staff car with four armed guards, and he wondered what he was thinking. All things considered, Paulie knew his chances of getting Tutsikov away from his guards alive were depressingly small.

Unfortunate.

Unlike most of the other political leaders in the area, Stefan Tutsikov was neither foolish, angry, self-serving, nor simply bent on age-old ethnic revenge and murder. That covert American support had been behind him had nothing to do with how Paulie felt. The man was just good. To abandon him to the certain torture and death that awaited him in Belgrade would be a lot crueler to Tutsikov and far more deadly to those he would surely betray under electric prodding than any bullets Paulie might have to pump into him.

The pink glow of dawn was spreading over the mountains as Paulie Walters rounded a curve and saw the staff car's brake lights brighten in the distance at one of the irregularly spaced rest stops along the road. It consisted of a low, rustic building with washrooms and a few scattered picnic tables and benches. Drawing closer, Paulie saw three huge trailer trucks lined up in the parking area: he assumed the drivers were asleep in their cabs.

Reaching under the passenger seat, he lifted out the blue-steel machine pistol he favored when the odds were this much against him.

He slowed as he made his approach on a long descending grade. The pines stood tall and dark on both sides; the sky was cloudless and getting lighter and redder above.

All four guards got out of the car and entered the building with their prisoner. Pretty stupid as far as good security went, thought Paulie, but that much better for him. Tutsikov had walked in with his hands behind his back, so he was handcuffed.

Cutting off the motor, Paulie rolled the last hundred meters and quietly came up alongside the staff car. He heard voices and laughter from inside the rest room. He glanced off to the right where the three tractor-trailers were parked. Nothing moved.

Setting the machine gun on full automatic, Paulie draped the sling around his neck and got out of the car. He took a sheathed hunting knife from his belt and ripped open two of the staff car's tires. Then he entered the rest room.

A pale white light froze the guards and their captive into a tableau.

Three of the guards stood at the urinals, their backs to Paulie. The fourth guard and Stefan Tutsikov were off to one side, with the guard busy unlocking his prisoner's handcuffs.

"Nobody move." Paulie Walters spoke more than rudimentary Serbo-Croatian.

They turned to look at him. One of the soldiers at the urinals was smoking a cigarette and it dropped from his mouth. They all wore holstered sidearms. The only naked gun was in Paulie's hands. He saw that Tutsikov was free of his handcuffs.

"Come over here beside me," he told him. "The rest of you, facedown on the floor."

The four guards glanced around at one another. No one wanted to be the first to do it.

Paulie leveled his machine pistol at the three in front of the urinals. "You guys really want to die with your little pretties in your hands?"

They dropped facedown on the floor together. The fourth soldier quickly followed.

"Get their pistols," Paulie told Tutsikov. "Be careful. Don't get between them and my gun."

Paulie watched as Tutsikov did as instructed. Every one of these soldiers more than half expected a bullet in the back of his head.

I hope they don't make me kill them.

He waited until Stefan Tutsikov had collected all the guards' weapons. Then, moving swiftly, he reversed his machine gun and swung its butt against the back of each of the four heads lined up on the floor.

Paulie checked. They were all unconscious. No great joy, but better than dead.

"Let's go," he told Tutsikov.

Outside, Paulie stopped to rip the phone out of the staff car. The three parked rigs were still quiet. Moments later the two men were on the road and picking up speed.

Stefan Tutsikov kept looking behind them.

"You don't have to worry," said Paulie, speaking English now. "I cut their tires before I went in."

Tutsikov spoke for the first time. "I was sure you were going to kill them."

"I didn't have to."

"*They* would have killed *you*. And worse."

"I know."

Tutsikov stared at Paulie Walters. "Who *are* you?"

"One of your American admirers."

The political leader gazed off at the growing lightness of the sky. "I know what you saved me from. I'm grateful."

Paulie drove in silence.

"Would you have shot me if you couldn't get me away from them?"

"Of course."

"I thank you for that, too."

Less than an hour later, in response to a coded signal from Paulie's radio phone, an unmarked helicopter picked them up in a small clearing not far from the Serbian town of Kula.

Four hours after that, Stefan Tutsikov was aboard a U.S. Air Force flight from Rome to Washington.

Paulie Walters, after being dropped off in Naples and reporting to Tommy Cortlandt by secure telephone, headed home to Ravello along the Amalfi coast. Nearing Positano in the early afternoon he turned off the main road to stop at his parents' house for a brief visit.

Paulie had been born and raised in the house, a white, flat-roofed, Moorish-style villa in the green mountains overlooking the Bay of Salerno.

Waking in the morning, his first sight of the day for much of his life had been Ulysses' fabled Rocks of the Sirens, rising out of the water about a mile offshore. He had painted the scene many times. This afternoon, the rocks stood golden and shining in a glassy sea.

Paulie saw the two cars in the parking area, so he knew that both his parents were home. Climbing the long, steep path through the rock garden, he felt the more than thirty-six hours he had gone without sleep.

When no one answered his knock, Paulie Walters opened the door with his own key and went in.

"Anyone home?"

He called out first in English, then in Italian.

Entering his father's studio, he saw the current canvas on an easel. No paint-filled brushes were in sight, which meant his father had not been painting today.

Paulie was curious, not concerned. Nothing appeared out of order. Friends sometimes stopped by to pick up his parents for a day out on their boat or whatever. More than anything, he was disappointed at their not being home to greet him.

He took a cold beer from the refrigerator and sat down with it at the kitchen table.

His day and a half without sleep suddenly hit him again, and he knew he was not about to get behind the wheel for another hour of driving to Ravello.

Pushing out of his chair, Paulie Walters started up the stairs. The idea of a nap in his old bed seemed very appealing.

The thought never got further than that.

All he saw at first were his father's bare arms.

They were on the floor.

Reaching.

Paulie breathed the coppery smell of blood.

He entered his parents' room and saw it all, saw it in that mix of color and black and white that happens in only the worst of nightmares.

Eyes closed, he knelt on the floor hugging himself with both arms, rocking gently.

The room itself was quiet, but the air was smeared with silent screams. They were all he heard.

Time had passed, yet he had not really looked closely at his parents. He knew he had to now, and he had always done what was required of him.

Paulie looked at his mother first, where she lay on the bed. A revolver was in her hand, and at a quick glance a stranger might have thought she had shot her husband and then taken her own life. Paulie knew better. He saw that his mother had been shot twice in the face, and that a third shot had splintered the bed's headboard behind her.

Knees shaking, Paulie approached his father slowly and with great care. He saw his naked body stretched out on the floor, facedown, both arms extended as in a dive. Only his old wounds were visible, no fresh ones. On the pale tile floor around him, an irregular red stain radiated out from under his chest.

Insanely, Paulie placed two fingers on his father's wrist, felt for a pulse, and silently called for a miracle.

His father's flesh was cold.

There was no miracle.

He stayed with them, turning his head from side to side, pretending he was looking for some tangible object. In truth, though, he was gasping through the fading afternoon light, smothering in the emptiness of the house.

Chapter 3

"Having sex," thought Kate Dinneson, was the wrong description for what they were doing. When one was engaged in this sort of carnal transaction with Nicko Vorelli, it had to come more under the heading of an art form.

They were in the master bedroom suite of Nicko's Sorrento villa, the blinds closed against the afternoon sun, a few pale, wavering rays still managing to break through. A bedside clock said it was just past four, which was something of a shock to Kate: imagine her cavorting in bed while the sun was still shining.

But today was different. Today she was still fighting the mixture of panic and remorse she had carried away from the tragic episode the night before in Positano. She had rushed straight to the bed of *Doctore* Nicholas Vorelli for his unfailing expert therapy.

Nicko *was* an expert. Not only in bed but in everything leading up to and surrounding it. Eroticism, he believed, could change disorder into harmony, fear into courage, despair into hope. Nicko should know. He had been living for all of fifty-four years—more than twice as long as she—and had become a practicing philosopher. He had learned that ruin came to flesh, inevitably, that time wore a person away bit by bit, and that all one faced was the void. So why not live life accordingly?

Now, moving with him through one of those sweet, far places that transcended sex, Kate Dinneson felt lighter than air, intensely alive. Nicko was still her mentor, still opening new avenues to her. Most important, he cherished and delighted in her, which he had been doing since she was seventeen, when she had all but forced her way into his bed and seduced *him*.

Being cherished and delighted in by a rich and distinguished man was very comforting. Nicholas Vorelli was a widely respected doctor of political science whose theories and advice were eagerly sought after for astronomical fees by corporations, financial and political advisory services, and major governments at a time when the collapse of world Communism had opened great gaps in the geopolitical order, which chaos was threatening to fill.

In addition, Nicko had a deft, clever way with people and was always being invited to parties at various embassies and famous town and country mansions. Kate often went with him to these gatherings, usually when there was a chance it might prove useful to her career as a features writer for several major news services.

Attending these events, she sometimes found herself staring at celebrated guests and deciding she did not like their faces. They looked too much like the faces of small-town merchants, growing a little too fat, too sleek, too overcomfortable. Nicko had once asked, "What are you so busy looking at?"

"The faces of our world leaders. I don't like them."

He had smiled. "The trouble with you is, you've spent so much of your life looking at the dark underside of things, you don't even know how the light at the top is supposed to look."

True enough. Yet it was just as true for Nicko. He had come out of some of the same dark places as she. Even darker. He had not been too far removed from her mother and father during the worst and bloodiest of their violence-filled days. Yet he had come out clean and seemingly untouched.

Nicko was above her now, all sweet flowing warmth to her flesh. A rare greed shone in his eyes: he had that special male look that said the world and everything in it was his. Kate knew she really was no part of it.

A moment later she felt the sudden rushing, that wild blend of scent, sight, and movement. Then with a great urgency, she took hold of Nicko and felt him dissolve, and herself with him, as everything she had been holding back broke loose.

They lay naked in the warm room, the sheets thrown off the bed. Nicko Vorelli's face lay on Kate Dinneson's breast.

"All right, let's hear about it." Nicko spoke in Italian, although he could just as easily have spoken in English, German, French, or Spanish. Just as Kate could have understood him in any one of those languages.

"Let's hear about what?"

"Whatever it was that drove you to this extraordinary hunger for me in the middle of an otherwise ordinary afternoon."

Kate was silent.

Vorelli moved his head to look at her. "It's that bad?"

"I'm afraid so."

Getting out of bed, she padded barefoot and naked to the liquor cabinet and poured some brandy into two snifters. Then she handed one to Nicko, sat down on the edge of the bed, and sipped her drink. She stared dimly at the pleasantly familiar room, at its elegant antique lamps and period dressers, at its custom armoires and bed tables.

"I shot a man and a woman last night," she said quietly. "I didn't really want to, though I did go to their house with a gun. The woman began shooting at me and I had to shoot back. When it was over, they both were dead."

Nicko Vorelli stared at her, obviously shocked.

"Who knows about it?"

"No one."

"No one saw you enter or leave their house?"

"No. It was the middle of the night, and dark."

"What about fingerprints?"

"I wore gloves and never took them off."

"Did you tell anyone you were going there?"

Kate shook her head.

"Could the man and woman have told someone you were coming?"

"They never knew. I broke in while they were asleep."

"Who were they?"

"Their names were Paul and Peggy Walters. He was the man who shot my parents, and she was his wife."

Nicko Vorelli's eyes were troubled. "From Positano?"

"You knew them?"

"I know Walters was an artist. I know his wife ran a gallery right here in Sorrento."

"He was also a shooter for the CIA. Or did you know that too?"

Nicko offered no answer. His silence alone was almost enough to convince Kate he knew.

"I think you'd better tell me exactly what happened last night," he said.

Kate told him, her voice flat. The only thing she left out was what she had begun to consider her curious overreaction to the Walterses' son, Paulie, and his paintings.

When she finished, Nicko said, "How did you find out Walters killed your mother and father?"

"A man named Klaus Logefeld told me."

"Who is he?"

"He was one of the old leftist, anarchist crowd I used to trail after when I went to school for a while in Germany. He must be about fifteen years older than me and he used to fancy himself an intellectual revolutionary. Probably still does. My parents were his gods, and I was their little daughter. I keep running into him in different places where the overage ex-Reds cry in their beer together. The last time was ten days ago in Rome. That's when he told me about my parents."

"Did he say how he knew Walters shot them?"

"Just that a friend happened to mention it."

"What kind of friend?"

"One who once did work for the CIA in Frankfurt."

"Why do you suppose your Klaus lied about your mother and father being unarmed when they were shot?"

"Maybe he didn't lie. Maybe that was what his friend told him."

"Or else it was his way of making sure you killed the Walterses."

"Why would that matter so much to him?"

"I'll tell you what I don't like," Nicko said. "Mostly, I don't like this German wildman knowing you've just killed two people. Neither do I like everything leading up to it."

"Like what?"

"Like God suddenly arranging for you to run into Klaus ten days ago in Rome. Like his friend just happening to mention that Walters killed your parents eighteen years ago. Like the facts somehow getting twisted into making you believe Walters was a cold-blooded murderer who deserved to die."

Nicko Vorelli palmed his brandy snifter in both hands. "Have you called Klaus to tell him what happened last night?"

"No. I wanted to talk to you first. And I guess I just needed time."

He looked at her. "How are you now?"

"Better. Don't worry, Nicko. I'll handle it."

"Where does Klaus live?" Nicko asked.

"Rome."

"You have his phone number?"

Kate nodded.

"Do me a favor. Take a nice hot bath, get dressed, then call him while I listen in. I want to hear how he handles it when you tell him what happened."

She had luxuriated in the skylighted marble bathroom many times before, but she had never gotten used to it.

How could she?

She had been the orphaned seven-year-old child of a pretty English terrorist mother and a zealous Italian terrorist father, the foster daughter of three sets of temporary parents in ten years, the perennial wearer of hand-me-down clothes, and uncertain eater of irregular, not especially nutritious meals. She did not take easily to the trappings of wealth.

Not that she had to put up with it all that often. Only when she was with Nicko, who took a far simpler approach to the entire subject. His credo was this: Once you're past the basics, the only true purpose of money is to smooth out some of the bumps in living. Very little came smoother than the polished marble of the tub in which she lay.

Still, there was no smoothing away the two deaths that should never have taken place. Yet if she had not been so well trained in violence by all those hard-edged revolutionaries who had raised her, she herself would be dead this minute.

Nicko Vorelli was on an extension in the next room when Kate heard Klaus Logefeld answer in Rome.

"It's me," she said.

"I've been waiting to hear. Did it go well?"

"For me. Not for them."

"You mean you killed *both*?"

"It couldn't be helped."

"There's been nothing on the news," said Klaus. "I guess they haven't been found yet."

"I appreciate what you did, Klaus. I have been waiting forever for this." Now she was following Nicko's script.

"Your mother and father were martyred heroes. You deserved your chance to put things right."

"Well, you're the one who gave me the chance," said Kate. "So if there's ever anything I can do . . ."

Kate played out her alleged gratitude for a few moments longer. When she finally hung up, Nicko came back into the room.

"What do you think?" he asked.

"I don't like his having lied to me. But in the end I shot those two because Peggy Walters was trying to kill me, not because of Klaus's lie. I'd say he's harmless."

"He's German, isn't he?"

"So?"

"History says there's no such thing as a harmless German."

"History doesn't know about Klaus Logefeld."

"He's that special?"

"He's eaten up with Nazi guilt. He wasn't born until well after the Holocaust, but he's still pouring its ashes over his head."

Kate looked at Nicko. "What's *your* feeling?"

"The same as always in such situations. It's never good to leave any loose ends."

"No, Nicko."

"It's the only way to be absolutely sure."

Kate's face was set. "I said *no*. I've already killed two people I didn't really want to kill. With Klaus, I'm sure enough."

Chapter 4

IN ROME, KLAUS LOGEFELD was in his apartment on the Via Sistina, studying a sheet of contact prints with a large magnifying glass. He was going over the pictures for the third time, trying to decide which would be best to enlarge. With a fully equipped darkroom in the apartment, he had done all the developing and printing himself during the late afternoon. The blowups would be next.

Klaus had used the latest in silent, high-tech cameras for the all-important shoot. Actually, he had used two cameras: one loaded with infrared film for shooting in the dark, the other holding film suitable for low-level artificial light. Both cameras were fitted with telephoto lenses. Because of the restrictive shooting conditions, he had been anxious about the possible results, particularly since clarity and detail were vital and there were no second chances. Judging from the contact prints, the enlargements would be giving him everything he needed.

He reviewed the pictures in their proper sequence, starting with the first shots of Kate waiting in the midnight dark of the wood, then catching her as she stood up and headed toward the house, pulling on her mask. He had pictures of her breaking into the house through the basement window, but no more of her until she was upstairs in the Walterses' bedroom, turning on a lamp and waiting for them to waken.

At this point Klaus hit the switch on a small audiocassette, and the sound of Kate's and the Walterses' voices gave sudden life to the pictures. Then there was the business of Peter Walters opening the safe, and his wife shooting at Kate, and all hell breaking loose as Kate finished them both from flat out on the floor.

That is some little lady, thought Klaus Logefeld, as he wondered how many shooters could have succeeded with that kind of speed and accuracy.

And there were the photographs of Kate removing the pictures of her parents from the safe, which was something for him to think about because she had never mentioned the pictures on the phone and even pretended not to know he had lied. Why?

Then came the especially important photos of Kate with her mask off, but still in the bedroom with the two bodies, and the pictures of her wandering about the house and looking at all the Walters family photographs and paintings, and the total devastation on her face as she looked.

Sorry, Kate, he thought, because he had never had anything but good feelings about Kate Dinneson and took no pleasure in having to use and deceive her like this. He had not been born devious. He believed himself to be essentially honest and straightforward by nature. It had taken a long, hard process of conditioning to change him.

The process had begun in the dark of a Berlin movie theater when he was just twelve years old. It was the day Klaus saw a documentary showing the end of the Third Reich through the eyes of an advancing American tank battalion. The battalion's lead units were the first to confront the evidence of what Corps Intelligence had designated only as Objective 3. Entrance had required no fighting. The SS guards had left the camp several hours before. Just the dead, the dying, and the walking skeletons greeted the Americans.

At the end, the guards had evidently butchered an extra few thousand as a farewell gesture, but had not taken time to dispose of the bodies. The Germans were an efficient people, noted the narrator, and the killing had, typically, gone well. But body disposal was always a problem. Stripped naked, the corpses were stacked in piles, like cordwood. Occasional sound and movement emanated from the piles, and the living had to be dug out.

Throughout the film, Klaus maintained an air of careful reserve. He clung to it the way a shipwrecked sailor might cling to a piece of flotsam in a lonely sea. He was afraid to let it go. He did not know what might take its place. Not until several weeks later, when he had read and seen everything he could uncover on what the German people, *his* people, had called the *final solution* to the Jewish problem, did he find out. What came was a very fine and continuing madness.

At the age of twelve, Klaus Logefeld was left with the cold certainty that nothing in his life was ever going to be as it had been before. All he could think of were the cordwood skeletons, and that it was Germans who had put them there, and that *he* was a German. He learned to control the feeling as he grew into adolescence, but it stayed with him. Finally he became disgusted. Why was he molesting himself with abstract issues of national guilt, of historical evil? He was no philosopher or priest. He was just a German with an aching soul. That was hardly a life's work.

Yet no one could say he had not been trying to turn it into just that. How? By becoming a schoolboy bomb-maker? A particular irony lay in that, too, since the bombs were always used for good causes.

Human qualities still had to be cherished.

They also had to be protected from the crazies.

There were always the crazies.

Their names and colors might change but they were always there.

At one point Klaus might have become one of them, until he had very deliberately pulled a switch and changed a lot of things.

Changed his name and identity.

Changed his personal history.

Changed his career path from revolutionary to establishment academic.

Changed everything but his long-term goals.

In the general nature of things, he sometimes thought wryly, that still left him pretty much of a crazy.

Except, of course, to his own grandfather, a once celebrated, war-maimed hero of the Third Reich, who mockingly referred to him as Little Jesus, yet understood and cared about him as no one else ever had.

Klaus still had the old scrapbook, reverently put together and passed on to him by his mother, that heralded his grandfather's glory. Tempted to burn it a hundred times, he had kept it as a lesson and a reminder. His legacy. As if he could ever have forgotten the yellowed news clippings and photographs, especially the one picture that had shown Adolph Hitler himself hanging the Iron Cross around the neck of Major Helmut Schadt, whose hideously patched together face bore testimony to the heroic actions that had saved an entire Wehrmacht battalion from certain annihilation.

It had become perhaps the most famous news picture of World War II, shamelessly exploited by all sides for their own purposes. Pathways of glory, leading straight to hell. For years, antiwar stamps and posters had carried that same silently screaming face.

Not only was his grandfather alive and remarkably well, but Klaus still loved him and carried him whole in his heart.

Chapter 5

THE ONLY WAY for Paulie to have prevented the public event that the funeral finally became was for him to have spirited away his parents' bodies in the middle of the night. He had not wanted to do that. His mother and father had lived on the Amalfi coast for twenty-seven years, he had been born here, and a lot of people cared about them. So he just let things take their course and tried to handle it as best he could.

Circumstances made even that nearly impossible. With the unsolved double murder of a major artist and his wife sending the media into an instant feeding frenzy, with hundreds of the morbidly curious gridlocking the roads and plazas surrounding the church, police from several neighboring towns had to be called in simply to maintain order.

Three big *carabiniere,* running interference, were required to get Paulie through the crush of reporters and photographers working the crowd as if they were at a championship sporting event. Inside the church it was much calmer, and Paulie was able to slide beneath the cool quiet that smelled of flowers and distance himself from the rest.

He had already said his own good-byes; the performances taking place here meant nothing to him. Nor would they have meant anything to his parents, who, for as long as he had known them, had never gone inside a church to pray.

So all this was only a charade—harmless enough, but false. Just as his parents' names and much of their appearance were false, having been altered exactly twenty-seven years ago to help keep them alive. Even these efforts had finally failed. The only unblemished truth about his mother and father, thought Paulie, was the feeling they had for each other.

Lord, had they been in love.

If there was anything at all fitting in how they had died, it was in their having died together. That part they might even have liked. It had been that way for them from the start.

Imagine.

A top American hit man is ordered to kill a beautiful young woman. He goes wild for her; instead of carrying out his contract, he fakes her death and carries her off to Italy.

Try and match that one, Paulie thought, and for the first time he let anyone who might be watching see him cry.

Among the watchers was Kate Dinneson.

She was sitting off to the left of Paulie and one row back, so she was able to see his face. When he wept, so did she.

Her reaction disgusted her. Cheap, guilty sentiment. For whom were her tears? Even worse was that she was there at all.

What was it she wanted so desperately from this tall, spare, dark-eyed young man she had dressed in mourning?

Absolution?

He would never give it to her. If he gave her anything at all, it would be a bullet in the heart.

The priest's voice broke through to Paulie. Father Angelo had been his mother's and father's friend, not their priest. He recalled their coming to Positano from the United States almost thirty years ago, raising their son here and never leaving. He spoke of the many friends they had made in their adopted land, and of their contributions to its culture. Peter through his painting, Peggy through her gallery. He celebrated their warmth and kindness, their devotion to their son and one another, their generous giving to those in need.

From the aging, gentle-voiced Father Angelo, all these overworked platitudes took on a sweet melancholy for Paulie. He found them a welcome contrast to the almost two days of sharp questioning from a no-nonsense lieutenant of *carabinieri* sent down from Naples. His name was Spadero, and he was far from your friendly, deferential, neighborhood policeman. He was not one to fool around with a bedroom double murder in which a sophisticated security system was effectively neutralized, a house was broken into, and nothing apparently was stolen.

Lieutenant Spadero was finally able to punch up enough computer printouts from Rome, Washington, New York, and Interpol to learn that besides being a celebrated artist, the man who had lived for almost thirty years in Positano as Peter Walters had lived an earlier life in the United States as a high-level mob assassin named Vittorio Battaglia, followed by a later period of covert action for the Central Intelligence Agency.

The same man who was being so warmly eulogized by the priest.

All of which Paulie had already known.

Lieutenant Spadero had turned up nothing so violent in his mother's past. She had merely been witness to a couple of killings. She had taken no part in them. Of course she had once been a New York lawyer, but no specifically reprehensible acts seemed to have resulted from that.

Only a comparatively small number of people were at the grave site. Paulie stood with them beneath a blue, summer sky and watched the springtime of his life being lowered into the earth.

Father Angelo, doing his prescribed job, recited an appropriate prayer for the dead, and Paulie silently repeated some of the words after him. He guessed it was about as good a prayer as any and better than most.

Nevertheless, it embarrassed him, because he did not really believe a word he was saying and his parents deserved better.

He glanced about the open grave at those who had come to share these final moments with him, and wondered what *they* really believed. Most of the faces he saw were familiar, but some were not. He saw the fragile looks in their eyes and understood that behind them lay as little true belief as his own, and that in its place was a kind of panic.

He noticed a slender, dark-haired woman looking toward him. Her gaze gave him the sense that he was briefly illuminated.

Her eyes were a pale gray-green. He knew he had never seen her before: he was certain he would not have forgotten. Yet he could be wrong, because she did seem to know him. Or she must have known his mother or father. Why else would she be here?

He stood very still, with the priest's voice no more than a soft sigh on the summer air, and let her eyes light his face.

Visitors came into his parents' house that afternoon and evening to pay their respects. Most of them had known Paulie since he was a boy; they embraced him and wept. The women brought food to keep him from starving in his grief, and the men did their best to get him drunk.

The last of them left at about nine o'clock.

Moments later Lieutenant Spadero appeared at the door, a hard-faced man with a cynical expression who had probably been waiting outside until Paulie was alone.

"Sorry to break in on you tonight," he said, "but I'm leaving town and I just need a few minutes."

Paulie showed him in, surprised by the small human touch of an apology. In the living room, Spadero stood unmoving until Paulie offered him a place to sit.

"My sincere sympathy for your loss." The lieutenant of carabinieri spoke formally, as if this were their first meeting. "How sad to have them both taken from you at once. And like *that*."

Paulie nodded.

"I'm not always uncivilized," said Spadero. "Only when I'm working."

"Anything new?" asked Paulie.

"Not a thing. Unless you know something you're holding back, I'm naked in the shithouse on this one."

"Why would I hold anything back?"

"Because you're their son."

"Meaning?"

"You might have some macho notion of getting their killer yourself."

"You think I'm that crazy?"

Lieutenant Spadero reached for an open bottle of Chianti, poured some into a glass, and swallowed it in a single gulp. "Let's cut the bull, Paulie. I know all about your poppa. Who he was, what he did, and for whom. I'd have to be an idiot not to believe he hasn't passed some of that on to you."

"I'm an artist, Lieutenant."

"So was your poppa. But that was never enough for him, and I don't think it's going to be enough for you."

"Is that what you came to tell me?"

"What I came to tell you is that I need your help. I've got no fingerprints, no bloodstains, no witnesses, no gun, no motive. All I know is that it was a professional hit by a single killer who entered your parents' bedroom while they were asleep, woke them up, and was probably talking to them at gunpoint when your mother started shooting."

"How do you know they were talking? And that it was my mother who shot first?"

"If the killer just wanted them dead, he'd have shot them while they were asleep. So either he wanted information or the pleasure of letting your parents know who he was before he killed them, which would mean it was personal. Maybe even a payback for a hit your father might have done."

Spadero poured himself some more Chianti.

"As for your mother shooting first," he said. "Well, she was hit twice in the face. So she wasn't about to get off her own three shots by firing second. Also, her first shot was through the bed sheet."

Paulie breathed deeply, but he still felt stifled.

"You were close to your father," said the lieutenant. "Didn't he ever mention possible problems, enemies, people he might have been worried about?"

"Not to me."

Lieutenant Spadero sat weighing Paulie's answer.

"That's too bad," he said. "Because unless you can come

up with something you suddenly remember . . . or we get lucky with an informer . . . I can't see much hope for us here."

The big surprise of the night was the arrival of Tommy Cortlandt.

The CIA director was standing in the Walterses' living room no more than an hour after Lieutenant Spadero had walked out of it, his arms clutching Paulie in a powerful embrace. There were tears in Cortlandt's eyes.

"You came," Paulie said. As always, he used English when he was with the director.

"How could I not? I was at a NATO meeting in Brussels when I heard the news." Cortlandt looked at Paulie. "Sorry I wasn't at the funeral, but it would have been stupid. I'd only have been recognized by the press, which wouldn't have done either of us any good."

He drifted about the room, touching things. Then he sat down, a controlled man with cool eyes that seemed to invite a challenge.

"You all right?" he said.

Paulie shrugged. "I'm still half in shock."

"Who found them?"

"I did. I'd stopped in on my way home from Serbia."

"What did the police come up with?" asked Cortlandt.

"Nothing," said Paulie, briefly describing the lieutenant's last visit.

"Was the lieutenant right?" asked Cortlandt. "*Were* you holding anything back?"

"Yeah. But it wasn't that much. Only my father's wall safe."

"What was in it?"

"Mostly personal and legal stuff. Except for·a couple of pictures. Blowups of a man and woman blazing away with a pair of Schmeissers. They meant nothing to me, but I was hoping you might know something."

"Let me take a look."

Paulie went upstairs to the safe and took out the manila envelope. When he returned to the living room, his heart was racing.

He handed Tommy Cortlandt the two enlarged photographs. Then he just concentrated on watching his face.

"For what it's worth," said Cortlandt, "I do recognize these two people, but they've been dead for almost twenty years."

"Who were they?"

"A couple of world-class terrorists. Angelo and Patty Falanga."

"What did they have to do with my father?"

"More than they would have liked. He killed them both."

"Together?"

"Yes. Seconds after these pictures were taken."

"What made him save them? The pictures."

"I have no idea. I never knew he had them."

"These were the only pictures in the safe," Paulie said. "They're the only pictures of that kind I've ever seen in this house. Wouldn't you say they had to have had some very special importance to my father?"

"Obviously."

Paulie blinked, suddenly feeling slow and tired.

"I see where you're heading," said Cortlandt. "But your father shot the Falangas almost twenty years ago. Why would anyone wait that long for retribution?"

"I don't know. Unless the guy just found out who killed them. How many people do you think actually knew my father was involved?"

"I can't answer that with any accuracy."

"Were you Dad's chief of station back then? Did you give him the assignment to get the Falangas?"

"Yes. To both questions."

"Something like this would have to be on a top secret, need-to-know basis?"

Cortlandt nodded.

"What kind of backup did my dad have? Or was he handling it alone?"

The director took a long moment. "He had two men going in with him. They were both killed in the final action."

"Can you think of anyone else who might have known he was the killer?"

"After eighteen years? At best, I'd have to dig back, check our data base, and get lucky."

"Would you please do me that favor?"

Cortlandt was silent.

"It's important to me," said the artist.

"You're really stretching on this one, Paulie."

"I know. But what else have I got?"

Paulie was no stranger to threat, mystery, and violent death. He had been just past his eighth birthday when one of his mother's youthful, premarital involvements came near to ending her life as well as his. The only reason he was alive today was that he himself had drawn a hidden gun and shot their intended killer.

Now he was nearly twenty-seven years old. He had stopped pretending a long time ago that the darker sides of life were unknown to him, or that he loved most of what he had witnessed. Lieutenant Spadero had caught it very quickly. He was his father's son, and his father had passed on a key part of his inheritance: the knowledge that life held more grimness and cruelty than one could ever find reason for or understand.

His father had been an American of Sicilian lineage who was born and had lived the first half of his life as Vittorio Battaglia, which means "victory battle."

Imagine having to live up to a name like that.

Still, his father had earned a reputation as the top Mafia enforcer in New York. No women and children, thank you. He had run off with his only assigned female target, changed their names and appearances, and settled down to new lives in Positano.

Like father, like son.

How naturally Paulie had fallen into it. Some bloodspell had to be there. First, of course, he was an artist, having done his early suckling on his father's own talent. Then he followed his father once more by going undercover for Tommy Cortlandt and the Company. Always partly lost in his own private kaleidoscope of death, he could never quite forget the man he had shot when he was eight.

Chapter 6

KATE DINNESON DROVE SLOWLY past the house where Peter and Peggy Walters had lived and died, and where their son was still in temporary residence. Three cars were parked in front but she knew they all belonged there.

When the road ended in a cul-de-sac, Kate drove back and parked beside the other cars. She sat there for a while, gazing off at the early sun sparkling on the sea.

Carrying a briefcase, she climbed through the rock garden to the house and rang the bell.

A moment later Paulie Walters opened the door and looked at her. He remembered her eyes lighting his face across his parents' open graves and remembered being touched. What he did not remember was that she was this beautiful.

"Good morning," she said in classic Roman Italian. "My name is Kate Dinneson. We've never met but I knew your mother and father. Please accept my heartfelt condolence. If this is a bad time . . ."

"No, no. Please come in."

Paulie led her into his father's studio, where an entire wall was floor-to-ceiling glass and the light was steady and clear. She was younger than he had thought, with a softness to her flesh and a vulnerability that time had not yet been able to cover.

Paulie seated her with as much care as he would have given to posing a model. He placed her with the light coming in at a good angle, flooding her hair and shoulders and spilling down over her breasts, which were small, high, and elegantly formed.

When he was satisfied by what he saw, he backed into a facing chair, sat down, and waited.

"I've been in this room before," she said. "It's probably my all-time favorite."

"Mine too."

Kate sat very straight, hands folded primly in her lap. "Did your mother and father ever mention my name?"

"No."

"It's hard to know where to begin," Kate said. "Unless I just say I'm a writer and start from there."

"What do you write?"

"Feature stories. Mostly for the Continental News Service. I was just getting into one with your parents when this terrible tragedy happened."

Paulie showed surprise. "You mean you were writing an article about my mother and father?"

"Yes."

"They were actually going along with the idea?"

"If they weren't, I wouldn't have been doing it."

Kate opened her briefcase, took out a clutch of handwritten notes and typed pages, and handed them to Paulie along with her press credentials.

"I know it wasn't their usual style," she said. "But if you'll just glance through some of this, you'll see how much they were into the whole idea."

Paulie barely looked at the material. "And now?" he said.

"Now I think it's doubly important to get it done. I was wondering how you might feel about helping me."

Paulie said nothing.

"I know what an awful time this must be for you," Kate told him. "Yet this could be the moment for an involvement that can keep your parents alive for you. Who would be better qualified? Who would know more about them than you?"

Paulie fought to calm himself. He had to remain composed. He had to show this beautiful young writer with the incredible eyes that she was acting wisely in seeking his help.

"I saw you at the cemetery," Paulie said. "I wondered who you were."

"Well, now you know."

"Do you look at everyone the way you looked at me over my parents' graves?"

"How did I look at you?"

"I could never describe it. But I know it touched me when I very much needed to be touched."

"Then I guess you're going to help me," Kate Dinneson finally said.

Chapter 7

KLAUS LOGEFELD KNOCKED on the door of a well-cared-for house in a suburb of Berlin and waited for the old man who lived there alone to answer.

The sun was not yet up. He felt chilled from having walked the half dozen or so blocks from where he had parked his car.

The door opened and the old man stared at him. At six-fifteen in the morning he was already shaved, combed, and standing erect and resplendent in his gray security guard's uniform.

"Ernst Oberman?" Klaus said in German.

"Yes. And you?"

"Lieutenant Spier. Berlin Police Department." Klaus showed him a badge and identification. "May I come in and talk to you, please?"

"Is something wrong?"

"Nothing like that. Just a few questions about your security work at Wannsee. It shouldn't take long."

Oberman led him into the kitchen. A pot of coffee was on the stove; he poured Klaus a cup without asking. They sat down at a wooden table with straw place mats, and Klaus noted the neatness of the clean, brightly lit room.

"I have to ask you about your keys to Wannsee," he said. "You haven't by chance lost or misplaced any, have you?"

The old man frowned, his face cracking into a hundred lines. "Are you serious? Those keys are never off my belt, never out of my sight."

"Nothing personal. It's just that a man, a known criminal, was killed in Berlin last night, and a set of the Wannsee Center's keys was found in his pocket. So we're just checking to see whose they might have been."

"Well, you can be sure they're not mine, Lieutenant."

Stiff with indignation, Ernst Oberman rose, unbuttoned his uniform tunic, and showed Klaus the ring of keys dangling from his belt. "Here's where they are and here's where they stay," he said. "Unless I'm sleeping. Then they're under my pillow. Someone would have to kill me to get these keys, and I don't kill easy."

"I know that, sir."

The old man rebuttoned his gray, gold-trimmed tunic and slowly sat down. It was a chief of security's uniform at the nearby Wannsee Museum and Conference Center, but he wore it with the pride and dignity of a *Reichmarschall*.

"You know *what?*" he asked.

"That someone would have to kill you to get those keys, and that you don't kill easy."

The old man stared at Klaus across the kitchen table.

"You're no stranger to me, Captain Oberman. I know of your heroic war record with the Wehrmacht, and the many wounds you suffered serving the fatherland. I know these things will never be forgotten."

"They're forgotten already. Turned to shit like everything else we did and tried to do. Master race." He laughed coldly. "Master money-grubbers. We've become a nation of weakling shopkeepers. We're out-Jewing even the Jews. The six million we buried must be laughing in their graves."

"You have no regrets about that?"

"You mean about killing the Jews?"

Klaus Logefeld nodded.

"Of course I have regrets. But not about the six million we killed. What I regret are the five million we never got to kill because we lost the fucking war."

"I admire your honesty. These days not many have the courage to say things like that."

"There are more of us than you think, Lieutenant."

Klaus did not doubt it. Tiredly, he put down his cup and rose from the table. "Thanks for the coffee, Captain Oberman. I'm sorry to have troubled you."

"No trouble, sir. It's good to know that a German of your generation can appreciate all that the Third Reich stood for."

Heil Hitler, thought Klaus, and he followed the ramrod-straight ex-soldier out of his spotless kitchen and into the foyer.

Moving quickly and silently, he grabbed the old man's head from the rear with both hands and, with a short, vicious push-pull motion, twisted his neck backward, upward, and sideways.

The cervical column snapped with a sharp, cracking sound. Klaus felt Oberman's body give one final contraction before it slumped against him.

He dragged the old man back into the kitchen and stretched him out on the tile floor. He looked at the pale dead face and staring eyes and felt nothing—not even the satisfaction of having removed one more hurtful German from the current scene.

Pulling on a pair of fine latex gloves, Klaus made sure that the front and rear doors were locked. He washed and put away his coffee cup and wiped all fingerprints from anything he might have touched. When that was done, he opened the old man's tunic, disconnected the ring of keys from his belt, and laid them one by one on a work counter. There were nine in all.

He took two rectangular packages of sliced, half-inch-thick wax from his jacket pockets, softened the contents over a stove burner, and made a careful impression of each key. Then he put the wax impressions in the refrigerator's freezing compartment to harden, cleaned any hint of wax from the keys themselves, and slipped their ring back on Oberman's belt. His need for the keys was still a fair number of days away; when the old man's body was found, the integrity of the keys would not appear to have been compromised.

To this same end, he now set about trying to give the police reason to believe that Oberman's death had been accidental.

The cellar door opened from a small hallway off the kitchen. The stairs leading down from it were steep, of smooth-surfaced wood, and ended on a concrete floor. A perfect fatal fall waiting to happen. Particularly for an old man with dimming eyes and erratic balance.

It took only a few moments.

Klaus lifted the late Captain Oberman from the kitchen tiles, eased him into the open cellar door, and launched him down the stairs. For added detail, he took a small wicker hamper of dirty clothes out of a bathroom and tossed it next to the sprawled body. Clearly the old man had been carrying it down to the washing machine when he missed his footing and fell. Klaus was careful to leave the cellar door open and the lights on.

Returning to the kitchen, he took his now hardened wax impressions out of the freezer, placed them in plastic sheeting and a cardboard box, and slipped the small package into his jacket pocket.

Klaus checked everything once more. When he was satisfied that no visible signs of his presence remained, he left the kitchen and found a small office just off the living room. In it were a desk and a file cabinet. He went through both until he opened a folder marked WANNSEE and saw what he was looking for: several blueprints and schematics that included details of rooms, air-conditioning and heating units, and wiring and plumbing.

Moments later he left the house the same way he had entered, setting the outside door to lock behind him. He saw no one as he walked through the quiet, early-morning streets, and as far as he knew, no one saw him.

It was just ten after seven when he reached his car.

Chapter 8

IT WAS LATE in the evening of the third day that Kate and Paulie had been working together on her story about the Walterses. That the piece was merely an artifice created for her own needs made it no less real in the doing. The words were real, the connection between them was real, and the freshly dug graves of Paulie's mother and father were most real of all.

What remained unreal was the fragile web of lies that supported the entire works, with Kate herself as the biggest lie of all. So much so that at times, in the very act of speaking, the combined enormities of what she had already done and what she was even now attempting to do would suddenly clog her throat.

As for Paulie's lies, they were mostly lies of omission. Whatever he might be telling Kate about his family for her article, he was forced to leave out an almost equal amount. Not that he didn't do his censoring effectively. He was well practiced. It was just that with Kate, he did it painfully, reluctantly, as if each true fact omitted was a betrayal of everything he was growing to feel for her.

They shared a late supper that evening in his father's studio, the big, glass-walled room lighted by just two candles and the moon, and their eyes and thoughts focused solely on each other. The great Luciano Pavarotti's heart was breaking in soaring tenor notes from hidden speakers.

"I love you." He whispered the three words as if fearful of waking someone sleeping nearby.

Kate studied his face. She touched it with the tips of her fingers, a silent searching.

Paulie held his breath. What would she discover?

Yes, I can see you love me, Kate was thinking. *What you'll never know is that I loved you first.*

Carefully leaning across the table, she kissed him.

He took her upstairs.

He took her to the room that had been his from infancy until he was a man and living in a house of his own. Only as they were passing through the doorway did he realize that in all his twenty-six years of living, he had never before said "I love you" to anyone but his mother and father.

Paulie switched on the brass, green-shaded student lamp he had once studied by, and which was now going to teach him about Kate.

Dressed, she had a cool, narrow look.

Naked, her breasts and hips were fuller, more sensual.

From the softness of her lips to the pliant curves of her body she might have been one of those erotic phantom lovers that lonely men invent for themselves in the long, unpeopled stretches of the night.

Presented altogether, she drove him a little wild.

"Gently," she said, and helped him. For once, after all Nicko's practiced expertise, Kate herself was able to feel a bit like the teacher. She loved it.

Entering her, Paulie saw an image of Kate's face turned to gold in the lamplight.

She was beneath him now, and Paulie looked again at her face. It suddenly seemed different, with a new, half-frightened little girl's look cutting into and marring its glow.

"What is it?"

Holding him, she hesitated.

"Tell me," he said.

"I'm scared to death of loving you. I'm afraid that what we have might be too good."

"What's there to be afraid of in that?"

"That it won't last," she whispered, her breath quickening.

"Who says so?"

"I ... do ..." She was barely able to manage the two small words.

He could feel her beginning, although she was still a few seconds away.

"What do you know about it?" he said.

More than I'll ever be able to tell you, Kate thought.

Then she went for the sky and took Paulie with her.

The old student lamp was off and they lay holding each other in their separate darks. For Paulie Walters, it had been a knowing, drowning, passionate experience, a rising tide of wanting that had swept away the past days of bereavement. For these moments at least, his grief had been lessened in the plain, lumpy bed of his boyhood.

It was very different for Kate Dinneson. Something seemed to be waiting for her in the dark, and it was less than good. She was going through one of those panic attacks that turned simple breathing into an act of balance.

She felt vile. Why? She had done only what she had set out to do, which was to love this warm, caring, very special man, and get him to love her in return. Whom had she hurt?

No one, she thought, but it was just the beginning.

So?

So we could end up with a very large investment in each other.

Wonderful. What could be better?

If he finds out you killed his mother and father?

He won't find out, she told herself, and dropped it right there.

A faint, far-off ringing in the dark woke Paulie. A luminous digital clock said 1:07 A.M. but the nearest telephone was across the hall in his parents' bedroom. Slowly, reluctantly, he pulled away from the warm, fragrant body beside him and went to take the call.

"Paulie," said Tommy Cortlandt's voice. "I guess I woke you. How are you doing?"

It was six hours earlier in Langley, and the CIA director usually worked late, so he was probably calling from his office.

"I'm all right, Tommy." Paulie waited briefly. "Got anything good for me?"

"I'm not sure how good. But I've had some people checking back through our data base and they did come up with one small possibility."

Cortlandt paused and the connection hummed between them.

"I have to tell you, I can see nothing but damage resulting from your even getting involved in this wild goose chase."

"Why?"

"Because it's a deeply emotional thing that can get obsessive."

Paulie stood naked in his parents' bedroom with the phone against his ear. In the wavering moonlight he looked at the bed in which his mother had died, and the broad stain left by his father's blood on the pastel-colored rug.

"Not to mention the danger," he heard Cortlandt say.

"The danger?" Paulie echoed dimly.

"Remember," said Cortlandt's distant voice, "you'll be going after a killer you won't know or see, while he'll certainly be knowing and seeing you."

"Anything else?" Paulie asked.

"No." The CIA director's sigh carried over more than six thousand miles. "So here's what I have. According to the still classified records, only three of our own people ever knew your father killed the Falangas. Two of them were killed at the scene, and we've been out of contact with the third since he retired to Switzerland about ten years ago. But I do have his last known address and the name he was using at the time."

"Go ahead."

"He was calling himself William Meister and living at 15 Ausdorf. That's in Zurich."

Paulie scribbled the information on his mother's telephone pad. "Who was he?"

"A good pro. Spent almost thirty years with us. Maybe a little burned out near the end, but who isn't?"

"What did he have to do with the Falanga hit?"

"Whatever your dad told him. It was your father's operation. A lot of people had very good reason to kill your father, Paulie."

"Maybe. But not to kill my mother along with him."

The CIA director left that one alone.

"Anyway," said Paulie, "I appreciate what you've done."

Paulie hung up and stood staring at the name and address he had written down. Too much depended on them. He wished he had more.

Kate stirred as he got back into bed beside her.

"Anything wrong?" Her voice was soft, remote with sleep.

Paulie kissed the soft, silvery place between her breasts.

"Not now."

Chapter 9

KATE DINNESON CAME HOME from the Walterses' place in Positano in the late afternoon.

Essentially nomadic, Kate currently lived in a small apartment in Naples with oversized windows, a wonderful view of the bay, and lots of light. The rent was twice as much as it should have been, but she was happy to pay it because of the view and the light. She had grown up in a series of dark, urban rooms that faced blank walls, and she could still get depressed at the thought of having to lean out of a window and look straight up to see the sky.

After checking her mail and messages, she took a leisurely bath. Then she poured herself some wine and sat watching the sun burn its way into the Bay of Naples.

She thought about the past few days. She thought about Paulie, about the best and the worst. Taken altogether, she felt a kind of mystic joy along with old graves opening inside her.

Was this how she was going to respond to the fate of being human and in love? Plus her accompanying fear of the future? Evidently.

Well, she could live with it. Not to would be stupid. Looking ahead and worrying was as bad as looking back and regretting. Both poisoned you and neither altered a thing. The main reason she had changed her name was to separate herself from her parents' bloody history, to start fresh.

*   *   *

She had just finished a light meal when a knock on the door surprised her. She knew few people in Naples, and no one ever came by without first calling.

Still, she opened the door without asking who was there, and found herself looking at a smiling Klaus Logefeld.

"Klaus!"

He had never been here before, so she was startled.

"May I come in, or do you have company?"

"Of course come in. I'm alone."

Once inside, he handed her a delicate bouquet of violets. "My apologies for walking in on you like this."

Kate laughed. "That's so sweet. I can't remember the last time anyone brought me flowers."

Klaus stood awkwardly in the middle of the living room. He looked too big and curiously out of place.

"Please sit down," Kate told him as she put the flowers in a vase. "How long have you been in Naples?"

"About fifteen minutes. I came to see *you*," he said. "You're the only reason I'm in Naples."

Kate slowly sat down. She felt a charge in the air.

"What's wrong?" she asked.

"Nothing. I've just come to ask a favor." Klaus gazed out at some ships' lights on the bay. "When you called me last week, you said you appreciated what I'd done, and that if there was ever anything you could do in return . . ."

Klaus Logefeld's mouth smiled but not his eyes. "Did you really mean that or were you just being polite?"

"You've known me too long to be asking such a dumb question."

"True. But this favor involves someone besides yourself."

"Who?"

"Nicko Vorelli."

Kate just stared at him.

Klaus laughed. "Why are you looking at me as if your relationship with the great Vorelli was a secret shared only by God?"

"What's the favor, Klaus?"

"I'd like to meet your famous Dr. Vorelli. I'd like the privilege of being able to actually sit in a room with him and talk."

"Talk?" Kate was more puzzled than anything else. "About what?"

"Geopolitics. The post-Communist world. The problems of ethnic cleansing and supernationalism." Klaus shrugged. "Whatever. I've read everything Vorelli's ever written. I think he's the most brilliant political theorist living today. For me to be able to just talk to him one-on-one, to ask him questions . . ."

Klaus grinned. "I know I'm being presumptuous as all hell, Katie. But this is very important. So will you try to arrange something? Will you tell him about me?"

"I'm not sure I'd even know what to tell him, Klaus."

"Well, you can start by just saying that Alfred Mainz has long been one of his most ardent fans, and he would be honored to meet him."

"Who is Alfred Mainz?"

"I am. At least for the past sixteen years. If that stuns you, I'm sorry. Not much of my life has ever been as open as I might have liked."

She considered him. "Is Nicko supposed to recognize the name?"

"Yes."

"How?"

"Because Alfred Mainz lectures on political science at the University of Rome and has published a couple of fairly well known texts on the subject."

Kate shook her head. "All these years and you never said a word?"

"There was never a good reason. Now there is. How about it, Katie? Will you do me this favor and please try?"

Kate nodded slowly. "I'll call Nicko right now."

The tiny apartment's only telephone was in the bedroom. Kate went in and closed the door behind her.

She called an unlisted number and heard Nicko Vorelli's voice.

"Listen, Nicko. Does the name Alfred Mainz mean anything to you?"

"Yes. Of course."

"In what context?"

"As a comparatively young political theorist with some bright ideas. Why?"

"He's in my living room. He also happens to be our Klaus Logefeld."

"Did I hear you correctly?"

"Yes," said Kate, and she went on to briefly explain.

"Fascinating," said Nicko. "Now we know why God arranged for you to run into him two weeks ago in Rome."

"You mean so I could get him to *you?*"

"What else?"

"I'm not sure. It just seems like an awful lot of trouble for Klaus to go through simply to talk to you."

"Well, we don't really know whether talking to me is all he wants. We won't know that until he gets here."

"You want me to bring him?"

"Damn right. And immediately. What I *don't* want is that tricky bastard floating loose out there, knowing you shot the Walterses."

Kate hung up, feeling in an almost trancelike state. Still, when she walked out of her bedroom moments later, her smile was in place and she appeared at ease.

"I guess this is your lucky night," she said.

Klaus had been gazing out at the bay. He turned. "You mean there's a chance?"

"Nicko wants me to bring you right over."

They made the half-hour drive along the coast road in the German's car.

Only a few downstairs lights were on in the villa. The rest of the house was dark, with none of the servants in sight. Nicko Vorelli opened the door. He kissed Kate on each cheek, greeted Klaus warmly, and took them into a walnut-paneled den.

Assuming the role of hostess, Kate poured some Remy Martin into three brandy snifters. Then she settled into the background to watch quietly and listen.

Despite herself, she was fascinated. Nicko, of course, was no surprise. But Klaus Logefeld, in his persona as Alfred Mainz, was new to her, and she was very quickly taken by his authority and perception. He spoke in a sharp, probing way about how the end of the cold war had left statesmen in a new and dangerous kind of smog, in which the true nature of threats was obscured by their very subtlety and numbers. He asked Nicko Vorelli insightful questions about national responsibilities and analyzed his answers with total understanding. Perhaps most striking of all, he showed himself to be sensitive and compassionate in regard to the human condition, yet unforgiving of its deliberate cruelties.

When almost a full hour had passed, Nicko Vorelli freshened their drinks and said quietly, "All right, Alfred. That was very enjoyable and I'm truly impressed. Now please tell me why you're here."

Klaus just looked at him.

"You're much too intelligent to be an awestruck hero-worshiper," said Nicko. "So you must want something from me. Correct?"

Klaus did not so much as blink. "Yes."

"Exactly what is it you want?"

"To be part of your staff at Wannsee on September 13."

No one spoke.

Nicko said, "The meeting at Wannsee won't officially be announced for another three days. How did you find out about it?"

"Educated gossip. I must have heard it from at least three different sources."

"I haven't heard a thing," said Kate. "What on earth is happening at Wannsee on September 13?"

Nicko's eyes were cold. "A high-level international conference."

"On what?" asked Kate.

"Broadly, on human rights. More specifically, on the plague of killing and ethnic cleansing in four major civil wars in central and western Africa, which *must* be stopped at once."

"Why at *Wannsee*, of all places?"

"We're hoping the ghosts of its six million murdered Jews might add weight and purpose to what we do there."

Kate looked at Klaus Logefeld. "Why did you have to lie to me?"

"I'm sorry, Katie. But this meant too much to risk your turning me down."

"What about *my* turning you down?" asked Nicko.

"I can only beg you not to, sir."

"Why?"

"Because I believe I've been preparing to be at this meeting since I was twelve years old."

"What happened then?"

"I sat in a Berlin movie house and understood what genocide really means."

"You think you're the only one who ever saw those horror movies?"

"No," said Klaus. "But I know of no one who can contribute more than I to keeping such things from ever happening again. It's been the focus of my entire adult life. There's nothing I wouldn't do to be at Wannsee."

"I believe you."

Klaus Logefeld took a long, deep breath. "Then you'll take me?"

"No. I'm sorry. Inasmuch as my gut feeling is that your passion and zealousness alone could probably do us all a lot of good, I'm afraid my answer still has to be no."

"*Why*, for God's sake?"

"Because quite frankly you scare the hell out of me."

Klaus's eyes were blank.

"You see," said Nicko, "I know how you manipulated Kate to get here tonight. I know that you not only tricked her into shooting two people she never should have shot, but that you're the one person alive who can implicate her in their deaths."

Klaus and Nicko stared at each other.

Kate heard a faint whisper of movement and saw Nicko's hand come up from behind a cushion with a silencer-lengthened automatic pointed at Klaus's chest.

"Don't, Nicko!"

Kate's cry was pure reflex.

Klaus smiled. "Thanks, Katie. You needn't worry. Your Nicko isn't about to soil his priceless oriental with my rich German blood. Once he's seen and heard my feature presentation, I'm sure he won't be doing any shooting at all."

"What feature presentation?" asked Vorelli.

"Pictures and tapes of everything that happened in the Walterses' bedroom. If you're interested, they're in my outside jacket pockets."

Kate looked at Nicko. He nodded slightly and she got the material out of Klaus's pockets.

She played the tapes while they both glanced through the photographs, which were synchronized with the dialogue.

Kate felt as though she were living through every second of it again.

"Forgive me, Katie," said Klaus when it was over. "If there was any way I could have done this without involving you, I swear I would have."

He considered Nicko, who was still pointing the automatic at his chest.

"Just so we understand each other, Dr. Vorelli. There are three other sets of these pictures and audiotapes in the hands of people I trust. If I should be hurt, disappear, or die, one set will automatically be sent to the chief prosecuting attorney of Naples. Another set will go to the Interior minister in Rome. And the third set will be hand delivered to the editor in chief of the International News Service in Milan."

Klaus Logefeld, aka Alfred Mainz, suddenly seemed tired.

"The same will apply," he said, "if I somehow fail to appear at Wannsee on September 13 as part of your staff."

Chapter 10

PAULIE WALTERS TOOK OFF from Naples on a 7:00 A.M. flight, changed planes in Rome, and arrived at Zurich International Airport at shortly before 9:00. He rented a Ford Fiesta from Hertz, plotted his route on a detailed Zurich street map, and half an hour later was parked almost directly across the street from 15 Ausdorf.

It was a small, undistinguished apartment house on a tree-lined block. Paulie entered the vestibule with only the mildest of hopes. Tommy Cortlandt had said the name and address were ten years old, and Paulie had been unable to find any telephone listing for a William Meister. Still, not many retired spooks ever really felt secure enough to trust publicly listed numbers, not even with the brand-new names they almost invariably adopted.

The vestibule wall contained ten mailboxes. Apartment 4-B was marked with a faded W. MEISTER. Paulie tried the vestibule door, found it locked, and quickly picked it open.

He rode upward in a smooth-running, polished brass cage. Getting out on the fourth floor, he passed a door behind which a little girl was screaming as though she were being beaten to death. Apartment 4-B was the last on the corridor. No sounds came from inside before Paulie rang the bell.

He heard a halting, clumping step.

"Who's there?" said a man's voice in Swiss-accented German.

"My name is Paul Walters," Paulie answered in English. "Peter Walters was my father. Are you William Meister?"

This time the man used English. "Who gave you that name?"

"Tommy Cortlandt."

Slowly two locks clicked, the chained door opened a crack, and a gray-bearded face peered out.

They stared at each other. Then the chain was disengaged, the door swung open, and Paulie went inside.

"You're handsome like your father," said Meister. "But you've got much more serious eyes."

Paulie saw a tall man, shortened nearly half a foot by leaning on a walker. He moved back into the living room with a painful lurch and shuffle. Arriving at a deep armchair he sat down, surrounded by stacks of books piled on the floor like barricades. The room didn't appear to have been cleaned in years. Age and neglect had turned once white curtains gray.

"Sit down, sit down," said the former agent. "Just toss the books off that chair. Can't remember when I last had a visitor. Must be important if Tommy Cortlandt gave you my name. Guess it has something to do with what happened to your mother and father. Heard about it on the radio. Terrible tragedy."

Paulie cleared the chair of books and sat down. The old spook had a pale, narrow face, translucent with age and surrounded by a fluff of white hair.

"So what is it?" he asked in English, his accent faintly midwestern. "You're sure as hell not here to look at my books and calcifying bones."

Paulie handed him the pictures from his father's wall safe. "I understand you were part of this operation. The Falanga hit."

Meister sat frowning at the photographs. "Where did you dig these up?"

"In my father's safe."

"You mean after he and your mother were shot?"

Paulie nodded.

"Now you're looking to connect them to your parents' deaths?"

"That's right."

"Based on what?"

"They happen to be the only pictures my father ever saved of anything connected with his work."

"And?"

"They're the single lead I have."

"What lead? They're not a lead. They're not even a prayer."

Paulie told him that, according to the main CIA database at the organization's headquarters building in Langley, Virginia, he was the one person alive who'd worked with Peter Walters on that hit. "That makes you the only one who might be able to tell me whether anyone closely connected to the Falangas actually knew that my father shot them."

"How would that help you?"

"I'm hoping it might at least give me an idea of who would want to kill my father."

"You mean a deferred act of vengeance, eighteen years after the fact?"

"I'm not up to the eighteen years yet. That's the second step. Right now I just want to find out who might have known my father was the shooter."

"Know what I think?" Meister said. "You're chasing your ass around an empty latrine."

Paulie was silent. A trapped fly buzzed between the dirty gray curtains and a window.

"Where did you come from this morning?" asked Meister.

"Positano."

"You came seven hundred miles for *this*?"

William Meister sank back into his chair, lost in memory.

"Listen," he said. "One other guy knew about your father shooting the Falangas. He was your dad's private mole inside the Falangas' crowd. That's how we knew where to hit them."

"Cortlandt didn't know about him?"

"No one knew. Not even the two other agents in our group. Your father told me only near the end, in case something went wrong and he was killed."

"Who was the mole?"

"A young Italian college student." Meister stared off at a small mound of dust-covered books. "Your father said the kid needed tuition money."

"What was his name? What college?"

"You think I remember after eighteen years?"

Pushing himself up out of his chair, the ex-agent groped for his walker and then lurched between stacks of books until he reached a pile in a corner of the room. Rummaging through it, he pulled out a couple of dog-eared notebooks and brought them back to his chair.

"My memoirs," he said dryly, thumbing through clusters of smudged and yellowed pages.

Paulie watched. When Meister rubbed his face, his flesh shifted like pudding. Here and there he paused to silently read a passage, shake his head in either wonder or disgust, and move on.

At last he straightened in his chair, licked his lips, and looked at Paulie with rheumy eyes.

"Anthony Pinto," he said. "That was his name. Eighteen years ago he was a student at Catholic University in Milan."

Almost the entire route from Zurich to Milan followed good superhighways, and Paulie reached the urban sprawl of the Universita Cattolica on the Via Ianzone in under two hours.

He showed a dark-haired young woman at the office of the registrar the false badge and identification of a Lieutenant Guido Ferlandina of the *carabinieri*.

"I'd like to see the file on one of your former students," he told the clerk. "His name is Anthony Pinto and he was at the university about eighteen years ago."

Moments later the clerk brought a folder to an empty desk and left Paulie to go through it alone.

A photograph showed a slender, fair-haired young man with intense eyes and a forced smile. His grades were excellent.

His home address had been in Padua. Later records revealed his having received medical training at the University of Bologna, along with further study in general and thoracic surgery. The most recent address listed for him was in Rome, where he was chief of thoracic surgery at Saint Peter's Hospital.

Paulie drove directly to the Milan Airport, returned his rental car, and boarded the 3:30 P.M. flight to Rome five minutes before its scheduled departure time.

He caught up with Anthony Pinto as he was leaving the hospital doctors' lounge.

"Dr. Pinto?"

The surgeon stopped and looked at Paulie. Time had taken much of his once fair hair and all of the forced smile he had worn in his college photograph.

"And you?" he said.

"Paul Walters."

Pinto frowned. "The artist?"

"Yes. Also the son of Peggy and Peter Walters."

"I read about your parents," said Pinto. "My sympathy. What can I do for you?"

"Is there someplace we can talk?"

The doctor hesitated. A vein pulsed in his temple.

"It won't take very long and it's important," said Paulie.

"My office is just down the corridor."

They walked through several busy anterooms before the surgeon closed a final door and settled behind his desk. Paulie sat down facing him. He suddenly felt tired and edgy. Chafing, he began without a preamble.

"Do you have any idea who might have shot my mother and father, Dr. Pinto?"

Pinto's eyebrows rose. "Why would you ask me a question like that?"

Paulie took out the two pictures of the Falangas' final moments and handed them across the desk. "Because I found these in my father's safe after he and my mother were killed."

Pinto studied the pictures. "What do these have to do with me?"

"Do you really want to do this the hard way?"

The doctor remained silent.

"All right," said Paulie. "Eighteen years ago you were working undercover for my father. During this time, you set up Angelo and Patty Falanga for a CIA operation that ended with my father shooting them both just seconds after these pictures were snapped."

He paused. "Now do you want to waste more time, or do we move ahead?"

Pinto looked away from Paulie and out a window.

"Whom did you tell that my father shot the Falangas?"

"I never told anyone."

"You're lying," said Paulie. "You did tell someone. Whoever you told killed my parents."

Paulie waited for some reaction to his bluff.

"Unless," he added, "I'm wrong and you did the shooting yourself.

"I want a name from you, Dr. Pinto," Paulie continued. "If I don't get it before I leave this office, I'm going to tell those who still revere the memory of Patty and Angelo Falanga that you were the Judas who sold them out to the CIA."

Pinto's lips worked dryly. "You wouldn't do that."

"Why wouldn't I?"

"Because you know I'd be dead in two days."

"So?"

"For God's sake! You're an artist, not an assassin."

"That was before my parents were murdered."

"I swear I wasn't to blame."

"Then who was?"

"There's no way I can know for sure. I wasn't there. But I did tell one man that your father shot the Falangas."

"What's his name?"

"When I knew him he called himself Klaus Logefeld. I don't know what name he's using now."

"German?"

Pinto nodded tiredly. He seemed to have aged a decade in minutes.

"What was he?"

"Everything from a terrorist to a savior of the world. You name it."

"Is he here in Rome?"

"He said he was."

"What did he ask you for?"

"The shooter who took out the Falangas."

"How did he know you knew that?"

"He never told me. But he's always had all sorts of lines out."

"Did he know you sold out the Falangas?"

"Christ, no! I wouldn't be here if he knew that. He idolized them."

"What made you hand him my father as their killer?"

"Klaus knows enough about my early student years to end my career tomorrow." The surgeon brought the fingers of both hands together. They were shaking. "I couldn't stand up to that. I've worked too hard to throw it all away."

"So you threw away my mother and father instead?"

"It wasn't like that. I was sick over it. I never expected them to be shot. Certainly not your mother. Please understand. I had no choice."

"There's always a choice."

"None that I could live with."

Paulie could think of no argument against that.

"Where does this Klaus Logefeld live?" he asked.

"About a twenty-minute drive from here. Not far off the Via della Lungara." Pinto hesitated. "At least that was the address he gave me."

"Then you're going to drive me there right now."

The parking lot was directly in back of the hospital.

Paulie watched Pinto get behind the wheel of his car, then he slid into the seat beside him.

The doctor's nervousness had increased. His movements were hesitant, shaky, and the keys jangled in his hand as he sought the ignition. Then the keys slipped from his fingers entirely, and he bent and groped for them on the floor under his seat.

"Easy," said Paulie. "Just do as I tell you and you'll be all right."

The surgeon lifted his hand from the floor. Paulie saw the automatic a split second before he heard a muffled shot. He felt a slight burning across his forehead.

He grabbed the barrel just as a second shot took him in the arm.

One more and I'm dead, he thought. Paulie struggled to turn the barrel in Pinto's strong hand.

Finally Paulie wrenched the automatic around and heard the soft sound of a shot smothered between their chests.

Pinto went limp against the driver's door. Blood stained his chest where his jacket was open. His eyes stared.

All I'm left with is a German name, thought Paulie, who had little doubt that even this would turn out to be false.

An ambulance siren drew him out of his reverie. He looked around the parking lot. No one was in sight, and the three muffled shots inside the car had apparently gone unnoticed. He felt light-headed and curiously without pain. Examining his forehead in the rearview mirror, he saw a shallow, angled gash above his right eye slowly oozing blood. Lucky. Lucky, too, with the wound in his arm. The bullet had passed through only flesh, and he was able to stanch the bleeding with a handkerchief.

Moments later he left Dr. Anthony Pinto alone in his car, dead seemingly by his own hand, his finger still on the trigger. Paulie walked fifty yards to his third Hertz rental of a very long day, and drove out of the parking lot.

Expecting nothing, he stopped at a public phone, asked the operator if there was a Rome listing for a Klaus Logefeld, and got just what he expected.

Paulie drove directly to a company safe apartment on the Via Boncompagni and took care of his wounds. He woke in a fever during the night, his mind a swirling montage of Kate Dinneson's face and an anonymous, perhaps even nonexistent German called Klaus Logefeld.

Chapter 11

THE PRESIDENT WAS ALONE as Tommy Cortlandt entered the Oval Office, a fact that was in itself significant.

The CIA director could recall only three other times that he had been summoned to the White House for a private audience. Each time had turned out to be special, although never a good sort of special. Once it had come near to being a full-blown disaster. Even now, Cortlandt could feel its remembered weight pressing his chest as he crossed the room.

"It's good to see you, Tommy."

James Dunster rose and came out from behind his desk to shake Cortlandt's hand. The president was a tall string bean of a man, homely and physically awkward enough to be attractive in a distinctly Lincolnesque way. Cartoonists usually had a field day portraying him in shawls and stovepipe hats, while the more Freudian of his image makers were certain that his resemblance to the Great Emancipator had gotten him elected in the first place.

"Good to see you, too, Mr. President."

Cortlandt searched Dunster's bony face for possible portents, but found nothing.

"What's happening, sir?"

"No more than our normal crises, so you can stop looking so worried." The president's voice was soft as a southerner's drawl, but there was no mistaking its touch of New England. "I just need your ear and possible help on something."

He motioned the CIA director into a chair and settled

his own length into a facing leather couch. He poured a couple of black coffees from an ever-present thermos and handed a cup to Cortlandt.

"I had a call from German chancellor Eisner a few hours ago," said the president. "It was routine. Nothing momentous. He happened to mention the conference he's hosting at Wannsee on September 13, and I was struck by something he said."

Dunster paused for a sip of coffee.

"Eisner said, 'This whole conference is going to be a dark and terrible mirror, and I have to wonder how many of us will be able to peer into it and not shudder.'"

The president paused once more, this time to mull over the words.

"Of course, the chancellor was speaking as a German," said Dunster. "How could he not? Just thinking about what the Germans have done in this century is enough to turn you green. But the sad truth is that much of the same horror is going on even now in at least four African countries, no one is doing anything about it, and there's plenty of guilt to go around."

The president shrugged, suddenly impatient with himself. "Anyway, the point of all this is that I've decided I want to be at Wannsee myself."

"Whom have you told about this?"

"Only you."

"Just one point," said Cortlandt. "Since Wannsee's been set up at the State Department and foreign minister level, do you really want to turn it into a summit conference?"

"Not at all. That would destroy my purpose. Other than for Chancellor Eisner's appearance as host, I intend to be the only head of state present."

"And what's your purpose?"

"To make a statement that'll be heard."

"By whom?"

"The oppressed."

"Where?"

"Everywhere. But especially in Liberia, Angola, Burundi, and Rwanda, where the suffering is fearsome and must be stopped at once. So I'm going to make some noise."

"You make me want to stand up and cheer, Mr. President. But it's not going to be that simple."

"I don't expect it to be simple, Tommy. That's why you're here."

"Frankly, I can see only one way to handle this, and that's with total secrecy and surprise."

"Which means?"

"You would just appear at Wannsee on the thirteenth, shake hands with Eisner, make your noise . . . as you call it . . . and leave.

"There'll be a trade meeting going on in Brussels at about that time," said Cortlandt. "Could you arrange to put in a brief, ceremonial appearance?"

"No problem. I was sending the vice president, but I'll go myself."

"That would be perfect cover for your whole trip. You could fly into Brussels on the twelfth, stay overnight, and make the short hop to Berlin early the next morning."

"Who would have to know in advance?"

"No one. The change in your overall schedule would come to less than four hours. You could tell your pilot just before takeoff from Brussels."

"And security?"

"I'd have that arranged for both at the NATO air base near Eberswalde, and Wannsee. In fact the secrecy itself would be your best possible insurance. What assassins need most is knowing a time and place in advance. And in this, you'd be giving them neither."

The president weighed Cortlandt's plan. "You actually make it sound feasible."

"It can be done. What I can't help you with is the flak you'll have to take afterward from every possible side."

"If all goes well, it'll be worth it."

Cortlandt said nothing.

Dunster's smile was cool. "Evidently not to you. Right?"

"Everyone has his own appointment with life, Mr. President."

Chapter 12

IF VICE PRESIDENT JAYSON FLEMING had not arrived early for his briefing with the president, he would have missed running into Tommy Cortlandt as the CIA director was leaving the Oval Office.

"Tommy!" he said, and looked to see who accompanied Cortlandt out of the president's office. The glance represented years of political conditioning, not just curiosity. The fact that Cortlandt appeared to have been alone with the president doubled Jayson Fleming's interest.

The two men shook hands.

"How are things, Jay?" said the CIA director.

"Until I saw you, I thought great. With our top spook coming out of a one-on-one with the Chief, I'm suddenly not so sure. Should I send my wife to the country?"

"Not yet. You'll be the second to know when I hit the panic button."

Fleming and Cortlandt had been friends for more than twenty years. In fact, they had actually worked together at Langley.

"How about tennis one of these days?" the vice president asked.

"As long as it's doubles and you give me a few decent line calls."

"You mean I can't cheat?"

"Only on your wife."

Fleming laughed. "Thank God for small favors. I'll call you."

Cortlandt left and Jayson Fleming went in for his meeting with Jimmy Dunster.

The president was on the telephone. He waved Fleming into his usual chair.

The VP listened to Jimmy Dunster's all-too-familiar voice pumping out its usual assortment of platitudes. *Just once*, Fleming thought, *I'd like to hear him say something that might actually surprise me.*

President Dunster put down the phone, scribbled some notes on a pad, and turned to Fleming. "Sorry to hold you up, Jay."

"No problem, Mr. President. What's on the agenda?"

"We'll get to that in a minute. First I have a change to make in our schedules."

Fleming took a leather-bound day journal out of his briefcase and flipped it open. "When is that?"

"The twelfth and thirteenth of this coming month. September. It's that trade meeting you were going to be covering in Brussels. I've decided I'd better handle it myself."

"Anything wrong?"

"More of our usual worsening trade figures. I may have to throw some weight around this time."

The vice president made the necessary adjustments on his calendar. "There goes Amy's shopping trip, which should save me a bundle."

James Dunster smiled. "She'll make up for it next year."

"I suppose Tommy Cortlandt will be going with you."

"Why do you say that?"

"I just ran into him as he was leaving. I figure that may have been why he was here."

"Yes," said Dunster. "Tommy is going with me."

"I ran into your boss this morning."

So said the vice president to Ken Harris, the deputy director of the CIA, over drinks at their Georgetown club early that evening.

Harris, who was Jayson Fleming's oldest and closest friend, responded, "Where was that?"

"Coming out of the Oval Office."

"Who was with him?"

Fleming grinned at the inevitable question. "Nobody. It was a one-on-one."

Harris, a tough-faced man with the still-lean body of an aging middleweight, sipped his bourbon in silence.

"Tommy didn't tell you?" said the VP.

"I'm afraid there are still a few small things the guy can't quite get himself to share with me."

It had become a wry, inside joke. All three men had started their careers with the Agency at about the same time, and Harris and Cortlandt were still in an unending, often scratchy contention with each other.

"Do you know what the meeting was about?" said the deputy director.

"I think so," said Fleming, and he repeated the Brussels story.

Ken Harris stared into his drink. "Sounds like a bit of high-level chess."

"How?"

"A couple of things. I can't see any substantive reason for Dunster going to that Mickey Mouse meeting in the first place. That's strictly *vice* presidential posturing. But if he *is* going, he'd never be dragging along his director of intelligence. Not unless he was planning something else along the way."

"Like what?"

The deputy director shrugged. "Who knows with him? He picks up Brownie points wherever he can. I think he started campaigning for his second term exactly two minutes after his inauguration speech."

Fleming laughed.

"It's not funny. The man holds the most powerful office on earth, and he hasn't a true core position on anything but the latest poll swing."

"So what else is new?"

Ken Harris took a long moment. When he finally spoke, his voice had dropped so low it was actually conspiratorial. "What's new is that you've just told me he's going to be in Brussels on the twelfth and thirteen of next month."

"So?"

"So that's probably the exact time and place we've been waiting for."

Jayson Fleming looked into his friend's cool gray eyes and detected a shimmer of madness. He wanted to shake his head. He wanted to shout No! He wanted to tell this controlled, always-calculating man that all those secret, Machiavellian discussions they'd been having over the past months had been purely hypothetical, nothing more. All he could do was sit mute and paralyzed.

"Easy," said Harris.

Fleming saw that his hands had started to tremble so violently that his drink was splashing onto the table. He put down his glass and a waiter quickly appeared, wiped up the small puddle of gin, and left.

"You OK?" asked Ken Harris.

The vice president nodded and swallowed what remained of his martini. "You just caught me by surprise."

"By now it shouldn't be a surprise."

"I guess I never believed it was real."

"It's as real as you want it to be, Jay."

Fleming breathed deeply. "Why Brussels?"

"Because Brussels has it all. It's a foreign city on another continent. It's home to a dozen terrorist groups eager to claim credit for any hit on a high-profile Western leader. The local security is about as lax as you'll find in any European capital. And I have some very dependable connections there.

"What's suddenly spooking you?" said the deputy director. "The morality or the fear?"

"To be honest, a fair amount of each."

"We've gone over every part of this a hundred times. If you're serious, we'll probably never get a better shot at it than now. If you're not serious, than just relax and accept the fact that you'll never be president of the United States. Hey, it's an impossible, egomaniacal job at best."

Fleming's smile was dismal. "There's still always the outside chance of my being elected after Jimmy's second term."

"Forget it," said Ken Harris. "After close to another seven years of being Jimmy Dunster's grinning errand boy, who the hell's going to want to nominate you?"

The vice president nodded slowly.

Chapter 13

KATE WAS AT HOME, reworking some of the material on her Walters article, when the telephone rang. It was 8:17 P.M.

"Do you have any memory of me at all?" said Paulie's voice.

Kate breathed deeply. "Oh, Lordy," she whispered.

"Does that mean you remember who I am?"

"What are you trying to do to me? It's been two and a half days."

"You've been counting."

"Every terrible second," Kate said. "Where *are* you?"

"Positano. My folks' house. I can't seem to cut the cord and go home to my own place."

"I'll be there in an hour." Then a trifle uncertainly, "Is that all right?"

"I just hope I'll be able to last that long," said Paulie.

Kate drove into Positano, parked in front of the Walterses' house, and with a pounding heart climbed the curving stone steps through the garden. The door opened and they held each other with an urgency like none Kate could remember. She felt weak, frightened, foolish, a thirteen-year-old wanting without knowing what.

"I guess you do remember me," Paulie said when he could speak.

Inside, they went for each other again and Kate saw the gauze taped to his forehead.

"What happened?"

"Nothing."

She grasped his arm to turn him toward a light and Paulie winced.

"What happened?" she asked again.

Kate took his hand, pulled up his sleeve, and stared at the bandage. Blood stained its front and back.

"Knife or gunshot?" she said.

"Gunshot."

"Are you still carrying the bullet?"

He shook his head.

"Has a doctor seen it?"

"I don't need a doctor. It's clean."

"Was the head wound from a bullet too?"

Paulie grinned.

"Very funny," Kate said. "Do you know what another fraction of an inch could have meant?"

"No. Tell me."

"What are you? Some kind of closet Mafioso?"

Paulie leaned over and kissed her. "Aren't all Italians?"

"You're American."

"Oh. Sometimes I forget."

Kate looked at him. "I suppose that's all you're going to tell me."

"Yes, Mother."

Kate took him upstairs and uncovered his wounds.

"They don't look too bad. Where did you pick them up?"

"Rome."

Paulie watched as she cleaned, treated, and redressed the injured areas. "You handle this stuff well, like you've done it before."

"I used to live in Rome."

They went into his childhood bedroom, sat beside each other on the edge of his bed, and touched fingertips. That alone made Kate feel better.

"You could have died," she said. "And I'd never have seen you again or even known what had happened."

"Yes. But I didn't die and you're seeing me just fine."

"Still, it's frightening."

Paulie nibbled a soft ear.

"What it does," Kate said, "is just make me aware of how little I know about you."

"Maybe it's better that way," he said. "Because we still know the important things, and whatever came before is just history anyway."

"What are the important things?"

"How we feel when we're together. Everything I sensed and wanted when I first saw you."

Her eyes looked vaguely wistful. "How I'd love to believe that."

"Try. It's easy."

Maybe for you, thought Kate Dinneson.

Then they reached and touched and were all over each other.

After a while, somewhere nearer the finish than the start, emerging from the strain and unease and the nest of lies she was slowly smothering in, like a prize she did not deserve, a fresh breath of hope entered her along with him. It was so sweet and appealing that she let herself be carried away, knowing exactly what it could lead to but not caring. She was willing to take as much as possible for as long as she was able and the devil take what came after.

Chapter 14

Professor Alfred Mainz was addressing a packed crowd in the University of Rome's largest lecture hall. One of the university's most popular speakers, Mainz seemed to attract almost as many faculty members and outsiders as he did students. In the often obscure realm of political science, no one knew how to grab and hold on to an audience like Professor Mainz.

He was more than just a good pitchman. The professor brought the intellect of a scholar, the passion of a zealot, and the world view of a prophet to the lectern. Because Alfred Mainz could make any audience feel he truly believed every word he was saying, he had a better than fair chance of making believers of those listening to him.

Afterward, he spent an hour doing some of the busywork that was part of being an academic. He completed it judiciously and without complaint; the fact was, he liked it. He found the work to be just about the only area of normalcy he had ever experienced in the course of his less than normal life. It allowed him the brief illusion of a continuing existence unthreatened by sudden, violent death; neither his own nor anyone else's.

Early that evening, about two hours after his last class of the day, Klaus Logefeld drove a short distance outside Rome and parked behind a small stone house that boasted a faded, peeling locksmith sign. He wore horn-rimmed glasses and an iron-gray moustache and hairpiece, which he carefully adjusted in the rearview mirror. Satisfied with his disguise, he left the car, crossed a littered, weed-choked backyard, and knocked on the rear door of the house.

The locksmith, a fat man with sagging jowls and a dead cigarette butt clenched between nicotine-stained teeth, let him in.

"Mr. Fagione," he said. "You're exactly on time."

"I'm always on time, Guido. You have my keys?"

"Sure. Why not? I'm always on time too. A few tricky problems with the wax impressions, but that's all part of it, right?"

Klaus followed the man down a flight of stairs into a cluttered cellar workshop so crowded with equipment—metal forms, vises, grinding tools, molds, electric ovens—there was barely room to move around.

The locksmith took a brown envelope from a cabinet drawer and emptied its contents onto a workbench.

"Here are your keys and your wax impressions, Mr. Fagione. If I do say so myself, as perfect a job as you'll find anywhere. Pick them up. Hold them. Look at them."

Klaus examined the keys. The workmanship was indeed meticulous, and the material was the best.

"Excellent. Would you put them on a ring for me, please?"

The locksmith rummaged through a drawer, found a key ring of suitable size, and slid all nine keys into place. Klaus pocketed them along with his wax impressions and took out his wallet. "I gave you a hundred and twenty-five thousand lire deposit, so there's an equal amount due. Correct?"

"That's it."

Klaus Logefeld counted out a wad of bills and handed them over. "Please count the money yourself so there's no mistake."

Guido did as instructed.

"Exactly," he said. "Thank you very much, Mr. Fagione."

Klaus shook the locksmith's hand. "I must say it's a pleasure to do business with you, Guido."

The fat man grinned. It broke his face into soft folds. "Just recommend me to your friends."

"What friends?"

They laughed.

The sun was red and still sinking as Klaus drove away from the house.

It was slightly before 8:00 P.M. when he parked his car at Rome's international airport.

Forty minutes later he was aboard an Alitalia flight taking off for Berlin.

The Wannsee Museum and Conference Center contained nothing of great material value. Whatever worth was attached to the landmark villa lay in its history and mystique, which could not be carried off and sold. The center's nighttime security reflected this, with only a single guard on duty at the gatehouse and none at all in the museum or on the grounds.

Klaus Logefeld knew all this and more from the documentation he had taken from Captain Oberman's study just after he'd killed him. Still, there was an air, a mood to the place in the moonlit dark that belied its casual security. Klaus sensed it as he worked his way through a patch of woods, climbed over a concrete wall, and edged in and out of shadows toward the villa. Even the damp night seemed to invade his lungs like a message of alarm.

Here, in this dark mansion, was where it had all started on a truly systematized basis. Of course the mass murder of Jews had already been going on for several years, but never following any broad overall plan, and never on the kind of scale that would eventually defy all rational belief.

On January 20, 1942, what was to become known as the Wannsee Conference was held in this particular villa in Wannsee, Berlin, to discuss and coordinate the implementation of the Final Solution. The villa, Am grossen Wannsee 56–58, was a former Interpol property confiscated by the SS. The conference was hosted by Heinrich Himmler's top deputy, Reinhard Heydrich.

Klaus Logefeld knew every fact, every detail, every element of this landmark event. Heydrich had invited the state secretaries of the most important German government ministries to attend the conference, which was significant for two reasons: first, it was the only meeting to involve such prominent members of the ministerial bureaucracy; second, it was the moment at which Adolph Hitler's decision to murder every last Jew in Europe—from Ireland to the Urals and from the Arctic to the Mediterranean—was officially announced to this bureaucracy, whose cooperation was considered necessary. It was not a meeting at which this decision was argued. Those present talked about the implementation of a decision already made for the "final solution to the Jewish question."

Here in this place, thought Klaus. Heading across a stretch of freshly mowed grass whose sweetness was still in the air, Klaus approached the rear of the museum. He had the villa's schematics folded in his pockets, but he had memorized many of the main features and had no need to check anything at this point. He found the outside alarm box on a wall beside a dry well and neutralized the entire system with the appropriate key on his ring. Then he paced off twenty meters to the right, came to a short flight of covered steps leading down to a cellar door, opened the lock with another of his newly minted keys, and entered the blackness beneath the building.

Klaus switched on a small flashlight. He unfolded the necessary diagrams and spread them on the floor to orient himself. This was only a dry run, strictly for planning. But the success or failure of whatever might take place here on September 13 would depend greatly on what he charted now.

According to his blueprints he was directly under the main conference room. He began checking out the walls and ceilings. Much of this area had been converted into reference rooms, with bookshelves lining knotty pine walls, and the ceilings made up of acoustic squares. Either material would serve his needs; both could easily be removed and replaced undetected. Assuming a final security check a day or two before September 13, Klaus planned on having everything in place by September 9. Any later, and he might run into additional night guards. Any sooner, and there was always the added possibility of his charges being discovered.

As for the explosive itself, Klaus had decided on French *plastique* rather than the comparable American C-4, which was a bit more stable but less malleable and not nearly as powerful. Not that the power factor really mattered; if things ever reached the point of actual detonation, the relative size of the resulting catastrophe would hardly be all that important.

Climbing on a chair and using a pocketknife for leverage, the professor carefully eased a square of acoustic board out of the ceiling and flashed his light into the opening. The exposed space was wide and deep enough to allow him more than enough room for the charge he would be using. He replaced the acoustic board and repeated the same procedure in three other sections of the basement, identifying possible backup positions.

When he was finished in the basement, he climbed an interior stairway to the first floor, which was where he would begin his operation.

Since he would enter the museum on the thirteenth unarmed because of the security check, he would need quick and easy access to a small handgun. The men's room off the main entrance lobby seemed the most viable location for such a cache, and he followed the pinpoint beam of his flashlight through its swinging doors.

The individual toilet stalls were enclosed by ceiling-high walls, perfect for his needs. Not only would he have privacy if others were in the washroom, but a small, removable ventilator grill was set into the ceiling, behind which he could tape a loaded automatic. Klaus felt an instant lift in his spirits. A good omen, he thought, and he decided to cache his remote detonator right here with the gun so he could pick them both up at the same time.

Klaus unlocked and entered the surveillance room, which was dark, deserted, and nonfunctioning tonight but would be the pulsing heart of the place on September 13.

It had no windows, so he made bold use of his flash to look everything over. He studied the banks of television screens, the audio and video controls. He figured out the rooms, corridors, and other areas covered by the cameras and microphones. He located the main and individual unit power switches, the fuses, and the circuit breakers and made notes on the color-coded wires connected to each.

Depending upon how well or how badly things went, the room could be a help or a liability. That was a judgment he would have to save for later. Still, when it finally came time for him to act, the decision and the wire-pulling would be his.

All right, what else?

He could think of nothing else.

For a moment, Klaus Logefeld found himself enjoying a shining little fantasy in which everything he planned went off beautifully, no one had to die, and his message finally reached a threatened world and helped light prevail over darkness.

Chapter 15

A GLITTERING, FULL-DRESS AFFAIR was in full swing at the Naples home of Count Enzo Bonamotti, a world-class shipping mogul. Soft string music played in the background and everyone appeared rich, distinguished, powerful, or at the very least beautiful.

Nicko Vorelli stood with the Italian foreign minister and a group of naval and military officers, none of whom were below the rank of admiral or general. Kate sat off to one side, watching. Catching her eye at one point, Nicko motioned her over but she shook her head. She needed a respite from high-level chatter.

Earlier that evening, as power, wealth, and gold braid shimmered around them, Nicko had gripped her arm and whispered, "Do you have any idea how wonderful it makes me feel just to have you here beside me?"

He was standing close, head cocked to one side, staring down at her very seriously. *He means it,* she thought, *he actually means it.* She felt disturbed, tender, and guilty all at the same time. *After what I've just made it possible for an obviously dangerous man to be able to do to him.*

A short while later Nicholas Vorelli broke away from the foreign minister and his potpourri of admirals and generals and came over to where Kate was sitting.

"I guess you're having a pretty terrible time," he said softly.

"I'm sorry, Nicko. It's my own stupid fault. I feel like the original specter at the feast."

"Then let's get out of here."

Kate hesitated.

"Well?" he said.

"Is it all right for you to leave?"

"All right? My dear young woman, if the count dares say a word, I'll buy up all his little ships and close him down."

Nicko took Kate to his villa in Sorrento, where she tried to make amends in bed.

In a way, she supposed she did, although even there she found distractions, not the least of which were her thoughts of Paulie. This was the first time she had ever loved one man and gone to bed with another. It was not a matter of infidelity: no vows had ever been exchanged with either man. The truth was, her body still responded to Nicko's practiced touch, as it had every right to do after so many years. Flesh was still only flesh, and the rest was nothing but friction.

Or so they said.

She held Nicholas Vorelli for one last embrace. Then they were finished.

"You have to stop brooding and beating yourself over this crazy German," Nicko said.

"I just feel so stupid and used. Worst of all is the hold I've given him on *you*."

Nicko lit a cigarette and blew smoke at the ceiling. "It's not all that cataclysmic."

"Maybe not now, but as long as he has those pictures and tapes of me, who knows what he'll ask for next?"

"You're worrying too far in advance," Nicko said. "All your friend has asked so far is to come along to Wannsee on the thirteenth. He's better qualified than most to be there."

"He's a zealot."

"Of course he's a zealot." Nicko smiled. "But zealots do have a way of getting things done."

Kate lifted herself on one elbow to stare at him. "You said yourself he scared the hell out of you. Twice you actually wanted to kill him. What's suddenly happened?"

Nicholas Vorelli sighed. "The thing is," he said, "I see your German as a very real threat, to the point where I've had people watching him around the clock. A couple of evenings ago Alfred Mainz left his university and went to see a locksmith just outside Rome. When he left the man's workshop a while later, Mainz took off on a flight to Berlin, where he picked up a car and drove directly to the Wannsee Museum."

"In the middle of the night?"

"At exactly 1:50 A.M."

"And then?"

"He parked his car in some woods, scaled a wall, switched off Wannsee's central alarm system—probably with one of the keys the locksmith had made for him—and entered the museum through a cellar door he unlocked with another key. He remained inside for more than an hour. Then he left the building and flew back to Rome on the first available flight."

A lock of hair fell across Kate's eyes and she stared at Nicko through it. "What do you suppose he was doing in there all that time?"

"Reconnoitering. Preparing."

"For what?"

"Christ only knows. I had someone call Wannsee's curator yesterday. I wanted to find out if any of the building's keys had been lost or stolen."

"And?"

"Nothing. But apparently the museum's chief of security had been found dead at home with all his keys still on his belt."

"When was this?"

"Some days ago. Certainly before Mainz's nighttime visit to the museum."

"How did the security chief die?"

"An apparent accident. He fell down some cellar steps and broke his neck. He was an old man."

Kate stared at the ceiling.

"The way I figure it," said Nicko, "Mainz must have

taken wax impressions and brought them to the locksmith to make into keys. He probably broke the old man's neck before tossing him down the stairs.

"Well?" said Nicko Vorelli. "Do you feel any better, knowing?"

Kate Dinneson shook her head.

Chapter 16

TWENTY-FOUR HOURS AFTER PAULIE HAD CALLED and spoken to Tommy Cortlandt about Klaus Logefeld, the CIA director telephoned him back with what he had learned. By this time the German's name was glowing like a giant candle in Paulie's private dark.

"Here's what our data base came up with on Logefeld," said Cortlandt. "The man seems to have been a rather shadowy German national with alleged radical connections. But very small-time, very minor, and he's never actually been booked. He's used two known aliases . . . Hans Schmidt and Walter Miller. But it's pretty certain he's not using either of them anymore and there's been nothing new on him for seventeen years."

"What about known associates?" asked Paulie Walters.

Papers rattled at the other end as Cortlandt checked through his printouts. "I have four names that cross-check and tie in with him," Cortlandt finally said. "I take it you want them all."

"Along with their last known addresses."

Cortlandt read them off and Paulie wrote everything in a small notebook. One address was in Berlin, another in Florence, and the final two in Rome. "I'd like you to do something for me when you're in Berlin," said Cortlandt. "And I'd appreciate your making that your first stop."

"What do you want me to do?"

"On September 13 there's going to be an international human rights conference at Wannsee. It'll be on the foreign secretary level, with the German chancellor acting as host. What I need you to do is to spend a few hours going through the place, and then give me as precise a security report as possible."

"Isn't security the host country's job?"

"Ordinarily, yes. But in this case I have to make it ours as well."

"Why?"

"Because Jimmy Dunster wants to put in a surprise appearance."

"Who knows about this?"

"The president and I. And now you."

"That's all?"

"That's all," said Cortlandt. "And it has to stay that way."

"What's Dunster's purpose?" asked Paulie.

"There were a few lofty references to some African bloodletting and human rights. But I suspect the bottom line may still be closer to personal ego."

"That's worth dying for?"

"Jimmy Dunster doesn't expect to die."

"Ever?"

Cortlandt's laugh was flat. "A certain whiff of immortality seems to come with the territory."

"You can't talk him out of it?"

"I'll give you his private number," said the CIA director. "*You* talk him out of it."

Paulie found himself gripping the telephone with a white-knuckled hand. "With all your resources, why am I the one you're asking to get involved with Wannsee?"

"It's important that this doesn't leak," Cortlandt said. "With you I know it won't."

"Go on," said Paulie Walters.

Cortlandt remained silent.

"How about your trying to get me out of obsessing over my parents' killer and into something more productive?" asked Paulie.

"You mean you think keeping the president alive might be more productive than chasing some unknown shooter through the dark?"

"No," said Paulie. "But *you* do."

Chapter 17

MIST HAD TURNED TO LIGHT RAIN as Deputy CIA Director Harris drove along the Potomac. About twenty miles west of Washington he entered a long stretch of Virginia pine.

It was a black night and he was alone in his own car, having left his official limousine and driver an hour earlier. He squinted against approaching headlights and swung north away from the river on a two-lane blacktop. Then he turned west for a short distance until he saw the remains of an old barn.

A gray sedan was parked behind it. Ken Harris pulled up alongside it and cut his lights and motor. His passenger door was opened and a man he had known for many years as Daniel Archer slid in beside him.

"Mr. Deputy Director," said Archer.

"Hello, Danny. How's the old pulse? Slow as ever?"

"Hey, if it was any slower I'd be goddamn dead."

A wiry man who looked a decade younger than his forty years, Archer was a dedicated distance runner. He took pride in his unusually slow pulse and checked it often, as he proceeded to do now.

"Thirty-eight on the nose," he said.

The deputy director considered Archer through the dark. "I have something for you, Danny. The biggest ever. Think you're up to it?"

The question was a modest attempt at humor. It was generally accepted between them that there was nothing in Daniel Archer's area of expertise that he was *not* up to.

"Let's hear it," he said.

"The president will be at a trade meeting in Brussels next month. He's planning to arrive early on the twelfth and leave for home the morning of the thirteenth." Ken Harris paused. "Your job is to see that he doesn't make it out of Belgium."

Archer whistled softly. "Who's behind it?"

"A few people who feel it'll be best for the country."

"You mean true-blue American patriots?"

The deputy director's smile was vaguely reminiscent of dirty river ice. "Now you've got it."

"What restrictions?"

"You're not to do it yourself. I don't want any Americans involved. Pick a hitter from one of the local or international groups. Afterward, toss the police a suspect with a history. We need someone to take the heat."

"Can you get me estimated arrival and departure times for Air Force I?"

"I already have them. They'll be coming into Brussels International at 9:30 A.M. local and flying out the exact same time the next morning."

"What about the routes to and from the airport?"

"Those are in the hands of Belgian security," said Harris. "You'll have to dig them out for yourself."

Daniel Archer pursed his lips, a man with multiple problems trying to decide which to consider first. He had a sharp-jawed face that gave him the look of a worried fox. "What kind of money are we talking?"

"It's open, but don't go crazy. It still has to come from covert, discretionary funds. You'll get a few hundred thousand to spread around as a starter. Then we'll work from there."

The light rain turned heavy and they listened to it drumming on the car's roof.

"How does it make you feel, moving into the history books?" Harris asked.

"Dunster's not really *my* target. You just told me I won't be the hitter."

"No, but you'll be the one setting it up."

"A hit's a hit, Ken. I don't personalize it." Archer looked at the deputy director. "You're the one who taught me that."

"And you've learned it well. That's why you're handling this."

Daniel Archer put a stick of gum in his mouth and sat gravely chewing. "Not that it matters," he said, "but the one thing I can't figure in the whole deal is Jay Fleming having the guts to go for it."

"Who said he's going for it? Who said he even knows?"

"I just assumed."

"Didn't I also teach you never to assume?"

Ken Harris laughed abruptly.

"Well this time you happen to have assumed correctly," he said.

Chapter 18

KEN HARRIS'S FIRST CHANCE to be alone with the vice president after his meeting with Archer came later the following night in the deputy director's bachelor apartment.

Earlier, a purely social evening of dinner and a concert with the vice president and his wife had ended when Amy Fleming suffered a sudden bout of migraine and had to be dropped off at home. The two men continued on to Harris's condominium in Chevy Chase.

They were silent until Ken Harris had poured the obligatory Napoleon.

"It's started," said the deputy director. "I've set things in motion."

Fleming briefly closed his eyes. He might have been offering a silent prayer.

"When?" he asked.

"Last night."

"Tell me about it."

Harris looked evenly at the vice president. "Are you sure you want to hear? There's really no need for you to know every detail."

"It could be worse not knowing. I've already begun dreaming about it."

"Just don't talk in your sleep," said Ken Harris. "I don't think Amy would enjoy the idea too much."

Fleming rolled his eyes heavenward. "Christ!"

"Anyway, I met with my contact, told him what had to be done, and gave him the dates."

"Just one man?"

The deputy director nodded. "Which means just a single link to me, and none at all to you."

"He's not one of your Agency people, is he?"

"Hell, no. I'd never use a Company man for something like this. That would give us too direct a connection if something went wrong."

"What if something goes wrong with this man involved?"

Harris shrugged. "He becomes expendable."

"Who is he?" asked Fleming.

"A pro. The best. With no moral judgments clogging his arteries."

"How long have you known him?"

"A lot of years. He believes we're good friends."

"And you? What do *you* believe?"

"Pretty much the same thing. Unless he becomes a threat."

Sipping his brandy, Jayson Fleming got up and began to pace. "What about Cortlandt and this man of yours? Does Tommy know him?"

"I doubt it."

"You're not sure?"

"What's ever sure in this business? In any case, it hardly matters. Whatever has to be done will be done. We're way beyond Tommy now."

The vice president stopped his pacing. "Is your man an American?"

"Yes. But he won't be the one actually doing it."

"Who will?"

"Some zealot with his own agenda. Someone who knows and cares nothing about either one of us and will probably end up dead himself."

It was nearly three in the morning when the vice president quietly slipped into bed and looked through the silvery dark at his sleeping wife. The small frown of pain from her headache was gone and she slept as though she were eighteen years old.

Amy.

More than thirty years of living together and how much did they really know about the darker parts of each other? How many secrets would they finally carry to their graves?

Just don't talk in your sleep, Ken Harris had warned.

Lord, if Amy knew.

Jayson Fleming's eyes blurred at the thought.

Which left him with only one truly significant question.

Did he really want the presidency badly enough to murder for it?

Obviously he did.

The whole concept of such a thing had not just sprung full-blown into his brain. It had been germinating ever since he was forced to accept the fact that Jimmy Dunster was not going to honor his solemn, preconvention pledge not to bury him in all the ceremonial nonsense that traditionally came with the vice presidency.

"Be honest with me, Jimmy," he had said before accepting the Number Two slot. "I don't want to spend eight years in a limbo that could finish me as a future contender for Number One. So if you can't offer me more than that, please tell me now."

Jimmy Dunster had made his pledge, never kept it, and everything that Jay Fleming had feared would happen to him as vice president had happened.

Except for this, of course. Who would ever have expected to be planning an honest-to-God assassination?

Clearly, Ken Harris. And probably his father, were he still alive.

Fleming smiled coldly. To his father, being Number One wasn't just the best thing. It was the only thing. While there he was, stuck with a son who had never gotten past Number Two.

This time would be different.

Yet Fleming knew that most of what he was into now was still coming from Ken Harris, who was strong, tough, and confident enough to get exactly what he was after. Or was he simply evil enough?

Never mind that. If it were his own dead father's approval he continued to chase after, killing for the presidency had to get it for him. Hell, he could still hear his father bellowing after him as he ran onto any one of a hundred ball fields: "Get in there and bust their legs, kid!"

That's it. Blame it on Big Daddy and Ken Harris. As if he couldn't come up with enough other reasons for wanting the president out of the way.

If anyone was a foolish, do-nothing, political hack, it was Jimmy Dunster. How many precious fragments of the human condition would finally be lost through the ineptitude of this one man who held the single most influential office on God's earth?

Still, Jayson Fleming could not avoid recognizing his own troubled pride, the poverty of conscience that reduced his soul. He had to know that what Ken Harris was offering him, and what he was offering himself, was only the darkest of illusions. But the soul wanted what it wanted and he still loved and fell for the myth he had made up about himself.

The glory.

The courage.

The grace and exaltation.

To soar above the dirt and degraded clowning and into the light.

Yes. *He wanted the presidency that badly.*

Chapter 19

PRESIDENT DUNSTER CAME UP OUT OF SLEEP SLOWLY, pausing at each new level. He felt the pressure on his chest, but there was no pain and he thought it might just be part of a dream. Then he heard himself groan and knew it was no dream and that he was awake.

Jimmy Dunster opened his eyes. He saw the silvered curtains at the window and the moon as a cold stone over Washington. Maggie lay asleep at his side, the soft rhythm of her breathing rising from her part of the bed. Waiting for the weight to leave his chest, Dunster held still so as not to wake his wife. These incidents frightened her. They frightened him too, but *her* fear was harder for him to take.

Then the pain came, and the feeling of suffocation, and he knew he was not going to get away with it very easily this time. The nitro pills were on his bedside table, but it took effort just to move and he could feel his heart skipping around inside like a small nervous animal. When he arched upward to meet the pain, he woke his wife.

"What is it, love?"

She was up on one elbow, blinking at him through the translucent dark. She saw what it was and an instant later she was out of bed and moving to his side. The floor seemed to pitch under her feet, but she caught her balance and got hold of her husband's pills.

"Open your mouth," she said, and put a pill under his tongue, where it would quickly dissolve.

Then Maggie Dunster lay close beside him, her body leaden on her bones. She imagined his heart kicking in his chest, bringing him pain, and she willed it to be still. After a few moments she felt his body relax, each part of it—chest, arms, legs—and he was back with her.

Still, she needed to hear it from him.

"All right?" she asked.

"Fine," he told her, and pressed her hand.

"Was it a bad one?"

"There are no good ones. I guess it was about middle range."

Maggie saw his face glinting with sweat and she dried it with the edge of her gown. She held herself close against him and silently wept.

"I'm fine," he told her again for reassurance.

"What are we going to do, love?"

"Just what we're doing."

"Yes, but for how long?"

"As long as we have to."

"I don't know what that means anymore," she said.

The president took a long, deep breath. "It means it's under control and there's no immediate danger. If it ever does get any worse, there's always the bypass."

He said it gently and almost by rote. He had been saying it often lately.

"We both know that's more of a political than a medical judgment," Maggie said.

Dunster stared dimly in the direction of the ceiling. She was right, of course. Had he not been president, with all that the office entailed, he would have been operated on weeks or even months ago. For him to enter Walter Reed for possible life-threatening surgery, followed by an indefinite period of convalescence and daily medical bulletins, would reduce the remainder of his term to a lame-duck shambles. As it was, only he, Maggie, and his personal physician knew about his occasional attacks of angina, and he intended to keep it that way for as long as he possibly could.

They lay quietly beside each other with their thoughts.

Maggie was the first to speak. "Do you love me?" she asked.

Jimmy Dunster smiled and for an instant he was full of peace. "It depends on what you're about to ask me to do to prove it."

"It's easy. Just stay away from Wannsee."

He turned to look at her.

"I mean it, Jimmy."

"I know you do."

Maggie was silent.

"You're making too much of this whole thing," he said.

"Am I?" Her voice sounded cold and angry to her, not how she wanted to sound. "And all this time I thought *you* were the one making too much of it."

Dunster sighed.

"Don't you dare sigh at me like that."

"Like what?"

"Like a long-suffering husband with a nagging wife."

He laughed.

"And don't laugh at me either."

"All right," he said.

"It's not all right. It's all wrong. I'm so frustrated and frightened I feel sick."

"Just because of a brief trip to Berlin and a little harmless speech-making?"

"If that's all it was, I wouldn't mind. It's what you've turned it into that terrifies me."

"What have I turned it into?"

"A mission from God."

Jimmy Dunster considered his wife in the reflected light of the moon. About to reply with a flip remark, he thought better of it. "Come on, Maggie. Aren't you getting a little carried away?"

"Think about it, love." She spoke more quietly now, working against her creeping panic. "All you lack is your own burning bush. They'll just break your heart for your trouble and ship you home in a box. Only I won't be here to sign for you."

Maggie paused. "Do you know where I'll be? Right there where they finished you. At lovely, historic Wannsee. History's ultimate charnel house."

"Maggie, you can't go with me."

"The devil I can't. From here on, and until you're either dead or check into Walter Reed for surgery, you're not going anywhere for a single night without me along to feed you your little nitro fix."

Maggie Dunster glared through the dark, engulfed by love, fear, and a sudden, icy fury. "If you so much as try to stop me, I swear to God you'll find yourself reading about your secret angina and plans for Wannsee on the front page of the *New York Times*."

Later, Maggie was calmer as she lay beside her husband, guarding him in his sleep.

That poor, imperfect, struggling heart. One of these days, she knew, the pills were not going to work. She mocked the intensity of his spirit, yet she loved it. But hearts could be pushed only so far.

Chapter 20

BERLIN WAS STILL BERLIN to Paulie Walters, and at best he had never been comfortable in the city. Too many Germans, he thought, and had to admit to one of his uglier areas of lingering bias.

Stop being stupid, he told himself.

So he concentrated instead on the map and street signs that he hoped would bring him a bit closer to Klaus Logefeld.

He had just driven in from Tempelhof International Airport; a fine rain was settling over the roads as he headed for the western rim of the city. Klaus Logefeld intruded, his presence almost shadowlike on the windshield. Paulie tried to make something of it, tried to put together some sort of face. But he could not even begin to imagine what the German looked like. All he could do was try to trace him through one or more of the four names that Tommy Cortlandt had given him, along with addresses listed in three different cities.

For Berlin, the old comrade's name was Dieter Hoffman. His address, 97 Olbers Strasse. According to the map, it was only about ten miles from Tempelhof.

The place was a half-timbered, stucco house with an attached carpentry and general woodworking shop.

A young, heavyset woman was working at a desk in a small, glass-enclosed office. She had a playpen set up in a corner, with a child asleep in it. There were the sounds of sawing and hammering, and Paulie looked through the glass and saw men working in back.

The woman glanced up and smiled at him. "Good morning," she said in German.

"Good morning. I'm looking for Dieter Hoffman." Paulie's response was in German.

"Ah, you're American," she said, switching to English.

"My German is that bad?"

"No, no. It's very good. In fact, excellent."

"You mean for an American?"

She laughed. "I'm sure it's better than my English. Does Dieter expect you?"

"I doubt it."

"Do you know him?"

Paulie shook his head.

The woman turned and pointed through the glass. "That's Dieter back there with the power saw. The big fellow. Go right in."

A husky, balding man with light gray eyes, Hoffman stopped working and switched off his saw as Paulie Walters approached.

"The lady in the office said it was OK," Paulie told him, starting right off with English this time.

Dieter Hoffman grinned. "The lady in the office is my wife. Everything is OK with her. What can I do for you?"

"I'm looking for a man you used to know," said Paulie.

"What are you? An American cop?"

"No." Paulie took out the business card of a New York law firm and handed it to the carpenter.

"You mean you've come all the way from"—Hoffman glanced at the card—"Park Avenue, New York, to find a man you say I used to know?"

Paulie breathed the fragrance of fresh-cut wood. "That's right."

"He must be a very important man."

"He might be. I don't know. The only thing that's important to me right now is that I find him."

Hoffman looked at the men drilling, hammering, and sanding wood around them. "Let's go where we can talk."

He led Paulie into a back room that had a table, chairs, and a Coke machine and shut the door. By the time they were seated at the table, Hoffman's initially friendly face had turned cautious.

"So are you going to tell me this man's name, or what?"

"It's Klaus Logefeld," said Paulie.

The carpenter's pale eyes were cool and steady. "What do you suddenly want Klaus for?"

"Nothing bad, Mr. Hoffman. My firm represents the estate of his late aunt, who lived in New York. The woman died not long ago and left Klaus a considerable sum of money. All I'm trying to do is see that he gets it. We have no valid address and I have to find him first."

Hoffman nodded as though settling something within himself.

"I don't know where Klaus is, mister," he said. "I haven't seen or heard from him in about eighteen years. So I'm afraid I can't help you give him all that nice money from his aunt."

"I'm sorry to hear that," said Paulie. "When you did see him last, would you mind telling me exactly where it was?"

"Right here in Berlin." Hoffman paused. "As if you didn't know."

Paulie ignored the addendum. "Did anything in particular happen at that time?" he asked.

Dieter Hoffman stared at him. "You mean like that big bombing near the Tiergarten where five people were killed and Klaus and I were among those picked up afterward?"

The carpenter's voice was soft, but Paulie could feel the stopped-up anger in it.

"I don't know who you are or what you're after," said Hoffman. "But you don't have to play these fucking games with me. I've got nothing to hide."

"I never said you did."

"You don't have to goddamn say it. You're here questioning me, aren't you?"

Paulie studied the carpenter's face, watching his needs grow. "Listen," said Hoffman. "You're looking at the luckiest sonofabitch in the world. From where I once was, I could have been dead or in jail a hundred times. Look where I am now."

Paulie looked around.

"I mean I've got a goddamn dream life. I've got a wife I'm crazy about, a kid I could eat up, and a business that's getting better by the day. Do you know why I've got all these things?"

Paulie shook his head.

"Because I woke up one morning, looked at my fucking pissed-off face in the mirror, and decided I'd had enough."

"Enough of what?"

"Of trying to change the world into what it's not and can never be."

Dieter Hoffman took a deep breath. "The point of all this is that I know you're real bad news and I just want you to forget about me in connection with Klaus Logefeld and whatever we once were and tried to do."

"And Klaus?" asked Paulie. "Do you think he feels as you do?"

"What I think," Hoffman said, "is that Klaus is not me."

"Which means what?"

"That the crazy bastard is either still trying to change the world or he's dead."

"You sound as if you hate him."

Hoffman looked surprised. "Where did you get that idea? Hey, I love the guy. Always did and always will."

"Then why did you break away?"

"Simple. I just wasn't ready to die with him."

Paulie Walters arrived at Wannsee in the late morning, just as the sun broke through the last of the clouds. He parked among a bunch of cars and tour buses and strolled casually about the grounds. Everything looked fresh and green in the sunlight, with the women in their summer clothing adding their own brightness. Paulie saw two uniformed guards walking beside a perimeter wall, and another guard posted at the entrance gate. They were the only visible security.

Finished surveying the grounds, Paulie entered a main-floor office where he presented CIA credentials under the name of John Hendricks to a tall, trim man in a gray uniform who introduced himself as Major Dechen, the chief of security, and welcomed him in impeccable English.

Paulie sat down to the smell of pine-scented air freshener. "When did you receive word I was coming, Major?"

"Yesterday."

"Were there any special instructions?"

"Just to offer you every courtesy and make sure your identity is kept quiet."

"You understand that includes staff and anyone else connected with the conference?"

"Yes, sir. But you needn't worry about that, Mr. Hendricks. In large, multinational meetings of this sort everyone arrives with their own security needs. One way or another, they're handled."

"Any particular worries about this one?"

"Only my normal nightmares."

"Which are?"

"Either a truckload of dynamite crashing the building or a low-flying plane coming in fast under the radar with a couple of thousand-pounders."

"What are your defenses against them?"

"Mostly prayer."

He said it with a straight face, and Paulie liked that. "If that fails?"

"Concrete barriers on the land approaches, heat-seeking missiles covering the immediate airspace."

"What's your estimated effectiveness for all that?"

"About ninety percent. Unless we get some crazy kamikazes coming in. Then we drop to seventy. But I'm not really looking for any of that heavy-hitting for the thirteenth. So most of our concentration will be small-scale and interior. There'll be the usual body checks and metal detectors covering everyone for weapons as they enter the building. All security people will be issued special lapel badges no earlier than an hour before the first delegates are due to arrive."

"Where are the cameras?" Paulie asked.

Dechen stubbed out his cigarette and rose. "Just about everywhere. Come. I'll give you the tour."

Outside the security office, the rooms and corridors hummed with the hushed voices of tourists. Their faces were solemn, their eyes wide, their feet shuffling.

The major unlocked a door off a central corridor and took Paulie into the surveillance room. Two uniformed guards sat with earphones on, watching banks of closed-circuit television screens. Paulie saw many of the same people on the screens he had just passed in the corridors and other rooms.

"We have cameras covering almost every usable space in the building," said Major Dechen. "Other than for the actual toilet stalls, they even cover the rest rooms."

He took a set of headphones from one of the guards, let Paulie wear it, and had the guard switch on the audio for one location after another as Paulie listened to the sound connect with the video. Breathing the same air freshener he remembered from the security office, Paulie followed Major Dechen out of the locked surveillance room with its banks of silent screens and continued the tour.

"Understand, Mr. Hendricks," the major said, "the surveillance room is normally manned and functioning just for high-security occasions. I have it operating today only to demonstrate its coverage to you and some other security people I'm expecting this afternoon."

He led the way down into the lower-level library section, where about a dozen researchers were bent over books and microfiche screens.

"As a matter of fact," continued the major, "two of the people I'm expecting later are from your own State Department's inspector general." He looked at Paulie. "Did you know they were coming?"

"Yes."

"But of course they don't know about you."

"That's right, Major."

"I understand."

You only think you do, thought Paulie.

They circled the stacks of books and went into the utility area. Then they came back to the library and stood silently in a corner.

"How do you feel about spending so much time in this place?" Paulie asked. "Or is it just another job to you?"

"This could never be just another job to me."

The major looked hard at Paulie Walters. "Let me tell you something, sir. Every day I spend about half an hour just watching the faces of those passing through here. I see how they look and what they feel. That in itself is enough to keep me from blowing my brains out for at least another day."

Chapter 21

KLAUS LOGEFELD LAY ON HIS BACK, the young woman fitted smoothly over him, her mouth sucking on his as they neared the end.

He tasted the Chardonnay on her tongue and the wine tasted better to him this way than it had from a glass. His hands were on the soft spread of her hips and he felt the trembling there first as she began her final run. Then the shaking was all through her and she was taking him right along, until they cut loose whatever was left and cried out together.

They lay in the sudden stillness, gasping for breath in the cool, blue-green dark.

They were in her apartment, not his. Klaus never took a woman to his own place. That would have been a breach of an essential security. Let a woman into your burrow and she was halfway into *you*. One of his more inflexible sexual precepts. Along with never making love to the same woman more than three times, and never spending the entire night with her.

My basic survival code, he thought.

Or was he simply mad?

At times, it had begun to seem so.

Especially in the brighter lights of his memory, when moments with some wondrously appealing woman would return and they would be merged in moonlight. Then a hundred details would be set loose: strands of perfumed hair, a soft loving voice, a young body just learning to feel, its nerve endings still curled like fernheads in the first days of spring.

Faces and words came back to hurt him and he cast them away like some ghostly plague. Why? He had retreated into an emotional deadness, and he wanted no one to call him out.

He did have love and caring in him, but he let it be for the greater number rather than just one.

Only once had it been for one, and that was enough. Too much. Sometimes, in dreams, it was still too much, with her bending to him as he lay alone. He would make the mistake of reaching up through the dark to touch her face and feel only his own wet eyes. That was better, he supposed, than touching the blood and torn flesh to which she had finally been reduced when they were both sixteen and he was still making bombs until a bad fuse went off too soon.

Maybe I should have died with her.

Near midnight he got out of bed and began to put on his clothes.

"I wish you could stay till morning," said the woman.

She was very young, barely past twenty, and looked even younger. As he became older, younger became better.

"Are you sure you can't stay?" Her voice was soft, almost pleading.

"You know I can't."

"I don't know anything. You've never even told me why. Are you married, or living with someone, or what?"

"None of the aforementioned, Pigeon."

"I wouldn't mind if you had someone else," she said. "That wouldn't bother me. I just love being with you."

Klaus switched on a small lamp to help him find his socks. "Why on earth do you love being with me?" he asked.

"Because you know absolutely everything."

"That's all?"

"And you're wonderful in bed."

Klaus laughed. "At least *that* makes some sense." He leaned over the bed and kissed her forehead.

She looked up at him, unsmiling, her dark eyes wide. "When am I going to see you again?"

She never would, of course. This was their third time together.

"I'll call you," he told her, and went out of the room, out of the apartment, and into the midnight quiet of Rome's streets.

There was not a taxi in sight, but it was not too far to where he lived. His body suddenly felt weightless, and he was just as pleased to walk.

Moments later, a shiny black Mercedes glided slowly past him and stopped at the curb about fifty yards ahead. A man got out. He paused to light a cigarette and stood smoking under a street lamp.

As Klaus drew closer, he saw that it was Nicko Vorelli. He saw, too, that no one else was in the Mercedes, and that every move had been deliberately thought out so as not to startle him. The pulling up to the curb a fair distance ahead, the street lamp to make Nicko instantly recognizable, the lighting of a cigarette to keep both hands in clear view were all for reassurance. Yet none of these things were enough to dispel the cloud of foul intent that Klaus could feel himself entering.

"Dr. Vorelli," he said.

"Hello, Professor."

Neither man offered to shake hands: they just stood staring at each other in the small island of light. Klaus glanced around at the passing traffic and a few late strollers along the Tiber.

"It's all right," said Nicko. "I'm alone. I just thought it might be a good idea if we talked a little."

Klaus considered Dr. Nicholas Vorelli. Standing there in his dark, impeccably tailored suit, his manner cool and poised, his eyes knowing, he made Klaus feel the difference between them. It might have been that of a malodorous peasant with sweaty palms, confronting a member of the reigning aristocracy.

"How did you know I'd be coming out at this time?"

Klaus asked. "How did you know I wouldn't be spending the night with her?"

"Because you never spend a whole night with any woman."

Klaus knew the worst of it then. "How long have you had me under surveillance?"

"Long enough."

Klaus shook his head in disgust. "I thought I was watching my back every second."

"You were. I just have good people. Quite honestly, Professor, other than for a few of the more current details, they haven't told me anything about you that I hadn't already known. They've done little more than confirm my own judgment of you."

"What's that?"

"You're very dangerous."

Nicko touched the German's arm, gently urging him forward. "Shall we walk? I always feel more comfortable in motion."

Klaus was unable to imagine Nicko less than comfortable under any conditions. In the near distance, he saw the floodlit walls of the old Colosseum and the Palatine Hill where emperors once built their palaces. Things change, he thought.

"I'm not going to ask what you were doing inside Wannsee the other night," said Nicko. "You would only lie, and there's nothing I can do about it anyway. It might be helpful to us both if you gave me some idea of what you hope to get out of the conference on the thirteenth."

"The same things you want from it."

"You're so sure you know what I want?"

"I *should* know. There's nothing you've ever written or said on the subject of human rights that I haven't swallowed whole."

Nicko stopped and looked at Klaus. "You're a strange man, Professor."

"You mean besides being dangerous?"

"It's all part of the same package."

Nicko began walking again. "Since you're so sure of yourself," he said, "suppose you give me four specific motions of your own you'd like to see adopted by the conference before it breaks up."

"I can give you a lot more than four."

"I don't want a lot more. Just the four you feel most strongly about."

Klaus thought it through as they walked.

"All right," he said. "I'd like to see a permanent, international committee established, a quick-reaction strike force to back them up, a multibillion-dollar fund to give them independence, and an immediate move into Liberia, Angola, Burundi, and Rwanda to impose cease-fires and end the slaughter and suffering."

"You don't like the United Nations?"

"What's there to like? They're an exercise in futility, politics, and speech-making."

"If I were to ask you for a brief, one-line message to be sent to the world by Wannsee," Nicko said, "and to be adopted by your committee as its guiding principle, what would it be?"

Klaus did not have to take time to think about this one. "We must love one another or die."

"*This* from a bomb maker who kills?" said Nicko.

Klaus looked surprised. "Who would know better?"

Chapter 22

PAULIE WALTERS FINISHED a solitary dinner in his Rome hotel room and poured a third glass of Chianti, feeling tired, hurt, and depressed.

He had spent a futile, frustrating couple of days in his hunt for Klaus Logefeld, and he was fast approaching a dead end. Dieter Hoffman had given him nothing in Berlin, Sebastiano Pucci turned out to have accidentally blown himself to bits in Florence more than two years ago, and the first of his two leads in Rome, Amelia Vorto, had disappeared from his only known address. Roberto Spaderi was the last of the four links to Logefeld that Tommy Cortlandt had given him.

He planned to check out Spaderi later that night.

In the meantime, wanting Kate, he carried his Chianti over to one of the twin beds, propped a couple of pillows behind him, and called her number in Naples.

"Tell me something nice," he said when she answered.

"I miss you terribly."

"A good beginning."

"I adore you."

"Go on," he said.

"I'm only half alive without you."

"Now you're getting it." Paulie sighed, delighted with Kate's voice: warm, familiar, and full of affection over the phone. "Except I'm afraid they might pass some sort of law against you."

"Why?"

"Because you're addictive. I can't get through a day anymore unless I hear your voice."

"When are you coming back to me?"

"Soon."

"Where are you tonight?"

"Rome."

"At least you're getting closer." His other calls had been from Florence and Berlin. "I'll bet you're really a traveling lingerie salesman," she said.

"You've finally found me out."

He had concocted a story about having to look over some new galleries bidding to represent his work, but it sounded hollow even to him.

"Have you been changing the dressing on your arm?" Kate asked.

"Of course. Every day." Actually he hadn't, and the wound was starting to bother him.

"I know when you're lying."

"You mean you're some kind of witch?"

"Please, Paulie." Kate's voice had turned serious. "You can't fool around with that kind of lesion. You could end up losing an arm. Promise you'll take care of it as soon as you hang up."

"I promise," he said.

Paulie tried to picture Kate as he had seen her last, but somehow he was unable to conjure her up, resulting in an instant of panic.

"What are you wearing?" he asked.

"Why?"

"I want to be able to see you."

"A T-shirt and jeans."

"Does it say anything on the T-shirt?"

"Yes. 'Life stinks. Then you die.' "

Paulie laughed. "You've just made my night."

"I got it before I met you."

"What does your latest one say?"

" 'Life is a dream. Don't ever wake me.' "

"I love you," Paulie told her, needing to say the words.

"I love you too. Just take care of your arm. *You* may not need the two of them, but *I* do."

When Paulie hung up moments later, he put the receiver down slowly, smiling, remembering Kate. He sat propped against his pillows for a while, thinking of her, sipping his wine.

Then he went out to a public phone near the hotel and called Tommy Cortlandt in Washington, where it was close to 2:00 P.M. His last call to the CIA director had been made two days ago, when he reported on his security visit to Wannsee. Cortlandt had asked him to check back again tonight for possible follow-up information.

"Where are you calling from?" Cortlandt asked when Paulie reached him.

"Rome. I'll be trying my last lead tonight. Roberto Spaderi."

Staring off at the Via Sistina, Paulie waited for the roar of a passing scooter to fade. "I don't suppose your computers came up with any other possibilities."

"I'd have told you if they had."

Paulie wondered. He was in that bad a mood.

"About Wannsee," said Cortlandt. "I'm going to be there myself on the thirteenth, and I'd like you with me. Any problem with that?"

"No."

"I've just heard the president's wife wants in too, which will be another complication."

"What is she afraid of?" asked Paulie. "That he'll be chasing the *Frauleins*?"

"Not her style. Nor his. But something is evidently bugging her. At least, according to the boss, who doesn't want her along on this any more than we do."

"The president told you that?"

"By implication. But that's *his* problem. We have a few other things to worry about. Keep in touch, Paulie. And take care."

That makes two people who want me to take care.

*   *   *

The taxi dropped Paulie in front of an old apartment building within sight of the Ponte Palatino shortly before ten o'clock. Moments later, he saw the name Spaderi on one of the tarnished brass mailboxes in the vestibule and felt as if he had struck gold.

He climbed the stairs slowly, wanting to preserve the feeling as long as possible. On the third floor, he stopped in front of apartment 317, breathed deeply, and knocked.

A broad, aging woman with iron-gray hair opened the door and looked at Paulie without expression.

"Mrs. Spaderi?" he said.

Dark, watery eyes squinted at him behind steel-rimmed glasses. "Do I know you?"

"No. We've never met. I'm looking for Roberto."

She went on staring at Paulie. "You're looking for my son?"

He nodded.

"Well, you're looking in the wrong place," she said.

Paulie felt his good feeling drain.

"Do you know where I can find him?"

Mrs. Spaderi's face showed nothing. "Try Saint Angelo's Cemetery. He's been there for six years."

Paulie just stood there.

Evidently taking pity on him, the woman stepped back from the door. "Come in," she said. "You look terrible. Have some wine. It was mean of me to tell you like that. I seem to be getting meaner by the day."

Mutely, Paulie followed her into a small living room crowded with dark, heavy furniture. He sat down and watched as she poured two glasses of red wine.

"I've been out of the country a long time," he said. "I'm sorry to do this to you."

"I'm used to it. Roberto had friends all over. They keep dropping by like you, not knowing he's dead." Mrs. Spaderi's eyes pinned Paulie to his chair. "I suppose you're like the rest. One of the bunch. Still waiting your own turn to get popped."

Paulie went along with it. "How did it happen with Roberto?"

The woman shrugged. "The way it happened with his father ten years before him. The way it always happens. He just did one too many."

Paulie took a sip of wine and waited.

"What's your name?" she asked, then quickly held up a veined hand. "No. Better not tell me. I still get visits from the *carabiniere*. The bastards don't leave me alone. Not that they'd get anything out of me. I spit on them. They try to scare me with death threats, and I spit on death too."

Paulie was silent.

"And now you come looking for my Roberto," said Mrs. Spaderi, and she came close to smiling. "I suppose you have something big planned, something that could probably get him killed all over again but that he'd have loved doing."

"He'd have done it well, too," said Paulie, his voice carefully tinged with regret. "Roberto did everything well."

"I know. There are a lot of crazies around these days, but my son was never like that. He was always controlled, dependable."

"I was wondering," he said. "Did you ever meet or did Roberto ever mention a man called Klaus Logefeld?"

The woman looked off somewhere. "I've heard the name. It was a long time ago but I remember because it's German and I've never wanted anything to do with Germans. In this I was right, because one of the few times Roberto was ever picked up by the police was when he was doing something with this Klaus."

"Do you know where I might be able to reach him?"

Mrs. Spaderi shook her head.

"You need this German for something important?" she asked.

"Very important."

"Why a German? Why not a nice Italian? Or maybe even a good Greek or Palestinian?"

Paulie forced a smile. "For this, I need someone who speaks fluent German."

"I know two Italians and a Greek. The best. They open their mouths, Hitler himself would swear they were his sons."

Paulie rose and began to pace the worn carpeting. "I wouldn't want to get you involved."

"Don't talk dumb. I'm involved my whole life. We all run in the same blood. We carry the rich on our backs and fight the brutes and hypocrites in power. So how can I help?"

Paulie stopped in front of a table of framed photographs. She's a tough old comrade, he thought, gazing at fading pictures of what he figured to be the dead son and husband she had already given to her lifelong cause.

"Well," he said, still considering Mrs. Spaderi's personal memorial exhibit, "do you think some of Roberto's other friends might know where I can find . . ."

Then Paulie spotted a particular picture on the table, picked it up to study more closely, and stopped thinking about Klaus Logefeld.

It seemed an ordinary enough photograph of a man, woman, and little girl caught in a moment of summer sun. What made it special to Paulie was that the man and woman were Angelo and Patty Falanga.

Still holding the photograph, Paulie turned to Mrs. Spaderi. "You knew the Falangas?"

"We were close friends." She rose to look at the picture with him. "I'm surprised you recognized them. They've been gone a long time."

"They were my boyhood heroes. I never knew they had a child."

"Prettiest little thing you ever saw. Everyone called her Firefly. When her parents were killed, she even lived with us for a while."

"What happened to her after that?"

Mrs. Spaderi shrugged. "God knows. We were on the run and had to pass her off to another family. They dumped her with others. Poor baby was a real hand-me-down. At some point she just disappeared."

"You never saw her again?"

"Never. Those were wild years for us all. We had to keep going underground, moving in and out of the country."

Abstractedly, Mrs. Spaderi took the framed picture from Paulie and began polishing the glass with her sleeve.

"Of course there was that item in the newspaper just a few months ago," she said.

"What was that?"

"I ran into this woman I hadn't met in years, and she asked if I'd seen Firefly's picture in the paper. What a dumb question! I mean how could I have recognized the child as a grown woman even if I *had* seen her picture?"

"How did the woman recognize her?"

"It was different for her. She had last seen Firefly at the age of eighteen. I haven't seen the child since she was seven or eight." Mrs. Spaderi looked at Paulie. "Anyway, I was happy to see how things turned out for her. She was all dressed up at La Scala in Milan with this crowd of real big shots."

"You mean you got to see the picture?"

"My friend sent me a copy."

Paulie felt a faint stirring. "Do you still have it?"

"Probably."

"May I see it?"

Mrs. Spaderi opened a table drawer and rummaged inside. Pulling out a folded sheet of paper, she smoothed the creases and handed it to Paulie. "I'm afraid it's a bad copy."

It was very bad, blurred with most of the halftones washed away. Still, Paulie was able to make out a group of elegantly dressed men and women in dinner clothes, laughing, talking, and sipping champagne at what was captioned as a grand opening for the opera season. Those in the picture were identified simply as the Honorable Evan Billings, the American ambassador to Italy, with his wife and their guests at a post-performance reception.

"Which is Firefly?" Paulie asked.

"The one in the white dress."

Paulie saw a slender woman with ink-black hair and an unidentifiable, dead-white face. The ambassador and his wife looked only marginally better.

Disappointed, he gave the copy back to Mrs. Spaderi. "Did your friend know what Firefly is calling herself these days?"

"No, but I'm sure it's not a name that any of us old-timers would recognize." Mrs. Spaderi studied the picture. "Look who she's hanging out with. You think she wants any connection to a bunch of broken-down bomb-throwers? Who can blame her? Look at all we put her through."

The old woman dropped tiredly into a chair and poured more wine.

"Then the girl was with you after her parents were killed?" asked Paulie.

"That's right."

"Did she know how they died?"

"She knew as much as anyone, which was almost nothing. Just that some shooters had killed them. My God, how she wanted to know. All she did was ask questions."

"What kind of questions?"

"Who shot them? Why? How did it feel to get shot? Poor baby couldn't leave it alone. You should have seen this little girl," she said. "Pretty and delicate as a rose. And as long as I knew her after her momma and poppa were killed, she was never without her pistol."

"She actually had a gun?"

"It was just a broken old piece she'd picked up someplace. The firing pin was gone and of course it couldn't shoot. She was always practicing with it. You know how kids do when they play. Drawing and aiming at the bad guys. Bang, you're dead! Except Firefly was never just playing. She was always preparing."

"For what?" Paulie asked, although by now he knew.

"For when she grew up and found the bad guys who took away her momma and poppa."

Close to midnight Paulie reached the United States Embassy on Rome's diplomatic row, presented his credentials to the duty officer, and requested what he needed.

Twenty minutes later, he had the relevant public relations files spread out before him on an empty desk and was going through them.

To locate what he was after was not hard. Once he had the past season's opening date for La Scala, he simply cross-checked it against the embassy's publicity releases for that evening. He found the original news clipping from which Mrs. Spaderi's blurred photocopy had been made and sat looking at it for several minutes.

There was no instant, clear-cut reaction. Paulie saw, yet he failed to see.

When he realized who the woman in the white dress actually was, it came to him slowly and in parts. Hair, eyes, nose, mouth, chin, all joined by an oval face.

Isn't she lovely, was his first complete thought.

Then he felt her withdrawing from him like a retreating wave over a quiet sea.

Until she was gone.

Chapter 23

USING A UNITED STATES PASSPORT under the name of George Lucas, the man that Deputy CIA Director Harris had called Danny Archer passed through customs at Brussels International Airport without incident and made a brief telephone call to a local number. It was 10:35 on the morning of September 2.

About forty minutes later Archer had rented a dark blue Ford Sierra and was driving north at a leisurely eighty kilometers an hour. When he neared the outskirts of Brussels, he turned off the main highway and drove through a series of narrow, winding streets. As always he watched his rearview mirror. No one was on his back.

Reaching the house he wanted, he drove several hundred meters past its front door. He parked and spent the next twenty minutes watching the neighborhood and the house from behind a newspaper, while sitting on a curbside bench in the small public park at the end of the street.

Everything seemed quiet and in order.

Even so, since he had not been here for several months, he approached the house carefully and rang the bell three times. One long and two short. A husky, cherubic-faced man in a T-shirt opened the door and grinned at him.

"Cautious as ever," he said in French-accented English. "I've been watching you sit out there for twenty minutes. Who's after you today?"

"These are dangerous times, Jean. Or haven't you noticed?"

"Shit, we're both alive, aren't we?"

"Barely."

The husky man named Jean locked the door, secured it with a chain, and took Archer into the kitchen.

"Where's your wife?" asked Archer.

"You wanted to be alone, so I sent her out to spend money." Jean poured two coffees and put them on a white enamel table. "So what do you need?"

"A name."

"What kind?"

"Arab, fundamentalist, and known American hater."

"That's all one word. You want a bomber or a shooter?"

"Bomber. And good. No fuck-ups."

Jean looked mildly offended. "You hurt me when you say things like that. You know I only give you the best."

"Sure. But this is special."

"They're all special."

The Belgian put down his coffee and raised both hands as if to block a punch. "I don't want to hear stuff like that anyway. I don't want to know a thing more than I have to."

"You won't."

"What's the money?"

"A hundred thousand American up front. Twice that when it's done. That's for everything, including you. Since you'll be the one handling the cash, you can cut it any way you like."

Jean feigned a smile. "You're a pleasure to do business with. I think I have the perfect man for you. Just one thing. Is there a firm date?"

"Either the twelfth or thirteenth of this month."

Jean rose and started from the room. "Wait here while I make some calls."

Daniel Archer sat there. He was just pouring more coffee when Jean came back into the room.

"It took three calls to track him down," said the Belgian. "But I finally reached him in Athens and arranged for a meeting here in Brussels tomorrow night. There'll be just the two of you."

"Who is he?"

"Abu Mustafa."

Archer was impressed. Wanted by no less than four governments, Mustafa had yet to be picked up by any of them. That Mustafa would even agree to such a meeting was an indication of Jean's reputation.

"What did you tell him?" asked Archer.

"Very little. Just that I'd known you for years, your word was good, the target was an important American, and the date was the twelfth or thirteenth of this month in Brussels."

"I never said the American was important."

Jean shrugged. "So I lied to him. If you want someone with Mustafa's reputation, money alone won't do it. His target has to mean something to his cause."

Archer was silent.

"You can handle it any way you want," said Jean. "If I were you and wanted to keep my real target a secret as long as possible, I'd make up something impressive and stick to it right down to blast-off."

At a bit past nine o'clock the following night, Daniel Archer was strolling along the Rue Royale where it edged the Parc de Bruxelles when a black Saab slowed and stopped at the curb a few meters ahead of him. Archer had seen the car pass twice in the last ten minutes, but this was the first time it had stopped.

He approached the Saab's open passenger window, glanced in, and saw a slight, dark-haired man at the wheel.

"Excuse me, sir," said the man in soft Arabic-accented English. "Could you tell me how to get to the Gare Centrale?"

"How did you know I spoke English?" asked Archer.

"Because you walk with the kind of arrogance that only comes with an American passport."

Archer smiled and got into the car. "Is that why you hate all Americans, Abu?"

"Not all Americans, Mr. Lucas. Just your leaders."

Abu Mustafa put the engine in gear and they drove for several moments in silence.

"So who do you want eliminated on the twelfth or thirteenth of September, Mr. Lucas? Please, do us both a big favor and don't lie to me. If you do, we've just wasted valuable time and I'm out of here."

"Why would I come this far just to lie?"

"Because most people who do what we do lie as a matter of principle. Anyway, I already know your target is the president of the United States."

"Do you do card tricks too?" asked Archer.

The Arab laughed. "It's not really all that good. Jean told me it would be an important American on either September 12 or 13 in Brussels. The rest came from news reports of President Dunster being here for just those two days because of a trade meeting. *Voilà*."

They drove in a wide, easy circle around the Parc de Bruxelles, passing the floodlighted Palais de Beaux Arts on one side and the Palais d'Académies on the other.

"OK," Archer said. "What do you want to hear from me?"

"Let's start with the president's airport arrival and departure times."

"He's coming in at 9:30 A.M. on the twelfth and is due to leave for home at the same time on the thirteenth."

"His motorcade routes into and out of the city?"

"They're not known yet. I'll get them for you as soon as I can." Archer looked at Mustafa's hands on the wheel. Small, almost delicate fingers. "How are you planning to do it?"

"A car bomb parked somewhere along Dunster's arrival or departure routes. Set off by remote as his limousine passes. Any objection to that?"

"No."

"The casualties will be higher than I'd like," said Mustafa, "but it's always the surest way."

Archer nodded.

"Good," said the Arab. "I know Americans generally prefer guns. It's more their stuff of myth. But the odds are bad."

"All I want is a dead president. You can keep the stuff of myth. Along with full public credit for yourself and your cause."

"I intend exactly that, Mr. Lucas." Abu Mustafa's smile was all sweetness. "Remember, I'm Palestinian."

"Of course you are, Abu. And may Allah be with you."

Chapter 24

KLAUS LOGEFELD FOLLOWED THE AUTOSTRADA north, from Rome, for about an hour, to Montefiascone. Leaving the main route, he drove west until he passed the town of Marta. From there, he saw the curving shore of Lago di Bosena in the near distance, and he kept the big lake on his right for not quite twenty minutes. Moments later, he turned onto a dirt road through a patch of woods so dense that he could barely see the water between the trees.

When he came to a stone wall, he left his car and entered an overgrown field by way of a rusted iron gate hanging from one hinge. There had once been a road here, but no one had driven on it for a long time and it was almost hidden in the high grass. A rabbit dashed away in front of Klaus, and a pair of doves broke cover off to the right. Other than the brief sound of beating wings, everything was silent in the sun.

It was a five-minute walk to the house, a two-story, stone and stucco villa half covered by vines. Rusted garden furniture was scattered across a slate terrace, and Klaus felt the cooling shade of tall cedars crowding together. He knocked on a heavy door and waited, letting the coolness enter him.

The door opened, revealing a tall, lean old man with a rebuilt but still terribly mutilated face and a missing arm and eye.

"Hello, Grandfather," said Klaus in German.

"So it's Little Jesus."

The former Wehrmacht major's speech was slow and careful. With the destruction of so many facial nerves, muscles, and tendons, every syllable had to be tortuously rerouted. As if to compensate for the multiple disasters below, his hair was thick, flowing, and magnificently silvered. From the sides and rear, the old man's hair gave him the look of an Old Testament prophet on an embassy from the Sinai. Head-on, he resembled nothing human.

Klaus walked past his grandfather into a big room over-looking Lago di Bosena. World War II battle photographs and paintings covered the walls, and several of the lamps had been made out of 88-millimeter shell casings. A gun rack held a Schmeisser machine pistol and two bolt-action sharp-shooter rifles. A glass cabinet held a large display of medals, with the Iron Cross at its center.

"It's been a while," said the old man. "I thought maybe one of your fucked-up, homemade bombs might have finished you."

"Not yet."

Klaus opened a shopping bag he was carrying, took out four bottles of Napoleon brandy, and lined them up on a liquor cabinet. Then he sat down.

"If you're not careful," said the former officer of the Third Reich, "you might outlive even me."

"Never, Grandfather."

From lack of use, the old man's laugh had a croaking sound. "Still out there saving the world, Little Jesus?"

Klaus shrugged.

"In the end, they'll just kill you for your trouble. You know that, don't you, boy?"

"I guess so."

"Why don't you quit while you still can?"

"And do what? Become a soldier like you?"

"You could do worse. If the world is ever going to be saved, it will be by clearheaded, disciplined soldiers, not by wild-eyed hotheads."

Klaus looked at a battle photograph on the opposite wall, showing German Tiger tanks and steel-helmeted infantry advancing through exploding shell fire. He knew the picture well. It represented his grandfather's most significant combat experience. The action had earned him his Iron Cross and cost him his face, his eye, and his arm. It had all happened in the area immediately surrounding the house in which he now lived. When he bought the house and land some years after the war, he said it was to stay as close as he could to his missing parts.

"Do you really think I'm a wild-eyed hothead, Grandfather?"

The old man shifted in his chair to better focus on Klaus with his one eye.

"No," he said. "I don't. That's what bothers me most. You're the best of us. Always were. You've got it all . . . brains, guts, heart, and you fucking care. And you're pissing it all away. Pure goddamn waste."

Klaus took a box of cigars out of his shopping bag, opened it, gave one to the old man, and took another for himself. Then he lit them both.

"Did you hear what I said, boy?"

"Yes, Grandfather."

"That's all you've got to say? 'Yes, Grandfather'?"

Klaus was silent.

The Wehrmacht major's eye glared fiercely. "I know what you think of me. Just another of Adolph's butchering Nazi turds. But I was never that. I was a soldier fighting other soldiers for my country. You think I had any idea what they were doing at those camps? You think I'd have just looked away if I knew? You think . . . I'd . . . have . . ."

The old man's voice trailed off and the remains of his face went slack. The twisted scars, the tendons, the seared flesh, all seemed to diminish and give up the ghost right there.

"I don't blame you, sir," said Klaus quietly. "I know there was nothing you could have done. I've always known that."

My ritual granting of absolution, thought Klaus, wondering if it would sound better in Latin. It was an old litany, worn smooth by repetition and finally polished into a minor art form. This time, though, there was a difference.

"Grandfather?" he said.

The pale blue eye opened and looked at him.

"I have to tell you something," said Klaus.

"So? Tell me."

"I'm going to Germany soon and I'm not sure when I'll be able to get here again."

"When are you ever sure? When you get here, you'll be here."

"This time there's a good chance I might never get here at all," said Klaus. "I just wanted you to know."

"All right. So now I know."

They sat quietly for a while, smoking their cigars.

"This trip to Germany," said the major. "No doubt it has something to do with saving the world?"

Klaus grinned.

"I said something funny?"

"No."

"Then why are you sitting there grinning like an asshole with teeth?"

"Because you have such a wonderful way with words."

"To hell with you, boy."

"I love you too, Grandfather."

The old man stared at Klaus seriously for a moment. "*Do* you?"

"Yes, sir."

"Why?"

About to give a flip, knee-jerk answer, Klaus decided not to. Not if this might be their last conversation.

"Because you're my grandfather," he said. "Because you loved me and took me seriously when no one else did. Not even my mother and father. And all *I* ever did was spit on the best of you."

The old man nodded slowly. "As I deserved. As you should have done. Exactly right.

"You always knew I was lying, didn't you, boy?"

Klaus pretended not to understand. "About what?"

"About our national slaughterhouse. About my never knowing what was happening. About my just being a good soldier who fought cleanly and with honor. About all the rest of what our 'master race' left behind to stink up the earth for the next thousand years."

"You were no worse than seventy million others."

"I should have been *better*," the old man whispered. "I was the worst of cowards. I knew, yet I pretended not to know. I fought, but I fought the wrong enemy, in the wrong places, for the wrong reasons. I should have been out screaming the truth on street corners. I should have been out grabbing Germans, and shaking them, and telling them we weren't fucking barbarians. When that failed, I should have grabbed a couple of Schmeissers, strapped on a dozen grenades, and gone after the lunatics at the top. At least I'd have died for a good purpose."

Klaus looked past the old man's head and stared at the lake shining in the sun. He saw a flight of ducks come in low over the trees and land so gently on the water that they barely made a ripple.

"Like *you're* about to do," said the major. "Or aren't you going to Germany to die for a good purpose?"

"I'm not going to Germany to die for *any* purpose, Grandfather. This has a lot more to do with living than dying."

"Still, you did imply you might not make it back."

"In such things, there's always that chance."

"In this case, I take it, there's a lot more than just a chance."

Klaus was silent.

"I wish I could go with you."

Klaus smiled. "You're that eager to die, sir?"

"Only for a good purpose. Only if it could help me make up for what I never had the balls to do when I was young, beautiful, and in one piece."

"What makes you so sure you'd find your good purpose with *me*?"

"Because since you were twelve all you've been after is to save the world."

"I haven't done much of a job of it, so far."

"At least you're trying."

Klaus drew on his cigar, found it dead, and spent a long moment relighting it.

"I'll tell you something I once used to think about," the old man said. "It was when I was in the hospital fifty-four years ago, when I first saw what they'd given me for a face. I wouldn't eat or speak for three days and was just waiting for a chance to kill myself.

"Then I thought maybe if I lived, I could do some good. I thought maybe I could take my face and parade it through the capitals of the world. I figured I could walk up and down roads for the remaining thirty or forty years of my life and frighten every man, woman, and child who saw me into remembering what they'd otherwise forget: that this was what hate produced, that this was its true face."

The major looked at his grandson. "Of course I wasn't anywhere near brave enough for that. I just crawled back here where it all happened and waited to die alone in my own puddle of piss."

Some crows called from outside until their sounds faded into the silence.

"Let me finally be of some use," said the old man. "Take me back to Germany with you."

"Be reasonable, Grandfather. You don't even know what I'm going to do."

"I don't have to know. You're betting your life on this, aren't you? That's enough for me. I want to make the same bet."

Klaus shook his head. "I'm sorry. There's nothing for you to do in this."

"You listen to me, boy!" The old man's voice rose. "I'm not a useless piece of shit. I can still do things. Even with one eye, I can outshoot you. I can lob a grenade fifty yards and make it land on the money. And I can put together a bomb in the dark with my one goddamn hand and no help from anyone."

The major breathed deeply. "And if nothing else works, I can always scare hell out of any bugger alive with my fucking face."

Klaus looked at his grandfather and believed him.

Chapter 25

IT WAS LATE EVENING and just growing dark when Paulie saw Kate leave her place high above the Bay of Naples. He was parked about a hundred meters up the block, and he watched as she got into her little red Fiat and drove off. A moment later, he started his own car and followed.

Paulie drove with his stomach in knots and his knuckles white on the wheel. He hated what he was doing about as much as he had ever hated anything. For the better part of two days and nights, he had been keeping Kate under long stretches of surveillance. If and when he ever learned the truth about what she had or had not done to his parents and what sort of game she was playing with her alleged feelings for him, he would decide what action to take.

Where was Kate leading her fool tonight?

At the moment, she was taking him south on the coast road edging the Bay of Naples.

Half an hour later, Paulie saw Kate turn off the coast road near the outskirts of Sorrento.

He set a longer interval between them and followed the Fiat as it climbed a winding, two-lane blacktop that crested high above the sea. When Kate entered the floodlit grounds of an imposing villa perched upon a grassy knoll, Paulie continued on past the gates and parked in a patch of woods a few hundred meters down the road.

He waited for about fifteen minutes before leaving the

car, lifted himself over a high wall surrounding the estate
Kate had entered, and dropped softly to the grass on the other
side. There were three separate buildings on the grounds: a
big garage with servants' quarters above it, a storage shed for
gardening and grass-cutting equipment, and the villa itself, a
two-story, stucco mansion built in the classic Mediterranean
style.

Approaching the complex, Paulie saw that the upper
story of the villa was totally dark; lights showed only for several ground-floor rooms. A few lights also were on in the servants' quarters over the garage.

Paulie crouched below the first lit window he reached
and peered inside. It was the kitchen, and it was empty. As
were the living room and the entrance foyer. The last of the
lit rooms was on the far side of the house and appeared to be
a combination study and library. This one was not empty.

Paulie saw Kate first. She sat alone on a dark leather
couch, a lit cigarette in one hand and a snifter of brandy in
the other. Her head was turned to the far side of the room,
where a man whose face Paulie could not see was fixing a
drink. She was talking, but the windows were closed and
Paulie could not hear a word.

Then the man finished preparing his drink and turned.
Paulie recognized him as the celebrated political scientist
Nicko Vorelli.

That probably meant that Kate was here to interview
Vorelli for some sort of current affairs article. Paulie had seen
the man a few times over the years at his mother's Sorrento
gallery and he knew him by reputation, but they had never
met.

Paulie Walters looked at Kate as Nicko Vorelli sat down
beside her on the couch. She seemed relaxed, comfortable, as
if she had spent time with the man in this room many times
before. Perhaps she was working on an extended piece, maybe
even a memoir of Vorelli's life and career.

Paulie saw her talking brightly, animatedly. Nicko
Vorelli leaned against the back of the couch and sipped his
drink as he listened. Occasionally he nodded, and Paulie

again had the feeling the two had been working together for a long time.

When she appeared to have finished her story, they laughed together and Nicko Vorelli touched her hair where the lamplight caught it. He put down his drink, drew Kate close, and kissed her.

"Oh, Jesus Christ!" whispered Paulie. Punishing himself, as if he needed to atone for every sin, real or imagined, he had ever committed, Paulie stayed and saw it all.

He saw them cut the lights and undress, leaving just a single lamp burning.

He saw the lovely body he knew as well as his own respond to the touch of flesh that had absolutely nothing to do with everything he had believed they shared.

What he finally felt was a total extinction.

Chapter 26

KATE DROVE HOME from Nicko Vorelli's place through pale, early-morning light, opened the door to her apartment, and found Paulie Walters staring at her.

"Paulie!"

Kate started toward him, arms open, reaching.

Then she had her first good look at his face and stopped.

"What is it?" she asked. "What's wrong?"

The next thing she saw was the gun. It lay on the small end table to the right of his chair, a blue-steel, 9-millimeter automatic with an attached silencer. It frightened her less than Paulie's face.

"Sit down," he said.

Even his voice sounded different, as if it were coming out of a tomb, Kate thought.

"Whore," Paulie said in his new, sepulchral voice. "How long have you been fucking Nicko Vorelli?"

For an instant, Kate felt overwhelming relief. *This* was all it had to do with?

She shook her head. "I love you. No one else. Don't you know how much I love you?"

"I saw how much last night. Through Vorelli's window."

Kate stared at Paulie apprehensively. "I've known Nicko since I was seventeen. He's helped me. He's taught me things that—"

"I saw what he taught you—all of it."

"That had nothing to do with us. In a way, he's never really touched me."

"Liar!"

Instead of calming Paulie, her words just seemed to ignite him. "Slut! You don't know what love means."

"Why did you have to follow me to Nicko's?" Kate asked tonelessly. "I don't understand why you were following me at all."

"To learn about you. To find out what you wanted from me."

"There was no mystery there. I just wanted to love you and have you love me."

Paulie looked at Kate. "When did you decide that? Before or after you killed my mother and father?"

He said it without change of expression. Kate saw that the automatic was no longer on the table beside him: it was in his hand.

Now I have it all, thought Kate, and wondered which of the two acts, her shooting of Paulie's parents or her sexual betrayal, she might finally have to die for.

"Who told you I killed your mother and father?"

"Nobody told me. I've learned enough to know it had to be you."

Kate grabbed onto the *had to be*. It implied no hard evidence, no smoking gun. "What have you learned?"

"That you're the Falangas' daughter. That since you were seven, you've been obsessed with the idea of shooting the killer of your parents."

Kate realized there was no room for the truth here. Never mind mitigating circumstances, or love, or the possibility of forgiveness. To admit her guilt at this moment would mean the end of her; if not literally, then in every other way that mattered.

"If that were true," Kate said quietly, "why would I have waited eighteen years?"

"Because until now you never knew my father shot your parents."

"How am I supposed to have finally found that out?"

"From your friend Klaus Logefeld."

This one hit Kate squarely in the stomach. Still, she held on.

"Did Klaus say he told me your father was the shooter?" Kate asked.

"I haven't been able to find the sonofabitch, but I did find the man who told Logefeld it was my father."

"Did *this* man say he told *me*?"

Paulie shook his head. He glanced at the automatic in his hand, then at Kate. "All this talk isn't going to do you any good. I know you killed them, Kate."

"Then why are you just sitting there with that gun in your hand? Why haven't you shot me?"

When Paulie finally spoke, he seemed drained of all emotion. "How could you have done it?" he asked. "Oh, I don't mean your shooting them. When I'm not totally crazy inside, I can almost understand your need. What I mean is, how could you have knocked on my door afterward and started on *me*? Did you expect to find a special thrill in making me love you after you'd just shot my mother and father?"

Kate said nothing.

"Or was it your way of atoning?" Paulie asked. "Of trying to give me back some of the love you'd just blown away with your gun?"

Kate looked straight at him. "Why do you suddenly believe that *I* am the killer?"

"It's not sudden. I've known you were the Falangas' daughter for almost three days."

"Why did you wait this long to rush in here with a gun in your hand? Why didn't you come three days ago? Maybe it had more to do with your seeing me with Nicko last night," said Kate, "than your actually believing I killed your mother and father."

Before Kate's eyes, Paulie seemed to shrink.

"Ah, Kate," he said, his voice almost a whisper. "I admit I have no hard evidence, but I am absolutely certain that you shot my mother and father. The worst of it is, you're still burning inside me."

Slowly, he lifted the automatic until it was pointing at her head. Using his thumb, he released the safety.

"Did you care anything at all about me?" he asked.

Unable to trust her voice, Kate nodded.

"Don't lie," Paulie said. "If you lie just before dying, your soul will never be at rest."

"I'm not lying. I loved you as I've never loved anyone."

"Not anymore?" Paulie's voice was faintly mocking. "You don't love me now?"

"You're frightening me too much."

"You've made such a pathetic fool of me. How can a fool be so frightening?"

Kate did not dare to speak.

"You're not even crying," he said, still keeping the automatic aimed at her head. "At the final moment of your life, why don't you at least cry?"

"I can't."

"Of course you can't. You haven't enough feeling in you for tears."

"My God, how you hate me."

Paulie stared at her for a long moment. "I don't hate you, Kate. I even weep for you. I listened to what happened to you as a little girl and it broke my heart. I just can't quite see myself letting you walk away from this."

Kate raised her hand.

"Close your eyes," said Paulie.

"No. You want to shoot me? Look at me."

Kate saw him bring up his other hand to steady his aim, saw the dark hole of the silencer pointed directly between her eyes, saw Paulie's finger tighten against the trigger.

She heard the soft, whooshing sound of the silenced explosion and felt death brush the hair on the left side of her head.

"That's for my mother, who deserved better," he said.

The second shot breezed through her hair on the right.

"And that's for poppa," said Paulie, "who would have loved you as much as I . . . given the chance."

He rose and put away his gun.

"I don't want to see or speak to you again," he said softly. "Not ever. Not in this world."

"Paulie . . ."

Paul Walters crossed the room. When he reached the door, he stopped and turned.

"I can forgive an awful lot," he said. "Maybe even your relationship with Vorelli. But you deliberately set out to make me love the killer of my mother and father. And you did it. *That*, I can never forgive."

Paulie left, quietly closing the door behind him.

Chapter 27

TOMMY CORTLANDT LOATHED the sprawling, diplomatic circus on the White House lawn, and he was just edging toward an early escape when the First Lady appeared in his path.

"Not yet, Tommy. Not until you give me at least ten minutes."

Maggie Dunster had her best politically correct smile in place, but her eyes were serious.

A tall, gracefully aging woman, the president's wife led Cortlandt past a string quartet gently playing Brahms, then guided him as far as possible from where her husband was holding court.

"I guess Jimmy told you I know about his secret plan for Wannsee," she said, "and that I'm going with him."

"He told me."

"I'm sure the news didn't add to your day's level of joy."

Cortlandt shrugged. "It's just that in something like this, I'm afraid you become one more high-risk security complication."

As they walked, Cortlandt was aware of the First Lady studying his face.

"I don't suppose my husband told you *why* I insisted on going along."

"No."

"Well, I'm going to tell you now. I need your word that it won't go any further."

The CIA director nodded.

"That includes not letting Jimmy know I told you."

"I should be able to handle that too."

Maggie took a moment. She evidently needed to compose herself. Cortlandt could feel her tension from a foot away.

"All right," she said. "Jimmy has been having some angina attacks. Chest pains. A few of them have been pretty severe."

Cortlandt's face froze.

"Only I and his personal physician know. He should be having bypass surgery, but he refuses. He's afraid it would blow the rest of his term to bits."

"How long has it been going on?"

"Almost two months. Sometimes he gets an attack in the middle of the night and I have to put a nitro pill under his tongue. It's terrible. Every time we go through it, I'm afraid he won't last till morning."

Strolling through the manicured grass, Cortlandt steered Maggie Dunster away from several approaching guests. When one of them called to her, she smiled and waved and kept walking.

"Knowing our president," said Cortlandt dryly, "I'm surprised he agreed to let you go with him. How did you manage it?"

"By swearing that if he tried to stop me, I'd call a news conference and plaster his secret angina and plans for Wannsee over every newspaper in the country."

"Would you really have done that?"

"You probably know me as well as anyone, Tommy. What do *you* think?"

"I don't think you'd have done it," Cortlandt said. "If for no other reason than that you know how much Jimmy distrusts his vice president."

"Well, you're wrong." Maggie stopped walking and leaned closer to Cortlandt. "And I'll tell you something else. I'm getting worried enough to be thinking about blowing everything wide open anyway. I might do it within the next day or two."

Tommy Cortlandt stared at her. "Do you know what something like that could do to the man?"

"Certainly. It could keep him away from Wannsee. It could force him to go to the hospital and have his bypass. And God willing, it could keep him alive for another twenty years."

"Or it could just finish him as president and break his heart. You can't fool with stuff like this, Maggie. A lot more is at stake here than saving Jimmy from a possible coronary."

"Not to me."

"Whatever your motives," said the CIA director, "you can't do this to him, Maggie."

"Who could stop me?"

"I could. And you know it."

Maggie's long, deep sigh seemed to ease the worst of her tension out.

"In any case," said Cortlandt, "I think you're way over the top in your reaction to Wannsee. You're making too much of the whole thing."

"I'm not the one. That's Jimmy. He's suddenly Christ on a mountain with his arms open to the world. When the world spits in his face, I'm afraid of what it could do to him."

"Come on, Maggie, you're not performing grand opera. Don't sell the guy short. Angina or not, he won't be doing any dying at Wannsee. We're all a lot stronger than anyone ever expects. With a little nitro here and there, we've even been known to rise above occasional chest pains."

"Do you honestly believe that, Tommy?"

"I guarantee it," said the CIA director.

There are times, he thought, when a man can get his mouth to say just about anything.

Fifty yards from where Tommy Cortlandt and the First Lady were talking, Vice President Fleming left a small group that included his wife, the secretary of state, and the French ambassador, took a glass of champagne from a passing waiter, and drifted over to where Ken Harris sat alone with his double bourbon.

"Have you been watching them?" he asked the deputy director.

Harris nodded.

"They've been going on like that for more than twenty minutes," said Fleming. "They're definitely not happy."

"Probably a lovers' quarrel."

The vice president failed to smile. "Did you know Maggie's going to Brussels with Dunster?"

"Who told you that?"

"Amy. She had lunch with her yesterday."

Ken Harris just sipped his bourbon.

"You know what that means, don't you?" said Fleming.

"No. Explain it to me."

The vice president wiped a few beads of sweat from his upper lip. "It doesn't bother you that Maggie dies too?"

"I'm not overjoyed at the prospect. But neither will it keep me from sleeping tonight." Ken Harris took a long moment. "Why? Do you want to cancel out?"

Fleming stared off at the First Lady and said nothing. He watched the hold she had on Tommy Cortlandt's arm, saw the way her fingers dug into and worked the fabric of his jacket sleeve. *Well, Maggie . . .*

After a while he said, "Have you heard from your man?"

"Yes. It's moving along."

"Meaning?"

"He's contacted someone."

"Who is it?"

"A Palestinian. A known American hater who'll claim full credit for himself and his movement. Exactly what we want."

Fleming nodded slowly.

He had just spotted the president working the crowd a short distance away. It was one of Jimmy Dunster's strong points. A handshake here, an amusing anecdote there, a light personal comment somewhere else, never at a loss. All artifice, of course, but the coin of the realm for any public figure. *I have more substance and brains,* Jayson Fleming thought bitterly, *but I'm also too intense, sweaty-palmed, and humorless. Like poor Nixon.*

Perhaps he could change once he was in the Oval Office. Perhaps he could develop a kind of soulful wit, learn to relax more with people, talk to them about what he thought and felt. Fleming bargained with himself. He would work night and day for the country, be apolitical, ignore all party lines and act only for the common good.

He was even able to feel a deep, unspeakable sorrow for Maggie and Jimmy Dunster, pressing at the limits of composure he desperately needed to maintain.

I'm sorry, he told them. That alone came near to making him feel at peace.

Chapter 28

KLAUS LOGEFELD FINISHED his final lecture of the week late
Friday afternoon and drove away from the university with
only a small bag in the car.

Klaus had been especially careful about watching his
back since Nicko Vorelli had surprised him in that unset-
tling midnight dark, and he was careful now as he headed
out of Rome and along a series of thinly traveled country
roads. When he was certain beyond any doubt that he was
not being followed, he picked up the road leading to the airport.

At 7:10 P.M. Klaus drove into the airport parking lot. He
had bought his ticket in advance, so he sat in the car for
twenty minutes, waiting until it was near boarding time.
Then he entered the terminal and arrived at his flight's departure gate just as the passengers were lining up to board.

His grandfather was halfway down the line.

The former Wehrmacht officer stood tall and erect, his
flowing gray hair silvered by the lights, his empty jacket
sleeve carried like a special badge of courage. He had on a
pair of oversized dark glasses, and a large surgical bandage was
taped over the more frightful areas of his face. People glanced
at him, then were careful to look elsewhere, except for two
young boys, who appeared fascinated until they were spoken
to by their mother.

Aboard the plane, Klaus sat seven rows behind his
grandfather. The old man did not once turn to look at him.

When they finally took off, his head was bent forward and he seemed to be asleep.

They landed at Berlin's Tempelhof Airport at 10:15 P.M. Klaus started the engine of the rented pale gray BMW and sat there until his grandfather opened the passenger door and slid in beside him. Moments later he drove out of the airport and headed south on Kleist Strasse. Only then did he speak. "So, Grandfather? How does it feel to be home?"

"Germany isn't my home. I have no home. But at least I'm here doing something."

They rode without speaking, and Klaus lowered a window and felt the coolness of the night against his face. About ten kilometers later, he turned off the main highway and onto a two-lane country road that soon ended in a dirt track. Then he swung to one side, parked next to a cluster of heavy brush, and cut the headlights.

"Where are we?" asked the old man.

"A few kilometers from where I used to live. I played here when I was a boy. It was my secret place."

Klaus took a flashlight out of his bag and circled around behind the brush. His grandfather followed. Klaus aimed his flashlight at a high outcropping of rock. Then he put the light in the old man's hand.

"Hold it steady right here," he told him.

Klaus scraped away a pattern of embedded dirt and leaves in the rockface, revealing a deep, irregularly circular crack. He dug a crowbar out of the soil, jammed the pronged edge into the crack, and kept prying until a large boulder was drawn far enough out of position to expose the opening to a cave.

"I'll be damned," said the major.

Klaus Logefeld took back his flashlight.

"Wait here," he told his grandfather, and he crawled into the cave with the beam lighting his way. Inside, it was as cold as an old icehouse, and Klaus felt the chill enter his bones.

He shifted his light until it picked up a large, olive-drab barracks bag lying deep in a far corner. The canvas was stretched tight with everything he would need at Wannsee. It was wrapped in two layers of heavy plastic to keep out the dampness. It had all been there, waiting, for almost three weeks.

Klaus unwrapped the plastic, then tugged the bag out of the cave.

The old man stared at it without comment. When Klaus began shoving the boulder back into the hole, the major put his full weight behind his one arm to help. Then he helped his grandson carry the bag to the BMW and lay it in the trunk.

"What are we going to do?" he asked. "Blow up Berlin?"

Klaus laughed. "Only if we have to."

He took out two cigars, handed one to his grandfather, and they lit up.

"Tell me how you feel about all this, boy." The old man's voice was quiet, easy, free of his usual emotion.

"Excited . . . nervous . . . frightened . . . angry . . . depressed."

"Not blissfully happy?"

Klaus smiled. "If you mean am I jumping with joy, the answer is no."

"You do know they're never going to let us out of Wannsee alive, don't you?"

Klaus Logefeld shrugged. "That's not how I'm planning it, but it's possible."

"That doesn't bother you?"

"Of course it bothers me. I'm not crazy. But we both know it's not going to stop me."

At 12:47 A.M. Klaus parked the BMW in the same patch of woods adjoining Wannsee that he had used on his previous visit.

Leaving his grandfather with the car, he checked security and found there was still just a single guard on duty at the gatehouse. When he returned, he eased the old man over the perimeter wall in slow, careful stages. Then he followed him over with the barracks bag.

The two men walked slowly, the weight of the bag shared between them. Klaus glanced at his grandfather and felt a little less lonely than in all the years since he had been a child. *Imagine him actually ending up with me in this.*

At one of the larger outbuildings Klaus unlocked the door and they carried the bag inside, where the air was rich with the smell of fertilizer and oiled equipment.

Klaus had explained to his grandfather everything that would have to be done at Wannsee this night, and they began in the outbuilding with the old man helping as best he could. Mostly, his job was to keep the light focused and hand Klaus things as he worked with the *plastique*, packing good, solid charges of the powerful explosive into two separate locations in the storage building, setting their electronically controlled detonators, and finally making certain that both units were completely hidden from sight.

When that was finished, they moved to the museum and conference center itself.

Like a man following an old trail, Klaus led his grandfather across the same stretch of sweet-smelling grass he had traveled on his practice run, neutralized the museum's alarm system, and entered the building though the cellar door.

Once inside, his breath labored heavily through his lungs and his hands tingled as they did their work in the four sections of the basement ceiling he had selected on his last visit. When the *plastique* charges were set in the cellar and the acoustic ceiling panels replaced, Klaus and the old man carried their half-empty bag up the interior steps to the first floor. Klaus continued his work there.

In the men's washroom off the main lobby, he removed the ventilator grill from the ceiling of a toilet stall and taped two small automatics and the remote for his detonators to some hidden studs.

His grandfather watched every move closely.

"Good," he said at one point.

It was the only word he spoke throughout.

Finally, they unlocked and went into the surveillance

room with its banks of closed-circuit television screens and audio and video controls.

Explaining everything to his grandfather, Klaus was struck again by the same sense of uncertainty about the area that he had experienced on his last visit. Would all this high-tech surveillance equipment be good or bad for them when the time came? Despite his careful planning, key elements still remained unpredictable.

Man plans and God laughs.

Nevertheless, Klaus Logefeld felt remarkably calm.

Chapter 29

FOR THE FIRST TIME since his parents were killed, Paul Walters was at home in Ravello, working in his studio.

Mostly, he stood and shuffled about in front of the same half-finished canvas that had been on his easel for weeks, and wondered what he was doing there in the first place. Paulie knew, of course. He was a painter, and painters were supposed to paint. He was trying to go through the motions, but the effort was worthless.

After a couple of hours Paulie put down his palette and brushes and just sat fighting his private darkness. A knock at the front door of the house roused him.

With relief, Paulie opened the door and looked at Kate Dinneson.

She stood uncertainly with the sun lighting her hair.

In the approximately twenty-four hours since Paulie had seen her, he had forgotten how the bones in her face seemed laced together rather than joined. Her eyes found and held his, lightly, ready to fly away if what she saw there remained as hard, dark, and unforgiving as her last sight of them.

Paulie stood there numbly.

"May I come in?" she asked.

"Why?"

"Because I can't just leave it like this."

"You mean you want to tell me more lies?"

"No. I want to tell you the truth."

"I already know the truth."

"All you know is what happened," Kate said. "That's bad enough, but still a long way from the truth."

Paulie remained silent.

"You may as well let me in," she said, "because I'm not going away until I've told you everything."

Paulie abruptly turned and walked back to his studio. He heard the door close behind him, then Kate's footsteps on the tile floor as she followed.

Paulie sat down and watched her enter the big, sky-lighted room. She looked at the paintings scattered about, studied the unfinished canvas resting on the easel, and gazed through the wide picture window at the sea sparkling in the sun far below. This was the first time she had ever been to his house, and he thought she might be trying to memorize everything because she knew she would never be there again.

Finally, she sat down. "I did kill your mother and father," she told him. "I shot them, but it wasn't the way you think. I was tricked . . . used. I was played for the worst kind of dunce."

"By whom?"

"By the man you've been looking for. Klaus Logefeld."

With effort, Paulie kept his emotions as controlled as Kate's. "Exactly how did he do all this to you?"

"By lying about how my parents died. By telling me your father shot them in cold blood when they were unarmed and coming out to surrender."

"So you went to avenge their deaths by shooting my father while he was asleep in bed?"

"No. I wanted to talk to your father. I wanted to hear from his own lips exactly how my parents died."

"With a gun in your hand in the middle of the night?"

"How else? By knocking on the door and inviting myself to dinner?"

Paulie swallowed dryly. "What did my father tell you?"

"That I'd been lied to. That my parents had actually come out shooting from behind a white flag. That they killed two of his men and wounded him three times before he began firing back."

"Did you believe him?"

"No, not really. But your father said he had photographs right there in a safe that would prove it was true."

"So?"

Kate looked at Paulie. Her expression was one of thoughtful, cool reserve.

"So I let your father get out of bed and open his safe," she said. "But then your mother started shooting from under her bedsheet, and your father was diving at me, and I was rolling on the floor shooting for my life." Kate paused and breathed deeply. "When it was over, I'd ended up doing what I swear to God I hadn't wanted to do at all."

Paulie said nothing.

Her eyes were moist. "You think I'm lying, don't you?"

"You've lied about everything else. Why not this?"

"What if you saw photographs and heard tapes of everything I've just told you?"

"You mean you actually have such things?"

"No. But I know who does have them."

"You mean we're back to Logefeld again?"

Kate nodded. "Those pictures and tapes are his entire reason for setting me up."

"So he could do *what?*"

"So he could pressure Nicko Vorelli through me. So he could tell Nicko I'd be jailed for two murders if Nicko didn't do as he asked."

"What was he asking for?"

"For Nicko to include him on his staff for that big human rights conference at Wannsee on the thirteenth."

"Vorelli agreed?"

"Yes. If he didn't agree, or if anything were to happen to Klaus, three extra copies of the pictures and tapes would be hand-delivered to the authorities. What else could Nicko do?"

"What your dear Nicko could have done," said Paulie softly, "is just say to hell with you, and either turn the bastard over to the police or quietly blow him away and bury him somewhere."

"Is that what you would have done?"

Paulie blinked, feeling slow and tired. "I have a much more important question. I'd like to know why an old-time terrorist hood should be going to so much trouble to get himself invited to some bullshit human rights meeting."

"Klaus doesn't look at it as a bullshit meeting. He sees it as something he's been preparing for all his life."

"How has he been preparing? By making bombs?"

"In all fairness, he's been away from that sort of thing for more than sixteen years."

"Doing what? Preaching the Gospel?"

"Hardly. According to Nicko Vorelli, he *has* made something of a name for himself as a professor of political science."

"Where?"

"Currently, at the University of Rome."

"I've never heard of him."

"Have you heard of Professor Alfred Mainz?"

"I've read one of his books. What about him?"

"He's Klaus Logefeld."

Paulie was stunned.

"When did he change his name?"

"I don't know. I never knew him as Alfred Mainz until he set out to use me," Kate explained.

"Do you at least believe what I said about how I shot your parents?" she asked.

Paulie turned to look at her. "How would my believing change anything? My mother and father would still be dead. And you would still be the one who killed them."

Chapter 30

PAUL WALTERS DROVE PAST the building on Rome's Via Sistina where Professor Alfred Mainz had his apartment, parked three blocks away, then walked back through the early afternoon sunshine.

A block from the house, he stopped at a pay phone and called Mainz's home number. He did not expect any answer. Having checked the professor's lecture schedule, he knew that Mainz would be busy at the university for another four hours. But Paulie was still cautious about possible surprises.

After six rings, he hung up and began walking again, trying to keep himself still inside. He had decisions to make, and thinking about them had kept him awake for most of the night. Now all he was left with were tired eyes and an aching head.

He opened a huge, nineteenth-century door, crossed a cobbled courtyard, and entered a dimly lit vestibule. A brass-trimmed directory listed Dr. Alfred Mainz as being in apartment 4-B, and Paulie climbed three flights of stairs without meeting anyone. When he reached Mainz's apartment, he picked the lock and entered.

Paulie did a quick run-through: foyer, living room, kitchen, dining area, bathroom, study, bedroom, a closet made into a photographer's darkroom. Klaus Logefeld lived alone, a seemingly orderly man with no frills or female touches. The bright apartment had sunlight streaming in from the south and high-key prints and paintings on the walls.

Paulie began a detailed search of one room at a time. In a closet of the study, he came upon a locked metal file cabinet. He worked it open with one of his skeleton keys. The cabinet had three drawers, which Paulie went through front to back. He found a cluster of notebooks filled with handwriting, along with groups of manila file folders and some video-and audiocassettes.

Paulie found what he was looking for at the rear section of the bottom drawer, in a folder labeled with the single word *Kate*. A large white envelope contained still photographs and two small audiocassettes held together by rubber bands. He put them on Logefeld's desk, took a cassette player from a wall cabinet crammed with audio and phonographic equipment, and sat down with what he had.

Paulie started with the infrared pictures of Kate in the dark of the woods and slowly followed each shot in sequence as she entered his parents' house and climbed the stairs to their bedroom. The first voice he heard on the audio was his father's, saying, "Peg? We have company."

From there on Paulie did his best to synchronize the dialogue with the photographs. His hands were shaking so badly that everything was soon hopelessly out of synch.

Not that it really mattered. Little doubt remained as to what was happening and who was saying what to whom.

So Kate had *not* lied. Logefeld *had* tricked and used her. She *had* fired only when she would have been shot dead herself if she had not. Logefeld had all but squeezed the trigger.

Heart pounding, he rose from Klaus Logefeld's desk and replaced the pictures and audiotapes in the files exactly as he had found them. Then he took a last careful look around to make sure that everything was just as it had been when he arrived, and left the apartment.

Paulie had seen where Klaus Logefeld lived. Now he wanted to see him in the flesh, hear the sound of his voice, listen to what Professor Alfred Mainz had to say.

* * *

A lot of standees were pressed into the rear of the university auditorium. Paul Walters edged in among them and looked at the man behind the lectern.

Dr. Mainz was tall and well-built, with a strong, sculpted head and a graceful way of using his hands, arms, and even his body as he spoke. His Italian held no trace of a German accent, and his amplified voice was both grave and portentous.

The professor was the quintessential public man, a speaker, a solid presence. His audience of hundreds was totally still. Alone on the platform, he projected his beliefs with the weight of an unstoppable force. This afternoon his words were delivered in the nature of a warning: fascism, once thought to be dead, suddenly had a new and frightening future in the world.

He declared that Hitler and Mussolini had descendants springing up after all—that their legacy did not just condone violence, that it *was* violence; that fascism was a form of revenge that history adopted in an age of indifference and moral failure; that its second springtime was a new plague, flowering as a doctrine of vengeance; that ethnic cleansing was simply thinking with one's blood instead of one's brains, while more and more blood was being spilled.

From Professor Alfred Mainz, these ideological declamations carried the sound of bugles.

Paul Walters found the accumulated pain of actually seeing and hearing his parents' final moments, of his unspeakable sorrow, and of his rage at the man responsible pressing at the limits of his control.

I'd better go before I blow his fucking head off.

He was well outside the hall and moving fast when he heard the applause behind him.

It sounded like rain.

Not bugles.

Chapter 31

KLAUS LOGEFELD WAS IN HIS GRANDFATHER'S HOUSE. It was late afternoon and they were going over the diagrams and floor plans of the Wannsee Museum and Conference Center. The doorbell rang.

The two men looked at each other.

"Sometimes people get lost and need directions," said the major. "I'll go and see."

"No. Just wait here. I'll go."

Klaus slid his charts into a drawer and walked to a front window. Peering out between closed curtains and some bushes, he saw the partially obscured figure of a man at the door. He could not see the man's face. Nor could he see anyone else.

He took an automatic out of a shoulder holster and released the safety. Then he put the piece inside his belt, buttoned his jacket over it, and opened the door.

Nicholas Vorelli smiled at him. "How nice to see you again, Professor."

Klaus stood there.

When am I going to learn about this man?

"May I come in?" asked Nicko.

Klaus Logefeld stepped aside and Nicko entered the house. He walked into the room where the old man was sitting and made a small formal bow with his head.

"I'm Nicko Vorelli," he said. "You must be Klaus's grandfather."

The old man said nothing. Nicko chose a wooden chair facing some windows and sat down.

"What a wonderfully peaceful place you have, Major," he said. "Just sitting here and looking out over the lake must be comforting."

"Like the grave," said the old man.

Nicko nodded. "That too."

His throat clotted with tension, Klaus spoke for the first time. "You do have a way of surprising me, Dr. Vorelli. What's happening now?"

"We're getting close to the thirteenth, which means we have to do some serious talking."

"I thought we had already done that."

"Not really, Professor."

Klaus went over and sat down opposite Nicko and his grandfather. He had the sense of being shoved onstage in the middle of a play without a script.

"So far," said Nicko, "neither of us has been entirely honest. Now it's time to stop playing games."

Nicko settled himself in his chair and deliberately studied Klaus. "I know considerably more than you think. I know that you went into Wannsee again the other night, this time with your grandfather. I know about the weapons and explosives you brought there. I know exactly where you cached everything. And I certainly know you have a lot of explaining to do."

Klaus Logefeld sat unmoving, and for several moments he felt as if a devil's toll had been exacted from his flesh.

"I must say you're taking it well," he finally said.

"What makes you think that? Because I'm not ranting and raving?"

Klaus did not answer.

"I'm not a ranter and raver, Professor. If I'm provoked enough, I simply remove the provocation."

"You mean you've removed everything we brought into Wannsee the other night?"

"No. It's all still there."

"Why?" asked Klaus.

"Because considering who and what you are, I pretty much expected it."

"Then it doesn't bother you?"

Nicko's smile approached the benign.

"If it bothered me, you'd be floating in the Tiber right this minute."

"We both know better than that."

"You mean because of those pathetic pictures and tapes you have of our little Kate?"

Klaus was silent.

"That's not what's kept you alive," said Nicko.

"What then?"

"My feeling that your zealousness, properly controlled, can actually help get us both what we want out of Wannsee."

They sat in the following silence. A breeze came through the windows, stirring the curtains, and Klaus felt increasingly hopeful.

"I'll be wanting my grandfather along too," he said.

Nicko considered the old man. "I see no problem in that. But what about your start-up plans? Do you have any precise schedule to follow?"

"My grandfather and I will pick up our automatics and detonator from the men's room right before Chancellor Eisner goes into his opening address. After that, we'll allow an hour or so while the world watches and we choose our primary hostages."

"How will you choose?"

"Mostly by opportunity. If possible, I'd like to include Chancellor Eisner and the U.S. secretary of state for the extra leverage they give us. If all goes smoothly, though, we should end up with whatever hostages we want."

"Meaning what?" asked Nicko.

"If there's any hitch, any refusal to fall into line, I threaten to press one of the little red buttons on my remote."

"You can't just 'threaten.'"

"I know that."

"You're prepared to sacrifice lives if necessary?"

"You know I am, Dr. Vorelli."

"Even your own?"

"If I wasn't ready for that, I would never have started the whole thing."

"You can still change your mind."

"And give up my one chance to do something really worthwhile?"

Nicko looked at the old man. "What about you, Major? Are you ready to die along with your suicidal grandson?"

"I've been ready for fifty years."

"Well, *I'm* not," said Nicko. "Dying plays absolutely no part in what I want from Wannsee."

Klaus stared evenly at Nicko. "To be truthful, Doctor, I still wonder what you really *are* after from this meeting."

"All the same sanctified things that you and your grandfather are after—except, of course, for the one very important item I haven't mentioned yet."

"What's that?"

"Fifty million German marks."

Klaus Logefeld frowned. "I don't understand."

"It's not complicated. Just a simple business transaction." Nicko's smile was warm, open. "Call it my finder's fee if you will."

"Your finder's fee for *what*?"

"For getting you and your grandfather into Wannsee to begin with. For giving your blessed epiphany its one chance to fly."

Klaus could only stare at Nicko.

"Why are you having such a problem with this?" asked Nicko. "Compared with the devious, labyrinthine lengths you went to entrap Kate and me, what I'm talking about is practically at kindergarten level."

"Exactly where would your fifty million marks be coming from?" Klaus asked.

"It would simply be included in your overall hostage settlement."

"I never thought about our hostages in terms of money."

"Then start thinking about it now."

Klaus felt himself sweating. "Why are you doing this? Why are you cheapening everything?"

"I wouldn't call fifty million marks cheap."

"That's not what I meant."

"I know what you meant, Professor. But this happens to be *my* decision and *my* personal need. So you're just going to have to live with it."

Klaus swallowed something cold and bitter.

"Are you telling me you have a sudden personal need for fifty million German marks?"

"I'm afraid so," said Nicko Vorelli. "You see, we all have our problems, Professor. My own current problem stems from the recent collapse of that huge land development deal in Marbella, which not only wiped me clean but left me millions in debt. You probably read about Arturo Mendotti blowing his brains out before they could arrest him for embezzlement. I just wish he'd have given me the pleasure of pulling the trigger. I've worked too long and hard for my way of life to abandon it now. So with a little prodding here and there, I'm counting on you to help me maintain it."

"You mean you had everything planned from the beginning?"

"No. Not until I found out what you really were up to. Then I figured why the devil not? Why not do myself some good while bettering our less than joyous human condition? With all the billions and trillions in unlimited currencies bubbling out of the communal pot, with all the bottomless waste and destruction of our unending tribal wars, my paltry fifty million marks are less than fly specks."

Klaus looked up to find Nicko smiling at him.

"It's not all that bad, Professor Mainz. Before we're through," said Nicko, "you're going to be very happy I've made myself part of this."

"Why?"

"Because in one way or another, I'm the one who'll be keeping you and your grandfather from falling on your own bloody swords."

This time Nicholas Vorelli's smile was for the old man.

"I'm sorry, Major. But any personal dying you may have been counting on is going to have to be done on your own time."

Chapter 32

AT ELEVEN-THIRTY on the night of September 10, Daniel Archer drove through the narrow, nearly deserted streets of one of the older sections of Brussels.

He drove very slowly, watching for an opening in the solid wall of buildings on his right. He had been here before over the years, but the tiny alley he was looking for was still easy to miss in the dark. When he did finally see it, he turned in and parked behind a waiting Peugeot.

Moments later, Archer was inside the other car, gripping the hand of a uniformed lieutenant of police.

"How goes it, Charles?" he said in fairly good French.

"Improving. Now that *you're* here bearing your usual generous gifts." The lieutenant grinned. "So what do I call you *this* trip?"

"Anything you want. But my passport says George Lucas."

"Christ, you've got the life. Travel, money, excitement, hot women."

"Sure. And always a good chance of an equally hot bullet in the head."

Charles offered a philosophical shrug. "Everybody dies, Danny. At least you're living great till you do."

"You're doing pretty well yourself."

"Not on my stinking cop's pay. The garbagemen earn more."

Daniel Archer took out a thick envelope and handed it to the officer. "Well, this should help."

"It sure as hell will," said Charles, and he gave Archer a folded sheet of paper in return.

"Check it out," said Daniel Archer. "There's a little bonus this time."

The lieutenant opened the envelope, counted the bills, and stared at Archer. "Jesus. This one must be very important."

The amount was supposed to be ten thousand dollars. Twice that much was there.

"They're all very important, Charles. Any trouble getting it?"

"Hell, I just opened a safe, copied a sheet of paper, and put back the original." The lieutenant's smile was weak. "Now all I have to do is try to live with it."

Daniel Archer studied the paper under a map light. A neatly typed paragraph detailed the exact route of President Dunster's motorcade from the Brussels airport to his hotel. A second paragraph described Dunster's projected return to the airport the following morning. The two routes were totally different.

"Everything there?" asked the lieutenant.

Daniel Archer nodded. "What are the chances of a last-minute change?"

"Emergencies can happen. But they're rare."

Charles lit a cigarette and looked at Archer in the flare of the match. "Good luck." He was silent for a moment. "To both of us."

Less than an hour later, Daniel Archer sat in Abu Mustafa's Saab in another part of Brussels. He was watching the Palestinian examine the two proposed presidential routes with the aid of a flashlight and an enlarged street map of the city.

"Let's drive through them," Mustafa said.

They started from the Chanteclaire Hotel, where the president would be staying. Daniel Archer drove while Abu

Mustafa read off street names and instructions and made notes of key points along the route to the airport.

It was well past midnight and there was little traffic moving, but they drove cautiously. From time to time the Palestinian had Archer pull over to the curb while he studied a particular street, building, or stretch of road. When they reached the outskirts of the city and the spaces began to open up, they stopped more often.

At the airport, they circled the main terminal area and started back to Brussels using the other route.

They finished at close to three o'clock in the morning.

"Well?" said Archer.

"I've got two locations that look good. They're both on the return route to the airport."

"When will you decide?"

"Tomorrow morning," said Abu Mustafa. "After we've made a final run to see what the traffic will be like at the exact time the motorcade will be going by."

Chapter 33

KATE WAS WITH NICKO VORELLI on his yacht, cruising the Bay of Naples. The sun sparkled on quiet water and Vesuvius was a gray ghost in the distance.

They sat under an awning on the stern deck, enjoying a lunch prepared and served with near reverence. That was pretty much how Nicko Vorelli approached most things that had to do with his personal pleasure. Yet to Kate, something exceptional was afoot today.

When they were alone and sipping their espresso, Nicko Vorelli finally said, "I have a few things I'd like to go over with you."

"About what?"

"About you and me and your friend Klaus Logefeld. About the coming meeting at Wannsee."

"Has something happened that I don't know about?"

"A great deal has happened."

Kate listened calmly as Nicko told her of his two additional meetings with Klaus Logefeld, as if even the cached weapons and explosives at Wannsee were all perfectly ordinary items that bore absolutely no connection to either Nicko or herself. Finally she realized that whatever potentially lethal events might still lie ahead, she would ultimately be to blame for causing them.

"My God, look what I've done!"

The words broke out of her, cutting Nicholas Vorelli off in midsentence.

He looked at Kate. "You haven't done a thing. You're one of the real victims in all this. If anything, you were done *to*."

"No. If it were not for those pictures and tapes of *me*, you could be turning Klaus over to the police this minute."

Nicko squinted into the sun at a passing sailboat. "You're wrong. Those pictures and tapes aren't what's keeping Logefeld out of jail. I am."

"I don't understand."

"That's because I haven't told you everything," said Nicko, and he proceeded to tell Kate about his demand for fifty million marks.

"So?" asked Nicko when he had finished. "What do you think?"

"What I think," said Kate Dinneson slowly, "is that you've probably just told me one of the saddest stories I've ever heard."

"Why?"

"Because as far as I can see, you're about to throw away your life and good name for a big pile of money you can manage to live without."

Nicko Vorelli laughed. "If that's what I was about to do, it wouldn't be sad. It would be just plain stupid."

A white-coated steward appeared from below with fresh espresso, and they waited in silence until he had served them and left the deck.

"Please understand this," said Nicko. "I have absolutely no intention of risking my life and good name for this big pile of money you claim I can live without. Whatever I do at Wannsee will be set up to leave me safe and seemingly uninvolved. As for my being able to live without those fifty million marks, that just wouldn't be my idea of living."

Considering each other, they sat with their separate thoughts. A breeze came up and ruffled the sea, causing the big yacht to roll slightly. Vesuvius had faded into a growing mist and was no longer visible. Still, the water remained a pure, stainless blue.

Nicko took a card from his wallet and handed it to Kate.

"This is for you," he said.

She saw that it was an official press pass to Wannsee. With the media presence cut way back and limited to mostly pool coverage by the major networks, Kate knew the kind of pressure Nicko must have applied to get this for her.

"Don't you want it?" Nicko asked.

"Of course I want it. What journalist wouldn't? But I can't help feeling this pass isn't entirely for me."

"Your name is on it. Who else would it be for?"

"You."

"I don't understand."

"Yes you do, Nicko. What are you going to want from me at Wannsee?"

"Nothing."

"I'll do whatever you ask," said Kate. "Only please stop playing with me and tell me what it is."

"Am I really that transparent?"

"No, I guess you've let me hang around you a little too long. What's going to happen at Wannsee, Nicko?"

"There are a lot of variables so I can't be sure yet. But I admit I may need you at some point."

Nicko studied the planking on the deck as if important secrets lay hidden there. "I'm sorry, Kate. I may be putting you in harm's way with all this. If you say no, I'll understand."

"How could I say no? You've put yourself in this position only because you were trying to help *me*."

"It may have started out that way," said Nicko, "but things changed."

Nicko sat there brooding, showing real pain. Kate had never seen him so exposed. Even worse, he appeared diminished. And he knew it.

"You shame me," he said.

Chapter 34

IN THE EARLY MORNING QUIET, Paul Walters climbed the stairs leading to Kate's apartment. Reaching the third floor, he knocked on Kate's door and waited. When he was about to knock again, the door opened and Kate was there in a terry robe with a towel covering her still dripping hair.

"Sorry to get you out of the shower," Paulie said.

Her face flushed a deep pink, Kate stood studying him. "I'm glad to see you."

They were polite to the point of suffocation.

"Why don't you sit down?" Kate suggested.

Paulie settled into a large sectional couch.

"Would you like some coffee?"

"No, thank you."

"How about orange juice and a bun?"

He shook his head.

"Then all you want is to shoot me?"

"No," said Paulie.

As she slowly worked her hair dry with the towel, Kate's eyes never left him. "What then?"

"I'm not sure."

"You seemed sure enough the last time we talked."

Paulie didn't respond.

Kate sat down on the same couch, but well apart from Paulie. "I suppose you've heard the tapes and seen the pictures Klaus Logefeld made. Is that it?"

"Yes."

"And?"

"You were not lying. Everything you told me was true."

"Where are the tapes and pictures now?"

"Exactly where I found them."

"You didn't show them to the police?"

Paulie looked at her hair, damp and shiny against her face. "Why would I do that?"

"To punish me."

"If I wanted you punished, I wouldn't have left it to the police."

Sitting carefully apart, they remained unmoving in the silent room. A guilty relief expanded inside Paulie's chest. It pressed his heart.

"You once said—" Kate began.

"I know what I once said. I can be as foolish as anyone else. You may have squeezed the trigger, but Klaus Logefeld killed my parents. Even I can see that now."

"Then you're going after Klaus?"

"No. I can't. If I did, the police would receive copies of those tapes and pictures and I'd just end up hurting you."

"I was sure you would never forgive me."

"I tried that: it didn't work."

Paulie stared helplessly at her. "I want you too much. I've never wanted anything so much in my life."

"I was afraid of so many things," she said. "I was afraid of how you felt about Nicko. I was afraid I—"

"To hell with Nicko. All I care about is you."

"You called me a whore and made me feel like one. I thought of how I'd hurt you and I wanted to die. Forgive me, Paulie. I know everything I've done. What more can I say?"

Paul Walters looked fully at her, a beautiful tragic woman pushed down by the weight of events.

He felt her pressing close, felt all that sweet warmth and softness that was the absolute center of everything when it was with him, but that he was never able to recall when it was gone.

And somewhere in the middle, afloat in this almost mythic young woman with the hurt, knowing eyes, Paulie sensed hope begin in him again, sweet and hard to follow. He clung to that hope, flying out over the same darkness he had been lost in just hours before.

They lay there.

For the moment, Paulie was content just to hold Kate close, to feel her heartbeat. Then the itch returned and had to be scratched.

"Have you ever told Nicko about me?" he asked.

"No."

Paulie was silent.

"Your name was never mentioned," said Kate, "and I wasn't about to bring it up. What could I say? I've fallen in love with the son of the two people I've just killed?"

The sun had moved upward and splinters of orange light filtered in and brightened the room.

"A small piece of news," she said. "I have to go away for a while."

"Where?"

"Germany. Nicko was able to get me a press pass for the Wannsee Conference. I'll be doing a daily feature from the scene."

Paulie needed a moment to let it settle. "Exactly how much do you know about me?" he asked.

"Enough to make me adore you."

"Apart from that."

Kate picked up the change in his voice. "Is something wrong?"

"Not really. I'm just curious about how much you may have learned, guessed, or thought you've figured out about me."

"Suddenly?"

Paulie smiled to lighten the moment. "Not so suddenly. But since we're slowly being forced into new areas of honesty with each other, I'd like to be sure I haven't misled you into adoring someone I'm not."

Kate thought about it for several beats. "This wouldn't have anything to do with your father, would it?"

"It would."

"Of course." Kate sighed. "You're wondering whether I've guessed you've taken on some of your father's ties to the CIA."

"I had the feeling you weren't just another pretty face."

"You could never have found out about Klaus and my parents and me without a certain amount of help from Langley's database."

"I deny any such connection."

"Naturally. But what made you bring it up now?"

"I didn't want you walking into Wannsee and just seeing me."

Her eyes went wide. "You mean you're going to be there too?"

Paulie nodded.

"Why?"

"In case some crazy tries to take out our secretary of state."

Chapter 35

NICKO VORELLI WAS AT WORK in his home office that evening when the call came through on his private line.

"It's Bruno," said the voice in German.

"What's happening?" Nicko asked.

"I have it all together for you."

"Good," said Nicko. "Leave a car for me at Tempelhof. I should be there in about four hours. Give me exact directions to where the car will be and where I'll be driving to meet you."

When Nicko hung up, he called his pilot and told him to prepare to take off for Berlin in an hour.

That done, he took twenty thousand German marks from a safe and loaded the money into a bag. Then he told his housekeeper he would be gone overnight and drove himself to the Naples airport.

Nicko slept through most of the flight; he left the plane refreshed and excited by what lay ahead. *Better than fear.* Although he knew there had to be a bit of that mixed in with it as well.

He found the car Bruno had left for him exactly where it was supposed to be. The driver's door was unlocked and the keys were under a mat. Starting the car's engine, Nicko shifted into drive and headed for the airport exit.

He had the dome light on and his sheet of instructions open beside him. At times he had to stop because he could not read his own handwriting—he was always impatient, always in too much of a hurry to properly form the letters. The only thing he never rushed was his lovemaking. He was increasingly grateful to Kate for making even that much possible.

The thought drew a smile.

Moments later, he crested a hill and made the first left turn into a heavily wooded area. When he had gone about two kilometers, he made a second left onto a rough dirt trail with heavy growth closing in from both sides.

Moving slowly, Nicko was watching for another dirt trail that would split off to the right. A full complement of nerves seemed to come alive in his stomach and he could feel them wriggling like a nest of worms.

Then he reached the cutoff he was watching for and turned onto it. His lights picked up a gray sedan waiting about two hundred meters ahead. Nicko parked and got out.

He heard the soft, night sounds of the forest and watched Bruno come toward him, a bulky man in jeans carrying a roll of blueprints and an unlit, battery-powered lantern.

The two men nodded and shook hands.

"How far is Wannsee from here?" Nicko asked.

"About a fifteen-minute walk. It's all woods." Bruno considered Nicko's jacket and slacks. "You shouldn't have worn such good clothes."

Bruno led the way. Nicko Vorelli stayed close behind. A three-quarter moon threw a cool, pale blue light, so the lantern was unneeded.

"You're fully satisfied with what you have?" Nicko asked.

Bruno answered without turning or changing pace. "Absolutely."

"Other than yourself," said Nicko, "how many were involved?"

"Just two."

"Who are they and what do they do?"

"One is a great-grandson of Wannsee's original owner. He's the one who had the old blueprints with the unrecorded alterations. The other is a retired archivist from the Berlin Hall of Records. He told me about the blueprints and who had them."

"Who else knows they exist?"

"No one living."

"Both men said that?"

"Yes."

"There are no other copies around?"

"Not that they knew of," said Bruno. "The Hall of Records and everything in it was wiped out during the Allied bombing of Berlin. But the alterations we're talking about were never officially recorded anyway."

Nicko's foot hit a rock in the high grass, and he stumbled. "What reason did you give them for your interest in the plans?"

"Some nonsense about history, the period, the human condition. What's the difference? All they cared about was the money."

They walked for a while in silence. Then Bruno stopped so abruptly that Nicko almost bumped into him.

"This is it." All Nicko saw was some bushes.

Bruno pushed through into a small, grassy clearing and switched on his lantern. He kneeled, dug both hands into the ground, and pulled aside a one-meter-square section of sod and leaves resting on a metal base.

A short flight of steps was exposed; the two men descended into a concrete-lined tunnel. The concrete was moist and discolored but in good condition. The passageway itself was about six feet high and cool, with enough fresh air coming in from an unseen system of vents to make its sunless odors bearable.

"How far does this go?" said Nicko.

"About five hundred meters."

"All on Wannsee property?"

"The museum owns all the land. But only the last two hundred meters are fenced in and under security."

"How many times have you been in here?" asked Nicko.

"This is my fourth trip in as many nights. It wasn't this good when I started. Most of the vents had to be cleared. Then all the supplies and gear had to be brought in and set up."

The tunnel ended against a dark, metal door.

Bruno opened it, his lantern illuminating a large, concrete-lined room with half a dozen bunks, a table and chairs, and a lot of canned goods and communications gear arranged on racks and shelves.

"Looks like an old air-raid shelter," said Nicko. "Where does it go into the villa?"

"I'll show you."

Bruno went into an empty closet and pressed a wooden panel at the rear. The panel swung back and the two men walked through the opening.

Nicko saw that they were in the rear section of a cellar storeroom. The wooden panel was of perfectly matched tongue-and-groove construction: when Bruno returned it to the closed position, no sign of a break was visible.

"Where do I press to open it?" asked Nicko.

Bruno guided his hand to the place and applied pressure. The panel opened. Nicko did it twice alone, studying the way it worked.

"Now let me see where this storeroom leads."

It led into a basement utility area, then into the museum's library and reference room.

Not using the lantern, they silently climbed the stairs to the main floor, guided by moonlight slanting in through tall windows.

This was where it would all be happening.

Then they went back down to the hidden room behind its secret panel. In his head, Vorelli could all but hear a wind come whistling up from out of the earth.

The sensation quickly passed as Bruno laid out his blueprints and diagrams and reviewed everything in Wannsee as related to their present position.

Next came the electronic gear, with Bruno explaining how reception and transmission would work with each piece of the cellular system he had brought in. The Berliner had a particular way of breaking down and clarifying everything to the point where Nicko could almost feel the magic of understanding enter his bloodstream.

Chapter 36

AT 6:30 ON THE MORNING of September 13 Daniel Archer and Abu Mustafa were fully prepared and in position, with nothing more to do for about two hours except wait.

As estimated, the president's motorcade would be passing their chosen location at approximately 8:30. Making allowances for possible delays, another fifteen or twenty minutes could be added. Since both Archer and Mustafa were prone to worrying about time, they suffered from visions of the president somehow passing before they arrived.

"Better to wait than be too late," recited the Palestinian.

They sat behind a cluster of trees and brush in an open, rural area about ten kilometers from the airport. The road on which the motorcade would be passing lay less than fifty meters away. At the edge of the road and slightly off to the right stood a small, abandoned farm stand that Abu Mustafa had packed with explosives just before dawn. Using a remote detonator, the Palestinian had only to hit a single switch as President Dunster's limousine drove by.

That would take care of it.

A little more than twenty-four hours earlier, the two men had waited for, then carefully watched the presidential motorcade driving toward Brussels from the airport. A pair of motorcycles appeared first, followed by a police patrol car with flashing lights and a wailing siren. Then came a black limousine with President Dunster, the Belgian prime minister, and their respective wives seated inside. A few more cars and motorcycles were at the rear of the column. But Daniel Archer had stopped paying attention by then.

Holy Jesus, he had thought, *the women too*.

By 7:30 A.M. there was a fair amount of traffic on the road, and the sun began burning through the early haze. With the first flights of the day taking off from Brussels Airport, the roar of their engines grew louder as they passed overhead.

Archer shifted his body in the grass to keep from stiffening.

Mustafa looked at him. "Getting antsy?"

"I never enjoy the waiting."

"Who does? Try some push-ups."

"The hell with that. I'm a runner."

"Then run."

"I will." Daniel Archer glanced at his watch. "In about an hour."

Abu Mustafa gazed off at the fields behind them at a point where the grass ended in a grove of trees. This was where they had hidden the Saab, and there had been a brief discussion about whether the distance they would have to cover on foot might turn out to be too great.

"I'm afraid we're going to be doing a lot more crawling than running. Thank Allah for the high grass."

"You don't have to worry, Abu. From the amount of *plastique* you packed into the charge, there won't be a whole person left in that motorcade to come looking for us."

At 8:40 they were tense and starting to sweat as the sun rose and became hotter.

"I don't like this," said the Palestinian.

Archer was silent.

They stared at the road in the direction of Brussels, watching for flashing lights and listening for sirens and motorcycle engines. Without speaking, they knew each other's thoughts.

Twenty minutes later, little doubt remained that the operation was either in serious trouble or dead.

"So?" said Mustafa.

"I don't know what to tell you, Abu."

"This man of yours. You've used him before?"

"For years. This is the first time he's crapped out on me."

"I don't think it's him. He was right on target for yesterday's route in from the airport. I think there may have been a last-minute change going back, and no way he could let you know."

Archer said nothing. Somehow, he was unable to believe that.

"Is there a number where you can reach him?"

"Yeah. But it's not secure."

"Use my car phone and talk around it. I'll stay here and watch the road in case there was just a delay." Mustafa's eyes were two shining marbles in the sun. "If you hear a big bang, hang up."

Dripping sweat, Daniel Archer pushed through the high grass to where the Saab stood among the trees. He called the lieutenant's private number at police headquarters; the phone was picked up instantly.

"Lieutenant Rougier."

"What happened?" said Archer.

There was dead silence for a long moment, then a sigh. "I'm sorry as hell. You should have done it yesterday," said the lieutenant, "while I still had my balls. I had all last night to think and it ate me up."

Archer waited to feel anger, but it never came.

"I'll return what you gave me," said Charles Rougier.

"Keep it," said Archer, suddenly anxious to get out of this car, this grove, and this country. "As a small reminder."

"Of what?"

"How fucking lucky you are," said Archer as he broke the connection.

He drove the Saab back to Abu Mustafa, who had only to glance at his face. "He lost his nerve?"

Daniel Archer nodded.

"What did he say?"

"We should have done it yesterday."

Abu Mustafa laughed. "The man's right. But he should have *told* us yesterday."

Archer liked his being able to laugh.

"You did a good job," he said. "The front money is yours. Maybe we can finish it up some other time."

"If we're around, Mr. Lucas."

They defused the *plastique*, loaded it into the Saab's trunk, and drove back to the city.

Archer reached Ken Harris at 4:00 A.M. Washington time on his secure home number.

"It's me," he said. "Are you awake enough to listen?"

The deputy director cleared the sleep from his brain and throat. "Go ahead."

"It's scrubbed."

There was a short silence.

"Anything or anyone compromised?"

"No. Nothing like that. Someone just chickened out at the last minute and there was no chance for another go."

"Where are you calling from?" said Harris.

"Brussels Airport. I'll explain when I see you."

Feeling curiously lighter than he had in more than a week, Daniel Archer hung up.

Chapter 37

PRESIDENT DUNSTER'S MOTORCADE rolled out onto the tarmac of Brussels International Airport at 9:25 A.M. on September 13.

Fifteen minutes later, with the ceremonial pictures and sound bites out of the way, the president and his party were settled aboard *Air Force One* for what was assumed to be their return flight to Washington.

They had been in Brussels for not quite twenty-four hours. During this period, Dunster had made his promised appearance at the world trade conclave currently in progress, met briefly with the leaders of several other large industrial powers, attended a formal dinner and concert given in his honor, and managed to squeeze in a bit more than five consecutive hours of badly needed sleep.

At 9:47 with the engines of *Air Force One* still warming up, Tommy Cortlandt told Colonel McNeil, the pilot, that the president wanted to see him in his private quarters.

McNeil, a big man with carefully barbered hair and a suntan, half turned from the controls. "You mean *now?*"

Cortlandt nodded.

"It's almost takeoff time, sir."

"I'm sure the president knows that, Colonel."

James Dunster was alone and at his desk when they came in.

"I have a slight change for you, Mac," the president told his pilot. "We won't be going directly to Washington. We'll be making a stop in Germany first. At our NATO air base near Eberswalde."

The pilot stood looking at Dunster. He glanced at Cortlandt as if for corroboration. Then he looked at Dunster again.

"Is everything all right, Mr. President?"

"Everything is fine."

"I'll have to file a new flight plan."

"No, Colonel." It was Tommy Cortlandt who broke in. "No new flight plan. We'll simply take off for Washington as scheduled. Then when we're at cruising altitude and off local radar, you can change direction and head straight for Eberswalde."

"That's not proper procedure, sir."

"Don't worry about it, Mac," said the president. "It's only a matter of security. It will be better if no one knows we're coming in until the last possible minute."

Tommy Cortlandt watched the pilot's face as he struggled between reason and training and a direct order from his commander in chief.

"May I have these orders in writing, Mr. President?"

Dunster scribbled a few lines and handed them to McNeil.

"A few precautions, Colonel," said Cortlandt. "No mention of this to anyone other than your copilot and navigator. And I want complete radio silence until you're picked up by Eberswalde's radar."

"How do you want it handled at that point?"

"Just request permission for an emergency landing," said Cortlandt. "Then I'll get the base commander on the phone and take it from there."

The entire flight was projected at a bit less than an hour, and Tommy Cortlandt waited until they were halfway to Eberswalde before he called in the four Secret Service agents who made up the president's security contingent.

"We're making what should be about a four- to five-hour unscheduled stop in Germany," Dunster told them. "We'll be

landing at our NATO air base near Eberswalde and driving to
the Wannsee Conference Center outside Berlin. No one
knows I'm coming, and security at Wannsee is tight for the
meeting opening there today. Just be sure you don't say a
word about this to anyone on board."

The silence in the cabin was heavy.

"Excuse me, Mr. President." The voice was that of Senior Agent Richard Gordon. "What do you mean by 'no one
knows' you're coming?"

"Exactly that. The only ones who know are my wife, Director Cortlandt, and one of his agents, who has been checking security at Wannsee."

"And how will we be getting from the air base to
Wannsee, sir?"

The president looked at Cortlandt. "Tommy?"

"We'll be using a four-car motorcade," said Cortlandt.
"It's only about a half-hour run, and two of my own people
will be in each car for added security."

"Eight of your agents will be there?" asked Gordon.

Cortlandt nodded.

"And they all know where the president is going?"

"No. They'll just follow the lead car. And I'll be in that
one, giving step-by-step directions to the driver."

The senior agent frowned.

"What's bothering you, Dick?" Jimmy Dunster asked.

"This man who's been checking security at Wannsee?
How long has he known you'll be arriving there today, Mr.
President?"

Dunster again glanced at the CIA director for the answer.

"A few days," said Cortlandt.

"Who is he?" asked Gordon.

"One of my best."

"What's his name?"

"You know I can't tell you that."

"I don't know a damn thing, sir. Except maybe that I'm
the one ultimately responsible for the president's life, and

that this nameless man of yours has had a few days to set him up."

Cortlandt's eyes were chipped glass. "I'd trust this man with my life, Gordon."

"That's your right, Mr. Director. But it's the president's life, not yours, that you're trusting him with."

"You're way out of line, Dick," said Jimmy Dunster.

"My apologies, Mr. President. But with all due respect, do *you* know who this mystery man is?"

"No. But if I can't trust the judgment of our director of intelligence, then we're *all* in trouble."

Chapter 38

THERE WERE HALF A DOZEN CARS lined up ahead of Klaus Logefeld and his grandfather when they reached Wannsee's first checkpoint, and they were barely moving.

Klaus glanced at the old man beside him. The dark glasses and gauze wrappings had been removed for purposes of identification, so it all hung out. The real article.

They finally pulled up even with the security booth.

"Which delegation?" asked a sergeant of the guard in German.

"Italian," said Klaus.

The sergeant flipped some pages on a clipboard.

"Names, please?"

"I'm Professor Alfred Mainz. This is Major Helmut Schadt."

Hearing two non-Italian names, the sergeant bent, peered into the car, and caught his first glimpse of the old man. Then he searched among the names on his clipboard until he found Mainz and Schadt.

"Passports, please," he said.

The sergeant studied the passports and their attached pictures, but he did not look inside the car again.

They went through much the same routine at the entrance to the parking lot. Then they left the car and started toward the villa.

Klaus walked with deliberate slowness. His hand gripped his grandfather's arm, although he was not aware of it.

This is the time and I'm here.

Long, sleek, chauffeur-driven limousines were pulling up in front of the historic villa to discharge their celebrated passengers, and Klaus recognized almost every one of them. He saw the photographers and reporters, loosely held in check by the heavy security but still hopping about with their cameras and microphones in a kind of ritual dance.

Klaus took a long, deep breath, held it briefly, and slowly let it out.

"Ready, Grandfather?"

"You know it, boy."

His hand still gripping the old man's arm, Klaus steered him along a route that would bring them directly in front of the newspeople.

"Jesus, look at that," he heard someone say in English.

And in a moment he and his grandfather were surrounded by Minicam units and still cameras.

Almost immediately three security guards were there to rescue them.

"It's all right," said Klaus. "This is what we're here for."

Questions flew in an assortment of languages and the old man began answering.

"Who are you, sir?"

"Major Helmut Schadt."

"German delegation?"

"No. Italian."

"With all respect, Major, are those war wounds?"

"Yes, sir."

"How were you wounded?"

"By a mortar shell while fighting for the Wehrmacht during World War II."

"Where, Major?"

"Near Lago di Bosena, Italy."

"I remember now," said a gray-haired newsman. "Wasn't your face used on stamps and posters?"

"Yes, sir," said the old man, and there was a buzz as others picked it up.

"Why are you here at Wannsee?"

Major Schadt stared evenly into the lens of the nearest camera. "To give people a long, hard look at me."

"Do you believe they'll learn anything from what they see, Major?"

"Probably not."

"Then why are you doing it?"

"Because I can." The old man was silent for several seconds. "And because not to suddenly seems unthinkable."

There was actually a scattering of applause when he finished.

Something genuine, thought Klaus.

As they entered the front door of the villa, they again had to show their passports. Then they were walked through a metal detector and patted down for any weapons that might have been missed electronically.

A guard pinned numbered identification badges to their jackets and wrote their numbers on the backs of their hands with an indelible marker. Another guard escorted them into the main conference room and pointed out the seating arrangements for their delegation.

They were the only members of the Italian contingent to have arrived. Klaus saw their names attached to a couple of chairs in the backup row around the conference table, and for the first time knew their positions in relation to everyone else.

They were directly between the German and Japanese delegations, with the United States and Canada following Japan on their left, and France and England off to their right.

Klaus sat down in his chair, dimly aware of his grandfather settling in beside him.

Major Schadt stirred and Klaus felt the old soldier's hand cover his own.

"It's all right, boy. Everything will go perfectly."

Perfectly.

But what in Christ's name was perfectly in something like this?

Chapter 39

IF I COULD PAINT THAT FACE and get it right, I would have it all.

So thought Paulie Walters as he considered the old man sitting next to Klaus Logefeld in Wannsee's gradually filling conference room. Indoors, the old soldier might have been the quintessential specter at the feast. Outdoors, earlier, he had been pure street theater.

Paulie had witnessed the entire episode with the media. He had listened to the simple, quiet answers given to their questions. And he had been impressed by the applause elicited from the world-class press corps that had made up the major's audience.

Or was he being too cynical?

The terrible battle wounds were certainly real enough. And the mere act of prying open that one pale eye each morning, of getting out of bed to deal with another day, took more hard courage than most men could scrape together in a lifetime.

Still, it was Klaus Logefeld who had brought the old soldier. And all things considered, that had to mean *something*.

It meant enough for Paulie to seek out Wannsee's chief of security in his office.

"What can you tell me about a countryman of yours?" he asked. "His name is Schadt. He carried your own rank of major in the old Wehrmacht, and he's evidently here with Professor Alfred Mainz of the Italian delegation."

Major Dechen hit some buttons on a desktop computer

and sat studying the screen. "I thought I recognized the name. He's a once famous antiwar poster model, and he seems to have been a late addition. Dr. Nicholas Vorelli was his sponsor."

"That's all?"

Dechen punched some more buttons.

"He's apparently a much decorated World War II hero with a full disability pension." There was a pause as the major considered what was coming up on the screen. "And according to information supplied by Dr. Vorelli, the man is Professor Mainz's maternal grandfather."

Paulie was alarmed. Klaus and the old man were of the same blood. Meaning what? Paulie had no idea. Except that if he sniffed around long and hard enough, he was absolutely certain he would come up with a smell he didn't like.

"Why all the interest in this Major Schadt?" asked the security chief.

"I guess you haven't seen him yet."

"No."

"His face is like nothing I've ever run into. It's a living indictment of all the horrors of war. A silent scream."

"Is that why he's here?"

"I can't think of a better reason," said Paulie.

A telephone rang.

Major Dechen answered, spoke briefly, and came out from behind his desk.

"Chancellor Eisner's limousine is just approaching the first checkpoint," he said.

Chapter 40

KATE DINNESON HAD NO IDEA what strings Nicko had pulled to arrange it, but she did find herself sitting in what was obviously one of the best press seats in the house at Wannsee.

With only limited space available, the media was confined to three short rows of chairs at the west end of the conference hall, and Kate was in the very first of these. She also was directly in back of Nicko Vorelli's own chair. Which, in turn, was right alongside that of the Italian foreign minister, Roberto Langione.

Of course this was all for Nicko's own benefit, for when he might need her, Kate thought, and the implication hit her like the sight of a large rock against which she was about to smash.

And that was simply for starters.

Klaus Logefeld and his grandfather were sitting even closer to her, the old man's ramrod-straight back giving off its own aura of unknown threats, while occasional glimpses of his disfigurement made the whole thing even worse.

How do you manage to live with something like that? Kate slowly shook her head and looked around the chamber for Paul Walters.

At the moment, Paulie was nowhere in sight. But Kate had spotted him earlier, in passing, and for an instant their eyes had met.

Her sustenance.

It was true. She was stirred, found a kind of support in merely knowing he was there. As if he somehow would be

able to help her should she be in the need of help, which in
itself disturbed her, made her feel less competent than she
knew herself to be.

A ridiculously outdated attitude. Romantic love, heart-
break, and dependency had traditionally been for women.

Not anymore, she thought, and was amused by her own
absurdity.

About her, the big conference hall buzzed with sound. It
was just about full. The German chancellor had not yet entered to make his opening remarks as host. Nicko, she noted,
was deep in conversation with the Italian foreign minister,
yet his eyes were all over, missing nothing.

So what was he going to do here? What was he going to
ask *her* to do? Sometime during the next few hours or days,
Nicko Vorelli was going to take some form of action that
would affect both their lives, and she had no idea what that
action might be. Still, she had agreed to be part of it.

Which meant what? That she was a fool?

At this moment it seemed so.

Then she saw Nicko leave the Italian foreign minister
and start toward her.

Nicko took Kate to a small area of clear space and said
softly, "I'm an idiot. Forgive me."

"For what?"

"For even thinking of getting you into this."

Kate stared at him.

"Forget everything I've told you," he said. "You're not involved."

"Then whatever it was, is off?"

"For you, it is."

"But not for you?"

He shrugged and half smiled. "I'll see."

"What does that mean?"

"That I care about you so much, it's utterly ridiculous,"
he said, and went back to the foreign minister.

Chapter 41

LESS THAN FIVE METERS in front of where Kate sat with other members of the press, Klaus Logefeld rose from his chair in the second row of delegates rimming the long conference table and touched his grandfather's shoulder.

"I'm going to the men's room before things get started," he said.

Major Schadt looked up at him and nodded.

Klaus circled the conference hall, crossed the main lobby, and entered the lavatory.

Two men stood at the urinals, staring blankly at the wall. A third man stood alone beside a window, watching Klaus as he walked in. Klaus recognized one of the men at the urinals as Arthur Green, the American secretary of state, and the man beside the window as one of his security people.

Four toilet stalls lined the wall opposite the urinals. Only one appeared occupied, but it was the one Klaus had to get into.

He stood there for a moment, feeling the flat gaze of the security man along with his own tension. Then he removed his jacket, hung it on a hook, and began rinsing his hands, face, and eyes in one of the washstands.

Klaus took it slowly, deliberately, working to kill time until the toilet stall became available.

When he at last reached for a towel, he looked up to find the American secretary of state smiling at him.

"Professor Mainz?"

Klaus nodded.

"I thought I recognized you from your book-jacket photo. I'm Arthur Green."

He spoke in English, extending his hand, and Klaus Logefeld shook it.

"I'm flattered that you've actually read my work, Mr. Secretary. Unless you just looked at my picture."

The secretary laughed. "Oh, I've read you, all right. I was impressed enough by your ideas to pass some of them off as my own."

"As long as you quoted me correctly."

"I wouldn't dare change a word, Professor."

Followed by his security man, Secretary of State Green left the room.

Moments later, Klaus entered the stall he had been waiting for, and locked it behind him.

Climbing onto the toilet, he used a small nail file to unscrew the ventilator grill from the ceiling. Then he removed his two automatics and remote detonator from the studs to which they had been taped five days earlier, and pocketed them.

When he had replaced the ventilator grill and left the toilet stall, the rest room was empty.

Klaus examined himself in the long mirror above the line of washstands.

He saw hair, eyes, face, chest. This strange creature. Yet human.

And inside, something else.

Hope.

The mirror showed his grandfather enter the room behind him.

Klaus turned, handed the old man one of his two automatics, and left the washroom without either of them saying a word.

Chapter 42

TOMMY CORTLANDT MADE HIS FIRST VOICE CONTACT with Paulie Walters by mobile phone at 12:36 P.M. The CIA director was with the president and two security men in the lead sedan of their four-car motorcade. Paulie was alone on the lawn just outside Wannsee's rear entrance.

"What's doing?" said Cortlandt.

"Eisner is well into his opening remarks. I guess he has about another ten to fifteen minutes left."

"I know. We've been listening on the radio. Any potential trouble spots?"

"None that I can see," said Paulie. "How far away are you?"

"About twenty minutes to the first checkpoint. I'd like to time it so we get there not too long after Eisner finishes up. Does the rear entrance still look best for us?"

"Perfect."

"Hold on a minute," said the CIA director.

He covered the receiver and spoke to Dunster. "Anything you want to say?"

The president sat in silence for a moment. He had spoken little during the drive from the Eberswalde air base and his eyes were distant. "Let me talk to your man," he said.

"The boss wants to talk to you," he told Paulie. "But no names or titles, OK?"

"Understood."

The CIA director handed the phone to the president.

"Are you hearing me?" said Dunster.

"Yes, sir."

"I'm just curious about the general mood. Is there any real sense of excitement, or is it all business as usual?"

"At this point I'd have to say business as usual, sir. But that might be a bit unfair."

"Why?"

"Because the chancellor is still making his opening remarks."

"And how would you judge what Eisner is saying?"

"More of the customary platitudes about human rights, of course. German edition."

"Meaning?"

"He's pouring ashes over his head about the Holocaust and the need to keep such things from happening again."

The president gazed out the window at the verdant landscape dotted with neat German homes.

"And that doesn't impress you?" he said.

"No, sir."

"Why not?"

"Because in one form or another these things *are* happening again. A few more platitudes aren't going to stop them now."

Jimmy Dunster looked less than happy.

"Thank you," he said, and gave the telephone back to Tommy Cortlandt.

The CIA director spoke again to Paul Walters. Then he broke the connection.

"Is something bothering you, Mr. President?"

It took Jimmy Dunster a long moment to answer. "To be honest," he finally said, "yes."

"What is it?"

"Just about everything."

At Wannsee, Paulie found Major Dechen at a far edge of the conference room and eased him into a nearby corridor.

"I'm going to need you to get me to your chancellor," he said. "The minute he finishes speaking. It's important."

"How important?"

"President Dunster wants to talk to him."

The major stared at Paulie. "Why do I suddenly have the feeling this is the real reason you're here?"

"Because you're smart."

"All right," said Dechen. "You can meet us in my office."

The security chief slipped away to better his position. Paulie stayed where he was to listen to Eisner.

Moments later the German chancellor completed his official remarks, and Paulie quickly worked his way out of the conference hall, along the central corridor, and into the security office.

Major Dechen had Eisner there almost at once. A heavy, ruddy-complexioned man, the chancellor stood mopping his face with a damp handkerchief as he shook Paulie's hand.

"Now what's all this about your president wanting to speak to me?" he said in lightly accented English.

"Exactly that, Mr. Chancellor."

Paulie punched some numbers into his handset and heard Tommy Cortlandt answer.

"I have your man here," Paulie said.

"Good," said the CIA director. "Give him your phone and the boss will take it from there."

In the lead car of the small motorcade, the CIA director nodded to the president, who had been listening to the brief exchange on his own phone.

"Are you there, Herman?" said Dunster.

"Hello, Jimmy. What's happening? Was my speech that bad?"

"No worse than usual. But this has more to do with *my* needs than with *your* speech." The president took a moment to moisten his lips. "The fact is, I need a small favor."

"Not too small, I hope. I'd rather have you owe me big."

"Listen to me, Herman. Right now I'm in a car just a few miles from Wannsee. And what I need is for you to meet me in fifteen minutes at your first checkpoint, and escort me straight through to the conference center."

There was complete silence at the other end and Jimmy Dunster spoke into it.

"Since this is not a secure call, Herman, I'd appreciate your holding all questions until we're together. Will that be all right?"

The chancellor's laugh, when it came, was flat. "I can't see how I'm going to know that for at least fifteen minutes."

Chapter 43

PRESIDENT JIMMY DUNSTER'S ENTRY into Wannsee's main conference chamber went all but unnoticed. The president simply appeared as part of a small group that included his wife and Chancellor Eisner, and was quietly seated in a far corner of the room.

Only when Klaus Logefeld became aware of an undercurrent of whispering along with a sudden swiveling of heads did he realize exactly who was there. Even then his initial reaction was little more than one of mild surprise.

Seconds later, the full force of it went off inside him like a small bomb.

He nudged his grandfather.

The old man nodded. "I saw."

The president's wife appeared younger and more attractive in person than in any pictures he had ever seen of her. It was just the reverse for the president. In the flesh, Jimmy Dunster looked a lot older and frailer than on film.

Klaus glanced at his grandfather and found his good eye staring back at him.

The old man shrugged.

A short while later, the German foreign secretary chairing the session picked up a signal from Chancellor Eisner and abruptly ended the parliamentary discussion.

The room buzzed with expectation. Then it went silent.

"Ladies and gentlemen," said the chairman, speaking German, "I have the singular privilege and pleasure of presenting the president of the United States, Mr. James Dunster, one of the prime initiators of this first Wannsee Conference on Human Rights."

The applause was instant, enthusiastic, and grew into a standing ovation.

Jimmy Dunster rose slowly from his seat. He looked at his wife, who was standing and applauding along with everyone else in the huge chamber. He saw that her eyes were streaming, and he felt his own eyes mist over.

Thou moveth me.

Jimmy Dunster walked toward the podium and lectern that had been set up for the German chancellor's opening remarks.

When he reached the podium he just stood there, letting the sound of applause pour over and into him.

He spread his carefully prepared speech on the lectern, but he suddenly had no interest in it. With his eyes blurring again, he doubted whether he could see well enough to read it anyway. He knew the cameras were picking up his tears and carrying them to uncounted viewers everywhere, and he was ashamed of the satisfaction he felt at such knowledge.

What's wrong with me? Why should I have such needs?

The world swam and his knees shook under him. Every breath he took felt like a blade making a cut, and he went through his recurrent nightmare of suffering a public angina attack. Then it passed and the room slowly became quiet, until only the soft whirring of the cameras and camcorders was left.

No platitudes, he told himself. *If that's all you've got, go home right now.*

He began slowly, softly building the force to cry out against the continuing slaughter of millions simply because of their race, religion, or nationality.

He invoked images of the mutilated and the dead in all their frightful numbers, showed their bones lying in unmarked graves, and the black holes where their eyes had been.

Gazing out over his audience, he had the sense he was actually seeing one of the corpses sitting right there in the room: the mutilated face and body of a white-haired old man stared back at him.

God save me, he's really out there.

The old man was backlit by a high, arched Palladian-style window, his mane of white hair luminous in a stream of sunlight.

Jimmy Dunster looked deep into the old man's eye, noting the grievous events recorded there.

"Sir?" he said. "Am I right in assuming you're a war veteran?"

The words hung in silence.

"Yes, Mr. President," the old man replied in English.

They might have been alone together. The media, taken totally by surprise, were busy shifting their attention and cameras from one man to the other.

"Would you do me the honor, sir," said Jimmy Dunster, "of joining me here on the podium?"

The old man sat unmoving, his head turned just enough to let him focus on the president. He seemed to be weighing the situation.

"The honor would be mine, Mr. President."

Major Schadt spoke his single line grandly, with a kind of old-fashioned courtliness.

He took a long and apparently difficult time getting out of his chair. With Klaus helping to support him, the two men deliberately made their way across the floor toward where the president stood waiting.

Every camera in the conference room was focused on them now, and Dunster could hear the old man's labored breathing.

Sweat quivered on Jimmy Dunster's forehead.

Here I am, manipulating and using him.

The two men stepped onto the podium and the president of the United States had more critical things to worry about.

It all happened so quickly that Jimmy Dunster did not have time to be afraid. One moment he was standing in the glare of media floodlights, facing a bunch of cameras and a room full of people. The next moment he had a 9-millimeter automatic pressed so tightly against his throat that it lifted his chin, while a second piece was jammed at his right temple. Klaus held one weapon. His grandfather held the other.

"Nobody move or draw a gun or the president is dead."

Klaus Logefeld's voice was sharp and hard. The words were in English.

"We intend President Dunster no harm," he said. "But even if we both die, he dies with us. So I beg all security, please, don't do anything foolish."

No one moved.

Poor Maggie, Jimmy Dunster thought, and silently prayed that whatever happened, she wasn't going to have to see his head blown apart.

"Chancellor Eisner," said Klaus Logefeld. "I want to hear you give the orders that will keep President Dunster alive."

"Who are you two and what do you want?" asked the German chancellor.

"I'm Professor Alfred Mainz of Rome University. And this is my grandfather, Major Helmut Schadt, formerly of the Wehrmacht. As for what we want, that comes later. For now, just do as I say. These first few minutes are on a hair trigger. I don't want any idiot would-be heroes spattering blood."

"Major Dechen?" said Eisner.

"Yes, Mr. Chancellor."

"Talk to your people."

Klaus saw the security chief's face. He saw the faces of the armed guards scattered about the room, and the faces of others whom he knew to be carrying weapons. If any one of them decided to make a move, it could all go to pieces right here. The urge was so strong they were shaking with it.

"You all heard Chancellor Eisner," said the major in German. "Nobody makes a move without orders from me."

Jimmy Dunster felt the nervous pressure of the automatics ease slightly and he was able to see his wife. Maggie sat white-faced, one hand pressed to her mouth.

"Very good, Major," said Klaus. "Now let's just take it one small step at a time. How many men do you have monitoring your surveillance room?"

"Two."

"And they're seeing and hearing everything going on in here?"

"Yes."

"What are they carrying?"

"Semiautomatic pistols."

"What we want now, Major, is for you to order your two men in the surveillance room to leave their weapons on the floor and join us out here."

Dechen glanced up at the lens of a closed-circuit television camera set in the ceiling. "Did you men hear that?"

"Yes, sir." The answer came in an uneven duet from a hidden speaker.

"Then do it," said the security chief.

Moments later the two guards entered the conference room and joined Major Dechen where he stood.

"How many men do you have stationed in the entrance lobby and main corridor?" Klaus asked Dechen.

"Three."

"With sidearms?"

"Yes."

"Please go out and bring them in here without their weapons."

Dechen left the room and returned almost immediately with the three disarmed guards.

"Here's what happens next," said Klaus. "We're going to very gently walk President Dunster out of here and into the surveillance room. Then with the door closed behind us, and everyone more relaxed, we're going to explain what this is all about."

There was a slight stirring in the room but no one spoke. Then Maggie Dunster rose. "Please, Professor," she said.

Heads and cameras turned.

"Oh, Christ," Dunster whispered.

Klaus looked at her. "What is it, Mrs. Dunster?"

"You have to take me with my husband."

"I'm afraid that's impossible, madam."

"Professor Mainz, this is very important. And I'm determined. Take my word for it. You wouldn't want me to make a bad scene over this, would you?"

Klaus's eyes were flat. "You would do that?"

"As God is my witness."

"And risk your husband's life?"

"My feeling is that his life would be at much greater risk if I weren't with him."

Dunster's neck was stretched so taut it twitched. He tried to speak but couldn't.

Klaus Logefeld stood very still, understanding that this bizarre little scene had to end at once or threaten everything.

"All right," he said. "When we get started, just walk slowly in front of us."

They finally moved, the four of them bunched together, with Maggie Dunster in the lead, Klaus and the president following close behind, and the old man as rear guard.

The two automatics were still pressed to Jimmy Dunster's neck and temple, but he was hardly aware of them. He was most conscious at that moment of the particular way his wife held her head, keeping it sightly tilted to one side. Like a lily on a stalk, he thought. The strength of her love warmed his heart.

Walking, he tried to keep his breathing easy, quiet.

He took as much air into his lungs as they would hold and slowly released it as the four left the conference hall, crossed the marble-floored lobby and corridor, and entered the surveillance room immediately beyond.

Then all he heard was the small, final sounds of the old man closing and locking the door behind them.

Chapter 44

PAULIE WALTERS STOOD BETWEEN TWO WINDOWS in the main conference room, sweating beneath his Kevlar body armor. He had taken no bullets intended for the president. He had simply watched Jimmy Dunster and his wife being walked out of the room at gunpoint. As had everyone else present. To have attempted anything more would have been disastrous. This way, the president and the First Lady were at least alive.

But I should have known.

How? By a signal from God?

I knew Klaus Logefeld. I should have acted on that alone.

And done what? Shot him in advance?

Why not?

You know why not.

Of course, he thought tiredly. *Kate.*

Such were Paulie's reflections, with the silence so total about him that he could all but hear his own interior dialogue.

Then a door was opened and closed a short distance down the corridor.

They were there.

A moment later, Major Dechen broke the silence.

"Everyone please stay as you are," he said. "When they start talking, I'll handle it. There's to be no random calling out of questions or comments. That's an order. Anyone who disobeys it will be ejected."

A few throats were cleared and someone reacted with a dry, hacking cough. That was all.

Paulie rode the swells of his own dread and looked around. The media representatives fussed with their cameras and tape recorders. Uniformed and plainclothes security avoided checking their weapons. Chancellor Eisner, ranking diplomats, and delegates sat sober-faced and brooding. The more devout among them moved their lips in silent prayer. Others crossed themselves.

The silence was broken as Klaus Logefeld's voice came through the public address system.

"This is Professor Alfred Mainz speaking," he said in English. "Am I being picked up out there, Major Dechen?"

"We hear you, Professor. Now we would like to hear exactly what you and your grandfather want."

"We want only what everyone else here allegedly wants. An immediate end to the killing in central and western Africa and a human rights treaty with enough muscle to make it work."

"And you and your grandfather will determine the agreement's acceptability?"

"Now you're with us, Major."

"And your deadline for signing?"

"Exactly seventy-two hours from midnight tonight."

"That's very little time," said Major Dechen.

"Not if people are serious about getting it done."

"And if your deadline is not met?"

Klaus worked the silence until it ran out of air.

"Then President Dunster will be shot."

A sigh passed through the room.

"And the president's wife?" said Major Dechen.

"We're not holding Mrs. Dunster. She's with us only because she insisted. She's free to go right this minute."

"Let's suppose you do get your treaty within three days," Dechen said. "What's to keep it from being scrapped as soon as President Dunster is out of your hands?"

"We've already taken certain steps as a safeguard. But we'll discuss all that later."

There was another long pause.

"Please understand, Major," said Klaus. "My grandfather and I take no joy in being branded villains. We're asking nothing for ourselves. We'll either be dead, in prison, or hunted fugitives when these next three days are over. All we're asking is a long overdue end to the hate-driven killing that's been turning so many of us into fratricidal butchers."

"But isn't that just what every delegate in this room is asking?" said Major Dechen. "You said it yourself, Professor. So why not give them the chance to do it?"

"We are, sir. We're giving them seventy-two hours." Klaus breathed deeply. "Forgive my cynicism, Major. But we've all seen these pathetic conferences before. They accuse, argue, make endless speeches—and do absolutely nothing. So my grandfather and I are betting that a couple of guns at the head of the most important leader in the world today will do more. In fact, sir, we're betting the president's and our own lives on it."

Chapter 45

MAJOR DECHEN CLOSED THE DOOR and locked it behind the four men he had summoned to his office.

It was 2:45 P.M. and Professor Mainz had just declared a break for what he described as "quiet thought and regrouping." With Dechen were Chancellor Eisner, Secretary of State Green, CIA Director Cortlandt, and Paul Walters, known to everyone there but Cortlandt as John Hendricks.

"Vice President Fleming is on the line from the White House," said the chief of security. "He's been trying to get through since the news broke. I'm making it an open conference call."

"Can Mainz cover this office from the surveillance room?" said Cortlandt.

"No. We're secure here."

The chancellor and the secretary of state sat down. The others chose to stay on their feet.

Dechen hit some buttons on his desk phone. "This is Major Dechen at Wannsee," he told someone at the other end. "We're ready to take the vice president's call."

A moment later the telephone audio box carried Vice President Jayson Fleming's voice. "Who do you have there with you, Major?"

Dechen told him.

"Who's John Hendricks?" Fleming asked.

"He's one of my people, Jay," said Cortlandt.

"Hello, Tommy." The vice president cleared a slight hoarseness from his throat. "I can't believe this whole thing. What the devil was the president doing at Wannsee in the first place? And why didn't I or anyone else here even know about it?"

"Let's save all that," said the CIA director. "Right now let's just worry about getting Jimmy out in one piece. I assume you've already taken over for him."

"Officially, eighteen minutes ago. Bud and Charlie are still right here with me in the Oval Office."

Bud and Charlie were Bradford Gaynor and Charles Rifkin, the president's national security adviser and White House chief of staff, respectively.

"What can you tell us," said the pro tempore president of the United States, "that we haven't been getting by satellite?"

"Not a thing. But we'll be going back for further information in about twenty minutes."

"Is there anything we can do from here?" asked Fleming.

"Not right now," said the CIA director. "Unless there's something Chancellor Eisner or Major Dechen want. They're the ones in charge at this end anyway."

A sharp line of static crackled through the audio box.

"What I can't quite get through my head, Major Dechen," said Fleming, "is how you and your people could have allowed two men to walk into that building carrying loaded pistols."

Dechen flushed. "Every precaution was taken, sir. The most rigid body checks were made. I absolutely don't understand how those weapons could have gotten through."

Paulie Walters felt compelled to break in.

"I don't think they did get through your body searches," he said. "I think those guns were planted inside the building sometime before today."

Everyone looked at Paulie.

"Who said that?" asked the vice president.

"I did, sir. John Hendricks."

"You mean you think the guns were planted in anticipation of President Dunster's visit?" said Fleming.

"No, sir. Mainz and his grandfather couldn't have known about that. I think they were planning to take *other* hostages. Then they saw President Dunster walk in and decided to take advantage of the windfall."

"Where would they have been able to pick up the guns without being seen?" the major asked. "Our cameras cover almost every square foot of the building."

"Do you have cameras in the men's room off the main lobby?" asked Secretary of State Green.

"Yes. Even there."

"What about in the toilet stalls?" inquired the secretary.

Dechen slowly shook his head. "No."

"I don't know if it means a thing," said Green. "But I did see Professor Mainz in the men's room just before the meeting started. When I left, he was still there. And he was alone."

Paulie was halfway to the door before Arthur Green stopped talking.

When Paulie returned moments later, no one in the security office seemed to have moved.

"You hit it, Mr. Secretary," he said. "I found this masking tape under the ceiling ventilator grill of one of the toilet stalls. That's where the guns were cached."

"Congratulations," said the vice president dryly. "But I want to know what we're going to do *now*."

"Quite frankly, Mr. Vice President," said Chancellor Eisner, "until we know a lot more than we do at this moment, I can't really see us doing very much of anything. Not if you want your president alive."

Chapter 46

THE BREAK WAS OVER at three-thirty, and delegates, press, and frustrated security were reconvening in the conference room.

From her place in the media section, Kate Dinneson watched everyone settling in. A lesson was being taught, she thought. If you were smart and paid close enough attention, you might even be able to learn something.

Like what?

Like how to make the mere threat of violence work for you. Look around.

Kate looked. Suddenly the entire place seemed to be one big free-fire zone. And without a single gun in sight.

Then her eyes fixed on Paulie, staring at her from across the room, and she looked at nothing else.

What must he be thinking and feeling? Had he not been so concerned about Klaus's threat to *her*, he would have put Klaus away days ago and no part of this catastrophe would have happened. *Dear God, I've become a one-woman plague on his house.*

Thus absorbed, she was unaware of the room quieting until she heard Klaus Logefeld's voice resuming its earlier dialogue with Wannsee's chief of security.

"To begin with, Major, an important warning. We know everything you and your people can go for in the way of heroics, and none of them will get you the president alive. That includes every kind of smoke, gas, and explosive device available. You'll just end up with bodies. *His* among them."

Major Dechen was silent.

"Next, a few housekeeping details," said Klaus. "Our sanitary facilities are fine, but we need food, drink, toiletries, things like that. We'll be slipping a list under the door."

How banal, Kate thought dimly. *While the earth quakes.*

"As for the conference itself," Klaus continued, "work sessions will run four hours on and four off, around the clock. Delegates may come and go as they choose. Let everyone just remember that the seventy-two-hour countdown for reaching an acceptable agreement will start at midnight tonight."

The room was quiet as the words settled.

"You haven't told us yet, Professor," Major Dechen said. "Exactly what will make the agreement acceptable?"

"You'll soon be getting a detailed draft of what we want. But first, my grandfather has something to say."

There were the small, scratchy sounds of a microphone being adjusted.

"This is Helmut Schadt," said the old man. "Earlier, we were asked how we would keep any agreement from being broken once President Dunster was safely out of our hands. I'm going to answer that now.

"In each of the seven countries represented here, a major high-rise has been mined with enough explosives to cause devastating tragedy. If any agreement reached here is broken, one of these buildings will be blown without advance warning. Other buildings will follow unless the agreement is reinstated."

The old man coughed dryly.

"My grandson and I abhor wanton killing," he said. "But if we ourselves are forced to kill in order to help end such killing, we'll do it. So please. Let no mistake be made about that."

The major's voice cut into a sudden murmur in the air.

"One more thing. If those in the conference room will please go to the north windows and look out, we'd like to show you exactly how serious we are about all this."

Feeling herself being played like an instrument, Kate rose and moved toward the windows along with everyone else. She saw a cluster of outbuildings, one far bigger than the rest, but all finished in the same sparkling white facing as the villa itself.

Suddenly, with a great crackling roar, the largest of the outbuildings burst into the air in a great cloud of smoke.

The villa's windows blew and pieces of glass rained in the conference room.

Kate found herself on the floor.

Slowly, tiredly, she sat up and picked tiny fragments of glass from her hair and clothing.

All this, she thought.

As if anyone had doubted their seriousness.

Chapter 47

THERE WERE NO WINDOWS in the surveillance room, but those inside it watched and heard the explosion on the closed-circuit monitors and felt its vibrations shudder through them.

They watched in silence. Maggie Dunster involuntarily cried out at the initial shock.

On one of the monitors, Jimmy Dunster saw billowing smoke, blackened ruins, utter devastation. Where moments before there had been a large, useful building, now there was nothing. Dunster did not know if anyone had been inside the building. Even without injury or loss of life, the act struck him as a baneful waste.

On another monitor, the president was able to look into the conference room. He saw people picking themselves up from the floor and helping those still too dazed to move. There were a few cuts from shattered window glass, but no one appeared to be seriously hurt.

The real damage, thought Dunster, being inside their heads, did not show.

Calmer now, he was beginning to appreciate the full implications of Mainz's act. *Let them know fear. If you frighten them enough at the start, they'll give you less trouble later on.*

The thought made him feel better. It had not been just a depraved, reasonless burst of destruction. At least there was a semblance of purpose behind it.

Small consolation.

Dunster reached for his wife's hand and felt it cool, moist, and minutely trembling against his own. Sitting side by side, this was their only means of touching. They were each manacled to their chairs by one hand. They were not uncomfortable and their captors had apologized for the need, but it was still the ultimate indignity.

Jimmy Dunster faced the very real possibility that in seventy-two hours or less, they could both be dead. Maggie, he saw, knew it too. So of course she smiled.

"Do you have any idea how much I love you?" he said, his words so quiet they were almost lost.

Maggie nodded.

"Then out of gratitude alone will you please do me a big favor?"

"No," she said.

"But you don't even know what I want."

"Yes I do. And the answer is still no. I'm not walking out of here until you're with me."

"That's so crazy, Maggie. It doesn't help anyone."

"You're wrong, love. It helps *me*."

They looked off to where their two jailers sat facing the banks of monitor screens, studying everything going on both inside and outside the building. Sound arrived from half a dozen different locations, and the room was filled with sirens, cries, angry and frightened voices. Fires were burning in the rubble of the blasted building and the smoke spread like a gray veil over fields and woods.

"Just out of curiosity," said the president, "how did you find out we were going to be here?"

"We didn't," said Klaus Logefeld. "We were just as surprised as everyone else when you walked in."

It was barely half an hour since the bombing, but things had quieted on the monitors. Hoses were wetting down what remained of the fires, the conference hall was being cleared of broken glass and returned to a semblance of order, and those in the surveillance room were taking advantage of their first real chance to talk.

"But you obviously had everything planned and set up well in advance," said Jimmy Dunster.

"Yes, sir. But not for you."

"Then for whom?"

"We couldn't really be firm on that. It hung on too many variables. But if all went well, it probably would have been Chancellor Eisner or your own Secretary Green."

Klaus Logefeld laughed. "Then God decided to gift us with you, Mr. President. And we knew there was no way we were ever going to do any better than that."

"How can you laugh?" Maggie broke in. "How can you think something like this is funny?"

Klaus looked evenly at her. "Do you really believe I think this is funny, Mrs. Dunster?"

Maggie sat very still. Then she slowly shook her head. "No. It's just that I don't understand how someone like you could have put himself in this position to begin with."

"Someone like *me*?"

"A professor. An intelligent, educated man."

"You mean only *un*intelligent, *un*educated men should take action against reasonless hate and killing?"

"It's what could have driven you to this *kind* of action that I don't understand, Professor."

"It's called desperation, Mrs. Dunster. And I'd be willing to swear that of all people, your husband understands it."

Chapter 48

"AS WE UNDERSTAND IT, Dr. Vorelli," said Major Dechen, "Professor Mainz and his grandfather were appointed to the Italian delegation at your request. Is that correct?"

"Yes."

It was 4:35 P.M. and Nicko Vorelli had been wondering how long it would take them to get to this.

He looked at the two men who were in the security office along with Major Dechen and himself. One of them was Director Cortlandt of the United States Central Intelligence Agency. The other, younger man, apparently an agent of Cortlandt's, had been introduced as John Hendricks. But Nicko had the feeling he had seen or met him someplace before. Possibly under a different name.

"Please tell us this," he heard Cortlandt say. "Of all the people you might have recommended for your delegation, what made you approach these two?"

"My infallible good judgment," said Nicko.

No one smiled.

"Actually," Nicko continued, "Professor Mainz approached *me*. The man could sell anyone anything. He projects the ultimate in passion and intelligence. That he's also proven to be a dangerous fanatic came as a big shock."

The man who called himself Hendricks stared at him. His antagonism was so open and intense that Nicko almost felt it was personal.

So where have I seen him before?

"I'm making no excuses," he said. "This has to be the most costly mistake of my life."

No one spoke. For several moments Nicko sat patiently in his chair, studying Paulie's face.

"How well do you know these two men?" asked Tommy Cortlandt.

"Obviously not well enough."

"But still a lot better than the rest of us," said the CIA director. "So let's talk a little. What about those seven buildings they claim they've set to blow? Do you think it's a bluff?"

"No. They're capable of it."

"Do you believe they'll release the president if they get what they want?"

"Absolutely. Why wouldn't they? They may be zealots, but they're not crazy."

"Do you have any idea what they'll be asking for?" said Major Dechen.

"Yes. And unless Professor Mainz was lying when he told me some of his ideas, I'd be happy to vote for every point he mentioned."

Nicko Vorelli half turned, met John Hendricks's curiously personalized rancor straight on, and suddenly remembered where he had seen him.

It had been in Peggy Walters's Sorrento art gallery. Although Nicko had never actually been introduced to the young man, someone had pointed him out as Peggy Walters's son, as well as an outstanding artist in his own right.

It was an odd coincidence, thought Vorelli, but still did nothing to explain the depth of the man's malice.

Until it came to him. *Kate had shot both his parents.*

Which meant what?

Another odd coincidence?

Nicko Vorelli did not believe so.

Chapter 49

AT 5:15 PAUL WALTERS WAS BACK in the conference hall awaiting a previously announced appearance by Professor Mainz.

Thunder rolled. A storm had come in and a driving rain rattled against the plastic sheeting that hung where the north windows had been.

Paulie breathed deeply, feeling the air heavy in his chest. He heard the rain behind him and let his glance drift back and forth between Kate Dinneson and Nicko Vorelli.

Looking for what?

Hot images of them fucking on Nicko's couch?

Idiot, he thought, and was disgusted with himself all over again for his stupidly abrasive behavior in Major Dechen's office.

Paulie could not help but be impressed by the grace and control of the man in dealing with his own far from happy plight. In an all too real sense, Nicko was as much a victim of Klaus Logefeld's nefarious plotting as Kate herself. Maybe more so, inasmuch as his personal sponsorship of Logefeld and his grandfather had the potential for making him an accessory to every criminal act they might commit. If his true reason for bringing them to Wannsee ever came out, it could well destroy him.

Klaus Logefeld appeared at exactly 5:20 P.M.

Paulie watched him walk across the conference hall with

Major Dechen, the two of them side by side. Then Logefeld approached the microphones alone, as strobe lights flashed and camcorders whirred.

"I hope we're finished with the ugly part," he said. "I hope the guns, the bombing, the melodrama are all behind us now. I hope now we can just get down to the business of taking some of the hatred and pain out of the world."

Klaus's eyes glittered in the lights.

"As promised," he continued, "we've given Major Dechen a full transcript of our treaty terms for President Dunster's release. Your photocopies are being made at this moment. When you read the terms, you'll find a lot to study and talk over. But these are mostly details and can be worked out. So all I'm going to mention right now are the three core commandments. If we can get agreement on these, there should be few problems with the rest."

Commandments, thought Paulie.

The sweet sound of reason delivered from Mount Sinai.

"All right," said Klaus. "Then what absolutely must be included are an autonomous executive committee, a strong, rapid-reaction strike force to carry out their decisions, and a multibillion-dollar revolving fund to make the whole thing viable. There'll be no compromise."

Klaus paused, tall and straight-backed behind the microphones.

"Now we come to the one group of killing fields we have to do something about right now. Not that we don't have plenty of choices. There are currently fifty-two places on earth where organized murder is going on. But we have to begin somewhere, and the wholesale butchery going on in parts of central and western Africa has been filling mass graves for years. So those places are going to be our starting points for an immediate cease-fire.

"What's wrong with us?" he asked. "We watch the bodies piling up—men, women, children—and we don't even bother to shake our heads. My God, it's within our sight.

"And that's probably the most depressing part of all," he continued. "We see it. Nothing is even kept from us anymore.

Now we just turn on the seven o'clock news and see dead Africans stretched out across the fields, lying along the rivers and roads, curled up in streets, houses, and churches."

Klaus was silent for a moment.

"And what do we do?" he asked. "We turn away as indifferently as we do no place else on earth. Why? Because they're all *black*."

Klaus Logefeld gazed abstractedly over the heads of those listening to him.

"But we're not turning away anymore."

Chapter 50

JAYSON FLEMING HAD ARRANGED TO BE ALONE in the Oval Office when Deputy CIA Director Harris was shown in. In the mind of the new pro tempore president, the impending meeting with his friend loomed as perhaps the most important in his life. He wanted no interruptions.

It was 12:23 P.M. Washington time. The two men had last spoken during the early morning hours, when Harris had called Fleming with news of the aborted assassination in Brussels.

Then the heavens had opened up at Wannsee, Fleming was swept into the Oval Office as pro tempore president, and he had barely been able to take a full breath since.

"Can you believe any part of it?" pondered Harris.

Fleming shook his head. "All I want to do is stare at that stupid tube in the corner."

"You and the rest of the world," said the deputy director.

The sound was tuned so low that it was barely audible, but the television screen was still glowing brightly. Both men turned to look at it.

About half an hour had passed since Professor Alfred Mainz had made his chilling statement. Now the cameras were focused on several of Wannsee's uniformed guards as they passed out transcripts of the professor's draft treaty. Some of the delegates had already started to read their copies. Others were gathered in small groups, talking.

In the telecast's audio, an English-language commentator with a British accent was reviewing the highlights of everything that had happened so far. He had been at it for hours and his voice sounded tired and hoarse.

Jayson Fleming stood staring fixedly at the lit screen. He had been staring for so long that he had begun to feel a kind of shimmering incomprehension. In the entire two hundred and twenty years of the country's existence, no American president had ever been taken hostage at gunpoint.

"Ah, enough of this," said Fleming, and cut off the audio entirely. "Let's talk."

Ken Harris glanced about the big room. "You're sure we can talk here?"

"You've been running spooks too long. We're in the Oval Office."

"Okay. As pro tempore president, what do you know that I don't?"

"Have you been watching the telecast?"

"Every minute."

"Then you know about as much as I do."

"Whom have you spoken to at Wannsee?"

Fleming told Harris about his conference call with Wannsee's security office, told him who was present and what was said.

"That's all they gave you?"

The pro tempore president nodded. He was staring off at the silent television screen. At that moment a reprise was being shown of President Dunster standing at a bank of microphones with one handgun pressed to his throat and another piece jammed against his right temple. For strictly dramatic purposes, the timing could not have been more perfect.

"Jesus," he whispered.

They watched in silence until the sequence ended.

"What's the protocol here?" asked Fleming. "Do I make some sort of attempt to get him out, or what?"

"There *is* no protocol for this. You're in uncharted territory. Whatever you try, good or bad luck and the hindsight of pundits can turn you into a hero, an ass, or a cold-blooded killer who'll do anything to make himself president."

"So I do nothing?"

The country's second-ranking intelligence officer took his time in answering.

"No," he said finally. "You do what's in your own best interest. And we both know what that is. In fact, with the right move, this entire Wannsee cataclysm could wind up as your personal hand of God."

"So why can't I just leave it to God and the two Germans?"

Harris shrugged. "There *is* always that."

"But you'd rather see me giving them some help?"

"This has been dropped right in your lap, Jay. It's a one in a million opportunity. And there's nothing like running with it and making sure."

Jayson Fleming slowly stood up, walked across the big oval room, and turned. "With how much risk?"

"Almost none."

"How do you figure that?"

"A single blast under the surveillance room would do it. Which would be blamed, of course, on some sort of accident, or tragic miscalculation by Mainz and the old man, who have already established their predilection for using explosives."

The pro tempore president could all but feel himself entering some new alley of the night.

"And your same good friend would be able to handle it?"

"Absolutely." Ken Harris smiled coldly. "In fact I've already briefed him."

Chapter 51

THREE HOURS AFTER Deputy Director Harris left the Oval Office, his alleged friend, Daniel Archer, boarded an American military transport at Andrews Air Force Base shortly before its scheduled takeoff for Berlin. His only luggage was a small canvas bag, which he stowed in an overhead bin. Then he fastened his seat belt and settled back for what had to be the quickest turnaround he had ever made for a return trip to Europe.

Staring out of his window moments later, Archer saw the edges of the runway blur and fall away. Soon there was brilliant sunlight on rolling clouds, a brief glimpse of city buildings far below, and finally a flash of light on Chesapeake Bay.

Good jump weather, he thought, and felt old sensations return. Even after so many years it was always the early drops he thought about most. How it felt waiting for the signal at the open door, the sinking fear as he went into the void, the sharp jarring as the chute filled and he sailed like a winged god. What could equal it?

Yet less than two hours earlier, Archer had felt some of that same mix of fear and exhilaration the moment he saw Ken Harris's face. The deputy director had come straight from his meeting with the pro tempore president, and it was all still in his eyes.

"It's all systems go," the deputy director had told him right off.

They were in Archer's car on a wooded trail not far from the airport.

"Did Fleming need much convincing?"

"Not really. I think his having gone along with the Brussels try made this one easier for him. And now that he's actually sitting in that office, he practically feels it's his."

Harris glanced at Archer's bag in the backseat. "You're all set?"

"I just have to get rid of the car and board the plane. What about the Berlin end of things?"

"You'll be met at the usual place. It will be a single man in a black Audi. He's tried and trusted and he'll have everything you'll need."

"He's German?"

"Yes."

"What about the blueprints?"

Ken Harris opened a briefcase and handed Archer a manila folder. "Here's a reduced-size set and a magnifying glass. You can study them during the flight."

Ken Harris had wished him good luck at the end and shook his hand with warmth and feeling.

Good luck, Archer thought now, remembering their last attempt and wondering how much the luck factor would finally have to do with whatever was about to happen. What he did not have to wonder about was his sudden loss of that curious sense of lightness he had felt when the Brussels hit on the president was aborted.

This time he knew.

Because even if everything does go off exactly as planned, Archer thought coldly, *and the president, his wife, and their two captors do finally end up dead, how long will Ken Harris be comfortable with my knowing he was the one behind the whole operation?*

A big question and a complex one, inasmuch as he and Harris not only went back a long way together, but shared feelings that had deepened into trust, respect, and even a unique sort of friendship. Yet there was no avoiding the fact that if this hit went off, he would be a loaded gun aimed at the deputy director's head for the rest of his life. How would Ken Harris ever be able to live with something like *that*?

Daniel Archer had no idea. Even if he thought he did, there was still no way he could be absolutely sure.

Unless he could *partially* carry it off: he could blast the two Germans, rescue the president and First Lady, and turn himself into a big national hero.

Certainly an interesting idea.

If a bit hard to explain to Harris.

Yet why would he have to explain anything at all? Wouldn't the deputy director end up looking equally heroic for supposedly masterminding the whole rescue operation?

Archer smiled dimly.

For a change it might be nice to be a genuine hero. Once, he had actually been one, thirty years ago in Vietnam, when he was seventeen years old and full of lovely illusions. All of which had finally turned to shit.

Maybe there were lessons to be learned from just that, he thought. But who could learn them?

Chapter 52

THE STORM HAD PASSED. Thunder no longer rolled and the rain had stopped rattling the plastic sheets over Wannsee's blown-out windows.

It was 6:30 P.M.; nearly an hour had gone by since Klaus Logefeld had appeared in the conference room, made his brief, searing statement, and left. During this period the detailed, thirty-two-page copies of his terms for President Dunster's release had been distributed and were in the process of being studied and discussed by the delegates and press.

The room buzzed with small pockets of sound. People left and returned, many of them with fast food and soft drinks. Some of the higher-ranking delegates went briefly to their hotels to freshen up and telephone their governments.

Paulie Walters kept himself in the background, moved about unobtrusively, and watched.

Mostly he watched Kate Dinneson and Nicko Vorelli, who held close to their separate groups and made no visible contact. When Kate got up at one point and headed for a rest room, Paulie drifted in the same direction, moved in close, and brushed by her.

Then he strolled past the guards at the villa's main entrance and lit a cigarette. He stood there smoking, watching some low scudding clouds. After a while he began walking. He followed a curving road for a few hundred yards until it passed through a patch of woods. A moment later Paulie left the road and placed himself behind a screen of brush.

He had just ground out his cigarette when he saw Kate approaching through the purple-shadowed dusk, a slender amorphous creature who seemed to glide slightly above the ground.

I love a woman who walks on air.

"Here," he said.

Then she was against him and they were holding each other, the air between them so full of feeling that it seemed to carry its own mist.

He went after her mouth and smothered it until they were both out of breath. Then he kissed her cheeks and felt her lips on his neck and her breasts against his chest and her instant wetness when he touched her.

"This is crazy," she whispered.

"Should we stop?"

"That would be even crazier."

Paulie lifted her.

He entered her standing up and Kate cleaved herself on him, taking all he had with a sharp intake of breath, her hair falling forward to brush against his face. She might have been weightless, the way she found his rhythm and worked against it, meeting him when he was aching to be met, then pulling back when not to would have been unbearable.

Somewhere near the finish they both realized that this might turn out to be their last time together, that anything could happen during the unpredictable madness of the seventy-two hours immediately ahead.

Moments later they were grinning and kissing and hugging as though they had done something wonderful, like bringing each other a dozen long-stemmed roses.

Kate came back to earth on trembling legs.

"I'd better not stay too long," she said against Paulie's face.

He breathed the sweetness of her scent. "Are you worried about your Nicko?"

"There's no point in making him wonder."

Wannsee's lights had come on in the settling dark and they gazed at them through the trees.

Kate sighed. "Wouldn't it be lovely if we didn't have to go back there at all?"

"Wouldn't it though."

"It's all too much. Who would ever have dreamed something like this could happen?"

Paulie just looked at her.

"Of course," she said. "You knew all along that Dunster was coming to Wannsee. That was the real reason you were here in the first place, wasn't it? To help protect him from exactly this kind of thing."

"I did a really great job, didn't I?"

"Be sensible, Paulie. You can't blame yourself for what happened."

"Who else can I blame?"

"Klaus Logefeld." Kate paused. "And *my* stupidity in letting him use me to get in here."

"It's easy to be smart with hindsight. But that's nothing but history now, so forget it."

"I can't."

"Yes you can."

"Can *you* forget I shot your mother and father?"

"I guess not. But the heart of that was really Logefeld's too."

Paulie slowly reached out his hand and touched her face. Was he still afraid she might disappear? "And there's no way I'm going to let him get away with it."

"What about the president?"

"This has nothing to do with Jimmy Dunster and what's happening here. This just has to do with Klaus Logefeld, my mother and father, and me."

"It's not that simple."

"I never said it was. I just said that's how it's finally going to be."

In the fading light, Kate's expression was troubled.

"That bothers you?" said Paulie.

"Yes."

"Why?"

"Because it sounds too much like my obsession with the killing of my own parents."

"Then you should understand how I feel."

Kate took his hand and held it, her fingers probing skin, bones, tendons.

"Oh, I understand it all right," she said. "That's exactly what's so frightening. I can still remember everything it did to me."

"Yes. But that was *you*, not *me*."

"Are you really that different?"

"Yes." The answer was instant. "At least in one way."

"What way is that?"

"The fact that I shot a man to death when I was only eight."

Kate's eyes reflected what remained of the dying light. Otherwise they were blank. "You mean by accident?"

"No. I meant to kill him."

"Why?"

"Because if I didn't he would have killed me, my mother, and another man who was with us. And to make it even worse, the man I shot was the United States attorney general."

Kate gripped Paulie's hand and waited.

"His name was Henry Durning," he said. "And since it happened, I haven't gone to sleep a single night without first thinking about what the then-president said in his eulogy. He said Henry Durning was one of the truly great men of his time, that his death was a tragic blow that couldn't help but lessen the lives of people everywhere. The president's exact words, Katey. You can imagine how *that* made me feel."

Paulie stared off, remembering. "I couldn't understand it. I knew this man. I knew he was the same man who not only had caused the deaths of a lot of people, but was just about to murder three more, myself included. A little pisspot of a kid."

Paulie shook his head. "I was eight goddamn years old and the whole thing was way too much for me. I think it still is. Although at the time, my father did do a pretty fair job of explaining it."

"How?"

"By telling me people aren't just one way, that there are different parts to us all. That some parts can be real great, but other parts can stink to high heaven."

"Did that make you feel any better?"

"What it made me feel mostly was very sad."

"Why?"

"Because I didn't mind shooting the bad part of Henry Durning. But what about all that great stuff I'd blown away along with it?"

They stood in the leaden quiet of the darkening wood.

"That's why you're so upset about maybe having to destroy all that great stuff you've begun to see in Klaus?" Kate suggested.

Paulie seemed surprised. "Who said I was upset?"

Chapter 53

AT 7:15 P.M. NICKO VORELLI once again entered Wannsee's security office. This time it was at his own request. Major Dechen, CIA Director Cortlandt, and Agent Hendricks were already there.

"I want to talk to Professor Mainz and his grandfather," he told them. "And I want to do it alone, in person, and without any microphones around."

"Why?" asked Tommy Cortlandt.

"Because I was the one who brought them in here, and I'd like the chance to try getting them out."

"What makes you think they would see you?" said Major Dechen.

"If you'll put through a call, we'll know soon enough."

The security chief looked at Cortlandt and Hendricks. "Any objections?"

"What's there to lose?" said the CIA director.

John Hendricks barely shook his head.

Dechen picked up a phone. "This is Major Dechen, Professor. Dr. Vorelli would like to talk to you in person. Privately. No microphones."

There was a moment of silence.

"Will he submit to a body search?"

The major repeated the question to Nicko, who nodded.

"He will," said Dechen.

"Give me a few minutes to get things in order."

Dechen put down the receiver.

"All right," he told Nicko. "But you'll have to let *me* pat you down first."

"Why?" said Nicko. "What if I *could* get in there with a gun? Do you think it would be such a terrible idea?"

The three men stared at him.

"I'm no expert on such things," said Nicko, "but you people certainly are. Wouldn't it be possible to conceal a small-caliber weapon somewhere on my person that might get through a nonelectric body search?"

"It's possible," said Cortlandt. "But it would take too much time and preparation to even think about right now."

"I wasn't thinking of now. I want to try talking first, anyway. But if nothing comes of that, I can always invent some reason to get in there again."

The CIA director turned to John Hendricks. "Remember your Greek assignment last year? Would you be able to rig something like that for Dr. Vorelli?"

"If I could get the parts."

"I'll find whatever you need," said Major Dechen.

"Exactly what are we talking about?" Nicko asked.

"It's a forearm pressure harness that carries a small-caliber pistol under your jacket sleeve," said Hendricks. "When you lower your arms after a body search, it can feed the piece into your hand."

Nicko considered the solemn-faced son of Peggy and Peter Walters. The open hostility he had shown at their last meeting was gone and he seemed almost friendly.

"The only problem," continued Hendricks, "would come from a hands-on body search that included your inner arms. But if you reacted quickly enough, you could get off a shot even then."

No one said anything.

Major Dechen gave Nicko a quick pat-down and walked him over to the surveillance room.

A moment later, Nicko was inside, with the door locked behind him and Klaus Logefeld aiming an automatic at his head.

"Welcome to God's corner, Doctor."

No one else was visible and Nicko realized Klaus had prepared for the visit by putting his grandfather and the Dunsters into a connecting bathroom to insure privacy. In addition, he had radio music blaring to further cover their conversation.

"Please excuse the precautions," said Klaus, and he went through a brief body search that did not include Nicko's arms.

Then with the banks of monitors flickering around them, they sat facing each other.

"A lot has certainly happened," said Nicko softly. "Imagine the president just dropping into your arms like manna from heaven."

"Does that mean God is with me?"

"How could He not be? You're doing His work for Him."

The music soared but Klaus was quiet.

"And your treaty terms are brilliant," said Nicko. "There's only one detail I find disturbing. Why was there no mention of my fifty million marks?"

"No problem, Dr. Vorelli. I just thought it unfitting to inject any specific mention of money at this point."

"But you have mentioned money. What about your multibillion-dollar revolving fund?"

"That's to support our strike force and infrastructure. Although it's also where your fifty million will be coming from. Don't worry, sir. It will be handled."

Nicko somehow doubted it.

"I'm only in here to supposedly talk reason to you and your grandfather," he said. "So it would be nice if you could give me something to take back to them."

"Like what?"

Nicko stared at the bathroom door. "How about Dunster's wife?"

"We've already tried to send her out. She won't go."

"Send her anyway."

"It's not that simple," said Klaus. "She threatens to scream, carry on, and do real damage to herself if we push her out. And that's not the kind of thing we need the world's attention focused on right now."

Nicko studied the backs of his hands as if seeking solutions there. "Has the president read your proposed terms for peace in Africa and their follow-up?"

"Before anyone else."

"What was his reaction?"

"Mildly ecstatic."

"Then how about putting him in front of a camcorder and letting him share those feelings with Wannsee's delegates and the world? Getting an all-out endorsement from the president of the United States would certainly help sanitize what you're doing."

Klaus Logefeld thought about it. "I don't know whether he would."

"I can't believe you said that, Professor."

"Why not?"

"Because you should know by now that as long as you have Mrs. Dunster here, there's probably nothing in this world the president wouldn't do for you."

Chapter 54

THE ATTACK STARTED VERY MILDLY this time, giving Jimmy Dunster plenty of warning and allowing him to keep control, move at his own pace, and not panic his wife.

The president just asked to be excused for a moment and let the old man free him from the single handcuff that still anchored him to his chair. Then he went into the adjoining lavatory and closed the door behind him. But by then his joints seemed to have locked together, and he had to struggle to get one of the nitro pills out of the bottle in his pocket and place it under his tongue.

Breathing hard, Dunster sat on the closed toilet cover and waited for the nitroglycerin to begin its work.

Crazy.

His first incident in more than a week and when did it hit him? Not with a pair of loaded automatics pressed to his head but during one of the most relaxed moments he'd had in a long time.

Sitting there, he clamped his jaws against a possible outcry and stared at himself in the mirror. His color was gray-green. His skin oozed moisture. He touched his cheek and it felt cold. His eyes in the icy fluorescent light appeared unseeing. The entire lavatory seemed made of glass. One wrong move would shatter everything.

He heard a groan and sweat soaked his neck, his shirt. The toilet tilted beneath him and he slammed his hand against a wall to keep from going over.

Then the door burst open and Maggie was staring at him, her handcuff dragging her chair.

"I'm all right," Jimmy Dunster told her.

Seeing Professor Mainz and his grandfather peering over his wife's shoulders, he forced a grin that came out a gargoyle's grimace.

They half walked, half carried him back into the surveillance room. Maggie grabbed a towel and mopped his face, his neck, his hands.

"Did you take a pill?" she asked.

The president nodded. "It's fine. It's working."

He saw the way Professor Mainz was looking at him, saw Major Schadt's eye blinking rapidly. *My new extended family.*

"Stop looking so worried," Jimmy Dunster said. "I won't die and ruin all your plans."

Klaus turned to Maggie. "What is it, Mrs. Dunster? What's wrong with your husband?"

Maggie remained silent.

"What sort of pills do you take, Mr. President?" asked Klaus.

"A painkiller my doctor prescribed."

"May I see them, please?"

"Why? Are *you* hurting too, Professor?"

Klaus stared evenly at Jimmy Dunster. "I don't want to have to go through your pockets, Mr. President."

Dunster felt his body change tone as the pressure in his chest eased. "They're nitro pills. Nitroglycerin."

"What's wrong with your heart, sir?"

"Nothing that can't be lived with."

"Or died from," said Maggie.

She said it softly, but it came out with the hiss of steam under pressure.

"Is that true?" the old man asked Dunster.

"My wife leans toward the melodramatic, Major. Actually, I've been living with this and functioning very well for months."

"Who else knows about it?" asked Klaus.

"Just my personal physician. And that's how I intend to keep it until I'm out of office."

Jimmy Dunster sat cooling himself, once again experiencing the relief of having made it safely to shore.

No one spoke. Something was happening and they were waiting to see where it would go.

It was Klaus Logefeld who finally said to Dunster, "My grandfather and I would like you to do something we feel would benefit us all."

"What would that be?"

"Earlier, you said you were impressed with the terms of our treaty demands. You said you thought they had real substance. Did you mean that?"

Dunster nodded.

"Would you make a statement to that effect before the cameras?"

Jimmy Dunster stared at Klaus and the old man. "You really think an endorsement made under a death threat means anything?"

"In your case, yes."

"I'm not that special."

"You underestimate the stature of your office, Mr. President. It overrides your mortality. Doubly so when you truly believe in what my grandfather and I are trying to do here. And nobody in this room could possibly doubt that belief."

Dunster let it all filter through him. He was beginning to feel like a prize game fish hooked deep. In the heart.

"You mean because you and the major have fixated on me as your blood brother?" he said flatly.

"No. Because you obviously risked your life just to be here."

Chapter 55

"SO WHAT HAPPENED?" asked Tommy Cortlandt.

Dr. Nicholas Vorelli was back in the security office to report on his visit to the surveillance room. Present once more were the CIA director, Major Dechen, and Paulie Walters in his persona as Agent Hendricks.

"It was downright depressing," Nicko said. "There wasn't the slightest give. I may as well have been talking to myself."

"Who *did* you talk to?" asked Major Dechen.

"Just Professor Mainz. I never glimpsed the president and his wife, or the old man. Mainz had them off in the lavatory before he let me in."

"Did you discuss their treaty terms?" pressed Cortlandt.

"Yes. I told him they were brilliant. I said I agreed with every major point and would back them all the way. Just let the president go, I told him, and I could all but guarantee conference approval and amnesty for him and his grandfather. But I said he had to do it now because all sorts of disasters could happen during the next seventy-two hours."

"How did he respond?" asked Cortlandt.

"By as much as telling me to go to hell. He said he had spent half his life making a careful study of reason versus force, and it really was no contest."

Nicko turned to Paul Walters. "So what I've been thinking, Mr. Hendricks, is that since we've just given reason a fair chance and failed, maybe it's time we tried the professor's own alternative."

Paulie looked deep into the doctor's eyes and said nothing.

"I was impressed by that device you described before," said Nicko. "Do you suppose you could set me up with something like that so I can get back in there with a gun?"

Paulie shook his head. "You're way ahead of yourself, sir. That's not how these things work."

"How *do* they work?"

"First, it has to be decided whether it should even be attempted."

"Who decides that?"

Paulie glanced at Tommy Cortlandt and Major Dechen, but they remained silent.

"To begin with, those of us right here in this room," said Paulie. "Later, perhaps Chancellor Eisner and the pro tempore American president."

"And if it's decided?"

"Then the mechanics of the operation would have to be worked out. Something that's always dangerous with lives at stake and no margin for error."

Cortlandt broke in. "You never told us, Dr. Vorelli. When the professor patted you down before, did he feel your arms?"

"No. He never touched them."

"Have you ever fired a handgun?" asked Major Dechen.

"Yes, Major."

"What about firing at someone who's shooting back?"

"I've done that too, sir. And the fact that I'm sitting here talking about it has to tell you *something*."

It told Paulie, for one, a great deal. But what it failed to tell him was the purpose of Nicko's playacting.

They sat like four tired hunters in the dark of some early-morning blind.

Nicko studied the three men facing him. "Well, gentlemen? Am I going to get a shot at this or not?"

"You mean you want an answer right now?" asked Cortlandt.

"If possible, Mr. Director."

"Then speaking for myself, the only thing I'd be willing to commit to at this moment is a very conditional maybe." The CIA director looked at Paulie and Major Dechen. "Could you gentlemen live with that?"

The security chief offered no more than a slight nod; Paulie, not even that.

"It's too dangerous to be anything but a last resort," said Cortlandt. "We still have seventy-two hours before we reach that point. Still, I can't see any harm in preparing a few things in case of a sudden emergency."

The CIA director appeared to consider Nicko with fresh interest. "You're actually ready to go through with this, Doctor?"

"I said I was."

"I know what you said."

"But you don't believe it?"

"I don't *understand* it. At best I see you with less than a fifty percent chance of getting out of that room alive. Why on earth would you want to place yourself in such a position?"

"I thought I explained all that at our last two meetings."

"You're a worldly, practical man, Dr. Vorelli. I just can't imagine you putting your life on the line out of a sense of guilt."

Nicko drew deeply on his cigarette, blew a trail of smoke, and sat watching it spiral upward.

"All right," he said. "If practicality is what you're looking for, then how about fifty million American dollars contributed to my favorite cause? World freedom."

Tommy Cortlandt stared. "Are you serious?"

"Very."

"You mean you didn't just scrape this off the top of your head?"

"Not at all, Mr. Director. It's been a dream of mine for almost twenty years. I'd certainly have put it on the table anyway before going much further with this. Since you're pressing for reasons you can understand, we might as well talk about it now."

No one spoke.

"Here's the deal," said Nicko. "If I go into that room and bring out the president and his wife alive and well, your government makes a cash donation of fifty million dollars to the Olympus Freedom Foundation in Naples sometime during the following twenty-four hours."

"If you don't get them out alive and well?"

"There's no obligation."

The CIA director's face was blank. "What made you pick fifty million?"

"Because it seemed a fair measure of the Foundation's current budget needs."

Nicko looked at Tommy Cortlandt. "Consider it this way, Mr. Director. I'm Wannsee's only hope of getting completely free of this calamity. Which means whatever amount I name, it has to be a bargain."

"Why?"

"Because unless I get in there and eliminate Mainz and his grandfather before they're granted amnesty and disappear, our respective governments are still going to have to face whatever future demands they might decide to make. Or have you forgotten their seven mined buildings?"

"I haven't forgotten a thing," said Cortlandt.

"So even if we hand them everything they're asking, and the Dunsters are safely back in their White House beds, Mainz and the old man will still be writing key parts of our agendas."

Nicholas Vorelli considered his audience of three. "I think that should certainly be simple enough to understand."

Chapter 56

AT 10:00 P.M. BERLIN TIME, Klaus Logefeld called his first four-hour conference break. He then announced that President Dunster would make an important public statement when the Wannsee delegates reconvened at 2:00 A.M.

Twenty minutes later, Paulie Walters and Kate Dinneson were in a hotel room just a few miles down the road from the conference center.

Fifteen minutes after that, they were asleep.

They slept holding each other.

Until in one of Paulie's brief, vagrant dreams, Kate suddenly was gone and he awoke calling her name.

Grief rasped out of burning eyes and a parched throat. "Kate!"

The bedside lamp came on and she was holding him again.

"What is it, Paulie?"

It embarrassed him. "A dream."

"That bad?"

"You were gone," he said.

Kate saw the touch of wetness on his cheek.

She turned off the lamp and they lay in the dark.

"How much more time do we have?" Paulie asked.

"About forty minutes."

"I'm sorry I woke you."

"I'm not."

Paulie was silent and Kate could feel him leaving her.

"So what's finally going to happen?" she asked.

"Who am I? God?"

"For me, in this, yes."

"In one way or another people are going to die," he said quietly. "Logefeld and his grandfather for sure. About a fifty percent chance for the president. Slightly better odds for the president's wife. And if we ever get as far as the blowing of just one of those mined buildings, Christ only knows how many hundreds more."

Paulie pursed his lips as though adding up a terribly expensive bill. "I don't suppose your friend Vorelli has told you, but he's been pushing to get in there and shoot Klaus and the old man himself."

He felt Kate stiffen.

"But how? I don't understand."

Paulie briefly told her about Nicko's meetings with them in the security office and his visit to the surveillance room.

"You knew nothing about any of this?" Paulie asked.

Kate shook her head.

"But what I *did* know," she said, "was that Nicko had worked a fifty-million deal with Klaus to let him and his grandfather go ahead with their plans for Wannsee."

It was Paulie's turn to be surprised. "When did Vorelli tell you that?"

"About a week before the conference. When he told me he had gotten me a press pass for Wannsee and that he might be needing my help there."

"What sort of help?"

"Nicko never said. Soon after we got here, he apologized for even wanting to involve me and said to forget the whole thing."

In the following silence, Paulie groped for signs of logic. "A couple of things I can't figure. If Vorelli has this big money deal with Logefeld, why is he so eager to kill him? And what's suddenly happened to his concern about those tapes and pictures of you going to the police if Logefeld dies?"

"I guess Nicko was worried about Klaus not paying off, and decided to do business with your CIA director instead."

"But that money would be going to the Olympus Freedom Foundation."

"Which Nicko controls."

Naturally, thought Paulie.

"As for those tapes and pictures of me," Kate said. "A few days ago Nicko located and destroyed Klaus's three extra copies."

"He told you that?"

"He more than told me. He let me watch them burn."

"And the originals and negatives I saw in Logefeld's apartment?"

"Nicko burned those an hour after Klaus left for Wannsee."

Chapter 57

KLAUS LOGEFELD OPENED THE DOOR to a single cameraman at exactly 1:45 A.M. and had everything ready for the planned telecast ten minutes later.

President Dunster sat alone, facing the newly set up lights and camera. The handcuffs that normally held him to the chair had been removed, and his hands lay loosely in his lap. He had no notes.

Maggie sat off to his right, out of camera range, trying to appear relaxed but failing miserably.

How pale she looked. How drawn.

Not for the first time, Jimmy Dunster was struck by how his wife was aging. Surprise. His twenty-one-year-old bride was no longer twenty-one.

Major Schadt fussed with the monitors, fine-tuning dials, keeping the audio down, and from time to time checking the sound from a particular area.

At one point, half turning, he caught the president's eye and offered a nod of encouragement.

Jimmy Dunster gazed past the glare of camera lights at the monitor screens covering the main conference room. Everyone appeared to have returned from their rest break and all seats were filled. Dunster saw that Chancellor Eisner had once more joined the German delegation, and that Tommy Cortlandt was standing with several security people against a far wall. At opposite sides of the room hung two large picture screens that had not been there earlier, and Dunster guessed that his own image would be projected on these when the telecast started.

"Anytime you're ready, Mr. President," said Klaus Loge-feld.

Dunster looked at him. Standing behind the pool cam-eraman, Klaus held an automatic in his right hand. His ex-pression was easy, pleasant. Only the thumb and forefinger of his left hand, which he rubbed together compulsively, be-trayed what was going on inside him.

"Let's do it," said the president.

Logefeld nodded to the cameraman and an instant later Jimmy Dunster saw the screens in the conference room brighten and come to life with his own picture. He looked better than he might have imagined.

"Ladies and gentlemen," said Klaus from where he stood off-camera, "the president of the United States."

Jimmy Dunster sat for a moment in silence. Then he turned and looked straight at the camera.

"I'm going to try to be brief and truthful," he said. "Both normally difficult for any politician. But this is far from a nor-mal time for me. And it might be my last chance to set things right."

Dunster swallowed.

"Whatever has happened to me at Wannsee is my own fault," he said softly. "I lied and deceived without shame to get here. I endangered my own life and the lives of others by hiding a serious cardiac condition and living with medication instead of going for surgery. I bought my wife's silence by agreeing to bring her here, thereby placing her in harm's way. Finally, I betrayed my high office by putting my personal needs ahead of my country's. None of which does me credit, either as a man or as a leader.

"Still, the purpose of our coming together here is far from lost," he said. "I've read Professor Mainz and Major Schadt's terms for an effective human rights treaty and peace in Africa and elsewhere, and they give me hope. Not so much for my own and my wife's safety, which mean little in the overall scheme of things, but for all too many millions of oppressed. Regardless of race or color."

The president stared blindly into the glittering eye of the camera. "Please understand," he said. "I'm really not a physically brave or heroic man. I've been frightened for weeks by the thought of walking in here as I did. And I obviously have a lot more reason to be frightened right this minute. Yet these two men with their guns and threats have given me a crazy kind of courage. Why? Because their thirty-two pages of carefully thought out terms prove something very important. They want exactly what the rest of us want. With one big difference. They're willing to do whatever has to be done to get it."

Dunster paused.

"Maybe that's what we need right now. If we're afraid to use our guns and risk our lives to stop oppression and killing, then we're truly condemned to chaos. Then we'll have to teach ourselves how to be blind so we can quietly ignore all our avoidable tragedies."

Someone in the room whispered a soft amen.

Chapter 58

DANIEL ARCHER'S FLIGHT LANDED at Tempelhof Airport twenty minutes ahead of schedule and taxied to one of the gates reserved for military and diplomatic transport.

About fifteen minutes later, Archer approached a man sitting behind the wheel of a black Audi station wagon at the end of section 6, aisle B in the long-term parking area.

It was 3:12 A.M. Berlin time.

"Do you have the time, Hans?" he asked in German.

The man looked at him. He had dark, nicely barbered hair over a tough, square-jawed face.

"Sorry," he said. "I'm afraid my watch stopped."

Archer nodded, walked around to the passenger door, and got in beside the driver. He tossed his bag in back and saw two pieces of luggage already there. One was a garment bag, the other a canvas duffel.

"You have everything?" asked Archer.

"Check it out."

Daniel Archer took a few moments to go through the bags. Among the weapons were two automatics (one with a silencer), a wire garrote, a razor-edged sheath knife, and a weighted leather sap. He saw flat packets of C-4 explosive, detonators, fittings, wiring, and timers. Additional brass tubing and two small metal containers of gas were separate and compact.

The garment bag held a gray military uniform, complete with service stripes, decorations, and a pair of black, highly polished, thick-soled shoes.

"That's a Wannsee guard uniform," said the German. "Size 40 long. It gives you access to anyplace inside or immediately outside the compound. The shoes are your own size 10. There are black socks inside them. Your official ID and name tag are in the left-hand tunic pocket."

Archer slid back into the front seat and they drove out of the quiet, early morning dark of the airport.

They rode without speaking, Archer's thoughts busy with what lay ahead. Suddenly doubt trickled from his breastbone to his belly.

Had he made the right decision?

It had to be right, because anything else would be wrong. At least wrong for *him*. And who else was there?

There was Ken Harris and there was the vice president of the United States, he thought dully.

The German spoke with his eyes on the empty road. "What are you going to want from me when we get there?"

"Nothing," Archer said. "All you have to do is wait in the car and get me away when I'm finished."

"I can do more than that."

"Sure you can, Hans," said Archer. "But not for me."

The German showed no expression. A car approached and its lights glinted in his eyes.

"I can help you," he said.

"Help me with what?"

"With what you're going to do at Wannsee."

"And that is?"

"Blow away the president, his wife, and those two crazies holding them."

Daniel Archer felt a sudden, almost sensuous fatigue. "Why would you think something like that?" he said quietly.

"Because I'm not stupid. And I've never heard of an American vice president who wouldn't do just about anything to get to be president."

"Even murder?"

"Even that. As long as someone else would be sure to get blamed."

"And who would be blamed in this?"

"Those two bomb-happy crazies."

"Interesting theory," said Archer. "But my orders are to just take out the two bombers and save the president and his wife."

"I don't believe that."

It was said with such quiet confidence that Daniel Archer was impressed. "Why not?"

"Because I know the conditions you'll be working under. And in that small a space, I'd have to say it was impossible to kill two without killing all four."

"Nothing is impossible."

"With all due respect, friend, you may be damn good, but so am I. And I wouldn't bet piss on my own chances of pulling that off. Not if I expected to get out alive myself."

Archer saw that they were entering a deep wood.

"So exactly what is it you think you can do to help?" he asked. "And why would you want to?"

"I know of an old underground passage. It can get you into Wannsee unseen and put you in perfect position to do what you have to and get out in one piece. And my reason for helping is simple. I'm just looking after my future. Your contacts come right from the top in all this. And if I can prove myself tonight, I'm hoping you might give me a lift and pull me up there with you."

Daniel Archer let a moment go by, then another.

"Who else knew about this passage?"

"Just two men. One is a delegate at Wannsee, named Vorelli. The other is a friend of mine. Bruno."

"And how do *you* know about it?"

"Bruno showed it to me." The German paused. "You want to hear the story?"

"Why not?"

"Vorelli hired Bruno to check out and equip this secret tunnel from the Nazi years. I don't know what Vorelli was planning, but it couldn't be anything good. Then Bruno got me to cover his back the night he took Vorelli down there to explain things."

"So what's been going on down there?" Archer inquired.

"Not a damn thing. All that electronic gear is still in place."

The German braked and slowed as the road began curving sharply between the trees.

"Then the conference started," he said, "and all this shit began happening with the president, and I got that call about doing what I'm doing for you. Now it looks like the whole business might do us all some good, if you'll let it."

Archer remained silent, a wire-walker in a shifting wind.

"So what do you think?" asked the German.

"Exactly where are we now?"

"About ten minutes from Wannsee."

"And the tunnel entrance?"

"Five minutes from here."

"On this trail?"

The German nodded.

"Then let's go for it," said Daniel Archer.

Chapter 59

STILL IN THE OVAL OFFICE at 9:10 P.M. Washington time, Vice President Fleming had eaten dinner from a tray and called his wife to say he would be spending the night at the White House.

There had been a steady parade of key staffers in and out of the office all afternoon and evening, but Jayson Fleming was alone when he again was joined by Deputy CIA Director Harris.

The two men had neither seen nor spoken to each other since the president's televised talk, and Fleming searched his friend's face as he came in.

"So how about Jimmy's little confessional?" he said. "I couldn't decide whether to cry or cheer."

"I just wanted to throw up. Imagine. A fucking heart condition on top of everything else."

Fleming opened a cabinet, poured two measures of President Dunster's private Napoleon, and handed one to Harris. "I've spoken to his doctor. Jimmy's lived with it for months."

Thinking identical thoughts, the two men stood looking at each other.

"And the prognosis?" asked Harris.

"He can go on like this for years, or die today. Only one thing is sure. He won't be running for any second term."

Harris swore softly. "*Now* he tells us."

Jayson Fleming stared at his brandy and the glass suddenly seemed alive to his fingers. A snake?

"I don't suppose you've heard anything from your man," he said.

The deputy director shook his head.

"When do you think you'll hear?"

"Not until it's happened."

"Is there any way you can reach him before that?"

"Not anymore."

The pro tempore president was silent.

"That's the wrong way to be thinking, Jay," said his friend.

"What's the right way?"

"Concentrating on what you're after. And not second-guessing yourself."

Ken Harris swept an arm toward the television screen, where Wannsee's delegates continued to hold forth. "Have you been listening to them since Jimmy gave his fireside chat?"

"Not really."

"Well, I have. They've got a bandwagon rolling. If it continues like that, they'll have a treaty signed and delivered within thirty-six hours, and the Dunsters will be on their way home."

"You mean in body bags."

"Only if we're lucky," said Harris.

"And what if we're not so lucky? What if someone grabs your man and he talks?"

"That won't happen."

"Why not?"

"Because he'll be terminated."

The vice president blinked several times. "By whom?"

"Someone far removed from either one of us."

Fleming stood motionless, his pulse suddenly in his temple. Was there no end to it? "I can't believe I'm actually party to all this," he said.

"Why?"

"Because it's so . . . evil."

"It's even hard for you to say, isn't it?" Harris's voice was mocking. "Yet there's really no such thing. Evil is just another

Sunday school word. Like God and the Devil. What it all comes down to is what we want, how much we want it, and what we finally have the guts to do to get it."

"I know," Fleming said tiredly. "Like my wanting to be president."

Ken Harris smiled. "Exactly. You're becoming part of history now, old buddy. And history is a priori amoral. All it cares about is whether something succeeds or fails. Then it raises statues to one and buries the other. So if you expect to stay in this office, better not forget that."

The vice president rolled his head slowly, trying to rid it of pain. "Let me tell you something," he said. "I was very young when John Kennedy had his skull blown away in Dallas. I heard all those ugly rumors and theories allegedly behind it, but I never believed any of them. And I especially didn't believe the ugliest of all. The one about Lyndon Johnson having set it up to make himself president. Sweet Jesus, I thought. . . . No man, not even a fucking Texas Democrat, could be that evil. Yet now I guess I have to start rethinking that, don't I?"

Jayson Fleming stared at his friend. "Except that now you're telling me there's really no such thing as evil. That should certainly make me feel a lot better about what I've set in motion here, shouldn't it?"

"Yes. It should."

"Then why do I still feel like such a damnable, murdering shit?"

"Because you've got the crazy idea there's redemption in just feeling that way."

Chapter 60

A WANING, THREE-QUARTER MOON edged past a long cluster of clouds and shone down on Wannsee.

In the surveillance room, Klaus Logefeld watched the television monitors and could all but feel the change of mood around the conference table. From an air of impending calamity, the prevailing spirit seemed to have turned to one of steadily building hope. Klaus saw it in the delegates' faces and heard it in their words and voices when they spoke.

Then he glanced at his grandfather and was able to pick out something that might actually have passed for a smile.

I think they're going to give it to us, said the facsimile of a smile.

And I'll believe it only when we have it in our hands, thought Klaus.

Still, Klaus had already demonstrated his own hope, his own easing of tension, by removing the Dunsters' handcuffs. But not without first reminding them to please, please, not try anything foolish when things were beginning to go so well.

President James Dunster needed no such warning. His perceptions, always acute, had never been so finely tuned. He was well aware of every positive indication being passed through the glowing monitors like the scent of some exciting perfume. He intended to just sit quietly beside his wife, gaze at the television screen, and make no waves.

Maggie simply kept looking at the president with such naked hope and feeling that it tore his heart. She gripped his hand and listened with growing impatience to the long-winded arguments, pomposities, and pure babble being produced by the various speakers at the conference table.

"Why don't they just shut up and vote?" she said after an especially lengthy harangue by the French foreign secretary. "Why must they always talk so darn much?"

"Because it's their profession. It's what they do."

"Even while you're sitting here under a death threat?"

"They all have their agendas, Maggie."

"That's disgusting."

"No more disgusting than my own agenda of just walking in here uninvited and unannounced."

"That was different."

"How?"

"*You*, at least, thought you were Jesus Christ."

"Are you telling me I'm *not?*" Dunster said.

Maggie looked at him for a long moment. "Considering the small miracle you seem to be working here, I'm beginning to wonder."

Making his own observations from within the conference room itself, Paulie Walters listened to the momentum growing in favor of Klaus Logefeld's grand plan for Africa and the world, and was not the least bit proud of how he was reacting. He seemed to be experiencing less joy at the prospect of the president's safe release than the anger and frustration he felt at the thought of Klaus flying off in a few days, free and unpunished.

I should be better than this, he thought.

How could he just let the sonofabitch get away with deliberately setting up his mother and father?

The answer to that was simple. He couldn't.

More complex, of course, was how he would finally manage to do what had to be done and get on with his life.

He knew that when the time came, he would figure that one out too. As his father would have done if the situation had been reversed. Or, for that matter, what his mother would have done as well.

They were that kind of family.

What about *vengeance is mine; I will repay, saith the Lord?*

Always an imposing thought.

He was evidently of a different *famiglia* entirely.

Kate Dinneson's attention was focused more on Paulie and what she felt he was thinking than on the delegates' speechifying.

There's no way I'm going to let him get away with it, he had declared in the woods early that evening, and the words themselves still frightened her.

Paulie met her gaze for a moment. Then he looked away, standing silent and still.

Kate had the sense of having seen him exactly this way before, and recalled it as having been at the freshly dug graves of his parents.

I was the one who put them there.

Still, he had cared and understood enough to grant her absolution. If he had not, Kate guessed she would now be dead. As Klaus would soon be dead. There was no doubt about that in Kate's mind. It was simply a question of Paulie deciding when, where, and how.

When that was done, no one would be able to stop him. Unless Klaus could, she thought, as this new fear coursed through her.

With what appeared to be the rising acceptance of Klaus Logefeld's agenda, Dr. Nicholas Vorelli was facing a problem of his own.

Seated at the conference table no more than ten feet from Kate, he stared coldly into the television lights, seemed to listen to whatever the other delegates were saying, offered appropriate remarks of his own when they were called for, and never for a moment stopped considering how best to handle the quandary ahead.

His own worst-case scenario would, of course, be the

swift approval of Klaus's treaty plan, an equally quick release of the Dunsters, and an instant end to any chance for his fifty-million-dollar rescue arrangement.

In a more positive view, he hoped that the delegates would milk as much time and media coverage as possible from the situation before voting themselves out of their starring role in the world spotlight.

That, in turn, would give him enough breathing space to sell those in command on the advantages of his own plan to shoot Klaus and the old man, thereby sparing everyone the almost certain blackmail of any future bombing threats.

Earlier, Nicko had checked back with Major Dechen, and the security chief had already carried out his promise to pick up the necessary parts for his pressure harness.

Now he just needed a bit of extra time, and he was confident he would get that.

If he failed to get it?

There would be other ways.

Somehow, there always were.

Chapter 61

THEY ENTERED THE TUNNEL at about four in the morning with Daniel Archer following his German contact through the camouflaged opening, down a short flight of steps, and along a concrete-lined passage smelling of time, dampness, and other things.

Death was among the other things.

They each carried a battery-powered lantern, and Archer held one of the two automatics the German had brought, the one with the silencer. The other piece was in his belt.

They walked without speaking until they reached a rusted metal door that marked the end of the tunnel. The German opened the door and they went into a large, concrete-lined room filled with bunks, canned goods, and communications gear.

Hans put his lantern down on a bare wooden table surrounded by four chairs, and turned.

"Vorelli's headquarters," he said.

"Headquarters for what?"

"Who knows? But it's stocked with enough electronic junk to tie in with half the world."

Daniel Archer glanced around and believed him. He unslung his canvas duffel and bag and set them down on the concrete floor. Hans put down the garment bag he had been carrying and smiled at Archer.

"You see?" he said. "Coming in and working from down

here, you won't even have to bother putting on your uniform."

"What about when I leave?" asked Archer.

The German looked at him and Archer suddenly got a
hint of the real reason the man was here.

"If we go out the way we came in," Hans said, "you won't
need it even then. But put it on if it'll make you feel better."

Archer opened the garment bag, took off his clothes,
and put on the gray uniform and shiny black shoes. With all
the fireworks that would be going on later, it was better to do
it now. He didn't bother asking Hans why he hadn't brought
a second uniform for himself. He had probably expected to be
wearing this one.

They started at once.

Hans now activated the miniature bugs and cameras the
German's friend, Bruno, had strategically placed throughout
the villa.

A split-screen television monitor suddenly lit up, and
Daniel Archer stared at four separate images. He saw the surveillance and main conference rooms, the first-floor corridor,
and the basement library and reference area. There were
headsets for the audio, but Archer had no interest in what
was being said. At that moment all he cared about was the
sight of those in the surveillance room.

Here they are, he thought, and felt his life and theirs
hanging by the same delicate thread.

The first thing that struck him was how they were positioned. Their placement in the room was so perfect for his
needs that he could not believe his good luck. Mainz and the
old man were sitting together in front of the monitors, with
the president and his wife side by side against a wall that had
to be at least fifteen feet away.

Two and two. And separate.

Archer saw clearly that what he had hoped to do could
actually be done. Not that it would be simple or certain.
With explosives, the size and placement of the charge was always tricky. Too much or too little, too close or too far away,
and anything could happen.

Still, to use the gas that Hans had brought as a possible backup would be even more dangerous, even harder to control with all four of them in the same room.

So it would be only the C-4.

"Show me the rest of the layout," he said to the German.

Hans went into what appeared to be an empty closet, and Archer saw him press a wooden panel that swung open.

They walked through the opening and were in the rear section of a cellar storeroom, which in turn led into a basement utility area and then into a library and reference room. All were unoccupied. Although in certain places footsteps could be heard overhead along with the faint murmur of voices.

Back in the electronics bunker, Archer reviewed the diagrams and blueprints he had studied on the flight coming over and decided exactly where and how to place his charge. He took particular pains in measuring out the C-4, and he set the detonator and remote according to a formula he had worked out himself and had used for years with good results.

In this, there were no second chances.

Hans watched, quiet and expressionless.

Finally, Daniel Archer sat down and looked at the German. His silencer-lengthened automatic lay on the table between them where he had placed it earlier; it had not been touched since.

"When are you supposed to do it?" Archer asked. "Before or after I blow the charge?"

"Do what?"

"Shoot me."

The German's eyes widened. That was all. "What are you talking about?"

"Listen," said Archer, "you have exactly thirty seconds to tell me what your orders are, who gave them to you, and who else knows about this whole thing. If you don't tell me, you're dead."

Hans never hesitated. "And if I *do* tell you?"

"Then you leave in one piece and you're out of it. We're both professionals. We don't die for this crap. Right?"

"Sure," said the German, and had the gun off the table and in his hand so fast that Archer found himself staring into the muzzle almost before he was conscious of it happening.

"Nice move," he said. "But the clip happens to be empty."

Hans stared deep into Daniel Archer's eyes. Then he took careful aim between them and squeezed the trigger.

There was only a faint metallic sound.

Hans quickly racked back the automatic's slide. But instead of moving forward into firing position, it remained locked open.

At that moment Archer caught the German in the temple with the butt of his other automatic, and Hans went down.

Archer picked up the silenced piece, placed a single cartridge in the exposed breech, pressed the slide release, and aimed the gun at Hans where he lay.

"OK," he said. "You know the questions. Let's try again."

Hans rose slowly from the floor and settled into a chair. A trickle of blood ran down the side of his face and stained his collar.

"You're running out of time," said Archer.

"Same deal as before? If I talk, I walk?"

"You've got it."

Hans nodded. "I'm probably two removed from the prime source, so the best I can do is guess at who that would be."

"Then make it a good guess."

"I already told you. The American vice president."

"And next to *him?*"

"The same man who hired you. Someone high up in the CIA."

"Let's hear a name."

"Foxcraft."

"Is that a guess too?"

"No," said the German. "I had a tap going and heard it on a phone call."

"Who did you have the tap on?"

"Someone in Berlin. He was using the code name Sam."

"Anyone else who knew?"

"No."

"What were your orders from Sam?"

"To help you as much as I could. To make sure it was done fast, right, and without messy complications."

The German paused and looked at some distant point.

"And then?"

"To shoot you before you were able to shoot me."

The German's voice was quiet and he was still looking off somewhere. He was waiting for something, and Archer knew what it was.

Daniel Archer rose, walked around the table to the man, and touched him on the shoulder. "You don't have to worry, Hans. When this is finished we'll go out of here together."

The German was silent. He nodded and did not turn. He was still nodding when the single bullet from the silenced automatic made its soft, whooshing sound as it entered his head.

Archer began.

He gathered everything he needed into his bag and pressed the wooden panel in the bunker closet. Then he went through the cellar storeroom into the utility area that his blueprints showed to be lying directly under the surveillance room.

Archer measured off the imagined spaces above him in relation to his own position. He pinpointed the south wall of the surveillance room that held the banks of monitors where he had seen Professor Mainz and the old man sitting. Marking what he estimated to be the most effective spot, he taped his prepared charge to the basement ceiling, checked his calculations once more for possible errors, and carried his bag back into the concrete chamber.

He looked at the split-screen monitor. In the conference hall, the delegates' discussion appeared to be going on as before. In the surveillance room, there had been a slight change in one of the occupants' positions. Professor Mainz was standing behind his chair and saying something to the president. But they were still separated by about fifteen feet, which seemed well within Archer's estimated safety margin.

Still, wanting to take no unnecessary chances, he waited another moment until he saw Mainz sit down.

Then Archer took a deep breath and pressed the bright red button on his detonator.

The big shock was the enormity of the explosion, a roll of thunder that echoed through the bunker and pounded the air with concussion. Along with his heart. And his brain.

It should not have been that strong.

Not with the amount of C-4 he had taped to the ceiling.

Not with all his careful figuring.

Unless his charge had touched off other explosives stored in the same area.

"Fucking God!" he said, and felt an old sickness enter him with the rush of dust and fouled air.

Then, with a flashlight in his hand, he began groping through the closet, the storeroom, and back into the utility area.

The power was out, and with all the soot and floating grime, Archer's light could cut through only a few feet at a stretch. His ears were still drained of sound; he heard nothing. When he was under the place where he had taped the charge, his flash picked out a jagged hole in the ceiling and the flooring immediately above it.

A body hung halfway through, arms down. It was Professor Mainz's grandfather, and he was dead.

Archer stood there, beginning to hear sounds as his ears cleared. There were distant voices and banging as people tried to get into the locked surveillance room. Needing to know the worst, Archer scrambled up some broken beams and poked and rooted about for whatever remained.

His light picked out three more bodies, and none of them were moving. He felt for pulses and signs of heartbeats.

The president was alive.

Maggie Dunster was terribly bloodied but had a heartbeat.

Mainz was still breathing. But barely.

Daniel Archer knelt there in his personal charnel house. Three alive and one dead. How long before the president, his wife, and Mainz would be dead as well?

It was impossible for Archer to tell from what he could see of their wounds, especially since so many blast injuries were internal and from concussion.

He heard the banging on the surveillance room's heavy fire door grow louder as axes came into play, and he started to leave the way he had entered.

Until a thought occurred.

And a moment later he was dragging Mainz to the opening in the floor and sliding him down one of the broken beams to the utility area below.

Then, lifting him as if he were a sleeping child, Daniel Archer carried the professor into the concrete bunker and closed the secret panel and the steel door behind them.

Chapter 62

THE CONFERENCE ROOM LIGHTS were knocked out by the explosion, but several battery-powered emergency floods came on and helped cut some of the chaos.

Still, shouting and screaming, people groped for exits without knowing what had happened or what might happen next.

Paulie Walters made his way toward the surveillance room. It was pure instinct. There was no telling exactly where the blast had taken place, but since the surveillance room was where the president was, that was where Paulie wanted to be.

He passed into the corridor, into thickening layers of smoke and dust. Bits of plaster were still falling from walls and ceilings. Two gray-uniformed Wannsee guards were hammering with their fists at the locked door of the surveillance room. There was no longer any doubt. This was where the explosion had taken place.

Paulie saw one of the guards draw his pistol and aim at the lock, and he dived for the gun before the guard could fire. "You want to goddamn shoot the president?"

The man stared at him.

"Anyone in there hear me?" Paulie yelled.

There was no response.

Paulie and the two guards slammed their shoulders into the door together, but it was made of metal and never budged.

"Get some damn axes!" Paulie shouted, envisioning only the worst on the far side of the door.

When entry finally was made, it was Paulie who shoved in first. But the room was totally dark and he had to wait for flashlights to be brought in.

Then he saw a big, jagged hole in the floor, a lot of debris, and three bodies. The bodies all looked like the usual bundles of old clothes that the newly and violently deceased seemed to turn into.

On closer examination, they became the old man, Maggie Dunster, and the president of the United States, and there appeared to be little doubt that they were dead. Paulie did not see what, if anything, remained of Klaus Logefeld.

Then nearing the president, he heard the small whistling sound of breathing made by a sucking chest wound and felt a sympathetic stirring inside his own chest. Maggie Dunster, too, turned out to be alive.

"Stretchers!" he called hoarsely.

They were there in moments, and Paulie lifted the president onto one of them himself. Then Paulie pushed into the ambulance with Maggie and Jimmy Dunster because he knew he had to personally insure their being alive when the ambulance reached the hospital.

Army medics had put tubes in the president's nose and arms and plugged the hole in his chest, so the sucking sound had stopped. There were bloody bandages on Maggie Dunster's head now and an oxygen mask covered her nose and mouth.

"Are they going to make it?" Paulie asked one of the medics, a sergeant.

"I couldn't tell you that, sir. There could be internal injuries and hemorrhaging."

A siren screamed as the ambulance picked up speed.

"Let's just be thankful they're breathing," said Tommy Cortlandt. "I was sure they were as dead as Mainz and the old man."

Paulie had not even noticed the director sitting there.

"What the hell happened in that room?" he asked.

"No one knows for sure. But did you see that big hole in the floor where the old man's body was lying?"

"Yeah."

"That was where they must have had the charge planted. I think either Mainz or his grandfather accidentally hit the remote and set it off."

Paulie gazed out of the back of the speeding ambulance. Behind them trailed a small convoy of American Secret Service agents and German police. In front of the ambulance was a line of motorcycles.

"I never did spot Mainz's body," Paulie said coldly. "Or wasn't there enough left to identify?"

"I don't know. The Dunsters were all I had on my mind when I was in there, so I never really looked. But if Mainz was at ground zero of the blast, his remains must have fallen through the hole and into the basement."

Paulie was silent.

He looked at the pale, unconscious face of the president.

I'm sorry about how things worked out for you and your wife, he told him, feeling intensely weary and a trifle mad. *But for God's sake, please don't quit on us now.*

Chapter 63

THE LORD GIVETH *and the Lord taketh away*, thought Nicko Vorelli. But he thought it wryly, without believing a word.

More to his own taste, of course, would have been *God helps those who help themselves*. Although he was hard put at the moment to see how he was ever going to help himself out of this one.

Avoiding the general panic that immediately followed the blast, he quietly drifted through the ebb and flow of confusion and picked up what little information was available.

Apparently the old man was dead, and the president and his wife were barely alive and on their way to the nearest hospital.

As for Klaus Logefeld, he seemed to have simply disappeared. There was no sign of him in either the surveillance room where the explosion had taken place or in the basement immediately below it. Both areas had been searched without turning up a clue. Nor had any of the guards posted around the building seen a trace of the curiously absent Professor Mainz.

The consensus on the blast itself was that it had been an accidental detonation of a charge previously set by Mainz and his grandfather. Considering how well everything had been going for them, any thought of their having deliberately set off the explosion made no sense.

Obviously something was missing. Since the absent piece had to lie somewhere inside the basement level, Nicko decided to do some quiet prowling of his own.

The central power system was still out, but Nicko had his own penlight to guide him. Voices and footsteps carried faintly through the flooring.

When he reached the rear section of the storeroom everything suddenly coalesced. He could only wonder why it had not come to him sooner.

Still, it was only a feeling, not a certainty. Nicko went straight to the perfectly matched tongue-in-groove paneling on the far wall that he had seen only once, placed his ear against it, and listened.

Not a sound came through.

He examined the surface for bloodstains but there were none.

Then Nicko switched off his light and pressed a hand against the place on the wall that Bruno had showed him.

There was not the slightest give.

He lowered his hand about twelve inches and pressed again.

This time he felt movement. Keeping the pressure on, Nicko eased the panel inward until he had a wide enough opening to see through.

Pitch blackness greeted him. He remembered that he was looking into an empty closet with its own steel door opening into the concrete bunker.

Then Nicko looked down toward the floor and saw a hairline of light where the door met it.

He stood staring for a moment, then he eased the panel back into place and left the basement.

Upstairs, everyone appeared to be milling about as chaotically as before. Chancellor Eisner had officially recessed the conference for two weeks to allow for emergency repairs and the clarification of events and agendas, but few seemed in any hurry to leave the building.

In the conference room, Nicko saw Kate with a group of delegates and correspondents. He waited until he was able to catch her eye, then he went out onto the front lawn.

Kate joined him a moment later and he led her into the shadow of a towering linden.

"I believe I know where our friend Klaus is," he said.

"You mean he's in one piece?"

"I haven't actually seen him, but I can't imagine his being in any too great a condition."

Kate stared at Nicko. "I don't understand."

"At this point neither do I. But I'm going after him and I need your help."

Kate was silent.

"I'm sorry," he said. "I don't enjoy having to put you in this position again. So if you turn me down, it will be all right."

"No. It won't be all right. After all you've done for me, I could never feel easy with you again if I turned you down."

"Well, things do have a way of changing, don't they?" Nicko lit a cigarette and the tip flared in the darkness. "But then there's always your mercurial Paul Walters to take up some of the slack. Isn't there?"

Kate stood absolutely still. "How long have you known?"

"Only about twelve hours," said Nicko, who went on to describe how he had made the connection.

Kate said nothing.

"Does he know about your killing his parents?" Nicko asked.

Kate nodded.

"And, I assume, about me?"

"Yes."

"Sounds like a match made in heaven."

"Don't you mean hell?"

Nicko Vorelli's shrug was eloquent. "We don't really know that."

They stood staring at each other. The sky was turning lighter in the east but the night remained dark under the linden.

Kate broke the silence. "So what do you need me to do?"

They picked up the limousine where the chauffeur had left it hours before, and Nicko explained as much as he chose to tell Kate as he drove.

He made his first left turn about a kilometer past the main security checkpoint. He remembered the heavy woods closing in from both sides and began watching for the rough dirt trail where he would take the second left. Reaching that, he swung onto the next right-hand track and kept going straight.

He handed Kate a key. "There are two automatics and two silencers in the glove compartment. Would you please put them together for me?"

Kate did as he asked.

"Just a precaution," he said. "You needn't worry."

Kate put one automatic in her purse and gave the other to Nicko.

Moments later they spotted a black station wagon parked in the woods just off the trail. Nicko braked to a stop and cut the lights.

"Damn," he said softly.

"What does it mean?"

"Nothing I expected. Cover me."

Nicko drew his pistol and approached the station wagon. He was back in a moment. "It's empty," he said. "But it probably means someone is down there with Logefeld."

"Couldn't there be more than one?"

"That, too."

Nicko drove for another fifty yards, parked behind some brush, and got out of the car. "The entrance is only a short walk from here. If I'm not back in twenty minutes, leave fast."

"You said you needed my help."

"That was before I saw the car. I don't know what I'll find down there at this point."

Kate slid out. "You're breaking my heart, Nicko. Let's go."

It took them exactly ten minutes to reach, enter, and traverse the tunnel. At the metal door of the bunker they were able to hear the faint sound of radio voices.

Nicko put his eye to a keyhole and saw a man in a Wannsee guard's uniform sitting at a table with an automatic on it. Then he saw the lower torso and legs of another man lying on one of the bunks.

He let Kate look. "Do you know the man?" he whispered.

"No. But I'm pretty sure that's Klaus on the bunk."

Nicko waited another five minutes to see if anyone else became visible in the room. Then, counting on the radio to cover any slight sound a key might make, he eased Bruno's key into the lock and gently tried to turn it. The door was not locked.

"Stay about three paces behind me," Nicko whispered to Kate, and pushed into the room.

Daniel Archer stared at the silenced automatic suddenly pointing at his head and did not make a move. Then, seeing Kate coming in with another gun, he just shook his head in disgust.

"Terrific," he said.

Kate and Nicko saw that the figure stretched out on the bunk was in fact Klaus Logefeld. They saw, too, that crude bandages were wrapped across his chest and midsection and that he was unconscious. Kate stepped toward the table, picked up the pistol lying there, and put it in her purse.

Then she nodded toward the bunk. "How is he?" she asked in English.

"Alive, ma'am," said Archer. "But I don't think for long."

"Has he been conscious at all?"

"No, ma'am."

Keeping an eye on Archer, Kate crossed over to the bunk and felt for the pulse in Klaus Logefeld's carotid artery. It was very faint and his breath made a rasping sound in his throat.

Archer watched and said nothing. Nicko was looking at a tarpaulin in a corner. He lifted it and stared at a dead man with a bloody head. Turning to Archer, he let the covering fall. "You shot him?"

"Yes, sir."

"Why?"

"For the best reason in the world. *He* was going to shoot *me*."

Nicko sat down facing Archer. "Do you know who I am?"

"Yeah. You're Dr. Nicholas Vorelli."

"Who are *you?*"

"An American citizen. Daniel Archer."

"Let me see your passport and wallet."

Kate stood against a wall, her pistol leveled, as the exchange was made.

Nicko glanced briefly at Archer's diplomatic passport and other ID. "Who sent you?"

"No one. I'm here as a private citizen."

"To do what? Blow up your president and his wife?"

"No, sir. To try to rescue them."

"I would never have guessed it." Nicko's voice was dry ice.

Archer was silent.

"Better understand this, Mr. Archer," said Nicko. "There are just two things keeping you alive: my need for answers, and the chance you might be able to do me some good. So the moment I feel you're lying to me, I'm putting a bullet in your head. Is that clear enough?"

"Yes, sir," said Archer.

"Then suppose we begin again. Are you CIA?"

"No, sir. But I've done special jobs for the Company."

"And this was one of them?"

Archer nodded, his face washed clean of all expression.

"Who was your contact?"

"Someone using the code name of Sam. No one I knew."

"And your orders?"

The former soldier breathed deeply. "To waste everyone in the surveillance room."

"Including the president?"

"Yes, sir."

"And you had no idea where the orders originated?"

"No, sir." Then, seeing the doubt on Nicko's face: "That's pretty standard, sir. It's how they protect themselves."

Nicko and Kate exchanged glances.

"Who else knew about your mission?" asked Nicko.

"Sam had said no one. When I got here I found he'd given my German contact orders to pop me when it was done."

"That's your German contact under the tarp?"

"Yes, sir."

No one spoke. There was just the sound of Klaus Logefeld's breathing beneath the murmur of a twenty-four-hour news program. Listening, Kate learned that the president and his wife were currently undergoing surgery.

"For the record," said Daniel Archer, "I never did try to carry out Sam's orders. My own plan was to just knock out Mainz and the old man, save the Dunsters, and be a goddamn hero. I had the charge and its placement carefully figured. But something went wrong and all hell broke loose."

"What went wrong," said Nicko, "was that the professor had explosives of his own cached very close to where you set off yours."

Archer sat there, unbending. "I thought it might be something like that. But you say it like you're sure."

"I am sure. It was reported to me about a week ago."

"And you did nothing about it?"

"I have my own agenda, Mr. Archer." Nicko considered the man sitting so straight and controlled only minutes from probable death and was impressed. "How did you know about this tunnel and bunker?"

"Hans, my German contact, knew. He was your man Bruno's friend and was covering his back the night Bruno took you down here."

Nicko looked at Kate. "Any more questions for Mr. Archer?"

Kate edged away from the wall. "Just out of curiosity, Mr. Archer. Why weren't you at least a hundred kilometers from this place before we ever showed up?"

"Because I've been hoping Mainz might come out of it long enough to explain what went wrong." Archer looked accusingly at the still figure on the bunk. "And now it looks like he's never going to."

Kate followed Daniel Archer's glance, but she found nothing different in that direction. Then she realized that the faint, rasping sound of Klaus Logefeld's breathing had stopped.

Good-bye, Klaus, she thought.

"So you made a mistake, Mr. Archer," said Nicko.

"I've made them before, sir."

"Yes, but I'm afraid this one promises to be fatal."

The room fell silent.

"Unless . . ." Nicko said slowly, and paused. "Unless there might still be a way for you to do us all a lot more good alive than dead."

Chapter 64

By 1:00 A.M. WASHINGTON TIME, the deputy director of the CIA felt he had received just about all the officially sanctioned news he was going to get concerning the explosion at Wannsee.

He knew that Jimmy and Maggie Dunster were alive but critically injured, that Major Schadt was dead, and that Professor Mainz had somehow managed to disappear without a trace.

All this information had come to Harris at home via phone calls from Wannsee, from the White House, and from his own office in Langley, Virginia. Scattered fragments had even come from Jayson Fleming himself, and the pro tempore president had sounded increasingly tense with each call.

I'd better get over to him, thought Ken Harris.

But there were other things for the deputy director to learn about and deal with before he headed back to the Oval Office.

Using the secure phone he kept in a wall safe in his study, Harris called a private number in a suburb about twenty miles north of Berlin.

A man's voice answered in German.

"Foxcraft here," said the deputy director, also in German. "What have you got for me, Sam?"

"Nothing you don't already know," he said.

"You haven't heard from Hans?"

"I wasn't supposed to hear from him. Not unless there was some sort of problem."

"So we can assume he took care of what he had to do?"

"Yes, sir."

The deputy director hung up slowly.

So much for Danny Archer.

Unfortunately, before dying, Archer had failed to carry out his assignment at Wannsee with his usual efficiency. So that with it all, Jimmy Dunster was still alive.

The deputy director allowed himself a few moments to think it through. Then he hit the buttons on a second direct call to the Berlin area.

This time it was a woman who answered.

"Do you know who this is, Anna?" said Harris, speaking his well-practiced German.

"How could I not?" The answer was instant, without hesitation. "One doesn't forget dear old friends, Walter."

"You're very kind," the deputy director said. "But it's been so long since we've spoken."

"Not that long. How have you been?"

"Reasonably well," said Harris, going through the pre-scribed litany with the skill of a veteran field agent. "And you?"

"Never better."

"Delighted to hear that. Especially since I'm very much in need of some of your more exceptional talents."

There was an easy, very female laugh at the other end.

"You do know how to talk to a woman, Walter. Not many men really do. Now exactly when would you like to make use of these talents?"

"Immediately. Or at least as soon as possible."

"No problem. Just fill me in."

"This one is not that simple, Anna. Actually, you'll be dealing with a very close and very important friend of mine. He's been badly hurt and right now is in severe pain." Harris paused and could see her face in front of him, that mobile, mocking, I-know-the-cost-of-every-bargain survivor's face. "Perhaps you've heard something about the unfortunate incident in which he was a victim."

The line was silent for several beats.

"You mean the one that just happened during the night?" she said.

"Exactly."

"Yes, I've heard," said Anna. "It was all too distressing. What would you like me to do for your friend?"

"What you do best. The thing so few women have your talent for doing. I'd like you to ease the poor man's pain. One hates to see one's friends having to suffer."

Anna took her time in answering. "Are we talking easing your friend's pain," she finally said, "or eliminating it permanently?"

"Eliminating it permanently would be so much kinder. If you think that's possible."

"Everything is possible, Walter. You know that. It's just a matter of difficulty and cost."

"If you can handle the difficulty, I can deal with the cost."

"We're talking top-of-the-line here, dear friend."

"I understand."

"Lovely. Now can we be a bit more specific?"

"How about doubling your usual honorarium?"

"How about quadrupling it?"

Ken Harris laughed. "You're all heart, Anna. But why not? Good friends deserve the best. And there's no one better than you."

"Deposited in advance at the usual dead drop," she said.

"You've never asked for *that* before."

"You've never had so important and difficult to reach a friend before."

The deputy director sighed. "The cash will be at the drop within the hour. Good luck."

The White House had enough lights burning at 1:40 A.M. for either a national celebration or a state funeral. Sometimes it was hard to tell one from the other, thought Harris, leaving his limousine. And tonight's efforts could still end up going either way.

The pro tempore president was waiting for him in a small family parlor on the second floor. Entering the room, Harris saw that his friend seemed to have finally settled into his more controlled mode.

"I've just spoken with the head of the hospital," Fleming

told Harris. "Jimmy and Maggie are still in surgery. If Jimmy gets through that, they're giving him a better than even chance of making it all the way."

"So how does that make you feel?" the deputy director asked. "Worried or relieved?"

"A little of both. At least it's out of our hands."

"You'd rather leave it to God?"

"And the German surgeons." Fleming sat down facing his friend. "Either way, it requires no further action from us."

"And you like that?"

"I can live with it."

"Well, I can't," said Ken Harris.

The vice president looked at him. "What's your other choice?"

"Making sure Jimmy doesn't leave that hospital alive."

"What are you telling me? That you've arranged for that too?"

"Yes."

It took visible effort, but Fleming's control held. "I hope you've arranged it more effectively than you did the other."

Harris shrugged. "We can only do what we can."

"You don't think you can reach a point where it might be better to just do nothing and wait things out?"

"I really can't see anything better for us in Jimmy Dunster coming home alive. Remember what the great Machiavelli, in his infinite political wisdom, once said?" asked the deputy director of the CIA. "_He who establishes a dictatorship and does not kill Brutus . . . or he who founds a republic and does not kill the sons of Brutus, will only reign a short time._"

A bitter, cynically wise quote, thought Jayson Fleming. But of course Jimmy Dunster was not even near to being Brutus, no meager American vice president had yet to turn himself into anything resembling a dictator, and the greatest republic in history had been founded more than two hundred years ago and was still going strong.

Chapter 65

IT'S JUST THE TWO OF US NOW, thought Paulie Walters.

Or so it seemed to him.

The other person was no less than the president of the United States, currently an unconscious, gray-faced conduit for assorted plastic tubes carrying fluids in and out of his body.

Paulie and Jimmy Dunster were not alone, of course. A continuing stream of doctors and nurses eddied about them, hovering and whispering as they consulted charts as well as each other. Stationed in the corridor outside the recovery room was an approximation of the same contingent of American Secret Service agents and German security guards that had so thoroughly failed to protect the president less than thirteen hours earlier.

Along with me, thought Paulie, still unable to let go of his own portion of the blame for the entire catastrophe.

But at least I've kept him alive. He directed his thoughts to Jimmy Dunster, encouraging him to just keep breathing, desperately willing it. Tommy Cortlandt had begun describing it as an apparently growing compulsion to enter into some sort of psychic pact with the besieged soul and struggling life forces of Jimmy Dunster.

"What the devil has gotten into you?" the CIA director had asked after Paulie demanded special permission to remain inside the intensive care unit with the still unconscious president. "Why are you carrying on so obsessively with this?"

Paulie had looked at Cortlandt for a long time. "All I know is that I don't want this man to die."

"You're not making sense, Paulie."

"I want to be here when he wakes up. I want to be the one to let him know about his wife. But even more than that," Paulie had told him, "I've gotten to believe that this is a very special man because of what he tried to do in coming here, what it's cost him, and just for trying to fly so beautifully close to the sun. Let me stay with him, Tommy. You can do it."

The CIA director had leaned on a few people and did indeed do it.

Now, wearing a pale-green sterile mask, Paulie sat in a solitary chair in the ICU, listening to Jimmy Dunster's breathing and waiting for his body to decide whether it was going to live or die.

None of the doctors and nurses entering and leaving the room paid particular attention to him. Because they were told Paulie was to be left alone, he became invisible.

He thought very little about the outside world until a few questions intruded harshly enough to force him to seek answers.

He learned that since no part of Professor Mainz's body had been discovered, it was generally assumed that he was alive and at large somewhere.

He learned, too, that the previously announced conference recess had been extended to a full month. Too bad, thought Paulie, who had the depressing sense that the temporary break in the meeting might well turn out to be permanent.

As for Kate, he suddenly found it impossible to remember his last sight of her, until he recalled catching her eyes on him as he stood in the conference room, listening to the momentum build in favor of Klaus Logefeld's grand plan and feeling disgusted by his own pathetically selfish reaction.

Now he just wished he could get that feeling back.

"It's just the two of us now," he thought once more, but this time aloud, looking at the unconscious president.

Chapter 66

"FEELING A BIT BETTER about things, Mr. Archer?" asked Nicko Vorelli.

Daniel Archer looked at him, looked at the bright pastel interior of Nicko's Lear jet, carrying them through the morning sky. He looked at Kate Dinneson's exceptional face and body, and looked, finally, at the graceful crystal from which he was sipping what had to be the best champagne he had ever tasted.

"Better than I felt back in the tunnel," he said.

The ex-paratrooper's gaze was wary. He had been brought here at gunpoint and Kate Dinneson was still holding an automatic loosely in her lap.

"From what you told us earlier, Mr. Archer," said Nicko, "you haven't got much of a future if your code-name Sam's people ever catch up with you. Or am I wrong?"

"No, sir. You're not wrong."

"Then exactly what did you plan on doing if Kate and I hadn't come along when we did?"

"Change my name and face and disappear. But we don't have to play games," Archer said. "Since you didn't finish me back there in the tunnel, I guess you decided I can do you more good alive than dead after all. So why don't you just tell me what it is."

"Suppose we talk a little first, Mr. Archer."

"About what?"

"For one thing, about how you ever got involved with this whole lethal undercover crowd to begin with," said Nicko.

"I soldiered with a few of them way back in 'Nam."

"That long ago?" asked Kate. "You must have been a child."

"I lied about my age to get in, ma'am."

Nicko looked at him. "You were that much of a patriot?"

"Hell, I was fifteen goddamn years old. I was sure we were the good guys."

"And now?"

"Now I'm not sure of anything."

The plane hit a patch of turbulence and they sat quietly through it. Nicko watched the champagne tilt and sway in his glass. When it had steadied, he turned to Archer.

"We're going to be landing in Naples in about an hour and a half," he said. "If I were to wish you luck, and set you loose there, what would you do?"

"Probably what I said before. Just try to take off somewhere and disappear."

"How are you fixed for money?" Nicko asked.

"A few thousand in cash and some credit cards that could be traced."

"Considering your line of work," said Nicko, "I must say you haven't prepared very practically for this kind of emergency."

"If I were a practical man, sir, do you really think I'd have been in this line of work?"

Nicko laughed. "Probably not. But I must admit I'm delighted to find you this hard up. It's going to make it that much easier for us to get along."

"How do you figure that?" asked Archer.

"Because for any partnership to be successful, it has to be based on mutual need. You're alive this minute because of mutual need, Mr. Archer. Let me explain," he said. "I have an idea that will take someone with your expertise to help carry out. But I have to be able to trust you. So I plan to guarantee at least half of that trust with the promise of ten million dollars in cash, a new identity and surgically altered face, and the prospect of a long, comfortable life wherever you decide to live it."

Daniel Archer gave it time to settle over him. "And how do you plan to guarantee the other half of my trust?"

"With a few carefully placed audiotapes of our conversation in that Wannsee bunker. The whole idea is still new, so bear with me." Nicko glanced at Kate to include her. "It actually came to me down there in that tunnel, when Professor Mainz died and we three were the only ones alive who knew about it. I realized that as long as the rest of the world believe Mainz has escaped, we'd been gifted with an extraordinary opportunity to do things we would otherwise be unable to do."

"Like what?" asked Kate.

"Like whatever we decide," said Nicko.

Kate and Archer just stared at him.

"Remember whom we're talking about," Nicko continued. "A man who was close to having seven of the most powerful nations on earth about to follow his orders. And now, by a fortuitous act of fate, we're in a position to take over much of that same capability."

"How do we do that?" asked Archer.

"By pretending to be Professor Mainz."

"I'm afraid we'd only be paper tigers, sir," said Archer.

"Why?"

"Because we don't have the professor's leverage. We don't have any guns at the head of the president of the United States. And we certainly don't have Mainz's seven major buildings set to blow at the press of a switch." Archer paused. "Or do you think he was just bluffing about that?"

"No. He wasn't bluffing."

"How do you know?"

"The same way I knew he had those explosives cached near yours at Wannsee. I had him followed when he was placing the charges."

"And they're all still in place?" said Archer.

"I can't see why they wouldn't be. So all you would have to do would be to go in there and synchronize your own detonator with the explosives in each of the seven buildings, and we would be more than just paper tigers."

Nicko waited a full thirty seconds while he drank his champagne. "Do you think you might be interested in such a possibility, Mr. Archer?"

For the first time, Daniel Archer smiled.

Chapter 67

AT FIRST JIMMY DUNSTER thought he might simply be drifting in and out of sleep.

He floated on a soft, dark cloud, unable to move and not really caring. At times in the past he had felt himself stretched out under a sheet, a nameless oppression clogging his throat, and the illusion of strange faces hovering. So maybe this, too, was a partial dream, and he would wake and get on with his life.

But increasingly, he began to sense that this had nothing to do with dreams, and that the tubes he suddenly found connected to his arms and body were real, and the blinking lights of the monitoring equipment were real, along with a strange man in a sterile mask who appeared to be sitting in a chair and dozing.

All were real.

Perhaps most real of all was the fear of regaining clear awareness and knowing exactly where he was and what had happened to him.

For a while he just let himself drift in and out of consciousness. Once, through slitted eyes, he saw that the dozing man in the sterile mask was awake and staring at him. A young, lean-faced man, with the darkest, saddest eyes he had ever seen.

Who is he and why is he so sad?

Jimmy Dunster kept his eyes closed and his breathing regular. Feeling very sly and superior, he took several moments to orient himself.

He had a vision of the four of them in the surveillance room at Wannsee.

As a college student, he had once tried LSD, and those sensations were not too different from those he was experiencing now. When he was high everything had quivered with a brilliant light, rainbows curved across the ceiling, and a fine mist had fallen. In the surveillance room, Professor Mainz and the old man were at the closed-circuit television monitors, he and Maggie had been quietly talking against a far wall.

And after that?

Nothing. Not until now.

Where was Maggie?

Jimmy Dunster lay squinting through heavy-lidded slits, silently considering the young man's sad eyes. Then the president fully opened his own.

For several moments they just looked at each other. Then Paulie Walters took a long, slow breath, rose from his chair, and approached the bed.

"Mr. President," he said softly through his pale-green sterile mask.

Dunster opened his mouth and tried to speak. But there was only a low, rasping sound. He licked his lips and tried again. "Where . . . where's my wife?" he whispered.

Paulie's eyes blinked above the mask.

Dunster reached for and gripped Paulie's hand. He held it without strength.

"Where's my . . . Maggie?"

"There was an explosion, sir. No one seems to know more than that." Paulie hesitated. "Your wife is still breathing, still alive."

It sounded better than "comatose and all but dead." But the implication of the worst was still there.

Jimmy Dunster swallowed dryly. Then he moistened his lips with his tongue. "And the others?"

"The old man is dead. Professor Mainz simply disappeared."

Dunster stared blankly.

"There was just no sign of him afterward, Mr. President."

The pressure on Paulie's hand eased as Dunster drifted off.

* * *

It was a while before the doctors finished with the president and he was asleep again. Nurses moved in and out of the room, checking on his tubes and vital signs. Everyone appeared hopeful. Paulie simply sat there in his chair, waiting.

"Who . . . who are you?"

The president's voice was barely audible.

Paulie went over to the bed, and Jimmy Dunster took his hand again.

"I'm one of Tommy Cortlandt's people, Mr. President."

"Have we ever . . . met?"

"No, sir. But we did speak once on the phone. You were in the car with Tommy Cortlandt on the way to Wannsee. You wanted to know what I thought about Chancellor Eisner's opening remarks."

Dunster closed his eyes to focus his thoughts. "I remember. More diplomatic . . . and spiritual platitudes."

Dunster's eyes remained closed, and for a moment Paulie thought he might be drifting off in a morphine haze again. Then he saw the glistening on his cheeks and knew better.

"Dear God," the president whispered, "I've killed . . . my wife."

"Don't say that, sir. What you did in coming here, what you said when you spoke, moved everyone. Besides, your wife is *not* dead. Everyone is praying for her."

Jimmy Dunster's mouth trembled and his pale face seemed on the edge of breaking apart. Whatever force was left in him appeared to fade. Then just as visibly, Paulie saw him rally.

"Maggie never wanted me . . . to come."

The monitors hummed and bleeped.

"What about after she heard you speak?" Paulie asked. "After she saw how things were going in the conference room. What did she say then?"

"She thought maybe . . . I was . . ." Dunster's voice faded.

Paulie leaned closer. "She thought maybe you were what, Mr. President?"

"Jesus . . . Christ," Jimmy Dunster whispered.

Chapter 68

ABOUT AN HOUR AND A HALF after Deputy Director Harris's call to Anna in Berlin, she drove past an old Lutheran church on the Liebling Strasse and parked a short distance down the street. She left her car and walked back toward the church.

She was a shapely, fair-haired woman with a face most men looked at twice, and the easy, swinging walk of an athlete. When she was younger, she had been a promising world class tennis player until she became bored with the discipline and training required. Most things bored her. Her work, however, was *not* boring, nor were the sums of money she received for doing it.

The church was dark, cool, and all but empty as she entered it. Anna slid into a rear pew, knelt, and genuflected toward the altar.

Kneeling there, head bent, she groped for and found a loose board at the base of the row of benches directly in front of her. She pulled the board open, reached into the space behind it, and felt her hand touch a bulging shopping bag.

She didn't look inside the bag until she was back in the car and driving away. Then she gave it only a brief glance to be sure the bills were in United States currency.

Her first stop was at the north Berlin branch of the Reichsbank, where she kept a large safe-deposit box. In the privacy of her own cubicle, she packed five thousand dollars into her purse and placed the remaining ninety-five thousand in her box. Then she returned the box to the vault attendant and left the bank.

Driving toward the hospital, she reviewed the few details she knew so far.

All she had gotten from "Walter" were the bare bones. No more, in fact, than that her target was the president of the United States, that he was gravely injured, and that he was in a hospital Walter had been careful not to name.

News reports had given her the rest. So at this point she knew that the hospital was Holy Cross General on the outskirts of Berlin, that President Dunster had come out of surgery with his vital signs stable, and that he was being given a fair chance of recovery.

Anna had also learned that the explosion that had injured the president had left his wife near death and killed one of the two terrorists who had been holding them hostage. She could only assume that Walter had been responsible for all this as well. Another surprise. She had no great regard for American political patterns. For all their professed ideals and pious rhetoric, Americans were historically among the most violent people on earth. But for the deputy director of the CIA to arrange the murder of his own president was a new low, even for them.

Not that Walter had any idea that she knew his identity. She would have been terminated a long time ago had he known. They had never met and had communicated only by telephone. But Anna had once heard him speak on television; she had recognized his voice.

Anna was at Holy Cross General in fifteen minutes. Security was all over the lobby, along with a small army of reporters and photographers watching for possible VIPs.

Anna approached a photographer. "What's all the excitement?"

"The American president is upstairs," said the man.

"Really? Where?"

"Hoffman Pavilion. Seventh floor."

Going up in the elevator with four visitors and two uniformed nurses, Anna stood hugging her elbows and feeling herself tingling a little. One nurse and two of the visitors left the elevator with her on the seventh floor. Anna headed toward a nurses' station off to the right. Nearing it she paused, as if searching through her purse. She studied everything in sight, detailing the staff, the uniforms, the ID tags they wore and where they wore them, the bulletin boards with their announcements and duty rosters.

Continuing along the corridor, she noted the utility storage closets and men's and women's washrooms, the emergency exits and the stairways leading up and down from them, and a room marked Nursing Staff. She pushed open the door, found it empty, and quickly slipped inside.

When she came out a moment later, she had a rolled-up nurse's uniform, several blank ID tags, and a stethoscope stuffed into her shoulder bag.

Anna continued along the corridor. After about fifty meters she turned a corner.

A sign read Surgical Intensive Care. Just beyond the sign were four dark-suited security men. And beyond them, she thought, the ailing president.

Anna sat down among other visitors in an open waiting area. She took a paperback novel from her bag and pretended to read. After about an hour, she felt she had a pretty clear idea of what was going on and how things were being handled.

Rechecking her escape routes as she went, Anna left the hospital.

Chapter 69

GETTING DANIEL ARCHER OFF NICKO VORELLI'S PLANE and past customs in a remote section of the Naples airport was so stereotypically cloak-and-dagger that Kate Dinneson was almost amused.

The limousine followed the coast road toward Sorrento. Its passengers rode in silence. The afternoon sun lit the sea and colored the hills orange. Angelo, the driver, had been with Nicko Vorelli for so many years he might have been part of the steering column.

Half an hour later, they were passing through the villa's electronically guarded entrance gates.

Angelo drove about five hundred meters past the main house and parked beside a smaller, more intimate, eighteenth-century stone villa surrounded by hemlocks. He took the bags from the limousine's trunk and led the way inside.

Kate breathed the familiar aroma of furniture polish and fruit. She liked being here better than at the big villa. Nicko worked on special projects here when he needed privacy, and this was where he usually brought her when they were spending extra time together.

They were in a graceful, high-ceilinged room. Light and textured walls contrasted with dark, heavy furniture, beams, and paintings. It was all solid and tangible enough, yet Kate's mood was such that nothing seemed quite real—not the house or the men she was with, and especially not all that had happened at Wannsee.

Angelo appeared with glasses and a bottle of red wine on a tray. He drew the cork and poured some for Nicko, who tasted it and nodded his approval. Then Angelo filled the other two glasses and left the room.

"I'd like to read you something," said Nicko. "I jotted it down during our flight and it's still rough. I plan to fax it to a leading newspaper in each of the seven countries represented at Wannsee, with the request that it be run on the front page of their next edition."

Nicko paused to glance at his audience of two.

"This is an open letter from Professor Alfred Mainz," he read quietly.

"As of this writing, my grandfather, Major Helmut Schadt, is dead, the president and First Lady of the United States are lying close to death in a German hospital, and I myself must remain burrowed away like a hunted animal. I have no idea how or why any of this happened, or who was responsible.

"But perhaps the most tragic result of this senseless bombing is the loss of our brief hope for a quick end to the killing in Africa, along with our chance for a world with love and peace at its core. This is unforgivable.

"So I repeat the following warning to prevent any further loss of life. In each of the seven powers represented at the Wannsee Conference, a major building has been mined with high explosives. At exactly twelve noon, local time, of the day this notice appears in your newspaper, one of those seven buildings will be blown. I will announce which it will be just one hour before that time to allow for evacuation.

"Please understand. This is only to establish my credibility. The second building will be blown without advance warning and result in hundreds of needless casualties. That is, unless my conditions, which will be stated in advance, are agreed to within a specific time period.

"Do not test me. After what happened at Wannsee, I am angry, anguished, and desperate.

"Professor Alfred Mainz."

Nicko put down his notes and looked at Kate and Archer.

"Well?" he inquired. "What do you think?"

"How much of that do you really mean?" asked Archer.

"All of it."

"What are the conditions you'll want agreed to before the second building is blown?" asked Archer.

"To begin with, a very substantial amount of cash. So that none of us will ever have to worry about money again."

"What would you call a 'substantial amount'?"

"A hundred million. American. We're dealing with seven major economic powers," said Nicko. "Any less would be demeaning."

Archer nodded gravely. "I wouldn't want to demean anyone."

"And after the money?" asked Kate. "What would be next?"

Nicko sipped his wine. "What do *you* think I'd be asking for?"

"Just about the same things Alfred Mainz wanted."

"You really believe I'd be that concerned about peace in Africa and saving us all from each other?"

"I *know* you would. Especially after you have all the money you'll ever need."

Nicko laughed and turned to Daniel Archer. "What about *you*? Once you have your money, how would you feel about pushing for the rest of Mainz's package?"

"To be honest, I'm afraid I'm long past all that good guy, save-the-world stuff."

"None of us are long past anything, Mr. Archer. Not until we die."

"That's another thing. The dying. What you're talking about could be very dangerous."

"And you've never done anything dangerous before?"

"Not with ten million in my pockets. I'm getting to feel being rich could make dying very hard for me."

"Then maybe we'd better think about making you poor again."

"Not even as a joke, sir."

*   *   *

Kate and Nicko were upstairs an hour later, unpacking.

"We're going to have to do a little talking about your friend," he said.

Kate did not bother to ask which friend.

"Are you in love with him?" Nicko asked.

Kate nodded. "Yes."

"When did you last see him?"

Kate considered. "Right after the explosion. When he carried the president out to the ambulance and rode off with him."

"He won't start worrying about you? Wondering where you are?"

"He'll know if he can't reach me at home that I'm probably here with you."

"That won't bother him?"

Kate shrugged. "He understands what you've been to me all these years."

"That's not what I asked."

"I would hope he could live with it."

"And if he can't?" Nicko asked.

"I'll deal with it then. But I'm sure that's a long way off."

"Don't be so sure. It could be sooner than you expect."

His eyes dark, searching, Nicko Vorelli took Kate's hands in his. "You do know why I have to ask you these things, don't you?"

"Of course. Because of all you're about to slide into with the rising of our newly sainted Klaus Logefeld. Although I can't say I know what my own part is going to be."

"Neither can I," said Nicko. "Other than that I'm going to need someone I can trust with my own and a lot of other lives." His gaze held steady on Kate's. "Unless I'm presuming too much and you really want no part of this whole thing."

Kate Dinneson realized that she had been preparing all her life for this moment.

"You're not presuming too much, Nicko."

"I appreciate that."

Moved by something in his voice, Kate stood silently in front of Nicko Vorelli.

"So how do you feel right now?" he asked.

"About what?"

"Everything you've just agreed to."

"I think I feel very glad you're holding my hands."

"Why?"

"Because otherwise I'm afraid they'd be shaking so hard they might fly off."

Nicko smiled. "Understandable."

"And do you know what else I feel very glad about?"

"No."

"That you're not going after only the money."

This time Nicko laughed aloud. "You do insist on ennobling me, don't you?"

"Not at all," Kate said. "That's something you always seem to end up doing for yourself."

Chapter 70

AT 2:30 A.M. in the upstairs family parlor of the White House, the pro tempore president Jayson Fleming was staring at his hands when his wife walked into the room.

He rose slowly. "What's wrong?"

Amy Fleming stood looking at him, a slender, delicately made woman. Her makeup was freshly and expertly applied and she had not a hair out of place.

Even in the middle of the night, Fleming thought.

"What's wrong," she answered, "is that I should have been right here with you through every second of this nightmare, and I wasn't. Why in God's name do I listen to you? You're never right about these things."

"Amy—"

But she was on him before he got any further than her name. All he seemed able to do was embrace her in a drowning, confusing, clutching bear hug that startled them both.

When he finally pulled away, he saw tears in her eyes and felt his own eyes mist over as Amy studied him.

"What's happened?" she said.

His knees abruptly weak, Jayson Fleming settled onto a couch and sat his wife down beside him. "Everything bad," he said. "The worst."

"No." Her voice was a whisper. "Jimmy's gone?"

Fleming shook his head. "Not yet. But it's going to be soon."

"That's not what I heard. All the reports say he's conscious and improving. It's Maggie who's probably going to die."

"Forget the reports."

Amy stared at him. "What are you trying to tell me?"

"Nothing."

"Talk to me, Jay. That's what I'm here for. That's what I should have been here for from the beginning."

The pro tempore president put his head in his hands for a moment. Then he raised his face. "How well do you think you know me?"

"After thirty-nine years? Better than anyone else alive."

"And you still care about me?"

Amy looked to see if he was serious. He was. "More than ever."

He was silent.

"What is it, Jay?"

"What if I told you I've done something so terrible, so ghastly, that it disgusts even me?"

She thought about it. "Maybe I'm being naive, but I don't believe you have it in you to do anything like that."

"Everybody has it in them." Anger had entered his voice. "It's just a question of not giving in to it."

"Then I don't believe you would give in to it."

"Jesus, you *are* naive. Because I must tell you. I *have* given into it. And to a degree that even I would never have imagined possible."

"What have you done, Jay?"

"Two things," said Jayson Fleming dully. "First, I knew about yet did nothing to prevent Jimmy Dunster from almost being blown to bits by that bomb at Wannsee. And second, I again know about, yet am doing nothing to stop, another attempt on his life that's about to take place at the hospital."

"I hear what you're saying," Amy replied, speaking with effort. "But I can't conceive of it being true."

"Yes you can."

Watching his wife's face, Fleming saw the whole poisonous truth gradually take hold inside her.

"Oh, God," she said.

She glanced around slowly at the small White House parlor in which they were sitting.

"You wanted all this *that* badly?"

"You know I did."

She nodded tiredly, as if this knowledge alone made her an accessory before the fact. "But how could you?"

"When it came down to it, it wasn't all that difficult."

Fleming sat unmoving for a moment, his eyes shut.

"The thing was," he said, opening his eyes, "once the idea was suggested, I didn't have to do a damn thing except let events take their course. I mean not a *thing*. Not a call made. Not an order given. I don't know whether it makes it better or worse, but I'm certain that if some specific action had been required of me, this whole abomination would have died unborn."

"I assume we have your blessed friend Ken to thank for all this."

Jayson Fleming did not answer.

His wife's gray eyes were cold. "Talk about snakes in Eden."

"Washington is nobody's Eden, Amy. There are no innocents in this town. Least of all *me*. And Ken never put a gun to my head. All I had to do was say no."

Amy took one of Fleming's hands in both of hers. She half turned toward him on the couch. "Why can't you still say no?"

Fleming looked at her.

"It's probably too late to do anything for Maggie," she said. "But Jimmy is still very much alive. Why can't you just tell Ken you've changed your mind and want him to call off the rest of it?"

"You're assuming I *want* the rest of it called off."

"I *have* to assume that," Amy said.

"Why?"

"Because I can't believe either one of us would be able to live with your *not* calling it off." Amy paused. "I certainly know *I* couldn't."

He looked down at her two hands, holding his, and said nothing.

"Besides," she said, "if you didn't want to save whatever remains of your own soul by backing out of what you yourself described as 'this whole abomination,' why did you tell me about it at all?"

"It's too late for Ken to call it off," he finally said. "The order has already gone down and there's no fail-safe button to hit."

"Then do it yourself. Call security at the hospital. Tell them you've been anonymously warned of another attempt on the president's life. Tell them you want Jimmy secretly moved."

Fleming's eyes were hooded. "It's not that simple. If I bypass Ken Harris on this I could be opening up a whole new can of worms."

"What is it? Are you afraid of the man?"

"Don't you think I should be?"

"What I think," Amy said quietly, "is that you should be a lot more afraid of quietly sitting still for the murder of the president of the United States."

The vice president's eyes turned gloomy.

"You're wasting precious minutes," said his wife. "If you don't move now, you could lose your one chance to save three lives. Jimmy's, yours, and mine."

Moments later Jayson Fleming had Tommy Cortlandt on the phone in Berlin.

Chapter 71

"PAULIE?"

Red-eyed, unshaven, and still in yesterday's clothes, Paulie Walters glanced toward the doorway of the intensive care unit and saw Tommy Cortlandt beckoning to him.

It was just past 9:00 A.M. Berlin time, and the hospital staff had finished the president's early-morning ministrations. Now Jimmy Dunster was dozing fitfully

Paulie rose stiffly from his chair, left the room, and joined the CIA director, who waited a short distance down the corridor from the morning shift of U.S. Secret Service agents and German police.

"How is he doing?" asked Cortlandt.

"Fine. As long as he's asleep."

"And when he's awake?"

"Mostly he asks if his wife is officially brain dead yet, and wishes *he* were."

"Listen," said Cortlandt. "I just had a call from the vice president. He's very upset. He's heard something about another try at Dunster and he wants him moved at once."

"To where?"

"Someplace where every crazy in the world doesn't know precisely where he is and how to get at him."

"You mean to another hospital?"

"That would be unnecessary and dangerous. I'm keeping him right here in this one, but in a completely different section. Only involved staff will know where that is."

"Are you going to add security?"

"I'm loading the hospital with agents, but not too visibly, not so the president will be easy to locate. There'll be two disguised agents in the corridor supply closet, outside his room, plus four more in two opposite rooms, looking like patients. You'll be Jimmy Dunster's roommate."

They started back along the corridor.

"Is this a real threat?" asked Paulie. "Or just another nervous rumor?"

"They're all real threats. Until they're not. Especially when they're called in by the pro tempore president of the United States."

To Paulie, it seemed to go off with the brisk, clean efficiency of a well-planned military operation.

At exactly 9:45 A.M., all corridor and elevator traffic between room 714 of the Hoffman Pavilion and room 561 of the Allstein Pavilion was halted at both ends for just seven minutes while President Dunster was being moved on a wheeled stretcher from one room to the other.

Paulie walked close beside him.

"Where . . . are they taking me?" Jimmy Dunster said.

"New quarters, Mr. President."

"Someone still trying to . . . blow me away?"

"Don't even think such things, sir."

"I wish him . . . luck."

The small group and their patient entered a waiting elevator.

Then they were down on the fifth floor and moving along another long, empty corridor with its doors closed on both sides.

They reached room 561 of the Allstein Pavilion without passing another person.

Inside the room, Jimmy Dunster's plastic tubes were attached to the same assortment of monitoring, breathing, and feeding devices to which they had been connected in his previous unit.

A bearded doctor checked his patient's charts and vital signs.

Paulie removed his clothes and put on a hospital gown and robe that were the same pale green color as his sterile mask. Then he took two 9-millimeter automatics out of their holsters, slipped one into a pocket of his robe, and placed the other under the pillow of the second bed in the room.

When the doctor and nurses left, Paulie stretched out on the bed and briefly closed his eyes. Then he opened them and lay there, waiting.

Five feet away, the president slept.

Chapter 72

COMING IN OUT OF THE SUN'S GLARE, Anna took a moment to adjust her eyes to the duller light of Holy Cross General's lobby.

Little seemed to have changed since her earlier visit. Maybe there were fewer reporters and photographers, inasmuch as President Dunster's death now appeared less imminent. But the number of posted guards seemed the same, along with the subdued air of bustle.

The big change was in Anna herself.

In a clean, freshly pressed white uniform, she was a prettier version of several hundred other nurses on the hospital's huge staff.

She wore a seniority badge pinned to her uniform, the gold pin of a nursing society, and an official Holy Cross nametag that identified her as Ilsa Stein.

Walking leisurely, she started toward the elevators that would take her up to the seventh floor of the Hoffman Pavilion.

She passed several nurses wearing the same uniform she had on. They nodded and half smiled, and she nodded back. *The sisterhood.*

The first hint of possible trouble struck Anna when she had left the elevator on the seventh floor, turned a corner, and did not see the four dark-suited security men who had been posted there last time.

Reaching room 714, she glanced in and saw that it was empty and that the bed had been stripped of its sheets.

Hurrying out of the corridor, Anna took an elevator down to a large, well-lit basement cafeteria. She picked up a mug of black coffee and settled herself at an empty corner table that offered a good view of the place and everyone entering or leaving it.

Why had they suddenly moved the president?

Going over the question calmly, Anna could see only two reasons for the move. One, of course, was medical. The other would have had to do with security. She was in no position to ask questions of anyone in a position to offer answers.

So she would just have to be patient, take whatever time might be required, and do it the hard way.

During her first visit, while sitting for over an hour in the ICU waiting area, she had carefully studied every nurse and doctor who entered the president's room. It was an old discipline that had not only helped her recognize key individuals on other assignments, but had once actually saved her life.

What Anna hoped to do now was simply to sit here until she saw some member of President Dunster's medical team enter the cafeteria on a break, and then follow when that person left.

This was the only place to eat in the hospital.

All she had to do was keep her eyes open, drink her coffee, and wait.

An hour later a young, dark-haired nurse with an even-featured face and a large mole high on her right cheek walked into the cafeteria. Anna remembered the mole.

The nurse sat down with a sandwich, a diet cola, and a copy of *Der Spiegel*. She barely glanced up from her food and magazine for twenty minutes.

When she finally rose and left the cafeteria, Anna was a short distance behind her.

They entered an elevator along with a few others and got out on the fifth floor. From there, they walked through busy corridors and passed a sign that read Allstein Pavilion. Anna kept a full twenty-meter interval between them. She extended it farther as she saw her guide stop at a nursing station.

Come on.

Anna leaned against a wall, pretending to read a notice.

At the nursing station, she picked out two doctors and another nurse whom she recognized as having been in and out of the president's old ICU.

She was in the right place.

But where were the missing security guards?

Anna watched the two doctors and one of the nurses leave the station, head farther down the corridor, and disappear into a room on the left.

From the way the room numbers ran, it figured to be room 561. Farther along the corridor, a couple of white-uniformed orderlies were casually unloading a wheeled cart into a large linen and general supply room.

They were clearly security guards.

Chapter 73

HERE I GO AGAIN, thought Kate Dinneson.

She felt the same excitement, anticipation, and fear she had felt immediately before her last nocturnal break-in.

It was a few minutes before 1:00 A.M. Naples time when Kate made her move, leaving her car in a twenty-four-hour permit-parking area and walking two short blocks to the small, four-story office building she was about to enter.

There was no security guard on duty, the alarm system was simple enough to neutralize, and Kate was able to pick open a rear basement door in less than five minutes.

Climbing a single flight of stairs, Kate was in the sprawling, floor-wide offices of the Neapolitan Commercial Real Estate Company.

She saw row upon row of matching desks, computers, and all the very latest in electronic communications equipment.

No fumbling and wasting of time, she warned herself. This had to be done quickly and efficiently. She had to be out of here before the location could be checked out and acted upon.

With only a small flash for light, Kate moved about until she had spotted the eight fax machines she would need for the almost simultaneous transmissions she was to make.

She took a manila envelope from her bag and removed eight copies of the open letter that Nicko had typed above the name of Professor Alfred Mainz.

Moving fast, she slipped a copy of the letter into the slot of each of eight fax machines, punched in the previously determined fax numbers for the seven managing editors of the leading newspapers in New York, London, Paris, Berlin, Ottawa, Tokyo, and Rome, and added an eighth number for the bureau chief of the International News Service in Washington.

Hurrying from one to the other, she hit the send button on all the machines.

The eight copies were transmitted in just under fifty seconds.

Seven minutes later, Kate left the building through the same basement door through which she had entered.

At about the same time that Kate was driving back to Sorrento from Naples, Daniel Archer was flying into Rome's Leonardo da Vinci Airport on Nicholas Vorelli's private jet.

It was raining as they landed, and a man with an umbrella was waiting for Archer as he deplaned. The man escorted him to a gray Mercedes parked less than fifty feet away on the apron.

I could get used to this, he thought.

Swinging his attaché case into the front passenger seat, Archer slid behind the wheel and headed for Rome.

At 2:25 A.M. he entered the lobby of the Del Guardo Building, whose many international brokerage and currency-trading tenants were open for business around the clock.

Carrying his executive attaché case, he walked past a pair of uniformed security guards, signed in as a visitor to the offices of the Provident Asset Management Corporation, and took one of many self-service elevators to the third floor.

From there, Archer slipped unobserved through an emergency fire exit and down five flights of steps to a utility area in a vast sub-basement. He heard equipment humming. There was no one in sight and the entire area was as brightly lit as a ballroom. Then he checked the schematic that Nicko had given him and moved on.

No dislocation in the heavens tonight, Daniel Archer thought, and sensed that everything was going to go smoothly—that the schematic would prove itself accurate down to the final square inch, and that he would do his own part as sweetly as he had ever done anything in his life.

Confidence. When you had it you had it, and it was like waltzing with the angels.

So it came as no real surprise when he worked loose the designated ceiling panel above the number 2 emergency generator and saw a great cache of *plastique* squeezed up there among the pipes, studs, and beams, all that tremendous explosive force just waiting to be fused and armed.

Which Archer now proceeded to do, calmly opening up Dr. Nicholas Vorelli's beautiful leather attaché case and taking out the required fuses, detonators, wires, and battery-powered clocks, and setting up two of everything just to have a backup circuit ready in case something went wrong with the first.

Checking the time, Archer set both circuits to detonate at noon, exactly nine hours and twenty minutes away.

He tightened a final connection, went over each step once more in his mind, and replaced the ceiling panel so perfectly that it was all but invisible as a separate unit. Then he counted his tools and leftover material as he returned them to the attaché case. Nine pieces out, nine pieces back in.

Everything was in order. It had to be. Tonight he could do no wrong. His clocks silently tracked the time.

Chapter 74

AT 2:40 A.M. Holy Cross General was bathed in an almost mystical, haunted quiet.

In room 561 of the Allstein Pavilion, President Jimmy Dunster's patched-together body drifted in drugged sleep. He was dreaming his wife came to visit him, but when he reached for her with miraculously tube-free arms, he awoke alone.

He must have been moaning, because he heard the young man in the other bed softly asking him something. Dunster didn't answer.

"Are you all right, Mr. President?"

Paulie Walters's question was louder now, more insistent, and this time Jimmy Dunster answered.

"No. I'm not . . . all right," he murmured.

"Do you want a doctor or a nurse, sir?"

"They . . . can't help me."

Paulie was silent. He studied the pink-and-white glow of the monitors on the ceiling.

"Beating yourself can't help either, Mr. President," he said finally. "That only makes it worse."

"How . . . can anything make it worse? If you licked . . . my heart . . . it would . . . poison you."

Then Jimmy Dunster's drugs, being more forgiving than his heart, let him drift off again.

Anna entered the fifth-floor corridor of the Allstein Pavilion at 3:04 A.M. dressed in her starched nurse's uniform.

For added authenticity, she had draped a stethoscope about her neck and carried a tray of medical material covered by a clean white cloth.

She had entered through an emergency door at the east end of the pavilion, which allowed her to approach room 561 without having to pass either the nursing station or the elevators.

Alone in the corridor, Anna moved quickly and silently on rubber-soled shoes. She slowed as she neared the open doorways of the two rooms directly opposite the president's closed door. Passing them on a practice run earlier, she had spotted the four Secret Service agents posted inside; two in each room. Their hospital gowns disguised nothing. Seen naked, they could not have been anything but what they were. The two guards disguised as orderlies were out of sight at the moment in the supply room. Their cart was still in the corridor.

She paused just before reaching the first of the two open doorways. Holding the tray with her left hand, she unfolded the cover cloth with her right.

Two pistols lay side by side. One was a 9-millimeter automatic lengthened by a silencer. The other weapon fired instant-acting tranquilizer pellets that could put out a two-hundred-pound man for a full half hour. Anna took pains never to kill unnecessarily. Not for any heavenly rewards; it was just her way.

When she felt herself ready, Anna moved into the first room so quickly that neither of the two men inside were aware of her. Until the soft hiss of the tranquilizer gun's initial firing caused the agent sitting in a chair to glance up from his newspaper.

His partner, reclining on his bed and caught squarely in his chest by the pellet, was unconscious before he could glance anywhere.

The man in the chair was still trying to understand what was happening when a second pellet put him out.

Start to finish, the entire action had taken precisely eight seconds.

Anna looked across the corridor at room 561. The two times she had walked past it the door had been closed. It remained shut.

She took four quick steps to the next open doorway and ducked in. The two Secret Service agents sat in chairs facing her. They had magazines in their hands. One rose instantly, reaching for his holster. Anna fired a pellet and he dropped back into his chair. His partner was dozing over his magazine and Anna put him out before he awoke.

That left just the president's room and the guards in the supply room.

One problem with the president's situation was that since Anna had never been able to look inside room 561, she had no way of knowing what she would find when she opened the door. Would there be two men guarding the president, or just one? If there were two, where would they be positioned, and which man would it be best to hit first?

In her favor, of course, would be their initial impression of her as a legitimate staff nurse coming in to treat her patient. By the time they saw her piece, she would have them both down. Then she would simply finish the president and be gone.

First she had to knock out the two guards in the supply room.

They were sitting on folding chairs, talking, when she walked in and squeezed off two more pellets. The men glanced up but never saw anything more than her breasts.

Chapter 75

EVERY SILENCE HAS ITS OWN PITCH, and the less than perfect silence in room 561 was no exception.

Paulie Walters lay on his hospital bed listening to it. He heard the faint hum of Jimmy Dunster's monitors along with his heavy breathing. He heard the sigh of an air conditioner and the gurgle of plumbing between the walls. He heard a metallic click that seemed to come from somewhere along the corridor.

A door latch, Paulie thought.

But surely not here.

As part of his own personally instituted security measures, no one—not doctors, nurses, not even the Secret Service—were to so much as turn the knob on the president's door without first knocking and identifying themselves to Paulie.

Then the door abruptly opened without either a knock or an identifying voice and he saw a tall fair-haired nurse enter the room.

The nurse was carrying a tray and for a moment she and Paulie locked eyes above it.

"Weren't you told to knock and . . ."

Paulie never finished the question. He glimpsed a pistol coming from the tray in the nurse's hand and dived off the bed, hands stretching but not quite able to make it to the gun itself, reaching only the near edge of the tray. He knocked it upward just as the first, soft, hissing shot from the tranquilizer gun went off, deflecting the pellet into the ceiling.

Paulie's body hit the nurse and took her down with the gun still in her hand, trying for another shot at him. He grabbed her wrist and twisted until the weapon fell free. The woman was surprisingly strong. They lay on the floor squirming together like two lovers, looking into each other's eyes.

Anna spat straight into Paulie's face and kneed him hard in his groin. Paulie gasped. Enough, he thought.

Drawing back his fist, he slammed it into the side of her jaw and felt her go limp under him.

Off to his right, he heard the president murmur something.

Paulie glanced toward Jimmy Dunster's bed and saw him staring down at them.

"What . . . are you doing, son?" Dunster whispered. "Fucking . . . my goddamn . . . nurses?"

Paulie managed a faint smile. "Not this one, sir."

Then grabbing some surgical tape, Paulie bound and gagged the unconscious woman and lifted her onto his bed. He checked her weapons and saw that the pistol she had been aiming at him fired only tranquilizer pellets. The other piece, obviously intended for the president, was a 9-millimeter automatic with a silencer.

Great. An assassin with scruples.

Paulie saw the president watching him. "I'll be back in a minute, sir. There are things I have to do."

"You mean . . . besides save . . . my idiot . . . life?"

Paulie looked at him.

"Don't worry," said the president. "I . . . appreciate it."

The man was definitely getting better, thought Paulie, and crossed the corridor to check on the six Secret Service agents.

No surprises. At least they were alive.

Using a phone in one of the security rooms, Paulie woke Tommy Cortlandt at his hotel. "Everything is all right," he told the CIA director. "But you'd better get down here fast with some fresh people."

"Another try?"

"Yes."

Cortlandt grunted. "I'll be there in twenty minutes."

Paulie got in touch with the chief of nursing, sketched in the bare facts, and swore her to silence. One good thing about Germans. They carried out orders.

Tommy Cortlandt arrived with six new agents and had them take over the president's security.

Only then did Paulie bring Anna into a prepared room at the far end of the corridor. He took the CIA director in with them and closed the door. Anna was conscious but still bound and gagged as Paulie sat her in a chair.

"Who is she?" asked Cortlandt.

"You know as much as I do," answered Paulie. "I gagged her while she was out and kept it that way. I wanted you with me on this from her first word."

Staring at Anna, Cortlandt was silent.

Paulie removed her gag, wiped a spot of dried blood from the corner of her mouth, and stepped back.

"What's your name?" he asked in German.

"Anna." She stared at both men—Paulie, still in his hospital gown and robe, and Cortlandt, dark-suited and distinguished. "And you two gentlemen?" Her reply was in good English.

"This is Mr. Tom Cortlandt," said Paulie, switching to English. "And I'm John Hendricks."

Anna turned to Cortlandt. "I thought I recognized you, sir. The director himself. I'm honored." Her voice was mocking. "Now if I can just have a drink of water," she said, "and my hands untied, perhaps we can start talking."

Paulie freed Anna's wrists while Cortlandt brought a glass of water from the bathroom. Then they watched as she rubbed some circulation back into her hands and carefully sipped her water.

"All right, who are you?" said the CIA director.

"No one as important as you, Mr. Director. Although I was once a better than fair tennis player until I got bored."

"And now?"

Anna gravely contemplated the question. "Now I just do

everything possible to avoid growing bored enough to blow my brains out."

"Is that the reason you were going to kill the president?" said Paulie.

"It was *one* of the reasons, Mr. Hendricks."

"And the others?"

"There really was only one other. A hundred thousand dollars."

Paulie and Cortlandt exchanged glances.

"You sell the president pretty cheaply," said Cortlandt.

"I'm only a poor German girl, Mr. Director. A hundred thousand seems a lot to me. What should I have asked?"

"At least five million."

Anna stared at Cortlandt. "Seriously?"

"Very seriously. So who paid you the hundred thousand, Anna?" Paulie asked.

Anna's jaw had swollen, making her smile crooked. "Please don't rush things, Mr. Hendricks. That information is all I have left to sell. So let's talk a little business first."

Tommy Cortlandt pulled up a chair and sat down knees to knees with her. "You may not have killed anyone," he told her, "but you're still facing up to forty years for intent. So let's also bear *that* in mind."

"How could I forget it, Mr. Director? But if you don't find out fast who was behind these first two attempts on the president's life, there'll be more. And the next one could succeed."

"*Two* attempts?"

"That explosion at Wannsee was no accident. It was only supposed to look that way so it could be blamed on Professor Mainz's carelessness and not the true assassin. But you can judge that for yourself when you hear who hired *me*."

"Are you implying we know this person?" said Cortlandt.

Anna sipped her water as though it were the finest brandy. "I am."

"All right, Anna," said Cortlandt. "What are you looking for from this?"

"What are you offering me, Mr. Director?"

"Depending upon what you finally give us, I think I can safely promise you no worse than your usual boredom."

"No prison term at all?"

"That's correct."

"Plus the five million you've just convinced me the president's life is worth?"

Paulie had to struggle to keep a straight face.

Cortlandt gaped at the woman. "Don't push it, Anna."

Anna shrugged. "Then President Dunster will probably be dead within days, I'll be in prison for the next forty years, and you'll be remembered as the cheapskate who bargained away the life of the world's most powerful leader."

No one spoke for a full half minute.

It was Paulie who finally said, "Come on, Tommy. Her performance alone has to be worth the money."

"And if she's playing us like a couple of hooked fish?"

"Then you toss her to the German cops and let her sue for the five million." Paulie studied the bulge on Anna's jaw where his fist had landed. "But my gut feeling is that we're going to get our money's worth."

Tommy Cortlandt turned to Anna. "All right, *Fraulein*. You've got it. Now let's hear what you have for us."

Anna looked at them. "The man we're talking about is your own deputy director. Ken Harris."

"That doesn't make sense," said Cortlandt. "Why would a high-ranking intelligence officer put his life in the hands of a contract assassin who could identify him anytime something went wrong?"

"Mr. Harris has no idea I know who he is."

"How is that possible?" asked Paulie.

"Because we've only talked by phone. It wasn't until I saw him interviewed on TV that I recognized his voice."

"But what's his motive?" Cortlandt inquired.

"You two gentlemen would know that better than I. How could Mr. Harris have benefited if the president died at Wannsee?"

"By getting my job after I got fired," the director said

dryly. "But that's hardly a driving reason to murder a head of state."

"What about the vice president?" said Anna. "Could there be any possible connection *there?*"

"Absolutely not."

"How can you be so sure?"

"Because it was *his* warning about another attack that probably just saved the president's life."

"It also could have been his cover," said Anna.

Cortlandt shook his head. "And I thought *I* was cynical."

"We're way ahead of ourselves," said Paulie. "At the moment we just have a failed assassin's word for all this. Where's the hard evidence?"

The two men looked at Anna.

"Give me a little slack," she said, "and I'll get it for you."

Chapter 76

KATE DINNESON WOKE to a bright sun, the sound of a man's voice, and thoughts that opened a grave in her stomach.

This was the day.

Then she saw Nicko Vorelli staring at the ceiling from another bed, and she remembered why she was here.

The sun was real enough. But the man's voice was that of a news commentator coming from a radio clock that Nicko had set to go off at exactly eight o'clock.

"Are you awake?" asked Nicko.

"Sort of."

"We're the lead item. He's coming to us now. Listen."

"Professor Alfred Mainz not only appeared to be alive and well," declared the commentator, "but was threatening a reign of terror if his soon to be announced conditions were not met."

The countdown had started.

The first building would be destroyed in any one of seven possible countries at exactly twelve noon, local time, today.

An hour before the deadline, the actual target would be named to allow for evacuation.

The commentator pressed on, but Kate had shut him out.

"Nicko?" she said.

He switched off the radio and half turned toward her. "Yes?"

"What if they don't give you what you want?"

"Considering the alternatives, how could they not?"

"I don't know. But what if they don't?"

"Then I'll do whatever they force me to do."

"Even though hundreds might die?"

"Even so."

Kate's fears turned her cold. "I don't know if I'd be able to stand up to random killing on principle, Nicko."

"Do you think *I'd* enjoy it?"

"No."

"Then what do you suggest I do if they force it? Back off?"

"I don't know, Nicko."

"Do you think your friend Klaus would have backed off?"

Kate shook her head. "No."

"Yet at the end you were rooting for him, weren't you?"

"I was rooting for the good he was trying to do. Not for the rest."

"And if there's no getting one without the other?"

Kate again ducked the question. "Klaus was a zealot. You called him that yourself. I guess I'm not."

"Neither am I, Katie. Yet I've cursed myself for not having the guts to be one."

Nicko took one of his cigarettes from a night table and lit up.

"Listen to me," he said. "I honestly don't believe they're going to be stupid enough to force a bloodbath no one wants. But if it ever does come to that, I promise to cut you loose before it happens."

Kate did not believe him for a second.

Daniel Archer left his hotel near the Piazza di Spagna at 10:45 A.M.

He walked a short distance to a public pay phone in a bustling shopping area and put through a call to the Emergency Service Division, police headquarters, city of Rome.

"Sergeant Giotti," said a man's voice.

"I'm going to say this only once, Sergeant," said Archer, speaking in Italian through a bunched handkerchief. "This is Professor Alfred Mainz. At precisely noon today, the Del Guardo Building on the Via Tuscana will be destroyed by a powerful explosion. You have just one hour to sound the alarm and see that the building is evacuated. This call is being recorded as evidence that you received warning."

Daniel Archer hung up and started to walk in the direction of the Del Guardo Building. He walked briskly but with seeming casualness, a calm, quiet-faced man who tried never to call attention to himself.

He heard the first sirens going off in the distance after no more than six or seven minutes. They grew louder as he walked.

By eleven-thirty the streets immediately surrounding the Del Guardo Building were being cordoned off by the police, with traffic detoured into a horn-honking maze of confusion. In places, fire equipment and ambulances jumped curbs and sped along sidewalks. *Carabinieri* were shouting instructions through bullhorns, but few paid attention.

Waving a press pass, Archer worked his way through the police barricades and crowds until he saw the site itself.

People were streaming from the building's exits and being shunted into nearby side streets by uniformed police. Adjacent buildings were being emptied as an additional precaution, which just added to the turmoil.

Archer saw a huge, armored, bomb-disposal truck parked in the road, and he knew that even now its crew was rushing through the building in a frantic, last-minute effort to locate and disarm the cached explosives.

At ten minutes before the hour, all civilians seemed to have been cleared. Those exiting now were uniformed police and firemen. The last to come out were the bomb-disposal personnel in their padded gear and helmets.

Daniel Archer stood against one of the more forward of the police barricades. He felt the quiet settling over the crowd, the press, the police, the firemen, everyone. There was something singular and magisterial about the event that seemed to demand a certain reverence.

Archer glanced at his watch. Two minutes to go.

Then someone began a controlled, rhythmic countdown that was picked up by the crowd at thirty.

"Twenty-nine . . . twenty-eight . . . twenty-seven . . ."

Its sound rising, the countdown spread through the streets, piazzas, and boulevards.

"Fifteen . . . fourteen . . . thirteen . . ."

What if it doesn't go off? thought Daniel Archer. In a moment of cold sweat, he mentally reviewed and checked off every detail that might go wrong at the last moment.

"Three . . . two . . . one. Blast off!" chanted the crowd, conditioned by more than thirty years of space shoots.

A dull, crackling roar seemed to emerge from deep inside the earth. It made Daniel Archer tremble. He felt air rush back against his face and saw whole sections of the Del Guardo Building's facade crumbling into the street below.

Clouds of smoke billowed black and gray.

The crowd gasped.

Fire came next. It broke through the smoke in spurts of orange and blue-green. Like licking tongues, the flames sank back then burst out again through shattered windows. Then the fire hoses got started, sending their looping geysers through black holes and seemingly affecting nothing.

Daniel Archer licked his lips. They tasted sulphuric. He looked at the faces of those around him and saw streaks of flame reflected in their eyes.

He saw other things as well. They were enjoying it. No. More than just enjoying it. They were having the time of their dull, tired lives. They would talk about it for years to come.

In all my life, they would say, I never saw anything like it.

Can you imagine anyone deliberately doing something like that?

Daniel Archer slowly worked his way out through the crowd and left the scene.

There was no need for him to imagine any such thing. He was the one who had done it.

Chapter 77

DEPUTY CIA DIRECTOR KEN HARRIS learned about the destruction of the Del Guardo Building at 6:14 A.M.

The news came via a call from the duty officer at Langley, who had orders to phone Harris at home the instant anything new developed.

Hoping for news of Dunster's death, Harris reacted to the bombing with a hard mix of disappointment and foreboding. Anna was taking too long.

He was just starting to shave when a call from the White House invited him to join Jayson Fleming at eight o'clock for breakfast in the presidential family quarters. The last-minute invitation made him feel no better. It could only mean that his friend needed propping up again.

Half an hour later, Harris found he was wrong. It was too late to prop up Jay Fleming. He had already fallen.

The deputy director knew this the moment he walked into the bright, sun-filled room and saw Fleming's wife sitting there with him.

"Amy, what a nice surprise," he said, and touched his dry lips to the cool and even greater dryness of Amy Fleming's cheek.

Amy just stared at him, and Harris knew instantly that she, not Jay, had set up the breakfast meeting. He knew, too, that not a single good moment was likely to come out of it for any one of them.

Sonofabitch. The poor fool's told her everything.

Ken Harris could only wonder at his own astonishment. He should have expected it. He had known them both for more than twenty years and Amy was by far the stronger and smarter of the two. That he and Amy had been secret lovers for almost four of those years only added weight to his judgment.

They were silent as a white-jacketed houseman poured coffee, took their breakfast orders, and left the room.

Amy sat considering the deputy director. "How could you?" she said, her voice quiet and very cold. "Do you really hate us so much that you finally had to destroy us?"

"*Destroy* you?" Harris glanced at Fleming, but the pro tempore president would not meet his eyes. "How? By trying to lift you to your ultimate place in the sun?"

"You had to know that neither Jay nor I could ever have lived with what you were doing."

"Even if it was successful?"

"Especially then." Amy paused to steady herself. "All I can do now is pray that nothing further happens to Jimmy Dunster. And if you're as smart as I think you are, you'll make absolutely sure it doesn't."

The threat was not even veiled.

"I'm not God, Amy."

"In this you are," she said.

Harris turned to Jayson Fleming. "All right, tell me what you've done, Jay."

"I'm sorry about this whole mess," said the vice president. "But Amy is right about cutting our losses. Right here. While we still can."

"Just tell me what the devil you've done."

Fleming studied his fingers. "I called Tommy Cortlandt last night. I said I'd heard something about another try at the president. I ordered him to move Jimmy at once."

"Outstanding," said Ken Harris softly.

The houseman returned with a full tray. The room was quiet as he served them. Then he left.

"Have you heard anything from Berlin?" Fleming asked Harris.

"Not a word."

"Then you don't know whether there was even another attempt?"

"That's correct."

"Will you be able to reach your contact and have the operation scrubbed?"

"It won't be easy. There are all sorts of complicating identity safeguards. But I'll try."

Amy Fleming threw the deputy CIA director a quick, hard look. "You'd better do more than just try."

Leaving the White House, Ken Harris had his chauffeur drop him at home rather than at Langley.

His housekeeper would not be in for another hour, so the apartment was empty. Checking the time, he figured it to be about three in the afternoon in Berlin. Then he went into his study, took the secure phone out of his wall safe, and put through a direct call to one of several numbers he had for Anna.

Ken Harris counted five, then six rings, and he was just about to hang up when he heard her answer.

"Anna, it's Walter. It's so good to hear your voice. You were beginning to worry me."

"But why?" she said. "What is there to worry about, Walter?"

"I hadn't heard a word and I was concerned about my sick friend. What's happening?"

"A few problems. You didn't tell me they were going to move him."

"I didn't find out until about an hour ago. Where did they move him to? Another hospital?"

"No," said Anna. "But they did put him in another room."

"How will that affect your planned treatments?"

"I'll manage. But I'm afraid it might take a little longer to get the kind of safe, permanent results you want."

"How much longer?"

"No more than a few days. Maybe less."

"There's no need to rush anything."

"I understand." Anna paused. "I've been waiting for your call. It was frustrating not being able to reach you. I thought you might want to cancel out entirely."

"Forget any such idea. The treatments are on."

The connection hummed softly.

"I don't suppose there's a safe number you could let me have for a possible emergency call," she said.

"Don't even think about it, Anna. If I don't find anything in the news, I'll try to call you at this same time each day. Then if you have something important to say or ask, you can be in touch. How is that?"

"Wonderful."

"Then good luck again. And here's hoping there are no more surprises for either of us."

The deputy CIA director hung up.

He had just made and acted upon what had to be one of the key decisions of his life and he felt good about it. The secret was to keep your eyes on the prize and freeze whatever might get in the way. His own prize would still sit him at the head of the table, right beside the brand new president of the United States.

Five thousand miles away, Anna hung up her own receiver, switched off the audiotape on which her entire conversation with Ken Harris had just been recorded, and looked at the two men who had been listening to every word.

"Well, do you still have doubts?" she asked.

Paulie Walters and Tommy Cortlandt sat without answering.

"I still can't understand his motive," Cortlandt said. "What does he get out of Jimmy Dunster's death?"

"How about getting his oldest and closest friend into the Oval Office?" said Paulie.

"Who is that?" asked Anna.

"The vice president."

The CIA director turned to look at Paulie. "I'd completely forgotten about their being that close."

"But why should it matter so much *why* the man wants the president dead?" said Anna. "Isn't it enough that he's trying to kill him?"

"No it's not enough," said Cortlandt. "Because if Ken Harris *is* trying to murder the president to get Fleming into the Oval Office, then Fleming himself has to be part of it." He paused. "Even if he *was* the one who warned me about your coming."

Chapter 78

NICKO VORELLI'S SCHEDULE had Kate Dinneson flying via Air France to Paris soon after the Del Guardo Building blew up.

After she landed and cleared customs at Charles de Gaulle Airport, she was able to stop at a terminal newsstand, buy a late edition, and read a headline that said "Mainz Keeps Word in Rome Bombing." She saved the story itself to read later.

A car had been left for her at a designated parking space in an airport garage. Its keys were taped behind the rear bumper and a bag in the trunk contained everything she would need to work with that night.

She took a moment to make sure it was all in order. Then she left the airport and drove directly to an undistinguished commercial hotel on the outskirts of Paris.

Kate was in her room by 8:00 P.M., feeling tired and dirty. She had not eaten since barely nibbling a light snack on the plane, but the thought of food repelled her.

And now? she thought.

Now she was in France to send out eight more of Nicko's faxes under the byline of Alfred Mainz. She took out a copy of the directive she would soon be sending to seven newspapers and a wire service in widely spaced cities, and read it through once more.

This is the second open letter from Professor Alfred Mainz.

The Del Guardo Building in Rome is down. I can only hope that this joyless act of destruction established my believability.

Here are my requests:

To begin with, a cash payment of one hundred million American dollars in used, unmarked currency of twenty-, fifty-, and hundred-dollar denominations, to be contributed jointly by the seven nations represented at the Wannsee Human Rights Conference.

The time, place, and manner of the delivery will be communicated to President Dunster shortly after this notice is made public. From that moment on, a clock will be ticking. If delivery of the money is not made within twenty-four hours, a second building will be blown in another of the seven nations involved at Wannsee.

This time there will be no advance warning.

The money will be used solely to support the practical needs and infrastructure of what shall hereafter be referred to as the Wannsee Project.

After the money transfer, arrangements will be made for a second human rights conference at Wannsee. This will be a summit meeting of heads of state, but with all my previously announced goals for central and western Africa and other trouble spots still in effect.

I pray for President Dunster's continued recovery from his grievous wounds, as well as for the survival of his courageous wife.

It is in honor of Mrs. Dunster, and in appreciation of the president's own efforts to validate what I myself was seeking at Wannsee, that I have chosen him as my trusted intermediary for whatever negotiations lie ahead.

I am putting the future of the Wannsee Project squarely in his hands. Considering the heart and spirit he brought with him to Wannsee, who could do better?

May God and good luck be with us all.

Professor Alfred Mainz.

The Wannsee Project, thought Kate Dinneson.
Nicko had christened it with a name and it had a fine

ring. Who could deny the nobility of its goals? But the potential for disaster suddenly seemed so open-ended, that all she was able to feel was a growing sense of dread.

Kate left the hotel at 1:00 A.M. and drove about five miles to the headquarters building of the Sevrès Insurance Company on the western end of the Rue de Montaigne.

She parked a short distance away and let herself into the building through the service entrance with her accustomed skill and dispatch.

Using the same procedures as in Naples, Kate faxed Nicko's second message to the same seven newspapers and one wire service that had received his first.

Driving away from the site when she was finished, Kate felt immeasurably better for having done a bit of physical busywork.

Just stay with the step-by-step details and don't think too much, she told herself.

Yet driving through the dark, deserted streets in the outskirts of Paris, she wondered who she was and what she was doing there.

Chapter 79

THE WASHINGTON BUREAU of the International News Service received Kate's latest fax at exactly 7:46 P.M. local time, and sent the alleged Professor Mainz's message out to its affiliates and subscribers about twenty minutes later.

CIA Director Tommy Cortlandt was awakened to the news by a call at 3:15 A.M. Berlin time, and passed the report on almost immediately to Paulie and Anna. They were all spending the night together in Anna's apartment, with Anna herself handcuffed to her own bed, and Paulie and Cortlandt sharing an oversize convertible couch.

Cortlandt made a quick call to Holy Cross General for the latest on the president's condition. When he learned that Jimmy Dunster was much improved and trying to order everyone to take him to see his wife, the three of them left at once for the hospital.

The president was awake when they arrived half an hour later. His eyes brightened when he saw Paulie and Cortlandt. Anna's presence, of course, puzzled him.

"What are you planning to do?" he asked. "Give her another shot at me?"

The doctor checked his chart and monitors, issued his visitors a warning not to tire him, and left the room.

Jimmy Dunster held out a pale, veined hand and Paulie took it, aware of the fragility of the bones. Yet the president did seem a lot more alert. When he spoke, his speech was no longer hesitant.

"All right, tell me what's going on," he said, "and why the hell I can't at least get to look at Maggie. Comatose or not, I want to see her."

Tommy Cortlandt stepped closer with Anna. "Mr. President, this is Anna," he told Dunster. "She has some things to say that we'd like you to hear. I promise we'll talk about your wife later, sir."

In her quiet, controlled voice and her near perfect English, Anna told the president of the United States everything she had previously told Paulie Walters and the CIA director. She spoke without emotion, and Jimmy Dunster listened the same way, except for the single moment when she said that Deputy Director Ken Harris had not only hired her to shoot Dunster in his hospital bed, but had probably been behind the explosion at Wannsee as well. Then a tear suddenly appeared in a corner of Jimmy Dunster's eye and ran the length of his face, dropping straight and fast.

The president looked at Paulie and Cortlandt. "You two can attest to everything she's said?"

They nodded.

"And you have this entire conversation with Harris recorded?"

"From beginning to end, sir," said Cortlandt.

"What else do we need?"

"Some proof that the vice president was involved in, or at least aware of, these attempts on your life," said Paulie.

"How do we get proof?"

"Anna thinks she can do it," Paulie answered.

"*Anna* thinks?" His head propped on fat pillows, Jimmy Dunster considered the woman who had come here to shoot him not too many hours before. "Can you also walk on water, Anna?"

"Just in extreme emergencies, Mr. President." She smiled. "And then I must admit it's only a simulation."

Jimmy Dunster closed his eyes. "See that the lady has whatever help she needs. But for God's sake, keep her on a short leash."

He opened his eyes and focused them on Tommy Cortlandt. "You didn't walk in here at four in the morning just for this. Let me hear the rest of it. Is it our dear professor?"

"Yes, sir."

"Of course. What's the bad news?"

A CIA duty officer had provided Cortlandt with the full wire-service report over the phone, and the director had taken careful notes. He read these now to the president, point by point.

Jimmy Dunster lay completely still, listening.

When Cortlandt finished reading, the president turned his head and looked at him.

"Imagine," he said. "The man has actually put it all in *my* hands."

"Are you going to do it, Mr. President?" Paulie asked.

In a movement so small that Paulie could not even be sure he saw it, Jimmy Dunster nodded.

Naturally, Paulie thought.

"Now take me to my wife," demanded the president.

They put him on a wheeled stretcher and went in a small convoy of tubes, mobile IVs, security agents, doctors, and nurses. When they reached the intensive care unit where Maggie Dunster lay swathed in bandages, Jimmy Dunster said, "Just leave me alone with her for five minutes."

Everyone stood silently in the corridor until the five minutes were over.

Chapter 80

KATE DINNESON HAD A QUICK BREAKFAST in her hotel room. Then she picked up her car and drove into the heart of Paris through a pale wash of morning sun.

On the seat beside her, the front page of the morning's paper carried a heavy black headline that read "Mainz Sets Terms."

One more example of Nicko's creative brilliance, Kate thought.

She parked a few blocks off the Champs Elysées. Then she walked to a group of public phones in a shopping arcade to make her calls.

Her first call was to the American consulate in Berlin, where she was able to reach an assistant to the consul general.

"Please listen carefully," she said in English. "I'm calling as a representative of Professor Alfred Mainz to deliver a message to CIA Director Thomas Cortlandt."

"Yes, madam."

"Please tell Director Cortlandt that I'll be calling President Dunster at Holy Cross General Hospital in exactly fifteen minutes. Tell him to alert the main switchboard to expect my call and to put me right through to the president." She paused. "Any questions about that?"

"No, madam."

"Then I thank you for your cooperation," Kate said, and hung up.

Fifteen minutes later, she made her next call from five blocks away.

"Holy Cross General Hospital," said an operator.

"President Dunster is expecting my call," said Kate. "Please connect me."

It seemed to take a long time. Actually, it was no more than twelve seconds.

"This is Jimmy Dunster," said a hoarse voice.

Kate was holding a page of scrawled notes and the paper was shaking in her hands.

"For the record, Mr. President," said Kate Dinneson, "my name is Beatrice and I'm only a messenger for Professor Mainz. I have no part in the Project."

The line was silent.

"In this same vein," said Kate, "any effort to trace this call or any future calls, or to interfere with the safe transfer of the cash payment we're about to discuss, will automatically result in the blowing of the next building."

"I understand."

"Then I'll get right to it, Mr. President. The monies in question are to be placed in three suitcases and left in the trunk of a gray Citroen sedan that will be parked in the garage at the corner of the Boulevard de la Chapelle and the Rue de Flandre in Paris. The car will be in space 26, on aisle B, of the third floor. The door will be unlocked, and the trunk key will be under the driver's seat."

"Excuse me, Beatrice," said Jimmy Dunster. "I'll need a moment to repeat all that for someone to write down."

"Take your time, Mr. President."

Waiting, Kate studied her detailed instructions. At least the paper had stopped shaking.

"All right," said the president. "But I'm worried about the professor's twenty-four-hour time limit. There are seven heads of state who have to consult on every decision. What I'd like is some extra time as a safeguard."

"How much time are you talking about, sir?"

"An additional twenty-four hours."

"You have it," said Kate.

"You can make that decision on your own?"

"Professor Mainz anticipated your request. Forty-eight hours from noon today, Berlin time, was his outside limit."

"How do I reach you if there's a problem?"

Kate read off the telephone number of an answering service in Paris. "If you call and ask for Beatrice, they'll beep me and I'll get right back to you."

"I'll have a conference call set up with the other heads of state and reach you as fast as I can," said Dunster.

"Thank you, Mr. President." Kate hesitated. "I'm so sorry about you, your wife, and your troubles."

Paulie had been out of the hospital for the past several hours, but things seemed to be going on in the president's room when he returned.

"What's happening?" he asked Tommy Cortlandt.

"Someone from Mainz just phoned the president to set up the money exchange. I'm about to run a tape of the call. Sit down and listen."

Moments later Paulie heard a curiously familiar voice saying, "For the record, Mr. President, my name is Beatrice. I'm only a messenger for Professor Mainz . . ."

Because Paulie knew that what he was hearing could not be possible, he had the sense of not hearing anything at all. Then the full shock set in.

Chapter 81

DANIEL ARCHER CAME INTO WASHINGTON'S DULLES AIRPORT at 8:07 A.M. on Alitalia flight 16 from Rome. It was an unusually bumpy descent and he checked his pulse all the way to touchdown. The beat never wavered.

Going through customs, he presented a passport under the name of Howard Beatty. The attached photograph showed an elderly man with a gray moustache and beard, dark shadows under his eyes, and ravaged cheeks, all of which matched his current disguise.

At the Hertz counter, he rented a Ford using an American Express card under the name of Howard Beatty and headed for Alexandria, Virginia.

It felt ugly being back in his own country as a fugitive, but Archer knew exactly how lucky he was to be back at all. He had a comfortable apartment in Bethesda, an agreeable, good-looking woman he had been seeing from time to time in Arlington, and he could not go near either one of them.

That fucking Harris.

Archer had no real ties here or any other place, yet the prospect of having to spend the rest of his life wearing disguises and looking over his shoulder had no great appeal either. Using a small portion of his carefully rationed malice for the deputy CIA director, Archer considered what, if anything, he should do about him.

No point in taking foolish risks, he thought. Yet if he did

decide to do something, how convenient that Nicko Vorelli had chosen Washington as his next bombing target.

For a while, the choice had wavered between Washington and Tokyo, with the American capitol finally getting the nod because of the psychological impact of hitting God where He lived. Not that either Vorelli or Archer believed it would ever come to that. After the fear struck by the demonstration blast in Rome, who would want to force Professor Mainz's hand with hundreds of lives at stake?

But since there was no figuring such things, not even that could be taken for granted. There were fools at every level. So the cached explosives still had to be fused and set to go by deadline time.

Daniel Archer had been driving for about forty minutes when he reached a neat, well-trimmed farmhouse that stood at the edge of a clearing a few miles south of Alexandria. He had been here many times before over the years and nothing ever seemed to change.

Archer found that in itself reassuring.

He parked beside a shiny pickup truck that appeared as lovingly cared for as the house. Then he got out of his rented Ford, knocked on the front door of the house, and waited.

A moment later the door opened and a spare, middle-aged man looked at him with watery blue eyes.

"Mr. Wilson?" he said, pitching his voice high and quavering, a dry, old man's voice. "Mr. Angus Wilson?"

"Yeah."

"I'm a friend of Danny Archer's."

The thin, tightly drawn face showed nothing. "So?"

"Danny said he thought you might be able to help me out with a few things I need."

"A few things you need for what?"

"To goddamn blow people's heads off. What else?"

Angus Wilson grinned and shook his head. "You sure had me fooled, Danny. You're still the best there is at that shit."

Both of them grinning now, they went inside.

"It's been a long time," said Wilson. "What are you up to these days?"

"Little of this, little of that. In Europe mostly. But I'm back now and can use some inventory."

"That's what I'm here for, Danny."

They talked for a while, trading inside gossip and lies. You never stayed too close to the truth in this line of work. Not if you wanted to stay in business and live.

Then Daniel Archer took out his shopping list and they went up into a windowless attic crowded floor to ceiling with shelves and drawers.

Archer read off what he needed and Angus Wilson filled a large, fine-looking piece of Samsonite luggage with a master bomb-maker's assortment of wires, cables, detonators, fuses, clocks, and remotes. For added measure, Archer tossed in a five-inch, razor-sharp switchblade and a 9-millimeter automatic with a shoulder holster, attached silencer, and two full clips of ammunition.

Back downstairs, they sipped Jack Daniels and talked some more. While Angus Wilson figured out the bill, Archer adjusted his shoulder holster and got the feel of the new automatic.

"I see you're still living alone," said Archer. "You're getting as bad as me. A nonfucking hermit."

Wilson shrugged. His wife had died long and hard of cancer a few years before, and he had never really known what to say to a woman anyway. "I'm too old to start all over again with that kind of crap."

"I know what you mean. I didn't have the patience for it even when I was young." Archer hefted the weight of the automatic, flicked the safety off, on, then off and on again. "You seen old Ken Harris lately? Or heard anything from him?"

"Nah. Nothing."

"Didn't he used to keep in touch?"

"Not for a long while. He's too big and important to waste time on me these days."

Archer slowly nodded. He aimed the 9-millimeter through a window at a bird swaying on a low branch.

Wilson licked the point of his pencil and scribbled a final figure. "The bad news is a grand total of seven thousand, five hundred and forty bucks. That's including the genuine Samsonite suitcase." He paused consideringly. "For you, let's call it an even seven thousand. How does that sound?"

"Like one of the last great bargains around," said Archer.

He paid Angus Wilson in cash and they walked out to Archer's car together and shook hands.

"Always a pleasure to do business with you, Angus," said Archer. "You and your place are about the last things around that haven't changed."

"Anyone tells you I've changed, you'll know I'm dead."

"I believe you," said Archer.

Wilson looked at him. "So when Ken Harris comes asking about you, what do I tell him?"

"Only the truth. That you haven't seen or heard from me in years."

Chapter 82

PAULIE WALTERS WAS GRATEFUL simply to be part of setting up the president's conference call. The fuss—the busywork alone—helped to keep his head straight. With any break in the action, his thoughts turned darkly to Kate.

What had happened?

How had she become involved with Mainz at this point?

Where did Nicko Vorelli fit into all this?

How much of what Kate was doing was with a loaded gun at her head?

The questions kept coming, kept working through him, and he had no answers.

Then the communications officer signaled for quiet and said they would begin in exactly two minutes.

While Jimmy Dunster's doctors fussed at all the activity, room 561 had been converted into a small but sophisticated telephonic nerve center. Cables snaked across the floor. Everyone involved wore headphones. And instant translations were available in English, French, Italian, German, or Japanese.

The president himself was stretched out in bed with only about half of his earlier tubes still attached. In the room, too, were Paulie, Cortlandt, and the chief communications officer. Outside in the corridor, other technicians sat at a computer consul with four security agents shuffling around them.

The two doctors in the room left and a moment later the president received his signal.

"This is Jimmy Dunster," he said. "Before we move ahead, I just want to thank you all for your warm expressions of sympathy and concern. They mean everything to me."

Then the president got right down to the business at hand. He described the call from Professor Mainz's messenger and the terms put forth and discussed. Some of the other leaders began offering their own suggestions, but the American president quickly cut them short.

"Gentlemen, please indulge me," he said. "Whatever we've been asked to do, we must do. This man is serious. And I'm sure none of us want to put uncounted lives at risk."

Jimmy Dunster paused to take a deep breath. Paulie saw how little he had in the way of reserves.

"This money has to be paid," the president told his group of six. "Whatever comes later, we'll talk about then. For now, I just want to call this messenger back as soon as possible and stop the clock on that bomb."

Cortlandt took over for the president in working out the details while Jimmy Dunster lay there with his eyes closed.

Paulie made it back to Anna's apartment by 2:45 that afternoon, close to the time when Ken Harris had said he would call each day.

With two agents keeping her under virtual house arrest and with no hint yet of her promised five million, Anna was growing increasingly restive.

"I don't see any suitcases of money," she said when Paulie arrived empty-handed.

"We're good for it. You don't have to worry."

"I'm not worried. I'm bored to death sitting around all day with those two retarded watchdogs you've stuck me with."

"You're very easily bored."

"That's true." Anna looked at Paulie. "Want to fuck?"

"That's how you keep from being bored?" Paulie said.

"Sometimes. If I'm lucky and happen to stumble over the rare man who seems slightly more interesting than a good vibrator."

"And other times?"

"I try to shoot the president of the United States."

"There has to be something in between, Anna."

"I do keep looking."

"I hope you find it soon," he said. "For all our sakes."

Then the telephone rang and Paulie put on a set of headphones and glanced at his watch. It was a bit past three o'clock. He nodded to Anna and she picked up the receiver on the third ring, which set the recording tape rolling.

"It's Walter," Ken Harris said.

"I'm glad you called. We have some serious talking to do."

Listening, Paulie felt himself tense up at just the sound of the deputy director's voice.

"Is something wrong?" asked Harris.

"A lot is wrong. And it's time we stopped playing this silly little name game." Anna paused. "You see, I know who you are, Mr. Harris."

The deputy director was silent for a long stretch.

"How did you find out?" he finally asked.

"About a year ago, I recognized your voice during a TV interview."

Harris said nothing.

"You don't have to worry," said Anna. "I've never said a word to anyone. And I won't."

"Then why are you telling me now?" said Ken Harris.

"Because you've just compromised my security and endangered my life," said Anna.

"How have I done that?"

"By telling your friend Jayson Fleming who I am."

There was more silence from the other end and Paulie could all but feel the deputy director sniffing around the bait.

"That's not true," said Ken Harris at last. "I never did say who you were."

"Then how was he able to warn your boss that I'd be coming to the hospital?"

"He never knew you by name. All he knew was that another try was being made."

"That in itself could have been enough to finish me," said Anna. "It almost did."

"I apologize. You have every right to be furious. I never expected the poor fool to unravel enough to blow the whistle on you."

Neither of them spoke for several moments.

"I can't tell you how sorry I am," said Ken Harris. "Forget the whole operation. I promise to make it up to you. In the meantime, if you stop by the dead drop tomorrow, you'll find an extra hundred thousand waiting."

Anna looked at Paulie as she hung up.

"All right?" she asked.

"Better than all right," he said. "Now just pack a bag and we'll get you to a safe house. Your generous friend will have someone here to blow your brains out in less than forty minutes."

Paulie brought Anna to a secure apartment on Hutten Strasse and personally checked out the three agents he had arranged to stay with her.

"Just be patient a while longer," he said. "If you try not to lay them all, I promise you'll be walking out of here rich and free in a few days."

Anna's golden, animal eyes considered him. "I don't want _them_. I want _you_."

"Only because I punched you in the jaw and you know you can't have me."

"How about after I get my five million?"

"Mail me a signed contract and we'll see."

"Where do I send it?"

"The White House," he said. "Care of the president."

An hour later, Paulie was back at Holy Cross General with Anna's recording of her conversation with Ken Harris.

In room 561, Jimmy Dunster was struggling to get his first dose of nonintravenous nourishment down into his stomach. Director Cortlandt was busy on the telephone. Secretary of State Green, who still knew Paulie only as John Hendricks, was just leaving the room and stopped to shake his hand and congratulate him for saving the president's life.

Then Green was gone, the president lay exhausted from his feeding, Cortlandt finished with the telephone, and the room took back its own field of force and silence.

"What did you get out of Little Orphan Annie?" asked Cortlandt. "Did Ken Harris call her back as promised?"

"Right on schedule," said Paulie. "And I have it all on tape."

"How bad is it?" asked Jimmy Dunster.

"You'll hear it for yourself, Mr. President."

A moment later Paulie put on the tape recorder and they listened without interruption.

President Dunster was the first to speak, his voice pure dry ice. "The vice president of the United States."

"Yet he was the one who called to warn us at the end," said Cortlandt. "Which probably saved your life."

"Only Paulie saved my life." Dunster's face was flushed. "But any way you look at it, the bastard still tried to kill Maggie and me at Wannsee."

"We really have no proof of that yet," said the director.

Jimmy Dunster looked at him. "Who needs proof? What am I, a goddamn court of law? My wife may die."

"What do you want to do about him and Ken Harris?" asked Tommy Cortlandt.

"Don't ask me that yet. Just get Jay Fleming the hell out of the White House and let the presidency revert to me here. I can handle what I have to."

Dunster sighed and his thin frame seemed to further diminish beneath the sheets. "In the meantime," he said, "we're literally sitting on a bomb. So let's just concentrate on that."

In the cafeteria later, Paulie and the CIA director carried some food to a corner table and huddled over a meal of sorts.

Paulie couldn't remember the last time he had eaten.

"I've been away from it all afternoon," he said. "How have the money arrangements been going?"

"The usual haggling. I finally told them we'd put up all the cash ourselves and collect later. They loved that. No matter what, we always end up as the world's banker of choice."

"When will the drop be made?"

"One o'clock tomorrow afternoon, Paris time."

Paulie watched Cortlandt over his coffee. "Then you've called the woman, Beatrice, at that number she gave us?"

"Twice. And she's gotten back to me each time in under ten minutes. She seems reliable."

"Who'll be making the drop?"

"Two of our Paris agents."

"They won't try to be heroes and tail the car?"

"Their orders are to dump the bags in the Citroen and take off. Period. If they try one thing more, they know they're finished."

They ate for several moments in silence.

"I have a favor to ask," said Paulie. "I'd like a few days on my own."

Cortlandt stared at him. "Does this concern Mainz?"

"Yes."

"That's all you're going to say?"

"Unless you insist on more."

They looked at each other in a curious way.

"You should know me by now," said Cortlandt.

Chapter 83

WITH LITTLE TIME TO WASTE, Paulie Walters moved fast. He wondered briefly what Tommy Cortlandt thought about his sudden desire to go off on his own. But from that point on, all he had on his mind was Kate.

He caught a 9:30 P.M. Lufthansa flight from Tempelhof and landed in Paris at a bit past 11:00.

Renting a Mustang at the terminal, Paulie drove to the Left Bank apartment of an old contact to arm himself. He broke into a cold sweat. What was he expecting to do? Shoot her?

At 2:35 A.M. he swung into the big, twenty-four-hour parking garage at the corner of the Boulevard de la Chapelle and the Rue de Flandre. He took a ticket from an automated dispenser and waited for the barricade to rise. Then he circled up the ramp to the third level.

The garage was mostly empty at this hour. But as Paulie drove past space 26 on aisle B, he saw that a blue Renault occupied that spot.

Probably Kate's switch, he thought, to keep her chosen space from being taken by another car.

Paulie parked his Mustang against a far wall and sat there for a moment. Then he took a small electronic homing device from his bag and slipped it onto the Renault's radio antenna like a tiny ring. Its matching chrome finish made it all but invisible.

There was an elevator off to the right. Paulie left his Mustang and rode the cage down to street level. Then he walked across the street into an all-night bistro that would allow him a clear view of any car entering or leaving the garage.

He ordered black coffee and sat at a small table watching the garage entrance. There were about a dozen people in the place, and a few couples were dancing to slow, recorded music.

I've never even danced with her, he thought.

At 3:20 A.M. he saw a gray Citroen turn slowly into the garage, stop at the ticket dispenser, and proceed up the ramp and out of sight. He was able to make out the shape of a woman at the wheel, but that was all. He could only assume it was Kate.

Less than ten minutes later, he saw the blue Renault that had been in space 26 come down off the garage exit ramp and stop at the checkout booth. Then the car swung right onto the Rue de Flandre and drove off.

This time Paulie was able to see that it was Kate. It was just a quick glimpse of her in profile, but it was enough.

Moments later Paulie left the bistro, walked back across the street, and rode the garage elevator to the third level.

With the blue Renault gone, the gray Citroen was parked in space 26. Paulie went to his Mustang, got another homing ring out of his bag, and slid this one down over the Citroen's radio antenna.

He was prepared to follow either car.

Four hours later Tommy Cortlandt's two agents arrived.

They came in a black van at the heart of the morning rush. Traffic was noisy and impatient and cars were circling the garage, searching for spaces.

Watching from the Mustang in its far corner, Paulie saw the van stop behind the Citroen and the two agents take out three large suitcases. Then they opened the Citroen's trunk, arranged the three bags inside, and slammed the lid shut.

With the transfer completed, the men got back into their van, drove down the exit ramp, and disappeared below.

Waiting now, Paulie flicked on a palm-sized computer screen and prepared the latest in high-tech tracking systems that he had picked up along with his weaponry.

He hit a button and a tiny red bleep appeared in the center of the computer screen. A graduated scale marked it as being at a distance of forty-three meters, which represented the signal sent by the miniature transmitter ring that Paulie had slipped over the Citroen's radio antenna. Its effective range went all the way up to a full kilometer, and it could indicate changes in direction as well as distance.

When the Renault in which Kate had driven off earlier came back within range, its transmitter signal would appear on the computer screen as a green bleep. Paulie was gambling that Kate would be driving one or the other of the two cars.

At exactly 8:32 A.M., the green bleep appeared in the upper right-hand corner of his screen at an indicated distance of just under a kilometer.

The bleep moved steadily closer, going very slowly because of the traffic, and changing direction several times. Ten minutes later, Paulie saw the blue Renault drive up the ramp and double-park in the aisle directly behind the Citroen.

The red and green bleeps on the screen were now side by side.

Kate slid out of the Renault and Paulie tugged the peak of his baseball cap lower over his eyes.

It was going to be the Renault.

Paulie saw Kate open the Citroen's trunk, wrestle out the three suitcases, and work them into the trunk of the other car. With that done, she got back into the Renault, started the engine, drove off down the exit ramp, and disappeared from Paulie's sight.

Watching his computer screen, he saw the green bleep of the Renault slowly pulling away from the red marker of the Citroen, abandoned now in Space 26, aisle B.

When the distance indicator on the green bleep showed a reading of exactly one hundred meters, a safe enough surveillance interval for heavy city traffic, Paulie turned on his engine and started after it.

Chapter 84

AT 6:30 A.M. the Virginia woods were still. There was not so much as a breeze. The only sound Daniel Archer heard was an occasional drop of moisture falling from a leaf.

He watched the path stretching in front of him at the place where it faded into gray mist. He felt his first rush of uncertainty.

Was this really so smart after all?

Leave it alone, he told himself. *You're here.*

Moments later, Archer heard the faint, distant sound of someone running.

Continuing to focus on the place where the path disappeared, he heard the runner's footsteps long before he would see the runner. The disciplined regularity of the beat was that individual. Even during his morning workout, Ken Harris allowed no break in his precision. There was a purity to the man that might have been beautiful if it were not so frightening.

Daniel Archer rose from the rock where he had been sitting. He stepped onto the path and stood waiting until he saw the deputy director of the CIA emerge from the mist. Then he started toward him.

Archer walked slowly, almost lethargically, keeping his hands in plain view at his sides. Although he still wore his elderly man disguise, his carriage and stride remained his own. To anyone watching, he would not have appeared at all threatening. All possibilities had to be considered, and

Archer could not be sure that Harris would not have some sort of security detail following him.

Nothing about Archer looked different from any other area resident out for an early-morning stroll.

Yet seeing Daniel Archer from a distance of almost a hundred yards, Ken Harris abruptly broke stride and cut his pace. Gradually he slowed until he was no longer running but walking, a tall, straight-backed man in a gray warm-up suit.

They were both moving so slowly now that the distance between them hardly seemed to be closing. They came together, two large carnivores of the same species, cautious but not unfriendly, meeting in a quiet mood somewhere in the jungle.

They stopped and just stood looking at each other.

Ken Harris spoke first. "Danny?"

Archer nodded. "Hello, Ken."

"It's a funny thing. At about a hundred yards I felt it was you. Your walk, your build and all. And fifty yards closer I knew it was you. Yet when I was close enough to see your face, I had doubts." Harris's smile was cold. "Good disguise. No wonder you weren't spotted coming in."

"You mean you had people watching the airports for a dead man?"

The deputy director was silent. If he had noticed the automatic that had appeared in Daniel Archer's hand, he gave no sign.

"Or maybe you weren't quite sure I was dead," said Archer. "Maybe you just wanted to play it safe in case it was Hans who somehow ended up dead, instead of me."

Ken Harris shook his head in a tacit denial of everything. "What happened, Danny? I've never known you to mess anything up as you did at Wannsee."

"Let's get off this path and I'll explain it."

Harris stood there.

"Move or I'll shoot you right here," said Archer.

Harris slowly turned and walked into the woods with Archer a few steps behind.

"All right," said Archer when they came to a small clearing.

They stood about six feet apart, but their eyes met and stayed together.

"Why are you going to so much trouble?" said the deputy director. "Why didn't you just pick me off as I jogged by?"

"Is that what you'd have done?"

"You know it."

"Then that's where we're different," said Archer.

"You actually think I deserve a few last words?"

"Whatever you'd like."

"I can't believe you're this sentimental."

"We've put in a lot of years together. Until Wannsee, you've never been anything but fair and decent to me. I was angry before, but not now." Daniel Archer shrugged. "Maybe because I've come out of this OK in spite of you."

The deputy director shook his head. "I have no last words. I'd rather hear what went wrong at Wannsee."

"Part of that was my own fault. But not the way you think." Archer stood with the automatic steady in his hand. "I never set out to kill the president and his wife like you said. Just Mainz and the old man. I figured to make us both heroes. Which was how I measured and placed my charge. But Mainz had some of his own stuff planted in the same area. That was what ruined everything. But at least the Dunsters are still hanging on. So it wasn't all bad."

Ken Harris gazed at Archer as if he were far off in the mist. "Christ! You're still trying to be a goddamn patriot."

"It's better than trying to blow away a friend, Kenny."

"It was nothing personal. I simply couldn't have you floating around, knowing what you did. You of all people should be able to understand that."

"I understand it all right. It's just that I can't see killing a friend as 'nothing personal.' "

Coming near to it now, Archer's mouth was dry and an almost pleasurable sadness worked its way through him.

The deputy director seemed to see it in his face. "You're getting soft, Danny boy. If you're going to do it, then fucking do it." He paused. "OK if I get a last smoke out of my warm-up jacket?"

"Which pocket?"

"Left."

Archer looked and saw a zipper on it. Also, the pocket was flat. "Very slowly and carefully," he said.

Ken Harris opened the zipper with two fingers. Then he gently slid the same two fingers inside the opening and fired three times through the pocket. The explosions were so fast and blurred that they might have come from a single shot.

It was a small-caliber pistol, but all three shots were squarely in the killing zone.

Working quickly, the deputy director stripped Archer of his wallet, money, identification, and some papers, which he stuffed into his own pockets to go through later.

Then he ran back to his car and returned with a tire iron.

Scraping out a shallow trench behind some bushes, Harris covered over Daniel Archer's body with soil, leaves, rocks, and dead branches. Eventually it would be uncovered by a prowling animal, but by that time it wouldn't matter.

Chapter 85

PAULIE WALTERS DROVE through the heart of Paris with only an occasional glimpse of the Renault in the heavy traffic ahead. He kept a long interval between the two cars, using the green bleep on his computer screen as both assurance and guide.

There were few changes in direction. Kate simply kept heading north until she reached the St. Denis area. Then she swung slightly northeast.

When the traffic began to thin, Paulie dropped back to a full four-hundred-meter interval, allowing about a dozen cars and trucks as a buffer.

At nine-thirty he saw signs indicating a turnoff ahead to Charles de Gaulle Airport. He knew this would not be where Kate was going. She was not about to be checking a hundred million in cash into the baggage hold of some commercial jet.

The city was behind them now and there were only scattered houses dozing peacefully in the sun. Between them were fields and patches of woods, trees black against the sky.

Paulie saw the bleep on his screen suddenly angle off to the right and continue in that direction.

When Paulie reached the crossroad, he turned onto a well-surfaced two-lane blacktop to Langley-le-Sec that wound through long stretches of woods. There were only three vehicles between the Renault and the Mustang now, and Paulie slowed until the interval had stretched to about half a kilometer.

The sun flickered among the leaves and grasses, and the air was piney and aromatic as if it had rained during the night. Paulie began to catch glimpses of lake water through the trees, and he cut his speed a little more. Because of the winding road, he began losing sight of the Renault for long periods.

Then he saw the green marker move to the left.

Moments later Paulie took the first left turn that he came to and slowed the car to a crawl. In the near distance he caught sight of the lake once more and the blur of a house in front of it. He did not see the Renault. But on his screen the bleep had come to a stop at an indicated range of half a kilometer.

He braked to a halt and sat watching the green marker. When it had remained still for several moments, he drove off the road and parked out of sight.

The only sounds were those of birds.

Paulie drew the automatic he had picked up in Paris. He checked the ammunition clip and slid a round into the firing chamber. Then he put the piece back into its shoulder holster.

Slowly, with effort, he opened the car door and got out. He suddenly was in no great hurry. Newly conscious of the loaded weapon against his body, he felt almost lethargic, as if the proper delay at this point would miraculously change everything that lay ahead.

I'm getting more foolish by the minute, he thought, and started toward the distant house.

Paulie stayed within the woods, keeping low and out of sight of the road. He moved slowly, listening to the forest sounds, the hum of insects, the calls of birds in the upper branches of trees. Occasionally he heard cars pass on the road, which was on his left. Then he heard a car traveling off to his right where the road curved parallel to the lake.

A flicker in the branches ahead made Paul Walters stop abruptly. But it was only a bird swinging on a branch tip, and he continued on. He could feel his heart pounding.

He saw the house through the trees and began to circle

around to the right. At one point he had to cross the road. He waited in the brush as two cars passed, then he ducked low and quickly crossed over.

At fifty meters, he peered around a tree and saw the blue Renault.

The only car in sight, it was parked on the side of a traditional stone house with high, shuttered windows. It was bordered by shrubs and trees. To Paulie it was suddenly the center of the earth.

Who was inside it?

Of course Kate was there. What about Klaus Logefeld? Was he with her, or off somewhere else? Might there not be others involved as well?

Paulie felt himself in need of calming. His brain suddenly brought too much agitation to every possibility. He almost believed that Klaus had been gifted with secret powers, a special grace. After all, he alone among the four in Wannsee's surveillance-room explosion had escaped death or serious injury. It was hard to imagine him being caught off guard like this.

Klaus Logefeld's nearness alone seemed to give off signals, seemed to create its own psychic warning in the woods.

As if forced to fulfill his own malevolent prophecy, Paulie thought he heard a faint sound behind him.

Before he could turn, a man's voice at his back said in English, "Put your hands over your head and don't move."

Paulie weighed his chances of going for his gun and getting off a quick shot. They were nonexistent.

He raised his hands.

"Now turn around. Slowly."

Paulie did as ordered and found himself looking into the muzzle of an automatic being aimed at him under the dark eyes of Dr. Nicholas Vorelli. All he could do was stare dumbly.

I'm close to dying and I've never learned a damn thing.

"Open your jacket," ordered Nicko. "Take out your gun with two fingers, and drop it on the ground."

Paulie obeyed.

Then they just stood gazing at each other.

"I know," said Nicko. "I'm afraid it's a very unhappy surprise for us both."

"Where did I go wrong?"

"By even attempting something this foolish in the first place." Nicko's quiet anger showed through his surface calm. "I'd have expected you to know better."

Paulie was silent. He could be dead in anywhere from seconds to perhaps half an hour. It depended on how much Nicko wanted to find out from him first. And if it was done out here in the woods, Kate might never learn what had finally happened.

Motioning with his gun, Nicko said, "Let's go inside."

He picked up Paulie's pistol in passing and slid it inside his belt.

Walking with Nicko's gun at his back, Paulie began breathing again. He felt a numbness all through him. And he still understood nothing.

Chapter 86

KATE OPENED THE FRONT DOOR of the house and saw the men walking toward her out of the woods.

"Dear, sweet God," she whispered.

They approached slowly, Paulie in front and Nicko about five paces behind with the gun in his hand. Watching them, Kate felt all brightness drain from her life.

No one spoke as they walked past her into the house, nor did anyone appear to look directly at anyone else. One wrong word or glance might have provided enough of a spark to send everything up in flames. Without knowing a single detail of how Paulie had ended up here like this, Kate knew he was dead.

Maybe we're all dead.

Nicko took Paulie into a room overlooking the lake and motioned him into a chair.

Kate trailed after them. A mute, forgotten waif.

"Your friend followed you all the way from Paris," Nicko told her. "When I finally picked him up, he was just about fifty meters from the house. Carrying a gun."

Nicko carefully sat down facing Paulie.

Kate remained standing. She stood a short distance behind Nicko at a point where she could see both men. Nicko held the automatic in his lap like an extension of his hand.

Paulie just sat there. He seemed nothing but eyes.

Those dark, solemn eyes, Kate thought, and suddenly saw them staring at her with so poignant a look that they ate holes in her.

So far neither of them had said a word.

"We need some answers, Paul," said Nicko. "Give them honestly, and you can still come out of this better than you might think. Lie, and you'll simply disappear. Clear enough?"

Paulie said nothing.

"To begin with," said Nicko, "can we assume you knew Kate would be picking up that money in Paris this morning?"

"Yes."

"How did you know?"

"Tommy Cortlandt had recorded her call to the president. When he ran the tape for me later, I recognized her voice."

"Did you tell that to Cortlandt or the president?"

"No."

"Why not?"

"Because it was Kate. And I wasn't sure what her involvement might be."

"What did you *think* her involvement might be?"

Paulie glanced at Kate, but she stood staring out the window.

"Klaus Logefeld had pressured her before," he said. "He might have been doing it again with some new kind of gun at her head. I had to find out."

"Find out for whom?"

"Myself."

"That's why you followed her here?"

"Yes."

"And what have you found out?"

Paulie's mouth was a thin, hard line. "Nothing. So far I haven't even seen Klaus Logefeld. All I've seen is you. And the only gun in sight is the one in *your* hand."

"Then you think *I'm* the one pressuring Kate into this?"

Paulie sat wordless. Where these two were concerned, he no longer was sure *what* he thought.

"If you have any doubts," said Nicko, "Kate is right here. Why don't you ask her?"

Kate turned and looked at Paulie. "You don't have to ask

me, Paulie. Nobody is pressuring me. Nobody has a gun at my head. Not Nicko, not Klaus, not anybody."

She spoke so low her voice was almost inaudible.

"I'm doing this only because I can't think of anything on God's earth that needs doing more. My only real pain comes from your having found out and blundered in here like this."

Paulie looked at Nicko, who had been studying him with total absorption. At that moment they could have been brothers. What two men deserved such closeness more? Hadn't they shared the love and body of the same woman? Surely a special intimacy existed in that alone.

Paulie saw how it would have to be. Nicko absolutely could not let him walk out of here knowing what he did.

In a sense, who could blame him?

Paulie was not even angry.

It was just that there was no way that he was going to let himself die sitting here in a goddamn, straight-backed parlor chair.

Paulie vaulted out of his chair without a sound, legs pushing off the floor, arms outstretched. He saw Nicko's eyes widen and his automatic rise up out of his lap. For an instant Paulie sailed free, until something exploded against his head and he hit the floor and rolled through sudden patches of light and dark.

When he stopped rolling, Paulie squinted past the blood trickling down into his eyes. He saw Nicko fumbling with the safety on his automatic and realized he had only been clubbed by the gun barrel and not shot by it.

"Nicko, don't!"

It was Kate crying out from behind a fine red haze as Paulie lay there on the floor, shaking his head to clear it.

"Nicko!"

Kate again.

Save your breath, Paulie thought.

Then Nicko had the safety off and was aiming with both hands. Paulie met his eyes above the dark hole of the muzzle.

"Go to hell," he said.

Paulie's eyes closed at the gunshot.

An instant later his eyes opened.

Nicko sat slumped in his chair, staring at nothing. Kate stood white-faced behind him. She was still pointing a revolver at Nicko's back.

As Paulie watched, she slowly lowered the gun. Then she came around and closed Nicholas Vorelli's eyes and kissed him on both cheeks.

"He knew how I felt about you," she said quietly. "I'd told him I loved you. But he wouldn't listen to me. He should have known I could never let him kill you."

Still blinking his own blood, Paulie struggled to his feet.

"I'm sorry," he told her.

"For what?"

"For making you choose."

Kate Dinneson came and held him. Finally, she wept. "Ah, Paulie, don't you know?"

"What?"

"It was never really a contest."

Chapter 87

GENTLE AS A MOTHER, Kate fed him brandy and cleaned and treated what was bleeding. Her fingers trembled and Paulie saw double. Still, it gave him two of her to watch.

The sweat on his back was as cold as snow.

Kate was no longer crying, although some tears still dimmed her eyes. *Look what I've done to her,* Paulie thought.

Paulie's forehead was swollen and discolored. But when Kate was through, it was covered by a neat, remarkably small bandage.

She took the brandy and led him to another room facing the lake.

"We have to talk," she said.

Paulie shook his head and felt slightly dizzy. "I'm not sure I can deal with any more surprises today."

"I'm afraid you're going to have to."

Paulie sat there.

"It's all a lie," Kate said. "There's no Professor Mainz anymore. And no Klaus Logefeld. He's dead."

Paulie was silent.

"It's true," said Kate. "He died in the explosion that killed his grandfather and almost killed the president and his wife."

"Where's his body?"

"In a hidden tunnel under Wannsee."

"And this whole idea of taking over in his name? Who came up with that?"

"Nicko, of course. Although I was happy to agree. Why let all the good that Klaus started go to waste?"

"Who knows about all this?"

"Just Nicko, me, and one other man who's been handling the explosives. And he's suddenly become a problem."

"How?"

"He has the clocks ticking on the next targeted building, and I can't seem to reach him to get them turned off."

"Where's the building?"

"Washington," said Kate.

Paulie looked at her. "You had no fail-safe arrangements?"

"Of course we did. But he didn't make his last three scheduled calls, and he hasn't been at his hotel to receive ours."

Paulie checked his watch. "He still has more than twenty hours to call in. It's not exactly panic time."

"No. But he's always right on schedule. I'm afraid something has happened."

"You know which building is set to go?"

"Yes."

"And the exact location of the charge?"

Kate nodded.

"You can always call the president and have him get someone to disarm it."

"And have us look like bumbling fools? No. Image is everything in this."

"Then what's your alternative?" asked Paulie.

"You."

There was a lot to be done at the house before leaving, and discipline was needed if they were to be thorough.

Paulie wanted to spare Kate as much as possible by taking care of Nicko himself, but she was not about to be spared a thing.

"I owe him at least that," was how she put it.

So they wrapped Nicko in blankets against the chill of the earth and laid him to rest beneath a grove of cypress. It was Kate who chose the site. Afterward, she cut a small cypress branch as a symbol of mourning.

They buried the three suitcases of money very close by.

No irony was intended.

It was merely that the house was a very short-term rental, and there was no telling when they would be back.

Nor was there any way to anticipate future threats. They spent a full hour scouring the house clean of fingerprints, bloodstains, and any other identifying signs.

Since the three cars, like the house, were all rented under false IDs, these were cleaned up as well. Finally, they took the added precaution of moving Kate's Renault and Nicko's Toyota a few kilometers away and rolling them into the lake.

Then they drove to Charles de Gaulle Airport in Paulie's Mustang, and were aboard a direct Air France flight to Washington at 7:00 P.M. Paris time.

They still had seventeen hours to detonation.

Chapter 88

KEN HARRIS DIDN'T GO through the contents of Daniel Archer's pockets until he came home from his office that evening. When he finally did check everything out, it was almost as an afterthought, over a drink.

There was nothing of true interest in Archer's wallet. Just an assortment of credit cards and IDs under different names. His passport carried the name of Howard Beatty, and the attached photograph showed him in his final, elderly persona.

Not until Harris was glancing over some folded sheets of paper was his attention caught by several drawings. Actually, they were more than just drawings. They were meticulously rendered and annotated schematics of what was clearly a maze of circuitry, detonators, and time clocks for a large-scale demolition operation.

Apparently Danny Archer had come to Washington to do more than just settle a personal score.

Mixing himself a second martini, the deputy director settled down with the schematics to see if he could find anything there that could tell him what the project was all about.

Moments later, they had told him.

The site itself was none other than the Taylor Building on Massachusetts Avenue.

The charges were pinpointed behind the number 4 and number 5 wall panels at the northeast end of the second basement.

Three timer clocks were arranged in a relay sequence set to detonate the next day at exactly twelve noon Paris time, which, it was stated in Archer's own cramped handwriting, translated to exactly 6:00 A.M. Washington time.

Listed, too, were the specific times at which Archer was to make his calls to determine whether a large cash drop had successfully taken place. If the drop had been made, he was to defuse and abort the entire project.

The deputy director read the instructions twice. Not because he found them difficult to understand—they were quite clear as stated—the whole concept just seemed beyond rational comprehension.

What he obviously had in his hands was a working diagram for the next target on Professor Mainz's hit list, with Danny Archer somehow assigned to carry out the operation—first to arm the explosives and set the timers going, then to pull the plug and stop the clocks after the hundred million was paid.

What remained impossible for Harris to fathom was how Archer had ever connected up with Mainz to begin with.

Nevertheless, the *plastique* was armed, the clocks were ticking, and Danny Archer was obviously unable to stop them.

And Professor Mainz?

No doubt waiting someplace in Europe for Danny's scheduled fail-safe calls that never came. But not for long. One way or another Mainz would have to stop the clocks or watch everything he had worked for go up in smoke along with the Taylor Building and hundreds of lives.

Harris checked the time. It was a bit past 7:00 P.M. That left Mainz with less than eleven hours to either get over here himself to stop the clocks or arrange for someone else to take care of it.

And I? he thought.

I sit here building an entire, detailed life story out of two pages of diagrams, notes, and pure speculation.

So before you lose it completely, Ken Harris told himself, why don't you just make a few calls and get down there to check the whole thing out?

*   *   *

The deputy director had three men meet him an hour and a half later in the parking garage beneath the Taylor Building. Like Daniel Archer, the men were not officially employed by the Agency but worked on especially sensitive clandestine operations that held the potential for negative fallout.

Best of all, their loyalty was to Harris rather than to the Company.

The garage was nearly empty at this hour, and their footsteps echoed as they left their cars and approached a metal fire door in an interior wall. The door was locked, but Peter, one of Harris's associates, took out a ring of keys and quickly opened it.

They were in a large, antiseptically white basement. George, the second of Harris's men, was built like a top-grade linebacker. Holding a photocopy of Daniel Archer's schematic open in his hand, he led the way through several corridors.

George and Peter were dressed in dark suits and carried leather attaché cases. The third man, Arthur, wore jeans and a zippered warm-up jacket with an olive-drab duffel bag slung over his shoulder. Passing a storage room, he spotted an aluminum A-ladder leaning against a wall and took it with him.

When the four men reached the northeast end of the second basement as indicated on the schematic, it took less than five minutes to locate the wall panels marked numbers 4 and 5, and an additional few moments to open them up.

The deputy director stared in silence at what he saw exposed.

All three clocks were ticking.

Chapter 89

THE AIR FRANCE 747 landed at Dulles International Airport at 8:45 P.M. Washington time.

Since Kate and Paulie had only carry-on bags, they got through customs ahead of the crowd.

But there were lines at the car-rental counters, and it was past ten o'clock by the time they picked up a sleek black Cougar, drove out of the airport, and headed southeast.

"Where are we going?" Kate asked.

"To arm ourselves," said Paulie. "Haven't you heard? Americans are the most violent people on earth. And their capital is their most dangerous city. Besides, I feel naked without a gun."

They had been traveling for about twenty minutes when Paulie pulled into the driveway of a white colonial with two yellow lanterns burning in front. To Kate, it looked like a house in which the president of the local garden club might live.

"Better wait in the car," Paulie said. "No point in your being seen unnecessarily."

Kate watched him walk to the front door. After a moment she saw the door open and a big man embrace Paulie before the two of them disappeared into the house.

Even gone from sight, she could feel Paulie Walters stirring inside her.

A warm, dry wind came through the open car window from the south, and Kate felt it move through her hair and touch her face. And she saw very clearly how the greater part of her life might have been leading only to this moment of sitting here in a rented car waiting for this man.

Half an hour later, Kate saw Paulie in the doorway beside the tall heavyset man. They appeared to be looking in her direction. When the man lifted his arm and waved a greeting, Kate waved back.

Paulie returned to the car with a bag bulging with ordnance and they drove off.

"That was my father's first cousin, Dino Battaglia," said Paulie. "Our family supplier of fine weapons to three generations of distinguished mafiosi and an occasional spook. He begs to send you much respect, affection, and gratitude."

"For what?"

"For loving me so much. He also begs me to please tell you he would be honored to be named godfather to our first-born."

Kate's smile was uncertain. "He didn't really."

"He did."

"Is that why he kept you in there so long?"

"No. That was just to demonstrate the latest of these crazy little gadgets he keeps inventing to help keep me alive. Dino still thinks I'm James Bond."

"You mean you're not?"

"As long as I have you backing me up, I don't have to be."

They drove toward Washington.

Kate kept one of her hands on Paulie's, where it gripped the wheel. "Is Dino your only relative?" she asked.

"As far as I know. What about you? Do you have any family?"

"No. But I think more than anything I'd love for us to start making one."

"I doubt if we'll have time tonight."

They rode for a while in silence.

"How do you think we'll do together, long-term?" Kate asked.

"Magnificently."

"I'm serious, Paulie."

"What makes you think I'm not?"

She either couldn't or wouldn't answer that.

"I'm going to say this only once," Paulie told her. "Given the chance to be with you, I'll never fail or betray you as long as I live."

They reached the Taylor Building shortly after midnight, which made it a bit past 6:00 A.M. in Paris and allowed them a full six-hour safety margin.

Still, neither Paulie nor Kate was complacent about what lay ahead. They would still be dealing with high explosives in a less than friendly environment, and they had enough knowledge of such things to respect their potential for disaster.

Kate had her own copy of the annotated two-page schematic that Daniel Archer had carried, and she studied it under a map light as Paulie drove slowly around the building. When everything appeared in order, he swung down into the underground garage ramp, pressed the special electronic door opener that had been in Cousin Dino's bag of magic tricks, and drove into the big parking area.

There were only about a dozen cars scattered about, probably belonging to late workers putting in overtime.

They sat in the Cougar studying the schematic. They noted the metal fire door through which they would enter the basement, and saw the door itself about fifty feet away.

They checked the guns and skeleton keys they were taking with them from Dino Battaglia's bag, hearing the reassuring click of the guns' slides being racked, then putting the pieces back in their holsters.

"Ready?" Paulie asked.

Kate Dinneson nodded.

He leaned over and kissed her. "For luck."

She looked at him in the cold light of the garage. "I know you don't really believe in any of this. I know you're doing it only for me. And I appreciate it."

"You don't have to tell me things like that."

"Yes I do."

"Don't you think I understand how you feel?" Paulie asked.

"Yes. But it's still important to me that I say it."

Paulie stared at her with his solemn eyes. "In that case you have my permission."

Kate smiled, and Paulie realized he had never seen a smile of pure love before.

Chapter 90

PAULIE AND KATE LEFT THE CAR, opened the fire door with one of Dino Battaglia's keys, and entered the basement.

Then, following the schematic, they started down a corridor that led to the right. With no anticipated threats, they kept their weapons out of sight.

They passed a storage room, then another, before finally reaching the northeast section of the basement. When they found wall panels 4 and 5, they worked together to get them open.

Paulie studied the exposed cache of *plastique*, wires, fuses, detonators, and clocks. He saw that the final clock still had five hours and twenty-two minutes to go before detonation. For a moment he stood unmoving, as if the clock had somehow fixed him in a mood he dared not break.

Finally, he reached for the off switch.

"Done," he said.

Turning to share the moment with Kate, Paulie saw the men. There were four of them and they made no sound as they approached from an adjacent room. Paulie's hand started for his automatic but he never drew it. There were four pistols with attached silencers pointing at him.

His hand fell of its own weight.

The men stopped walking and stood ten feet away in a loose semicircle. No one had spoken, but their timing and positioning seemed to have been choreographed.

Only then did Paulie realize that one of the men was Deputy CIA Director Harris. The other three were strangers to him.

Seemingly confused, Ken Harris frowned at Paulie. Then he stared at the exposed explosives and the timer that Paulie had just switched off. He considered Paulie once more.

"It looks like we're all a little unsettled by this, Paul," said the deputy director. "The last I knew you were at Wannsee, as John Hendricks. And I'm sure you never expected to be running into *me* down here."

Paulie said nothing. Now he understood why Daniel Archer had missed making his calls to Kate and Nicko.

Harris turned to Kate. "I don't believe we know each other."

"I know *you*, Mr. Harris." Kate's face was pale but controlled.

"And what's *your* name?"

"Kate Dinneson."

"Who are you? And what do you have to do with all this?"

Kate just stood there.

The deputy director turned to his men. "George, take whatever weapons they have and handcuff them both. Peter, see if you and Arthur can find some chairs. We could be here for a while."

No one else said a word, and Paulie watched as he and Kate were stripped of their automatics. The only picture in his mind right then was of a sawed-off bat beating on his brain. Poor Kate, he thought.

Moments later he and Kate were sitting side by side with their hands cuffed together in their laps, while Harris sat facing them.

"Explain it to me, Paul," said the deputy director. "I knew *someone* would have to be here soon to stop the clock, but why you?"

"Who did you expect?"

"Professor Mainz or someone near to him. How did *you* get involved?"

Paulie studied his cuffed hands. "Kate is an old friend of the professor's. He trusts her. But she was afraid she couldn't do it alone so she asked me to help."

"I'll ask you again. Why you?"

"Kate and I are close."

"Close enough for her to have told you where Mainz is holed up?"

Paulie thought quickly on that one. "Yes. If she knew. But she doesn't know."

Harris looked at Kate. "How do you communicate with Mainz?"

"We've been using dead drops and messengers."

"You don't have a phone number for him?"

"No," said Kate. "That would be as dangerous for him as a known address."

"I don't believe you, Miss Dinneson."

Paulie stared at the deputy director's three monkeys, with their smooth, expressionless faces and neat haircuts. Then, glancing at Kate, he realized that she too knew they were going to die.

"George, I think you'd better tie their feet," said Harris.

The man called George opened his attaché case, took out some nylon cord, and lashed Kate's and Paulie's ankles to the legs of their chairs.

"All right, Miss Dinneson," said Harris. "No more lies. I just want Professor Mainz's telephone number."

"How can I give you what I don't have?"

Ken Harris turned to George. "All right. Go to the next step."

The man reached for Kate's blouse with both hands and ripped it open down the middle. Then he unhooked her bra, exposing her breasts.

Two round spots of color appeared high on Kate's cheeks. That was all.

Paulie listened to his own breathing.

Harris spoke to Kate. "Don't be foolish. Everyone finally talks. So why not do it now and spare yourself unnecessary pain?"

"You're disgusting," said Kate.

The deputy director nodded as if that was the answer he had been expecting. "Show it to her, Arthur," he said, and the man in the jeans and zippered jacket took an electric prod out of his duffel bag and held it in front of Kate.

"Is this really what you want used on you?" asked Harris.

Paulie felt Kate's pulse as if it were his own. "Leave her alone," he said. "I'll tell you what you want to know."

The deputy director smiled at Paulie in a kind way. "Then you know where Professor Mainz is?"

"Mainz is dead," said Paulie. "He died in that explosion at Wannsee. This whole idea is just something a man named Archer dreamed up and got Kate to help him carry out."

Harris considered it for several moments. "Why? To what end?"

"For Archer it was the hundred million in cash. For Kate, it was the professor's human rights agenda."

The deputy director sat completely still. "Is this true?" he asked Kate.

She nodded.

"Then where's the hundred million?" said Harris.

Kate closed the front of her blouse with her cuffed hands. "In a safe place."

"Who knows about it?"

"Just Paul and I. Now that Archer is probably dead."

The deputy director rose from his chair and slowly paced the concrete floor. The three agents looked bored now that Kate's breasts were covered.

Paulie broke the silence. "There's something else you'd better hear," he told Harris.

"I'm listening."

"The president and Tommy Cortlandt know all about you."

Ken Harris stopped pacing. "What is that supposed to mean?"

"I think you'd better hear this alone."

Harris looked curiously at Paulie. Then he motioned to his men. "Wait in the next room."

They started out. "Be careful," warned George. "This fuck looks tricky." Then they were through the door and gone.

Ken Harris turned to Paulie. "OK. Let's hear it."

"The president has tapes of your last two phone calls to your friend Anna in Berlin. They're totally incriminating."

Harris wiped his lips with the back of his hand. "Then why am I still walking around?"

"This can make a lot of waves. The president wanted time to think it through."

"And the reason you're telling me now?"

"To keep Kate and me from dying where we sit. And you from dying in a federal prison."

Ken Harris stood very still. "Go ahead."

"I'll make it simple," said Paulie. "We have that hundred million buried in France. Fly us there and half of it is yours. Do you have any close family?"

"No."

"Even simpler. Just change your face, disappear, and live happily ever after in total luxury."

"How do you know you can trust me not to shoot you both when we get to the money, and just take it all?"

"I *don't* know," said Paulie. "But if I *don't* trust you, I do know that Kate and I are dead right now."

The deputy director nodded. "That much is true."

Seconds later, Ken Harris walked to the open doorway and called his men back into the room. They stood talking quietly in a corner as the deputy director passed around a pack of cigarettes. Paulie heard mild laughter.

It was cut short by a sharp whooshing sound. Paulie saw Peter's head snap back, part of his forehead missing.

Then there was the same sound, and this time Paulie saw the silenced automatic in Ken Harris's hand just as George's face seemed to fold and collapse inward.

The third man, Arthur, was still trying to free his piece from his shoulder holster when Harris's next two shots entered his chest and sent him tumbling.

The deputy director bent and felt for a pulse in each of the three bodies.

Then he rose and looked at Paulie. "You knew I'd have to do that, didn't you?"

"Yes."

"Exactly where in France did you bury the money?" asked Harris.

"About thirty miles from Charles de Gaulle Airport," Kate answered. "How will you get us there?"

"No problem. I'll just arrange for a plane and two of my own people as escorts."

Then, suddenly distracted, the deputy director walked over to the open wall where the bombs lay and stood considering it. Watching from where they sat, Kate and Paulie saw him carefully reach inside and turn on the timer clock that Paulie had turned off just ten minutes before.

"What the hell are you doing?" asked Paulie.

Harris seemed not to have heard him. He was busy moving wall panels 4 and 5 back into their closed positions and settling them in place. Then he turned. "What I'm doing," he said, "is making sure everything goes off in a little more than five hours. By that time, we should be about halfway to Paris."

Kate and Paulie stared at him.

"But why in God's name would you want to kill hundreds of people for no reason?" Kate whispered.

"It wouldn't be for no reason. It would be to teach the world's slow learners a lesson."

"About what?" said Paulie.

"About exactly how dangerous bleeding-heart, humanist crackpots like Mainz and Jimmy Dunster can be."

The deputy director, like a world-class lecturer on death for the waning days of the most deadly century in history, stared straight into Paulie's eyes. "Do you get my point?"

Paulie nodded and slowly turned his body a bit to the left, as if lining himself up with some invisible target.

Then just as slowly, he compressed the small rubber syringe that his Cousin Dino had insisted on taping slightly beneath his right armpit. The syringe, in turn, triggered the tiny pistol attached to it and blew away a significant portion of Ken Harris's brain.

Still handcuffed, Paulie and Kate fumbled free of the cords at their feet.

"You never told me anything about a gun." Kate whispered the words as though it were still a carefully guarded secret.

"There was nothing to tell. It was just one of Dino's crazy James Bond gadgets that I never thought I'd need, or would even work if I ever did need it." Paulie stared dimly at the deputy director where he lay, his gun still in his hand, one leg drawn up. "I guess it worked."

They held each other in the scorched air, which smoldered with the smell of cordite. Insulated in the silence of the dead, they allowed themselves a moment. Then there were things to do.

Paulie took the keys from George's pocket and unlocked their handcuffs.

Again, they removed panels 4 and 5, switched off the deadly, mindless clock for what they hoped would be the last time, and replaced the two panels.

That, at least, they had done.

They considered the best way to handle the bodies. But there really was no best way. So they decided to simply leave them as they were and see what the experts might be able to figure out.

Paulie remembered their guns, which were still in George's pockets. He pulled them out and packed them into the bag he had gotten from Cousin Dino.

They took a final look around and left.

Chapter 91

PAULIE WALTERS WALKED BACK into the astringent air and odors of Berlin's Holy Cross General only days after having left them, but it seemed more like years.

So much had changed inside him.

Still, the hospital was the same, with its bustling routines still telling less about the nature of life than about the urgency of death. And the clusters of media people hanging about were unchanged, along with the president's security.

Paulie had flown into Tempelhof from Washington two hours earlier, kissed Kate good-bye, and put her on a connecting flight to Naples. Then he had called Tommy Cortlandt at his hotel and arranged to meet him in the president's room at 11:00 A.M.

He arrived in the doorway almost on the minute.

"Ah, Paulie," said Jimmy Dunster, as he reached for his hand.

The president's cheeks were still gaunt, his color gray, his eyes deep-set and haunted.

Tommy Cortlandt sat off to one side, silently watching. "Welcome back," he said.

Paulie nodded, picking up something in the director's voice and manner. A certain reserve? "How have things been here?" he asked.

"Interesting."

Cortlandt looked at the president where he lay propped

up in bed, and some unspoken communication passed between them.

"Actually, there's a lot we have to talk about." The director went to the open door, closed it, and returned. "Sit down, Paulie."

Cortlandt looked again at Jimmy Dunster. "Would you like to take over, Mr. President?"

"No. You go right ahead."

Sensing an unseen weight about to descend on him, Paulie just sat there.

"I've known you since you were eight years old, Paulie," said Cortlandt. "And what you did, simply taking off alone the other day, was so disturbingly unlike you, that I felt forced to do something I would never ordinarily have done. I put a man on your back."

The CIA director paused.

"What did he learn?" Paulie asked.

Instead of answering, the CIA director handed Paulie a stack of photographs. Arranged in chronological order, each picture was stamped with the exact time, date, and place of origin.

Hands suddenly moist, Paulie started through them.

He saw shots of himself on the flight to Paris, shots driving to the arms dealer on the Rue de Vigney, then going on to the big parking garage where the money drop was made.

Knowing now exactly how bad this was going to be, he glanced up and saw the president and Cortlandt watching him.

"Listen . . ." he began.

The president lifted a pale, veined hand. "First look at the pictures, Paulie."

Was looking at the pictures to be part of his penance?

For Paulie, the most powerful were the shots taken through a window of the lake house with Kate and Nicko.

Kate's choice. Shooting Nicko.

The collection ended with Kate and Paulie boarding the 7:00 P.M. Air France flight to Washington.

"What happened to the remaining pictures?" Paulie said tiredly. "Or didn't your man follow us to Washington?"

"He followed you," said Cortlandt. "He just broke his camera. But he did give us a brief report on the four bodies he found in the basement of the Taylor Building right after you and Kate Dinneson left there.

Paulie sat clutching his stack of pictures.

"Shall we talk now?" suggested President Dunster. "There's obviously a lot that still needs explaining."

Paulie waited.

"Let's start with Professor Mainz," said the president. "Exactly where has he been through all this?"

Paulie took a long, deep breath. "Dead under Wannsee," he said. Then something seemed to give way inside him and it all broke loose.

When he finally finished, they sat in a kind of vacuum until Jimmy Dunster spoke.

"You must love this woman, this Kate Dinneson, very much," he said.

It was so unexpected, so human a reaction, that Paulie felt all his defenses breached. "I'd die for her, Mr. President."

"You very nearly did. More than once."

Paulie said nothing.

"Where is she now?" Cortlandt asked.

"At home. In Naples."

"And her plans?"

"That's obviously up to you and the president."

The CIA director considered Paulie for several moments. Then he looked at Jimmy Dunster, perhaps measuring the feeling between them. Finally, he just shrugged.

President Dunster picked up and sipped a glass of water. "What's your feeling about all this, Paulie?" he asked.

"About all what, Mr. President?"

"The big lie. The one that has the world believing Mainz is still alive and well and running the Wannsee Project. Do you feel there might be some profit to be squeezed from it?"

"Yes, sir. If it's handled right."

"Who knows the truth at this point?"

"Just the three of us. And Kate, of course."

Jimmy Dunster looked at his director of intelligence. "Talk to me, Tommy," he said.

"Why? You never listen to me anyway."

"That's probably true," said Dunster. "But you know there's no one whose judgement I respect more."

Cortlandt sighed. "Come on, Jimmy. This whole concept is even more insane than your showing up at Wannsee in the first place. And we've all seen how that turned out."

The president was silent.

"I'm sorry," said Cortlandt. "That was a real cheap shot."

"But deserved. My coming to Wannsee was a world-class disaster. That's why I'm grabbing at straws with this; I need something back."

Cortlandt shook his head. "But there's no guarantee it will even work, sir."

"It will have to work," said the president fiercely. "It's working already. We've seen it in the responses we've been getting to Mainz's latest demands."

"You're talking about a dead man, Mr. President."

"Yes. But he's alive for us. We evidently have that need. A man with guns at our heads. Even if he's only a lie."

The president looked at Paulie. "I want to meet your Kate. How soon can you get her here?"

"By early evening, Mr. President."

Dunster's eyes, still holding to Paulie's face, turned moist.

"Let me tell you something, Paulie. Less than an hour ago my wife came back to me from the dead. She actually looked at me, squeezed my hand, and smiled. So if for no other reason than that, how can I give up on Mainz?"

Chapter 92

AFTER THE USUAL SECURITY CHECK, they walked into the president's hospital room at 8:27 that evening. Paulie was holding Kate's arm as they came through the door. It was half pride of possession, half fear of losing her. Besides Jimmy Dunster, only Tommy Cortlandt was present.

Feeling strangely awkward, Paulie introduced her to both men.

"Mr. President," she said. "Mr. Director."

She shook their hands. Then she sat down facing the president in his bed. Cortlandt sat beside her. There was another chair, but Paulie remained standing.

How poised she is, he thought. How controlled, how beautiful.

"I assume Paulie told you what this is all about," said Jimmy Dunster.

Kate Dinneson nodded.

"As we understand it, the whole idea for this lie based on the existence of a dead man was Dr. Vorelli's. With you and Daniel Archer helping to carry it out. Is that true?"

"Yes, sir."

"And after Vorelli and Archer were killed? Did you plan to continue with it alone?"

"That was my hope."

"With Paulie to help you?"

Kate glanced at Paulie and found what she was looking for in his face. "That was my hope too."

"The two of you never discussed it?"

"Not in so many words," said Kate.

The president looked at Paulie. "Would you object to being part of a continuing lie like that?"

"I'm already part of it, sir."

"So you are," said Jimmy Dunster.

"Understand," said the CIA director, "that for all practical purposes this conversation has never taken place. If either of you claims it has, both the president and I will deny it. If you ever get into trouble, it will be entirely your own. Neither the Oval Office nor the Central Intelligence Agency must ever be involved. Is that clear?"

Kate and Paulie nodded.

"Another thing," said Cortlandt. "What happened with that bomb in the Taylor Building must never be repeated. Not anywhere. Make whatever threats you feel are necessary. But no bomb is ever to be armed and put on a clock again. Any questions?"

"Yes," said Kate. "What about the money?"

Cortlandt stared blankly.

"The hundred million we buried near the lake house in France," she said.

The director turned to Jimmy Dunster. "That could be a problem, Mr. President. We certainly can't return it to each contributing country. And it would be an embarrassment if someone stumbled over it."

"I don't see any problem," said the president. "Since the money was supposed to support the infrastructure and practical needs of the Wannsee Project, I suggest the new directors of the project simply use it for those purposes."

A hundred million dollars worth of infrastructure and practical needs, thought Paulie, and he waited to see whether he was the only one who found the irony of Nicko Vorelli's highly inflated style of living even remotely amusing.

Apparently he was.

But a couple of loose ends still remained.

"What about your vice president?" Paulie asked Jimmy Dunster. "Have you done anything about him yet?"

"I had Jay Fleming over here yesterday. He'll be resigning tomorrow for reasons of health. Then he'll just disappear someplace abroad."

"He's getting off easy," said Paulie.

"I know. But so is the country, which is all that really matters. And it sure beats hell out of a long ugly trial."

"And Ken Harris and his three goons?" asked Paulie.

"Killed in the line of duty," said the president. "Unfortunately they'll have to be buried with honors. But that's still infinitely better than the bloodbath you saved us from when you stopped those clocks."

Cortlandt looked at Paulie with tiredly sardonic eyes.

"My hero."

Chapter 93

THE NIGHT WAS BLACK. Kate Dinneson had only been there that once, with Nicko driving, so she was less than certain that she would be able to find the place again. Still, she was trying, although this time Paulie was at the wheel, and he had never been there at all.

They drove slowly along the dirt trail in silence, the forest pressing close on both sides. The only sound was the soft crunching of the tires.

Finally, the headlights picked up a narrow track cutting off to the left and Kate said, "Turn here."

"Are you sure?" asked Paulie.

"No. But it feels right."

My only true compass of direction, thought Kate. *How it feels*. That was why they were here in the first place. Because it had suddenly felt wrong to leave Klaus Logefeld to rot forever in that concrete bunker.

Paulie had a far more practical reason for getting Klaus and the other German out of there when Kate told him how she felt. Their combined odors would inevitably work their way into Wannsee's basement and up through the floorboards to the main conference room itself. Then where would their lie be?

So they had stayed over in Berlin, picked up what they would need to effect a more conventional burial, and returned to Wannsee to take care of it. That is, if Kate could ever find her way back to the tunnel entrance. After close to half an hour of blundering, she at last managed to do so.

Prepared with a wheeled dolly, Paulie lowered it down half a dozen steps as Kate lit their way with a lantern. Then he followed her along the concrete-lined tunnel until they reached the closed metal door of the bunker.

They stopped for a moment to put on sterile masks.

Then Kate pressed against the door, felt it give, and lit their entrance into the bunker.

Klaus Logefeld lay on the bunk where she had seen him last. But he did not look the same. A few small days made a big difference.

Yet even now he had a human look, thought Kate. From a heritage of German shame, he had fought to make something of himself. He'd had loyalties to certain pure states and he refused to compromise them. He knew there had been good Germans before him, that there would be good Germans to come, and he had died trying to be one of them.

And me? I'm trying for him still.

The other dead German, whose name had been Hans and whom Kate had never seen alive, remained invisible under his tarpaulin in a far corner of the bunker.

Paulie lifted the tarp and looked at the man beneath it.

"Who was this one?"

"His name was Hans. He had already been shot when Nicko and I got here. Daniel Archer killed him."

"Why?"

"Because Harris had hired Hans to kill Archer."

"Nice bunch."

Kate was silent. She was staring at Klaus. It was still hard for her to think of him as Alfred Mainz, although it was as Mainz that he had achieved his celebrity and his death. She noticed how well combed his hair was, how neatly in place, and tried hard to despise him. He had, after all, done despicable things. But the purity of his motives kept getting in the way.

"Let's do it," she said.

Along with the wheeled dolly, gloves, and a shovel, they had brought several large plastic bags, and they worked the two bodies into them. Kate caught a final glimpse of Klaus's face. The nostrils, the eye sockets, were very dark, the cheeks pale and waxlike. In the lips, frozen bitterness and a grimly reluctant humor.

They took out the bodies one at a time and buried them deep in the woods, in separate graves.

Kate had insisted on it, although Paulie pointed out that it was double the work and who cared anyway?

"*I* care," she told him.

Chapter 94

"IT'S STARTING!" Kate Dinneson called to Paulie Walters, who was working in his studio.

Paulie put down his palette and brushes and went into the living room to watch the televised opening of what had come to be known as the Second Wannsee Conference on Human Rights.

It had taken almost two months to arrive.

There had been delays.

Repairs to the bombed-out villa had been held up by unexpectedly severe structural damage. The seven leaders taking part had scheduling problems. President Dunster's recovery suffered setbacks.

Every complication along the way had to be worked out through a combination of publicly announced messages from a nonexistent Professor Mainz, and personal telephone calls to Jimmy Dunster from the phantom professor's supposedly anonymous representative.

The long-awaited moment had finally arrived. Kate and Paulie sat together on their couch in Ravello and gazed at President Dunster leaning over to kiss his wife, then slowly making his way toward the speaker's podium.

The president still limped, still had to walk with the help of a cane. But his progress across the floor of the big conference room was sure, and he received the same standing ovation he had been given during his surprise appearance at the first conference.

Except that this time there was something more. This time blood-filled history was included in the tribute.

This time he's paid his dues in advance, Paulie thought.

The president stood waiting for the applause to quiet. When it did, he lifted his head and gazed evenly into the magic eye of the camera.

"We're finally here," he said. "Now let's get to work and do what has to be done."

Paulie guessed it was about as good an opening to a speech as he had ever heard. Left alone, the two short sentences might even have been sufficient in themselves. But man had become an explaining creature, and the soul wanted what it wanted.

So instead of simply sitting down and getting to work, the president explained, in detail, his hopes for the conference.

Nevertheless, the speech was effective and stirring. On her couch in Ravello, Kate reached for Paulie and held him. She wept, soaring with a degree of hope equal to that of the president.

Not so Paulie. Hope was fine if there was some reasonable basis for it. Sadly, all he could see ahead for his own benighted species was hate, degraded clowning, and death.

Except for some bloody ethnic cleansing and at least one long-term civil war in central Africa. Volunteer strike forces had quickly moved in and established several genuine ceasefires that were still holding after five incredible weeks of peace.

Yet even here, Paulie chose to reserve judgement.

Chapter 95

PAULIE WALTERS HAD STARTED THE PAINTING on the same morning the Second Wannsee Conference began with such high hopes. There was no advance planning to it. The painting simply evolved bit by bit over a period of hours and days. The finished work was a surprise even to Paulie.

At first it was little more than a mass of swirling color, a dark abstraction from some hidden memory of the womb. Then Paulie had seen that first floating eye, so muddy and soiled, so perfectly somber and evil. But it was, after all, an eye. If only one. Then he and the emerging face were on their way, with a curving shadow for a nose and a dark opening below that would be the mouth.

Working his brush with care, he laid on red blood and green mud like medals of death pinned to the chest. Then a stab went in above the mouth and sucked the face in backward, as though upon the gouge of a bullet. The look was that of an old man, toothless, sly, reminiscent of fear and pain. An arm appeared, but only one, the other lost somewhere, or blown off, or eaten away.

Klaus Logefeld's grandfather?

But just briefly. Because there was no single particular creature reflected there. *Whap!* went the brush, and a hole appeared where the heart should have been. The face above grinned with a clown's deep gloom, as if there was pleasure even in this.

Paulie could no longer face the single eye. Now it contained it all—the blood, the carnage, the dark screams that never sounded. He faltered and had no stomach for the rest.

Enough, he thought.

Then the stubborn part of his brain took hold, and he went back to the painting to do what he had known all along had to be done.

He showed it to Kate after dinner one evening, bringing her into his studio, sitting her down in front of the canvas, and silently gazing with her at the big nude. This was what it finally had become, a life-size male nude painted in the stained and ugly hues of frozen flesh in winter tombs.

The figure was rendered broadly, freely, yet no detail of its early threat had been lost. The mouth still howled its maniac speech. The one demonic eye still glared. The stump of a missing arm still flayed the heavens. And from the chest cavity, from that dark hole where a heart should have been, crawled things black and viscous. If you believed in spirits and demons, in wizards and fiends and omens of evil, they would have dwelt in such a place as this.

Kate Dinneson sat staring for a long time, hands folded in her lap like those of an obedient child. Her face showed no emotion.

"Well?" said Paulie at last.

"You're a great artist."

"Is that all?"

"What else is there?"

"What do you *think*?"

"I'm no art critic," Kate said.

"I *know* you're no art critic."

She turned and faced him. "Shall I tell you how I *feel*?"

"Sure."

"Like killing myself."

He laughed.

"I'm not trying to be funny. I think if I believed what you've said here, I couldn't see much point in getting up in the morning. And if I thought you believed it yourself, I wouldn't feel much better."

"Don't you think I believe it?" Paulie asked.

Something strangled in her, some wistful desire to change what was beyond alteration. "For days, I've been hoping you didn't."

"You mean you've seen the painting before?"

"Every day since you started it. I've been coming into your studio and looking when you weren't around. I kept hoping it might brighten up a little, but it just kept getting worse. And so did the way I felt."

He sat numbly. "I didn't know."

"I was sure you'd notice some difference in me. I was sure it showed."

Paulie *had* noticed it. She *had* been different. But he had blamed it on how poorly things were going at Wannsee, with the glowing spirit of the opening seeming to fade by the day, and egos and petty political squabbling beginning to threaten further progress. Looking at Kate now, he could pinpoint the changes, could actually sense the anxiety in her face. Even the smoothness of her skin seemed vexed, troubled by hidden disasters.

Without knowing why, he felt he should apologize. "I'm sorry you don't like the painting."

"I don't just not like it. I hate it. Why in God's name did you have to paint such an abomination?"

It was fascinating to him to see her circling in, to watch her collecting the necessary anger for her attack. He fought a lover's wish to collaborate, to help make it easier for her to do what she so obviously needed to do. Still, her reaction puzzled him. It was much too strong.

"I don't understand," Paulie said. "Why do you let it bother you so?"

"Hopelessness always bothers me. I despise it."

"I wasn't really trying to be hopeless."

"My God!" Kate Dinneson stared at the silently howling mouth. "What *were* you trying to be?"

"Realistic." Paulie turned to stare with her at the canvas. "At least I thought I was trying to be realistic. You never know for sure while you're working. Emotion clouds. Especially in something like this. Maybe I shouldn't have touched the whole idea right now."

"What whole idea?"

"Wannsee's inevitable failure. All the same hate and killing going on as before. With the exception of a few parts of western and central Africa. And who knows how long those shaky bits of peace are going to hold."

Kate looked shocked, hurt. "They've just started. You're not even giving them a chance to make it work."

"Ah, Kate. It's never worked before. And I'm afraid not even you, the president, and your noble lie can make it work now."

She kept her lips tight, made her voice harsh. "When did you get so scared? I've never seen you so scared before."

"Is that what I am?"

"Or would you rather call it being realistic?"

"You might be right. They could be the same thing. Maybe it's impossible to be realistic anymore without being scared."

"Oh, damn it! Stop it!"

It came out a shrill shout that startled her as much as it did him.

"What is it, Kate?"

She shut her eyes as though the light had suddenly grown too bright.

"But what's the *matter?*"

Kate Dinneson opened her eyes and looked past Paulie at the mutilated nude.

"*That's* the matter," she said, and ran out of the studio and out of the house.

Paulie found her in the darkness on the crest of a hill that overlooked the sea.

He sat down next to her, but neither of them spoke. A small, warm breath of salt came off the water, which heaved gently under the moon.

"I'm sorry," she said at last.

He took her hand. "Just tell me what it is."

"It's us. We've done it. We've started the family I've been wanting more than anything."

Paulie waited for some sensation. But none came. "Are you sure?"

"Yes. I went to a doctor."

"When?"

"Four days ago."

"And you're just telling me now?"

"I was afraid."

"Of *what*, for God's sake?"

"Of you. Of how you'd feel about it. I was afraid from the minute I saw that painting. I thought, how could you possibly paint something like this and still want a baby? How could you see such ghastly visions ahead and want a child of your own to have to face them? Can you blame me for hating that picture? It's a rusty knife at my belly."

"It's only a painting, Kate."

"It's *not* only a painting. It's the way you feel."

"That has nothing to do with the baby," Paulie said. "I'm very happy about the baby."

"How could you be? You're so pessimistic about everything."

"Not about everything. Just about the world."

"What else is there?"

"There's us," Paulie said. He was almost smiling, realizing the insane dichotomy between his world pessimism and personal hope. "And now there's the baby."

Kate went soft against him. "Do you mean it? Are you really happy?"

"Yes," he said, and was astonished to find that he did mean it, that it actually did give him an extraordinary feeling.

Kate held him.

"I was so miserable," she said. "You'll never know how miserable."

Paulie stroked her hair where the moon caught it.

"I'll have a beautiful pregnancy, darling. You'll see. I won't cause any trouble. I won't bother you at all."

"Please," he said. "Bother me."

"No. Men don't like to know too much. They just want it to happen. They like the mystery. Darling, I'm going to give you the most mysterious, the most amazing baby you've ever seen."

"You're the one who's mysterious and amazing."

"No I'm not. But I love you to think so. Oh, Jesus!" She all but shouted the words. "I'm suddenly so happy I could die. Do you think I shouldn't be so happy? Do you think there's something wrong in it?"

"What could be wrong?"

"You know. The way the world is."

Paulie laughed. "You won't make things any better by being miserable."

He kissed her and she pressed him hard and touched him until he felt the magic of the rising begin. They lay back against the crest of the hill.

"*Here?*" he said.

"Where else, dummy?"

Then she was at him again, smothering the laughter in his throat and pulling at their clothes until they were naked in the cool grass, feeling it give softly against flesh and even the strangeness of it exciting.

A strangeness, too, in knowing of the tiny living thing inside, too fragile to believe. Paulie must have held back because Kate said, "Don't worry. You won't hurt him."

Still, there were three of them together instead of two. It was neither better nor worse than before, but different. And he could feel this child begin to engage him, this new invisible thing he had helped produce, giving wisdom to his touch and drawing fresh secrets from her flesh.

Afterward, Kate would not let him go, but held on against the final slipping away. "I hate when it ends," she said. "Why does it always have to end?"

"It doesn't really. It's just getting ready for next time."

"That's lovely."

"I told you I'm no pessimist."

"Just about the world."

As Paulie held her, this woman who had been tricked into killing his parents and was now offering him the gift of his own child in their place, he suddenly felt warm and accounted for, felt the almost mystic grace of the whole idea.

Then they dressed and walked back through the grass and found, when they reached the house, that nothing had really changed. The bitter threat was still there, still waiting for them.

Kate said nothing. But Paulie only had to look at her face to know what she was feeling.

Then, because all his usual disciplines were suddenly air, and he had nothing else to offer and no one else left to offer it to, he thought, *Why the hell not?*

It took only a moment to cut the canvas free of its stretcher and lay it out on the hearth. Then with Kate standing there wide-eyed, Paulie struck a match and let the poor howling creature seek its final peace in a shroud of smoke.

Paulie chose to look at it as part of his new contract.

An expectant father had to be more hopeful. It was the heart's only protection.

Which didn't mean that the hate and killing were not still out there. Perhaps they always would be. But for the first time ever, Wannsee was out there too. Along with the lie that was its fire and sword.

No small thing.